LIGHT *in the* EMPIRE

CAROL ASHBY

CERRILLO PRESS

ISBN: 978-1-946139-00-9 (paperback)
        978-1-946139-01-6 (ebook)

Cerrillo Press
Edgewood, NM

And when you stand praying, if you hold anything against anyone,
forgive him, so that your Father in heaven may forgive you your sins.
Mark 11:25

Be kind and compassionate to one another, forgiving each other,
just as in Christ God forgave you.
Ephesians 4:32

To my children, Paul and Lydia,
for their love, support, and encouragement and
especially to my husband, Jim, who says I'm incredibly lifelike
when I work on my laptop

And most of all, to Jesus,
who paid for my own sins so I could live forgiven.

Soli Deo gloria

Preface

Have you ever faced a situation where it felt impossible to forgive? When someone hurt or even killed someone you love? When the one you trusted most betrayed you so callously you're afraid you'll never trust anyone again? When someone crushed your dreams without even a particle of regret and you've lost hope?

Of all the commands Jesus gave to those who follow him, the command to forgive is perhaps the hardest to obey. It certainly is for me. It's not natural to turn the other cheek to someone who's just slapped you. It's not natural to work longer and harder to serve someone who never appreciates anything you do and enjoys taking advantage of you at every opportunity.

But natural isn't what Christians are called to. We're called to live a life enabled by the Holy Spirit. We're commanded to make the godly choice, not the natural one. Jesus said if we refuse to forgive, we forfeit the forgiveness of God that Jesus's death and resurrection bought for us (Matt. 6:14-15, 18:23-35).

When Jesus was walking the roads of Judea and Galilee, a Roman soldier who was tired of carrying his gear could grab anyone and make him carry his load for one mile. Only one, and there were road markers every mile so both would know when the drafted traveler could quit. When Jesus told his disciples to carry the load for two miles, not one (Matt. 5:41), he was calling them to a standard far beyond what anyone would want to do for a soldier of a brutal occupying army. He was calling them to acts of forgiveness and love, not vengeance and hate.

His call to us is the same today. When we choose to forgive a wrong for which we have every natural right to hold a grudge and long for vengeance, we are children of our Father, showing our love for Him

i

by obedience. And the reward? When we stop replaying the memories of how we were wronged and dreaming of vengeance, the Holy Spirit gives us the power to forgive. Each time I've chosen to release my enemy from the net of my unforgiveness, I find I really freed myself.

Forgiven is a story about people caught in the struggle between hatred and love, vengeance and forgiveness, and how Jesus makes it possible for them to choose the better way.

I hope you enjoy this story of God's faithful reward for triumphant obedience as much as I've enjoyed living in Rachel's and Lucius's world as I've written it. May God give us all the power to forgive the unforgivable and find the joy that waits beyond forgiveness.

Carol Ashby

Characters

CLAUDIUS DRUSUS FAMILY

Lucius Claudius Drusus: (24) Roman tribune serving in Judaea

Marcus Claudius Drusus: (22) Roman tribune, younger brother of Lucius

Lucius Claudius Drusus Fidelis (Lucius Fidelis): (40) Father of Lucius and Marcus

Tertius Claudius Drusus: (18) youngest son of Lucius Fidelis, still living in Rome

JOSEPH BAR JONAH FAMILY

Joseph: widower, Messianic Jewish follower of Yeshua (Jesus)

Nathaniel: (20) oldest son, zealot

Reuben: (17) second son, killed by Roman soldier

Rachel: (17) only daughter, Reuben's twin

Simeon: (12) third son

Asher: (8) youngest son

Samuel: brother-in-law of Joseph

Daniel: (24) zealot cousin of Nathaniel, son of Samuel

OTHER IMPORTANT CHARACTERS

Jacob bar Asa: innkeeper, friend of Lucius

Celsus: centurion, friend of Lucius

Eli: friend of Joseph

Cities and Towns

CAESAREA MARITIMA: major port city and capital of the Roman province of Judaea

GATH-HEPHER: town 3 miles SE of Sepphoris

LEGIO (MEGIDDO): legion headquarters half way between Sepphoris and Caesarea

NAZARETH: village 4 miles south of Sepphoris

PTOLEMAIS: port town north of Caesarea

SEPPHORIS: Galilean city of 30,000 rebuilt by Herod Antipas, local center of Roman government with garrison

TIBERIAS: city built by Herod Antipas on the Sea of Galilee

ZOTAPATA: Galilean city 20 miles north of Sepphoris where Roman troops killed 40,000 in AD 67 during 1st Jewish War

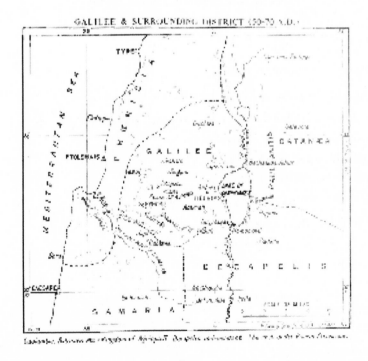

Chapter 1

Lost to a Roman Sword

Roman Province of Judaea, AD 122

The unarmed teenager lay dying at his feet, and Lucius wanted to vomit. That wasn't the response expected of a Roman officer, and he swallowed enough to keep his breakfast down. The ridicule from his fellow officers would be merciless if they thought he cared so much about killing a Jew.

Killing for Rome was not the problem. He'd killed in battle many times without regret. This time should have been no different. Zealots had ambushed a Roman tax collector, and the troops were hunting the murderers where they'd gone to ground in Gath-Hepher, a known zealot hideout. In the heat of battle, Lucius had thrust his sword into any and every man who came at him, already killing three.

He was pulling his blade from the third when he heard movement behind him. Someone stepped out of a narrow passageway. He spun and cut him down. His *gladius* slid deep into the chest. Blood flowed fast. So fast it coated his palm when he pushed the body off. Just one more zealot killed to keep the peace in Judaea.

Then he looked at the face. And the eyes.

Where was the hatred?

He wasn't a zealot. He was only a boy who'd been in the wrong place at the wrong time. His eyes held Lucius's. Surprise faded into... well, it looked like peace. He smiled—smiled up at the man holding the sword still crimson with his blood.

And then it happened.

He whispered something, and Lucius could almost swear it was "I

1

forgive you." But his ears must have fooled him. No one would ever say that to the man who'd just killed him.

Then the smile relaxed, and the emotion in the eyes changed to... nothing. The boy was dead, and there was nothing Lucius could ever do to change that.

He strode to his horse and mounted. Several zealots had fled down the narrow alleys where the horses couldn't follow. The troop would catch them on the other side of the village. With one final glance at the body, he kicked his horse and rode off in pursuit of the real enemies of Rome.

Rachel sat on the wooden bench outside the door as the canopy above her fluttered in the breeze. She pressed the heels of her hands against her jaw and her fingers tight against her eyes, but that didn't stop tears escaping between her fingers to form wet circles in the dust at her feet. More tears wet her thick brown hair that swung in rhythm with her rocking as gasping sobs convulsed her whole body.

Her twin brother Reuben lay dead inside, killed by a Roman sword. Her oldest brother, Nathaniel, had brought him home from Gath-Hepher. Why had Nathaniel let his zealot friends attack the Romans while Reuben was visiting?

Why hadn't Reuben listened when she begged him not to go there? He'd laughed at her concerns. He'd said he wasn't planning to do anything stupid. He only wanted to convince Nathaniel to stop fighting and come home. She'd told him Nathaniel wouldn't listen. Why hadn't he believed her?

She lifted her hands from her eyes and covered her ears. It wasn't enough to block out her father and brother yelling at each other. Abba's deep voice battered her head like a hammer on an anvil. Nathaniel's higher voice stabbed her heart like a dagger.

"See what your hatred of Rome has done? If you had chosen to follow Yeshua instead of that Pappus, your brother would still be alive."

"I didn't kill Reuben. Rome did. It's been killing us Jews for more than a hundred years. Don't blame me for the sins of Rome!"

"It is your sins I am worried about, not Rome's. Killing is not the way to freedom. The Lord's love through Yeshua is. Give up this way of death. Come back to the way of life before it is too late. Please, son. Come back to Yeshua."

"Your Yeshua hasn't brought freedom or life to Israel. I was a fool to think he would when I was a child. The only language Rome understands is the sword, and we'll use it to drive her out of our land."

"No, Nathaniel. You will only bring more death to the LORD's people, like Reuben."

"Enough, Abba! I won't stay and listen to you blame me. I'll take my own revenge on Rome for my brother's blood. I'm leaving, and don't expect me to return."

He stormed out the door and past her without a glance.

Rachel ran after him as he strode toward his horse.

"Nathaniel...Nathaniel!"

He stopped as he prepared to mount and turned to face her. She gripped his arm and leaned in as she tilted her head back to look up at him. A teardrop trickled across her cheekbone, then clung to the edge of her jaw. The fierce pain in his eyes softened as he gazed down at her.

"Please, Nathaniel! Don't leave like this. Abba loves you...I love you. We want you here with us."

He swept the back of his forefinger from her chin to her ear to wipe away the trail of tears.

"I know he does, little one, but I can't listen to him anymore. He blames me as much as that Roman butcher, even if he didn't say it." His mouth twitched as pain softened his eyes still more. Then his jaw clenched as the flinty glare returned. "I'm sorry Reuben followed me where the Romans could kill him, but I'm not sorry at all that I'm fighting the Roman dogs. A man can't stand by and let tyrants rule our land. Abba doesn't understand that. Tell him I still honor him, but I can't honor his choice not to fight. I can't stay."

He lifted her hand from his arm, mounted, and kicked the horse into a canter. Her shoulders sagged as he rode out the courtyard gate.

She tipped her face to the sky, and more teardrops trickled past her ears. "Why, LORD? Why?"

She'd already lost one brother to a Roman sword. Would she lose another to the Jewish sword raised against the Roman one?

Chapter 2

BROTHERS

Three months later

Marcus Claudius Drusus leaned against the bow rail of the trireme as it approached the harbor in Caesarea. He was sick of the slap of the waves against the hull of the ship. Sick of the up and down making his stomach queasy when the sea ran high. Sick of the throb of the drum that kept the rowers synchronized. Sick of the stench of three banks of men straining at the oars. The screams of the seagulls as they neared land were music to his ears. Soon the surface under his feet would no longer rise and fall, and he could purge the stink of sweating sailors from his nostrils with the aroma of a good, hot meal.

He was eager for his reunion with his older brother Lucius, who'd been serving in Judaea for three years. His generous, honorable older brother—the first man who stood between him and his inheritance of the vast Drusus fortune.

One corner of his lip lifted in a sneer. Lucius was like their dead grandfather Publius. Noble. Another word for fool. His nose wrinkled as his eyes steeled. Noble was no match for ruthless.

Father was a better model. A man who knew how to make things become what he wanted. Father had arranged Grandfather's execution for his Christian faith so he could escape his father's control and inherit sooner. A brilliant plan—all the benefits of murdering his father and none of the risk. The Emperor had even shown his appreciation by adding Fidelis to Father's name and awarding him a handsome sum of money for his loyalty.

Marcus fingered the raisins in his palm. A grapevine needed pruning to yield the best fruit, and that wasn't the only family pruning Father had done. Marcus had overheard two of the older slaves hinting that his uncle's death while racing chariots with Father hadn't been an accident at all.

His brow furrowed as he popped a raisin into his mouth and ground it between his molars. He'd been fifteen when he made his own first attempt at pruning. The swordmaster had just left, and Lucius wanted to keep sparring. It was the perfect opportunity, but big brother saw the stroke coming and slipped trying to avoid his blade.

Marcus's mouth twitched left and tightened. With the amount of blood that gushed from Lucius's cheek, that slash should have done more than cut his jaw from ear to chin and leave a wicked-looking scar. Malleolus had staunched the flow, but two inches lower and the blade would have slit his neck open. Not even the old steward who'd gone to war with Grandfather could have stopped a spurting neck wound.

Marcus's eyes narrowed as the next raisin followed the first. Lucius had sworn it wasn't anyone's fault, that Marcus wasn't a good enough swordsman to control his blade. That insult had infuriated him, but it had finally persuaded Father that it was an accident...maybe.

In a way, it was, but the only accident was that Lucius survived.

If he'd done anything after that to "accidentally" cause Lucius's death in Rome, Father would suspect he wanted him dead, too, and that would be the end. Father had killed his own father and brother for money. He'd kill his son to protect himself.

Marcus cupped his chin and stroked his cheek with his forefinger. A smile crept across his face as the galley maneuvered through the breakwater into the calmer waters in the harbor. He'd waited seven years, and the time was ripe to try again. Out here in Judaea, with a zealot under every rock and behind every bush longing to kill a Roman officer, covering up a murder would be easy. Even Father should never suspect anything.

Two months. That's all I'll need.

Once he knew how big brother spent his free time, he could pick the least suspicious way to remove Lucius from the line of inheritance. No reason to stay in Judaea after that. He'd request a transfer back to Rome. From there, he'd watch for the proper opportunity to prune younger brother Tertius as well.

The galley glided up to the pier, and the crew leaped to toss the bowline and sternline to the waiting slaves. As the dockworkers drew

5

the trireme against the fenders that protected it from the pier and the crew lowered the gangplank, his smile broadened, but his eyes remained flinty.

He'd developed a true appreciation for the old saying, "like father, like son." His father was definitely a man worth emulating.

Marcus shifted in the saddle as he leaned over to spit. He'd been in the province four days. Four days too long. The dust kicked up by the Roman convoy left the taste of dirt in his mouth. It would be a long, miserable ride, first from the port of Caesarea to the headquarters of the II Traiana Legion in Legio near Megiddo, then to the garrison in Sepphoris where Lucius was posted. So far, everything he'd heard about Judaea seemed to be true—everything bad, that is.

Serving in Caesarea Maritima could have been enjoyable. As the provincial capital since the time of Herod the Great, the port city almost felt like home. The public buildings and temples of white limestone gleamed in the sun. Mosaic sidewalks led to the theater. He could have relaxed at the luxurious baths and found entertainment at the Hippodrome, where chariots raced a course as large as the Circus Maximus, or the amphitheater, which was even larger than the Flavian Amphitheater in Rome.

Lucius was one of the tribunes specially assigned to the provincial governor, so he should have been posted in the capital. But no! Big brother had asked for a special assignment to find ways to reduce the spirit of rebellion simmering throughout the province. That sent him to serve in the center of Galilee, where there were constant problems with the Jews who wanted Rome out of the land. Lucius was attached to a cohort of the II Traiana garrisoned in Sepphoris, so Marcus had to ask the governor for a posting to Sepphoris as well.

Away from the coast, it was a hot, dusty land. He was covered helmet-to-sandal with a thin coating of Judaea as he rode into the legion fortress in Legio, where he would spend the night before proceeding to Sepphoris and his reunion with Lucius.

Worse than the dust was the unconcealed animosity in the towns and villages they passed through. No stones or taunts were thrown. In fact, almost nothing was spoken within earshot. The Galileans were like rats that scurry away when you carry a torch into the sewers after dark. Scurry off to hide in a dark corner, beady little eyes watching warily until you take the torch away. Watching and waiting...ready to chew on your living flesh if you were ever hurt and couldn't defend yourself.

A few women glared at him with warrior eyes, filled with hatred, but most were mousy little things, their heads draped, eyes downcast. Afraid to look at the might of Rome and her men. Maybe afraid to let a Roman man see there might be something pretty enough to be entertaining under those veils and decide to taste the hidden fruit.

Most men turned their faces down or away, like a rabbit cornered under a bush, pretending it didn't see the growling dog, hoping it would go away. Most men, but not all. Some stood straight and stared at him. They did nothing, but the hatred in the eyes—that was far beyond what he'd expected. It was quite disturbing—and gratifying as well. There should be no problem finding someone willing to kill Lucius for money. More than a few would be willing to kill a Roman tribune for free.

Marcus hadn't expected Lucius to be so happy to see him. When he and the other new soldiers assigned to the Sepphoris garrison passed through the gate in the late afternoon, Lucius was standing there talking with one of the centurions. The broad smile that overspread his face and lit up his eyes when he first saw Marcus should have warmed the heart of a brother.

It didn't.

Lucius strode toward him as Marcus dismounted. "Marcus! Welcome to Sepphoris. Have a good trip from the coast?"

Lucius gave him a hearty slap on the back. A small cloud of dust swirled around his hand.

Marcus unpinned the red cape that hung from his shoulder and shook it. The dust billowed around the pair. "I see now why no one wants to post to Judaea. I thought we'd never get here."

"It's not so bad after you get used to it. After you've reported to the commander, come find me. You must be hungry, and I know just the place for your first meal here."

Marcus smiled and nodded. Time to start acting like an affectionate brother. "That sounds good. I haven't had a decent meal since I left home."

Lucius chuckled. "Well, it won't be a Roman banquet, but I can promise you something much better than anything our garrison cooks dish up."

Before he left to resume his conversation with the centurion, he slapped Marcus on the shoulder.

Marcus smiled again. It was important for the other officers to think he liked his brother. He would want them to believe he was mourning Lucius's death in a couple of months.

Lucius led Marcus through the garrison gate to merge with the throngs of a city of 30,000. Sepphoris—Roman capital of the Galilee before the end of the Republic, center of trade for the region, a city that opened its gates to Vespasian's legions rather than fight for freedom in the Great Jewish Revolt, viewed by zealous Jews as a city of traitors and compromisers.

But for all its cosmopolitan character, Marcus still felt the daggers from the eyes of many who passed, and the eyes of many others masked true hostility with a friendly veneer. Despite its network of colonnaded paved streets, Roman public buildings, bathhouses, and even a theater, it was still a Judaean city at its core, and that meant it wasn't entirely safe for the Romans serving there.

Jews, Greeks, Syrians, Arabs, and Romans jostled together as the brothers wove their way through the crowd to an inn about half a mile from the garrison.

Lucius's hand rested on Marcus's shoulder. "This is one of the best places in Sepphoris to eat." He grinned. "I know how much you like good food. It won't be the three-course meal you'd get at home, but the food is truly delicious here."

Lucius pushed open the gate and motioned Marcus to walk ahead of him. The clamor of the street faded as they walked through a narrow passageway between two shops. Fifteen feet in, the passage flared open to reveal the dining area. The floor was a brilliant mosaic of intricate geometric patterns. Twenty or so tables were spread around a courtyard beneath colorful woven canopies that mirrored the reds and yellows in the mosaic and provided islands of shade while creating a bright, airy atmosphere.

The savory aroma of a lamb and lentil stew, enriched with onion and garlic, flavored with cumin and coriander and something special that only the chef knew, enveloped Marcus as he walked deeper into the courtyard. Lucius stepped past him and led him to a table by the back wall.

The middle-aged innkeeper, with a neatly trimmed, silver-frosted beard and a paunch that made him appear six months pregnant, approached the table with a welcoming smile. There was warmth in his dark brown eyes as well. That started to raise Marcus's eyebrows until he stopped them. Very few smiles had greeted him since landing in Caesarea, and not one was accompanied by eyes that smiled as well.

"Ah, Drusus." A string of strange words came from the man's mouth.

Unintelligible gibberish. Marcus's disdain peeked through a crack in his smiling mask. Greek was the universal language of trade in the eastern Empire. *Lucius should tell this ignorant Jew to speak Greek if he wants Roman money.*

"Jacob bar Asa..." The words escaping Lucius's mouth were gibberish, too.

Marcus's eyes widened as he swung his head to stare at his brother. Lucius speaking Aramaic? Why was he conversing with some innkeeper as if he were a Jew himself?

More Aramaic spewed from Lucius's mouth. He slapped Marcus on the shoulder, an affectionate big-brother grin on his lips. Except for Marcus's own name, Lucius's words might as well have been the babbling of a baby.

Jacob switched to speaking Greek. "It is a pleasure to have the brother of Lucius Drusus to serve. I will send your food and wine as quickly as I can."

Jacob's friendly eyes punctuated a genuine smile at Marcus, the first one he'd received from a Judaean since leaving the ship in Caesarea. He nodded, and he almost got the warmth of his eyes to match the curve of his lips. He'd worked hard to master faking it.

"Jacob..." Aramaic spewed out of his brother's mouth again. The innkeeper nodded and left after one more genuine smile directed at Lucius.

When the innkeeper was out of earshot, Marcus turned to Lucius. "You surprise me, big brother." A slight frown put a crease in his forehead. "Why ever would you bother to learn that language? Everyone knows Greek."

Marcus glanced around. His Latin should keep the Jews at the tables near them from understanding his words.

Lucius leaned forward, resting his forearms on the table. "Grandfather always said the best way to understand a man was to learn to speak his native tongue."

Marcus leaned in as well. "But why would a Roman even bother to understand a Jew? They're only a conquered people that we've crushed twice in the last sixty years."

"That way of thinking is a big part of the problem, Marcus. Maybe this province would be more peaceful if we Romans tried to understand the Jews better. We keep doing things that are guaranteed to make tensions worse. I asked to serve in Sepphoris to figure out how to change that."

Marcus rolled his eyes. "Nothing's going to change because of what you're doing. Getting too close to these Jews could get you killed." *Unless I get you killed first.*

◆

Lucius wasn't surprised that Marcus disagreed with what he'd said. His brother was too much the typical Roman who thought in terms of conquest and power, not peaceful co-existence. It had been three months since he killed the innocent youth in Gath-Hepher, and the memory still bothered him. Marcus would never have given it a second thought.

Marcus's mouth twitched. Time to change the subject before conversation turned into argument.

"Besides, there's not much around here for entertainment except getting drunk and gambling. I'd much rather spend my time learning a new language than wasting it like that."

"You sound just like Grandfather." The hint of a sneer dripped from Marcus's voice.

Lucius's eyes widened at his tone. "And you don't think that's a good thing?"

"No. His interest in the Jews got him killed. The Christians are only a bad kind of Jew."

"I suppose you think I should be more like Father. It wasn't Grandfather's interest in the Jews that got him killed. It was Father's greed. He sold out Grandfather for the estates and the Emperor's reward."

"Well, Father is rich and alive while Grandfather is dead. That should tell you something about who was the smarter one."

A trace of anger flickered in Marcus's eyes. Lucius had never liked it when his brother got angry, and he certainly didn't want to get into a full-blown argument in the middle of his friend's inn.

"Let's not discuss this anymore, Marcus. We're never going to agree."

Marcus nodded and forced a smile. Arguing with Lucius in public was unwise. Someone might remember after he arranged the accident that would make him the oldest son.

"You're right, big brother. No reason to let something so unimportant take any pleasure out of our reunion."

He slapped Lucius's arm and grinned for the benefit of some officers eating at a nearby table. Then he leaned back in his chair and watched their fellow diners.

Lucius leaned back in his chair as well and watched his brother. His face relaxed into a contented smile. It was so good to have Marcus sitting across the table from him. It had been a long three years so far from family and home. For all their differences in temperament and opinions, Marcus was his brother, and that counted more than anything.

Back at the garrison, Marcus left Lucius at his quarters. When he entered his own, he closed the door and leaned against the rough wood. He pulled a deep breath and blew it out slowly. Then a smirk lifted one corner of his mouth. After releasing the side latches between the breastplate and backplate of his metal cuirass, he lifted the body armor over his head and dropped it on the bed.

Marcus sauntered over to the small table where he'd placed a box of writing materials. He extracted a sheet of papyrus from the box, dipped the pen into the small bottle of ink, and composed the first letter to his father to begin setting the stage for Lucius's death.

> Marcus Claudius Drusus to Lucius Claudius Drusus Fidelis, my father, greetings. If you are well, then I am glad. I write to tell you that I have arrived safely in Sepphoris.
>
> It is good to be here with Lucius, although I find Judaea is very much worse than he has led us to believe. Judaea does not consider itself a Roman province at all. Not one Jew in ten is content to have us here. All eyes are daggers, and real daggers are used against us

if we lower our guard. The commander in Sepphoris has told us to wear armor every time we leave the garrison, even when off duty.

It is a good thing that I have come. Lucius does not take the danger seriously. He regularly eats at Jewish inns where he could be poisoned or knifed, and he goes riding for pleasure by himself. Perhaps now I am here, I can get him to be more careful. I will try.

I hope all will continue to be well with you. May the gods guard your safety.

He rolled the papyrus and sealed it with wax. As he wrote his father's address on the outer surface, he began counting the days until he could return to Rome as the oldest son.

Chapter 3

NOT THE ONE TO BLAME

Simeon and Asher strolled home after their morning studies at the synagogue. Simeon kicked up dust as they walked. It had been months since the last rain, but soon the early rains would come. That was good. The sheep liked fresh grass.

Asher looked up at his brother as they walked together. Simeon noticed and tousled his hair. Then Asher, too, began kicking up dust.

Simeon was twelve. Just starting his spurt into manhood, his feet were too big. He was thin, as if he'd been stretched like a sheepskin between two poles to dry. Reuben had always tousled his curly brown hair when he passed. He used to swat at his brother's hand, but it always pulled a smile from him...before Reuben's death. He'd give anything to have his hair mussed up by his brother again. The smiles were returning, but they were no longer the blissful smiles of a boy. He was still the first to speak encouragement to any of his friends. The sadness of the past three months hadn't changed that.

He was the favorite student of Rabbi Eliezer in *bet talmud*, where the boys between ten and fourteen were learning the oral law and mastering the deeper meanings of Torah, the Prophets, and the Writings. If it hadn't been for Reuben's death and Nathaniel's leaving, he would have continued his studies with the rabbi when he finished *bet talmud*. As it was, he would need to join his father, Joseph bar Jonah, full time in the workshop instead.

Asher was eight, and he was the image of Simeon at that age. On the outside, that is. His personality was the polar opposite of the older brother he adored. He was very quiet. Behind those serious eyes, deep thoughts swirled, but he wasn't likely to reveal them unless asked. And sometimes not even then.

When Simeon spotted his cousin Daniel riding toward their house, he sucked air between gritted teeth. His sister Rachel would not be pleased. Neither would Abba. It had been three months since Reuben was killed, and Daniel was a painful reminder of that terrible fact.

Daniel was four years older than Nathaniel. That was close enough that he'd been both friend and role model for Simeon's oldest brother. If Abba had realized Daniel was trying to convince Nathaniel to join the battle against Rome, he would never have allowed him to visit so often. Now the damage was done. Daniel was his nephew, so Abba wouldn't order him to leave, but he would never be truly welcome in their home.

◆

Rachel stood working at the loom under the canopy. She scrunched her nose at the sight of her cousin riding through the courtyard gate. Why did he have to come? The only good thing about Nathaniel not living at home was that Daniel had stopped dropping by. He was too angry, too eager to embrace zealot violence to oppose the Roman occupation.

Daniel was the reason Nathaniel had joined the battle and the reason Reuben was now dead. If she never saw him again, that would be too soon. Why did he have to keep trying to court her even though she had done her best to discourage him?

Daniel rode over near her before dismounting.

"It's good to see you, Rachel. You look very pretty today."

She longed to tell him to leave and never return, but to be so blunt would be unkind. Yeshua said to be kind to everyone, even this cousin who'd cost her two brothers. She pushed her disgust with him aside and spoke with civility instead.

"I'm surprised to see you, Daniel. If you're looking for Nathaniel, he's not here."

"I know. He's staying with us and working for a wagon maker in Sepphoris. I came to see how you were doing."

Rachel stared straight at him. "Not so well. We still mourn Reuben's death. We all miss him terribly."

Daniel shifted under her cool gaze. "I'm so sorry. I'll do what I can to the Roman dogs to avenge his death."

"That's the problem, Daniel. It's your hatred and desire for vengeance that got him killed. It's not Rome that's the most to blame."

Even Daniel shouldn't be so dense that he could fail to see she didn't want to talk to him today...or any other day.

Daniel's jaw dropped. It sounded like she blamed him for Reuben's death. She must be too deep in grief to think clearly. The sparks in her eyes promised an argument he didn't want, so he remounted.

"Time for me to go. I want to pay my respects to your father before I leave."

He paused to see if she had anything else to say. She'd turned her attention back to the shuttle she was weaving through the warp threads, so he reined his horse back toward the workshop.

As he dismounted to speak with Joseph, he glanced at Rachel. She was so pretty, and she used to be so happy. He didn't like to see her sad. When he came again, her grief should have faded, and he'd find the joyous Rachel he wanted to make his wife.

Two weeks later, Lucius was on his way back to Sepphoris with Marcus when they topped a hill and saw three mounted soldiers harassing two boys and their sheep. They were taking turns charging the sheep and jumping their horses over them at the last moment. The older boy was trying to move the flock away from the mounted men, and the smaller boy was hunkered face down on the ground, covering his head with his hands.

Marcus laughed when one horse barely cleared a ewe and the flock panicked, but Lucius was not amused. He was sick of these antics that inflamed the Jews against the Roman forces. This kind of stupid cruelty bred zealots like grasshoppers in the villages where such boys lived. He was tired of killing each new crop.

Lucius kicked his horse and galloped over to end their callous sport. When the soldiers saw a tribune riding hard toward them, the game ended, and they turned their horses to await his arrival. As he reined in, they sat at attention and thumped their chests with their clenched fists.

His stallion began dancing in place, excited by the anger radiating from its master. Lucius was livid. His mouth set to the thinnest of lines. His breath came fast, and the blaze crackling in his eyes would make even a man seasoned by battle draw back.

"Enough! You will not do this again. Report to the garrison immediately. I'll deal with you when I get there."

◆

The three saluted again and kicked their mounts into a trot. When they were out of earshot, the latest arrival turned to the man next to him.

"Who was that? We were just having some harmless fun. Why did he get so angry?"

The tallest one answered. "That's Claudius Drusus. He has no sense of humor if you upset some Jew. No other officer would have a problem with what we were doing."

The new arrival placed his hand over his mouth and drew it downward. "Will we be in big trouble over this?"

"Depends. If Drusus has anything to say about it, we'll be disciplined. But I wouldn't expect it to amount to much. He's only attached here, and the commander doesn't care what the Jews think."

The three rode on in silence. It was never good to get a tribune angry, even if the commander didn't share his anger.

◆

Simeon turned from the flock to see why the soldiers had stopped and ridden away. They were cringing while a red-faced officer on a prancing black stallion berated them. As they rode away toward Sepphoris, the officer swung his mount and trotted toward Asher, who was still balled up on the ground with his hands covering his head. The officer reined in and dismounted. In three steps, he was within sword range, and his hand rested on the pommel of the sword hanging at his side.

As the Roman stood towering over Asher, Simeon began running as fast as he could toward them. His knuckles whitened where he gripped his staff. A wooden staff wasn't much defense against a sword, but he would still fight to protect his little brother.

Then the Roman officer crouched down by Asher and gently placed his hand on his little brother's back.

Relief poured through Simeon, and he slowed to a trot.

◆

Asher's heart raced as he smelled the leather of the Roman's armor next to him. With everything he'd heard Nathaniel say about Roman troops, he expected the Roman to kill him. They'd killed Reuben. He began his death prayer. *Yeshua, take me to you as I—*

A hand rested on his back. No sword, like for Reuben? He turned his head to peek at the Roman's face. A scar along the soldier's jaw gave his face a war-like cast. He looked deadly, but his eyes were kind.

"Are you hurt, boy?"

Asher's eyes widened. The question was in Aramaic.

The corners of the Roman's mouth turned up. A soldier smiling at him?

"No." Asher had never been so close to a Roman soldier before. They were supposed to be cruel. This man seemed more like his friend Caleb's father.

The soldier stood and offered his hand to help Asher up. He took it tentatively. The Roman's smile broadened. Asher gripped his hand firmly, and the big man pulled him to his feet.

Simeon reached them. He jerked Asher back and positioned himself between the Roman and his little brother. He held the staff at a diagonal, ready to ward off any attack in case the officer changed his mind. The long scar on his jaw made him look vicious.

The soldier offered a smile and assumed a relaxed stance. He didn't look quite so dangerous with his weight on one leg and his arms hanging loosely at his sides. His eyes held Simeon's, and there was no threat in them at all.

The Roman's eyes flicked to Asher peering out from behind, then back to Simeon. "I'm not going to hurt him." He motioned toward the sheep with his head. "This should not have happened."

Simeon's eyes saucered. The Roman spoke to him in Aramaic, not Greek. He'd never heard of any Roman officer who bothered to learn the language of the Jews.

As the older boy stared at Lucius, a bleating lamb interrupted the silence, and all three turned toward the sound. It was dragging a broken hind leg and struggling to walk on three.

Lucius tightened his lips and shook his head. The loss of a single lamb could bring serious financial hardship to a poor family, and this part of Judaea was filled with such families. These boys probably came from one.

He reached into the purse hanging at his belt. "Here. To replace the lamb."

He held out some coins worth enough to buy at least two, maybe three lambs. The older boy held out his palm, and Lucius dropped them into it.

The boy smiled at him. "May the LORD bless you for your kindness."

Marcus rode up. "Let's go. I'm ready to eat."

With a nod, Lucius turned to his horse and mounted. He nudged the animal into a trot, and the Roman brothers headed for the garrison.

◆

Simeon watched them ride away. Nathaniel would never believe him if he told him what just happened. Well, he'd believe the part about soldiers bothering the sheep, but he'd never believe a Roman officer stopped them and paid for the lamb.

He turned to Asher. "Let's take the sheep home, in case the first three come back."

He scooped up the lamb with the broken leg. As it hung in his arms, he stroked it. "I bet Rachel can fix you. Rachel can fix almost anything."

As they started the flock toward home, Simeon glanced back in the direction the officer had ridden. There was now one Roman he'd be asking the LORD to protect when he said his prayers each night.

Chapter 4

Right Man for the Job

It can be difficult to find a good way to kill your brother when he doesn't have any bad habits, so Marcus decided to exploit his brotherly affection instead. He'd been in Sepphoris two months. It was time, and he had the perfect plan.

An ambush on a back road on the way to buy a horse would achieve his goal. He'd identified a few local men who'd been in trouble for starting fights. The blacksmith was his first choice. A bad gambler who liked to hurt people should welcome an easy way to cover his debts. It was time to enlist him.

Marcus sauntered into the shop and stood watching the blacksmith at his forge. He was an enormous man, muscled up like a champion ox. He should have plenty of strength to do whatever was needed. Lucius was muscled and strong, but he'd be no match for a brute like the blacksmith, even in a fair fight. Marcus wasn't planning anything even remotely fair.

"I hear you're a good man to see about a sword."

The blacksmith turned from the forge to face him. "That's true. Men come from fifty miles away for my swords."

Marcus drew his gladius from its scabbard of intricately carved wood and engraved brass. "So, if I needed it right away, how long would it take you to make a sword like this?"

As he held it out for the blacksmith to examine, he watched the man's eyes. They narrowed as the smith sized him up. *Yes, I'm rich enough to pay top money, and I'll bet that's what you need right now.*

When the smith's eyes relaxed, Marcus knew he had him hooked.

"That depends. If it's the only thing I'm working on, I can have it for you in a day. But it would cost you extra. Otherwise, it might take several."

"Extra is no problem for an excellent job done quickly." Marcus cleared his throat. "I hear you're also a good man if someone needs something special done to solve a problem. Something that could earn a premium price if it were done so no one knew who commissioned the work."

"That's also true." The blacksmith tipped his head, his eyes scanning Marcus. A close-lipped smile began to build.

Marcus suppressed his own smile. He'd made the blacksmith curious...and eager to find out what he wanted solved.

"I hear you might be the man to go to if that special job might involve hurting someone." He paused. "If someone needed that sort of man and was willing to pay good money to get a special job done, would you be interested?"

The blacksmith chuckled. "I might be. Hurting someone—that's not a problem if the money is right." A cruel grin twisted his lips. "I'm a man who keeps secrets as well. I might be your man if there's enough money in it."

"There's enough money in it." Marcus liked his response enough to continue. "There's a lot of money in it for the right man who can complete the job and then forget who hired him to do it."

"I'm the right man." The blacksmith grinned, revealing several rotten teeth.

Marcus scanned the shop to make sure no one was listening. He stepped closer and lowered his voice. "Here's the problem. There's this rich Greek widow I've been courting, but she's skittish about marrying again. Now there's another officer in the garrison who's interested in her, too. She's starting to pay too much attention to him. I need to get him out of the way before she decides she wants him instead of me."

The blacksmith nodded slowly, and another twisted grin appeared. "A man should take whatever steps he has to for the love of the right woman. I'd be glad to do my part to clear the path for true love...for the right price."

"Is 100 denarii the right price?"

"More like 300. I'll need a helper. Of course, he'll never know he's helping the cause of true love or who the lovers are."

Marcus tried not to smile at the counteroffer. He had been willing to go much higher.

"I want you to make me a sword as well. I'll bring my rival into your shop when I come to check your progress on the sword. That way you'll have no trouble recognizing him. He has an unusual scar on his left cheek. Can you start the sword this week?"

"I can start it today."

"Good. It has to look like an accident."

"An accident?" The smith's forehead furrowed as he tipped his head.

Marcus's lip twitched. He needed brute strength but not brute stupidity.

"On the day we pick, I'll arrange for him to be alone on a back road just south of here. There's a spot where it goes along a cliff. Get him off his horse with a slingshot, then throw him off the cliff. It needs to look like an accident, so send the horse on down the road. The fall will hide what the slingshot did. No one will suspect it's murder."

The blacksmith nodded. "I know that road. Almost no one uses it...I like it. No risk to me and the satisfaction of doing my part for true love."

His twisted grin confirmed his genuine appreciation of the plan. "I'm the man to solve your problem. Now, let's talk about the sword so I can start on it. I'll have it partly made by tomorrow. You can bring in your...friend whenever you want to. I'll talk with my friend tonight, and we'll be ready anytime you say."

Joseph had almost finished the metal rim that would hold the outermost wooden parts of a wagon wheel together. He stepped back from the forge and rested his forehead on his arm as he leaned against the post that supported the roof over the work area.

Each day had become a struggle to climb a sand dune, and every step forward made the sand shift, dragging him farther down the slope than before. Even worse, there was no relief in sight. It had been almost five months since Reuben was killed, and Nathaniel left to join the zealots almost a month before that. He and Reuben had worked harder to fulfill the promises he'd made based on three of them working, and they'd done fairly well. Now, with Reuben gone and Nathaniel refusing to return, he was behind on everything. He'd already had two orders cancelled that he'd counted on to support his family.

◆

Rachel's gaze fixed on her father as she came out of the house with some dates and watered wine for his midmorning break. She shook her head as she watched him standing there. He seemed older than he did before they lost Reuben. She blinked fast, but the tears started to form anyway. Then she flicked them away and put on a smile. It would be that much harder for Abba if he saw her crying, so she tried to never do it when he might see.

He glanced at her as if he'd felt her eyes upon him. Then he stepped back to resume his work on the rim. When she reached the workbench, she set the bowl and cup down and rested her hand on his arm.

"What's wrong, Abba?"

"Nothing for you to worry about, Rachel."

"I know that's not true. I'm not a little girl anymore. You can tell me anything you would have told Eema. Please let me help like she would have."

◆

Joseph gazed into her eyes. They were like the deep, still pool where the spring came welling up at its bottom—calm, reliable. She'd taken over the responsibilities of a woman when his beloved Hannah died five years ago. She was barely past her own childhood then, but she was no longer a girl trying to fill her dead mother's place. She had become a woman in her own right. She was just like Hannah. She was strong enough to hear his fears.

"The work. It is too much for me alone, and now my customers are having to wait too long. First Nathaniel leaves, and now Reuben is gone. I took on work for three, and now there is only me."

"Let me help, Abba. At least with some of the woodwork."

"No, Rachel. You already have enough to do."

"I can do more, Abba. I only have to arrange my day differently. Please let me help."

Her eyes were pleading. He cradled her face between his hands and tilted it up so he could kiss her forehead.

"I'll think about it."

"And then you'll let me do it."

She stood on tiptoes to plant a kiss on his cheek before turning to go back to her own work.

Until she disappeared through the doorway, he watched her. His Rachel was such a treasure. What would he ever do without her?

He turned back to the forge and pumped the bellows to bring the coals back to yellow-white heat. With hammer in hand, he gripped the rim with the tongs and placed the section he was shaping back on the coals.

Bittersweet would be the day he gave her to her future husband. Perhaps he should be glad she only wanted to marry a man who followed Yeshua. No such men of the right age lived in the village. He didn't want her to leave his home, but it was selfish to keep her with him. She deserved the love of a good man and the joy of raising her own children. A deep sigh escaped. He should be asking the LORD to bring the husband she deserved.

As he pulled the orange-hot metal from the coals and struck the first ringing blow, he offered up a prayer for the right man for Rachel.

As they walked through the streets of Sepphoris together, Lucius glanced at Marcus. It was so good to have his brother there. Life was ironic sometimes. He'd always wanted to be good friends, but Marcus had rebuffed his attempts when they were in Rome. Who would have thought when he posted to Judaea that Marcus would miss him? So much so that he asked to come to what was probably the worst place in the Empire to serve together. They'd finally developed a real friendship in the two months since Marcus arrived, and Lucius couldn't have been happier about it.

"The blacksmith is down this street. I've been told people come fifty miles to buy one of his swords. I had to have one." Marcus turned down the side street and led Lucius toward the shop at the end. "I want to check on his progress before we go eat."

The door to the shop was open, and Marcus led Lucius into the dimly lit interior. The blacksmith was working the bellows, each pump causing the red coals to glow orange and the orange to flame yellow. Marcus cleared his throat, and the smith turned to face them.

"Ah, Drusus. Come to check on your sword?"

"I have."

"Good. The blade's mostly finished, but I have a question about what you want engraved on it."

The blacksmith stepped over to a set of shelves and lifted the blade from the top one.

"It needs more tempering, but you can see how it will look."

Marcus took the blade and ran his fingers along it before handing it to Lucius.

"Didn't I tell you his work was exceptional?"

Lucius felt the heft of the blade. "Very nice. I may have to have one made myself after I see the finished sword." He looked up at the smith's face and offered a friendly smile.

The smith's eyes darted from Lucius to Marcus. "It'll be a few days before it's done. I've got to finish a special order as soon as the buyer tells me what day he needs it."

Marcus's eyes narrowed. The blacksmith's smirk irritated him. His annoyance grew when the smith's eyes flicked back and forth between him and Lucius as his finger traced out Lucius's scar on his own jaw. It might make Lucius suspicious.

On second thought, his dear, naive brother would never dream of suspecting him. It didn't matter what the smith looked like or implied.

"I'm having second thoughts about the engraving. Plain might be best for my purposes. I'll let you know as soon as I decide. I'll be back shortly to tell you how to complete the work."

The blacksmith fought a grin before he turned back to his forge.

Marcus slapped Lucius on the back. "Let's go eat. I'm starved."

As they headed back up the side street on their way to Jacob's inn, Marcus glanced at Lucius. He let the corners of his mouth turn up into a smile. *Enjoy this meal, Lucius. You won't have many more.*

Marcus's heart rate picked up as he contemplated his brother's profile. A few more days, and he'd be able to request his transfer back to Rome. The blacksmith really did make good swords, and his would be a reminder of his successful tour of duty in Judaea once he was the oldest living son.

Chapter 5

If You Want It Done Right

Lucius was sitting on his bed reading when Marcus burst into the room.

Marcus strode to the bedside. "I've been wanting a better horse, and I may have found exactly what I'm looking for. There was a stallion I liked in the market, but it sold before I could make an offer."

Lucius closed his codex. "Maybe you'll find a better one soon."

Marcus gauged the interest in his brother's eyes. Time to jiggle the bait. "I may have already. That's the good news. The breeder lives less than ten miles from here, and the man selling his horses told me his master is about to sell a magnificent three-year-old stallion. He said it was one of the best horses he'd seen come from that stable. Given what all the other horses he had looked like, it must be amazing. I told him I was very interested and wanted first chance at it. He said that was possible, but only if I can go look at it tomorrow."

He had Lucius's total attention. They both appreciated truly fine horseflesh.

"Since we're both off duty tomorrow, let's go look at the stallion. If it's even half as good as he says, I want it."

Lucius nodded as his eyes brightened. "Sounds like an excellent way to spend our day off. Maybe I can find something I like, too."

Marcus slapped his brother on the shoulder and gave him a beaming smile before he swung around and hurried out the door. The beaming smile turned into twisted grin as soon as he was around the corner. Easiest fish he'd ever hooked.

Early the next morning, Lucius withdrew 500 denarii from his account with the paymaster. He was walking back to his room when Marcus walked up beside him. His brows lowered when he saw the pained expression on his brother's face.

"What's wrong, Marcus?"

"My gut's twisting worse than on the ship coming from Rome. Hope it's only something I ate last night. We should have gone to Jacob's instead of eating here. I don't think I can ride too far today." He paused and clutched his stomach for effect. "I have a favor to ask of you, big brother."

"What is it?"

"I want a chance at that stallion. You know horses as well as I do, and you know what I like. Would you go take a look and buy it if you think it's the right animal?" He handed his purse to Lucius. "There are 500 denarii in here. If it's more than that, five hundred should hold it until I can get over there with the difference."

"I can do that."

Lucius took the purse and tucked it inside his tunic, where he had placed his own. He wouldn't carry that much in a purse on his belt to tempt a robber. With the nineteen aurei and twenty-five denarii he'd withdrawn and the same from Marcus, it was going to be a snug fit when he put on his body armor today.

When Lucius headed into the hills south of Sepphoris, he'd expected more people on the road Marcus sent him down. Until he left the road to Nazareth, he'd been riding past people heading both directions. In the past half hour, he'd only passed one person going the other way. That was fine with him. Unlike his brother, he enjoyed solitude, and a leisurely ride in good weather down a little-used road was the perfect way to spend time alone.

Since the rains had stopped five months ago, the shrubs and trees were islands of green in a sea of golden grass. Puffs of dust rose where his horse's hooves struck the dirt road.

The day was hotter than normal. He released the chin strap and lifted off his helmet. After he swished his fingers through his damp hair, the breeze was as refreshing as a dipper of water poured over his head. When he'd cooled off, he replaced the helmet but left the strap loose.

One moment he was watching the breeze ripple the grass. The next, pain exploded behind his left eye. He toppled, smacking the ground with a grunt, the breath driven from his lungs. Sparkles danced against the dim images of four black legs.

A rock had struck his helmet right where the left cheek guard was hinged to the bowl. A fraction of an inch to the left and it would have killed him outright or at least taken his eye.

Shaking his head to clear it—huge mistake. As he fought to focus on anything moving around him, he heard voices. Aramaic. Two men. If they'd suspected he understood, they would never have been so careless with their words.

A high, nasal voice spoke. "Hard to believe we're getting paid by one Roman soldier to kill another. Good money, too. I'd have been willing to kill a Roman even without getting paid."

A guttural growl responded. "Let's finish the job before someone comes along. Get the legs."

One of them grabbed his ankles while the other grabbed his wrists. They dragged him over to the edge of the cliff by the side of the road.

The blow to his head had disoriented him, but he struggled against them. One man was huge, and the kick he drove into Lucius's kidney could have come from the hind leg of a horse. It didn't knock all the fight out of him, but it almost paralyzed him for a few seconds. That was enough. They stretched him out between them so his thrashing gave him no leverage for breaking free from their grasp.

His stomach clenched when they lifted him in the air and swung him once, twice, three times before letting him sail out over the edge and plummet to the base of the cliff.

With arms and legs flailing, he watched the cliff face rush past.

The wind was knocked out of him when he hit on his right side and flopped onto his back, but he'd expected much worse.

He'd expected to die.

Odd. He'd been thrown from a horse as a child. Arcing through the air, slapping flat on his back, fighting for breath. But that was only a four-foot fall. This should have been much worse, but there was hardly any pain. Who would have thought it possible to fall twenty feet and not be seriously hurt? His metal cuirass protected his torso well against sword strikes. His fellow officers would be amazed that it helped so much against such a fall.

He watched his helmet hurtling down at him in slow motion. It blocked his view as it struck his forehead at the hairline. Odder still. That scarcely hurt as well.

He closed his eyes and lay still as death.

Dead. That's what the assassins needed to believe so they wouldn't come down to check. He strained to catch any voices, hoping to hear something that would tell him who at the garrison wanted him dead enough to risk hiring someone to kill him.

Faint words floated down to him. Growler spoke, "That was easy. Too bad we can't take the horse, but it's got to look like an accident."

Nasal man replied, "Are you sure he's dead? Should we go check?"

Growler again. "He must be. Look at him. Besides, even if he isn't now, the heat or the jackals will finish him off quick enough. No one around here would lift a finger to help a Roman. Let's go."

A few pebbles showered down as they moved away from the edge. He took a deep breath and blew it out slowly. His would-be murderers were gone...except for the one back at the garrison. A few more minutes pretending and then he'd climb back up to the road. It sounded like they'd even left his horse.

Then the immediate shock of his injuries began to wear off, and the pain started.

When he tried to sit up, stabbing pain ripped through him where the ribs on his right side had broken or at least cracked. Shooting pain radiating up from his right leg told him it was broken even before he looked down and saw it bent at an odd angle below his knee. Then the rivulet of blood from where the helmet cut his forehead made its way into his left eye.

He collapsed back onto the soft sand. The pain kept ramping up.

The assassins might be right. His injuries were so severe he'd never get back to the road on his own. If no one came along or if whoever came chose to ignore a Roman soldier's cries for help, it would be either the heat or the jackals that got him.

He'd fallen with his scabbard beneath him. The pain from his ribs surged as he raised himself enough to pull it out. At least his arms weren't broken, so he wasn't completely defenseless. He drew the *gladius* and placed it where his sword hand could reach it.

Given the choice between jackals and heat, he would choose heat. At least that would be his choice if he was still able to use his sword when the jackals came.

Chapter 6

Good Samaritans

Simeon and Asher watched the vultures tighten the circle and lower it in the sky. That afternoon, they were leading their sheep to the wadi near the base of the cliff. The rains were long since over, but the grazing was still a little better there. Rocks sometimes fell from the cliff wall, but it was worth the risk for some better grass.

Simeon walked ahead to drive away anything feasting on whatever had died. It might prefer fresh lamb to rotting flesh. He froze when he rounded the tall pile of rocks that had fallen after a spring storm. Asher trotted up beside him.

He gasped and clutched Simeon's tunic.

A Roman officer lay crumpled on the sand. A jackal was circling him, moving steadily closer. The Roman clutched his sword as it lay on his chest, but he didn't seem to have the strength to raise it to fight off the approaching jackal.

Lucius had been holding off the jackal for more than an hour, slashing at it each time it approached too close. His cracked ribs made each stroke produce an explosion of pain and slowed his attack enough that the beast was too fast for the blade to connect. It was becoming harder each time to rise up from the ground and swing the sword. How much longer could he keep the scavenger at bay?

The sun was in the wrong part of the sky for the cliff to give him

29

any shade. He'd been baking in its unrelenting rays for several hours, and his tongue stuck to the roof of his mouth.

A man was trapped inside his head, hammering on his skull to break out. Whether that was more from the lump from the rock that knocked him off his horse, the cut where his helmet hit him, or the lack of water as he lay in the blistering sun, he wasn't sure.

He'd heard only three people passing on the road, but none of them had responded when he called out. At least none had responded by helping. One had looked down, muttered a curse at him, and chosen to walk on, leaving him to die.

The jackal was coming once more, and he tightened his grip on his sword, hoping he still had enough strength left for one more swing. He wasn't sure he did.

Amber eyes locked on him, teeth bared, the jackal was less than five feet away. Pain ripped through him as he tensed his muscles, preparing to rise from the sand to strike one more time...maybe one last time.

Suddenly it catapulted into the air with a yelp. Another yelp and it spun and took off at a dead run. He turned his head to look in the opposite direction from the running jackal.

Two boys were trotting toward him, one about eight and the other maybe twelve. Both held slingshots. He closed his eyes and blew out a sigh of relief. It took some effort to reopen them to watch the boys approach.

Help may have finally come.

When Simeon knelt beside the injured man, his head bounced back as his eyebrows shot up. That long scar on his jaw—there couldn't be two like it. It was the Roman officer who'd given him money for the lamb. He'd been praying for this man's protection every night since. The LORD had surely answered his prayers by letting them find him before the jackal finished him off.

"It's good we saw the vultures." He lifted the water skin from his shoulder and untied the thong that closed it. "Here, drink some of this."

Simeon raised the Roman's head enough for him to drink. The half-dead man flopped his left hand onto Simeon's arm and rested it there as he gulped the water. When he'd drunk his fill, Simeon tipped the bag so some water washed across his flushed cheeks and neck. Then he lowered his head to the ground.

"Where are you hurt?"

As he looked down at the Roman's half-closed eyes, Simeon saw a spark of hope kindle. He must have thought no help was coming. The way most people felt about the Romans, he could have been right.

The Roman grimaced as he drew a deeper breath before he spoke. "Broken leg...ribs...think that's all."

Simeon nodded. The Roman had a purple lump near his left eye that stuck out more than half an inch and an ugly bruise around the two-inch cut at his hairline. The dried blood on his face hadn't all rinsed off.

There might be more wrong than the Roman thought. They'd come just in time even if the jackal hadn't been about to kill him.

He didn't know what to do next, but Rachel would. She always knew what to do.

He stood and turned to Asher, who stood at the Roman's feet, staring at the broken man. He'd only seen his brother stare at something like that once before—when Nathaniel brought Reuben's body home. He'd stared at Reuben exactly the same way.

"Asher." His brother kept staring at the Roman. "Asher, look at me." His brother's head twitched before his gaze switched from the Roman to Simeon. "Stay here with him and keep the jackal away. I'm going for Rachel."

Asher nodded.

Simeon turned back toward the Roman. "Don't worry. I'll get my sister, and she'll know what to do. Asher will keep you safe until we return."

The Roman's grateful smile spoke much louder than his voice. "Thank you...what's your name?"

"Simeon bar Joseph."

"Simeon...thank you." His voice was scarcely above a whisper.

Simeon nodded in response. He handed Asher the water skin before trotting away toward home.

Rachel was working at the loom under the canopy when she glanced up and saw Simeon trotting toward her. Her heart skipped, then raced. He shouldn't be coming home at that time of day, and he certainly shouldn't be coming alone. She dropped the shuttle and ran to meet him.

"Is something wrong? Where's Asher?" Her voice quavered as she gripped his shoulders. *Please, LORD! Not another brother lost!*

"Asher's well, but we found someone who needs help. In the wadi below the road. It's the Roman who gave me money for the lamb. One leg's broken below his knee and his ribs, too, and maybe more. He so weak he can barely talk. We found him just before a jackal got him. I left Asher guarding him and came to get you. I told him you'd know how to help him."

"A Roman cavalryman?"

She took a deep breath and blew it out. Knowing how and wanting to were very different things. Helping him could be dangerous. Knowing she'd even gone to help a Roman would upset most of the village if they ever found out. Bringing him home to care for him until the soldiers came to get him—that would be considered traitorous.

Support for the zealots was strong among her neighbors and among many members of her own extended family. Almost all of them would not simply refuse to help a Roman. They would rejoice if he were to die. Many would gladly hasten his death.

It had only been five years since Rome put down the Kitos rebellion at Lydda so brutally, crucifying hundreds when the city fell. The forty thousand who died less than thirty miles from her village in the siege of Jotapata fifty-five years ago were as fresh in the minds of Galilee as if it were yesterday. Hatred for Rome ran deep in the whole province of Judaea.

Before Reuben's death, she hadn't shared that hatred, but now...

Only the handful of people in the village who knew Yeshua was Messiah would understand why she would even consider helping an injured Roman soldier. Only they would know Yeshua's parable about the Good Samaritan and his commands to his followers to help even their enemies when they needed it.

But a Roman soldier...did she have to help one?

A sigh welled up from deep inside. She knew the answer even before she asked. But she would have to conceal his Roman identity to protect both him and her family until someone from the garrison could come get him.

She could send Simeon on the donkey to let them know he was with them. Getting rid of him shouldn't take more than two or three hours once she got him home. That shouldn't be too long to keep him safely hidden. Besides, if anyone saw the soldiers come, they'd only think he was being arrested as long as he wasn't in uniform.

Simeon stood in silence before her, waiting for directions. It was a big risk to help the Roman, but her brother was willing to take it. He wasn't questioning what they should do.

She took a deep breath and held it. *Oh, Lord, please don't let this be a mistake.* As she blew the breath out, a sense of peace filled her. She would help the enemy...for Yeshua.

"Get the donkey. I need to gather a few things." Simeon nodded and headed to fetch the animal.

She entered the house and opened the chest that held the clothes that had belonged to her dead brother. Looking into the chest was enough to start the tears welling up in her eyes. She flicked them away. There wasn't time for that right now.

One thing was certain. The Roman couldn't come to their house wearing his uniform. He'd need Judaean clothes to conceal his identity. It would be even better if she could make him look like an ordinary workman. She lifted out several of Reuben's tunics before selecting one that he'd worn in the workshop. It had some stains and mended tears, so it should serve the purpose well. Reuben had been big for his age and muscled from helping Abba at the forge, so it might be big enough for the Roman.

Her father's tunics might be too big, but she opened another chest and picked out one of his old ones. It would work if Reuben's didn't fit. She folded them both and placed them in a bag with Reuben's leather belt. She wrapped a sharp kitchen knife and placed it on the tunics. Finally, she added some cloth that she could tear into strips for bandages. She pulled the drawstring tight and slung the bag on her shoulder.

Next she selected two pieces of firewood of the right width and length for splinting a broken leg. She wrapped a length of rope around the wood, tying it off to form a loop that made it easy to carry.

She lifted her veil from the peg by the door and draped it over her hair as she headed out to find Simeon. He was waiting for her with the donkey saddled and ready to go. Together they started back to the wadi and the injured Roman who desperately needed her help.

Chapter 7

ONE HE CAN TRUST

Lucius lay still with his eyes closed. The slightest movement launched a cascade of pain. Simeon's water had replaced the stone-mason's mallet striking his skull with a smaller hammer, but his head still throbbed. The pain in his leg shifted between piercing agony when he moved it and a penetrating ache when he let it lie still.

He'd never hurt so much. Pain shot through his chest every time his ribcage expanded when he breathed in. It surged again when he breathed out. He concentrated on taking only shallow breaths spaced far apart. It was hard. He'd never had to think about breathing before. He had a high tolerance for pain, but between his head, his leg, and his chest, even just lying there was almost more than he could bear.

The jackal tried to come back once, but a well-placed stone from Asher's slingshot convinced it to look elsewhere for its next meal. At least he didn't have to defend himself anymore. He could rest and muster any strength that remained for when Simeon returned with his sister and they tried to take him away from this place.

Asher sat nearby on a rock, playing a small flute. Lucius appreciated the boy's silent company. It hurt too much to talk, but the music gave him something to focus on besides the pain.

It seemed an eternity since Simeon left to fetch his sister. Maybe she'd refused to come help a Roman. He couldn't expect that any Galilean woman would want to.

Asher stopped in the middle of a song. He held his hand over his eyes to block the sun.

34

"I see them."

Lucius turned his head to look in the same direction. With Simeon walked a short, slender woman in a light beige, long-sleeved tunic tied with a faded red sash. The ends of the long beige veil that covered her hair crisscrossed her chest and were tossed back over her shoulders. Between them walked a donkey.

She had come after all.

He would have breathed a deep sigh of relief...if it didn't hurt so much to breath.

She turned to her brother like she was saying something, and they increased their pace. As they drew close, Asher hopped off the rock and trotted over to his sister. She hugged him and kissed him on top of his head before resuming her brisk walk.

Rachel's stomach tightened at the sight of the officer. She cringed at the thought of touching any strange man, much less a Roman. But he needed help, so she would help him. She wouldn't even turn an injured dog away, so how could she turn her back on the Roman? Yeshua died for his kind, too.

When she knelt beside the officer, any thought that he was someone unworthy of help slipped away. *Poor thing.* Purple blotches all over him. The dullness of his eyes, the tightness of his mouth, his shallow breathing...he must be in horrible pain.

Please help him, LORD. Take his pain away, and let me know what to do for him.

She rested her hand on his left shoulder to comfort him. She spoke Greek so he would understand her. "All will be well now. We'll take care of you."

Her fingertips lifted his hair back from his forehead to give a clear view of the source of all the dried blood. A huge purple bruise surrounded a cut just below the hairline. At least the cut didn't look very deep, and the bleeding had long since stopped. The mottled purple lump that stuck out almost half an inch near his left temple must hurt terribly. She didn't touch it.

She surveyed his battered body. One leg broken, bent but the bones not through the skin. Both arms and the other leg—no sign of serious injury. Ribs broken—or so he'd told Simeon. Internal injuries—only the LORD knew. He had so many bruises that his arms and legs and face looked more purple than tan, but there didn't seem to be any blood anywhere else on him. At least she wouldn't be needing the bandages.

◆

Despite the pain that tore at him with every breath, Lucius relaxed as she knelt beside him. Her gentle touch and the warm look of compassion that filled her large brown eyes—they brought a wave of hope that washed away the despair that had gripped him after the hours of pain and the indifference, even hostility, of those who'd refused to help him.

Long, thick lashes framed those eyes. It seemed a long time between blinks. Her gaze so steady and calm—like nothing was wrong that she couldn't fix. And something more—like she was seeing deep into him, feeling herself how much he hurt. Those eyes drew him in like no other woman's had. Just looking into them gave him the feeling that Simeon spoke the truth. His sister would know what to do, and he didn't have to worry.

Her veil didn't completely conceal the rich dark brown of her luxuriant hair that hung past her shoulders. In her haste to help him, she had neglected to pull it across her lower face. A heart-shaped face with high cheekbones and a narrow, straight nose. Her lips were that rich dark pink of the plums at home when they were almost ripe, and a sympathetic smile had drawn them into a gentle curve. His rescuer looked somewhere between sixteen and nineteen. She wasn't beautiful, but that smile and those compelling eyes made her a very attractive woman. She must be a kind one as well, or she would never have come to help.

His left hand lay across his stomach. She placed her hand upon it and stroked it with her fingers before patting it twice. "Where are you hurt?"

She'd spoken in Greek, so he replied with the same. "Leg broken… Ribs, too."

He tried to smile; it was closer to a grimace. His chest hurt more when he breathed deeper so he could talk. "Thank you for coming…to help me."

He'd decided no one would just before the boys appeared. He'd accepted his death as inevitable, and he hadn't expected to see another sunrise. He could see his future again in her kind eyes.

She laid her hand on a spot on his left arm where there was no bruise and patted it. "I'm glad to help in any way I can. Don't try to talk too much. I'm going to splint your leg so we can take you back to our home. Then we can send word to your garrison for them to come with a wagon to get you. You'll be with the garrison physician very soon."

36

A frown pulled his mouth down after her last statement. The words of the assassin played again in his mind. The person who wanted him dead was someone in the garrison, and he had no idea who that might be.

"Can't go to the garrison."

She stared at him. Those long lashes were blinking much faster. "Why not? You need more care than I know how to give. Your physician will know what's best to do."

"Men threw me off the cliff...hired by a soldier to kill me...No idea who...Can't go there like this."

She might be right about the physician, but how could he risk the garrison before he could defend himself again?

Talking drove daggers into his chest, so he paused before proposing what seemed the obvious solution to his problem. "Let me stay with you...until my leg heals...Five hundred denarii...for seven, maybe eight weeks?"

He expected the offer to be irresistible. That was almost two years' wages for many working men in that region. A woman like her probably earned less than a tenth of that, if anything. To him, that amount of money was nothing. It was only ten days of his officer's pay, and his father's fortune was more than twenty thousand times that amount. He even had the money with him since he'd planned to pay up to a thousand for the horse he was going to buy for Marcus.

Her eyes widened as she drew a quick breath. "But I'm not sure I can keep you safe if you stay with us. My neighbors hate Rome... especially her soldiers. It might be even more dangerous for you than returning to your garrison."

"Understood...But with you...I'll know who to trust."

She looked away, her eyes bouncing to each of her brothers. She bit her lower lip as her eyes, still soft with compassion but not as calm, settled back on him.

"Five hundred not enough?" No words, but her eyes spoke volumes. The problem wasn't the money. "Too much to ask...Too dangerous for you."

He closed his eyes. If she couldn't take him in, he'd just have to risk his unknown enemy trying again. He could trust Marcus to watch out for him, but his brother sometimes had to go to legion headquarters in Legio or to Caesarea on the coast.

The Roman's request shocked Rachel. Tending his wounds and giving him shelter for a few hours until his fellow soldiers could come get him was one thing, but looking after him for several weeks? That was much more than she'd planned. Even if she wanted to do it, which she didn't. That could prove very dangerous for all of them.

She gazed upon him as he lay there, eyes closed, struggling against the pain. She tried to steel her heart against his plea, but he was so helpless. He could be right that returning to the garrison now would put him in mortal danger. Maybe it would be safer for him if he stayed with her family, at least for a while.

LORD, do you want me to do this? To put Asher and Simeon and Abba in danger? Do I have to care for him longer than I planned?

Certainty of the answer she didn't want flooded through her. She shook her head, then squared her shoulders. For Yeshua, she would do it for however long the poor Roman needed her to.

She rested her hand on his shoulder again, and he opened his eyes.

"I can't accept so much money for only doing what my Lord Yeshua commands, and whether it's dangerous or not doesn't matter."

She took a deep breath and held it before blowing it out slowly. If she was going to obey her Lord at all, she must do it all the way.

"You're welcome to stay with us. I'll do my best to keep you safe while you heal, but no one can know you're a Roman soldier."

◆

Lucius stiffened when she spoke of obeying Yeshua despite the danger. Grandfather was torn apart by lions in the Flavian Amphitheater in Rome for his devotion to that same Jesus. He hadn't cared about the danger of doing what the Christian god commanded, either. That ended up getting him killed. Would helping him get her killed?

"Is it safe...for you?"

Her eyes widened and her breath caught when he asked about her safety. Her shock at his question didn't surprise him. No Judean woman would expect that from a Roman. Especially not from a Roman who needed her to let him stay as desperately as he did. Then her eyes settled back into that calm state that made him feel like she had everything under control. How did she do that so quickly?

And why did her face radiate that gentle look of compassion? It was as if she truly cared about what would happen to him. That was unique in his experience since posting to Judaea. Galilean women looked at him with animosity or fear, never like they cared.

◆

"Safe enough."

His question surprised Rachel. Everyone knew the Romans didn't care what happened to any of the Jews they ruled. Well, he was the one who gave Simeon money for the lamb, so maybe he was different. But it didn't matter if he was. She would help him no matter what. Yeshua had commanded her to love her enemies, and she would obey.

"You can be thinking about what we should tell people about you. Everyone who sees you will wonder, you know." She tilted her head and contemplated his appearance. "With a beard, we might pass you off as a Greek...maybe..."

His short brown hair was cut military style, and it wasn't the least bit curly like the Greeks she'd seen. At least it was longish...for a soldier. He looked like he was overdue for a haircut. With that aquiline nose, he really did look terribly Roman, so she wasn't sure whether they'd have any success at claiming he was Greek. And that scar...it branded him as a warrior. A beard might hide it...maybe, if it grew fast enough and thick enough. He did already have thick stubble.

A deep sigh escaped. Well, he looked like what he looked like. They'd just have to make the best of it and pray that the LORD would protect them all.

Besides, Rahab had managed to hide two Israelite spies when all of Jericho was searching for them. She should be able to hide one Roman from her village when no one suspected he was there. He was hurt badly enough that he wouldn't even be leaving their house for many days. Maybe he'd look more Greek by then...or at least less Roman.

"First your name. What shall we call you?"

"Perhaps Lucas...of Corinth...I've spent time there."

She patted his left arm and smiled to encourage him. "Very well, Lucas of Corinth. Let me set your leg, and then Simeon can help you out of that Roman tunic and into one of my brother's before I take you home. We'll have you looking Greek before you know it."

He nodded once and closed his eyes again. Exhausted from fighting the pain, poor thing. Maybe even keeping his eyes open was too much work at the moment.

She remained on her knees but moved down by his right thigh. She'd set the broken leg of the lamb, and it healed with no problem. His leg was bent more, but it should set as well after they straightened it. At least the bones hadn't come through his skin.

"Simeon, I need your help here."

Her brother knelt beside her. "What do I do?"

"We need to pull his leg to get the bones lined up right. Can you pull while I pin him down?"

Simeon nodded and took hold of his right ankle. "Ready."

She looked once more at the Roman's battered face and closed eyes. The thought of hurting him, even though there was no way around it, pained her.

"I'm sorry, Lucas, but this is going to hurt. Are you ready?"

His eyes didn't open. "Yes." His voice was scarcely above a whisper.

Rachel leaned all her weight on his upper leg and pinned it to the ground. While Simeon pulled, she watched his leg straighten as the bones slid back into place. The Roman clenched his fists and jaw and held his breath. His thigh muscles tensed under her palms and fingertips as he fought to keep from arching his back against the pain and making his ribs hurt more. Somehow he kept from crying out, but how did he ever manage that? Just looking at him made her want to cry.

"Stop. I think that did it."

The tribune winced as she slid her hands along his calf, trying to be as gentle as possible as she felt to see if the bones were back where they belonged. With the swelling, she couldn't be completely sure, but at least his leg looked straight now.

"I'm so sorry, Lucas." Her fingertips pushed some hair back from his forehead. "We didn't mean it to hurt so much, but we're done now. All I have to do is splint it, and then we'll get you on the donkey and take you home."

He was a tough, brave man to have made it this far, but he seemed so weak. *Oh, Lord, please don't let the ride be too much for him. He's suffered too much already. Please give him strength for what he still has to bear.*

◆

Lucius opened his eyes at the soothing touch of her fingers and saw that gentle look of compassion, magnified by the moistness of her eyes. Were those tears for him? The corners of his mouth tipped up ever so slightly.

"Thank you...sorry...forgot your name." He knew her brother had said it, but the pain made everything hazy.

"Rachel."

"Rachel." When he repeated her name, the best he could manage was a whisper.

He watched as she positioned the splints on opposite sides of his leg and lashed them in place with a length of rope. She seemed to know what she was doing. No smile while she worked, but as soon as she tied the last knot, there it was. Something about it made him feel better even though nothing hurt less. Those calm, kind eyes cheered him even more than the smile. He wasn't sure how it could be, but he was already starting to feel a little stronger.

"That should keep everything in place for the trip home. We'll fix it better when we get there. Can you sit up now if we help?"

The corners of his mouth twitched up, and he nodded slowly to keep his head from throbbing more.

Simeon took one arm, and she took the other so they could pull him into a sitting position. Once there, he was able to remain upright. His ribs hurt, but the pain was no worse than before.

"We're going to get you out of that uniform and into my brother's tunic. It will be much safer."

First she undid the fasteners at the shoulders of his armor. Then she leaned in close and began undoing the fasteners on the right side that held the breastplate to the backplate of his metal cuirass, beginning under his arm and moving down. As she released the last one, the two purses with the horse money shifted inside his tunic. The soft jingle raised her eyebrows and brought her eyes to his, but only for a moment. As the armor fell away from his body, she caught it and lowered it to the ground.

He pulled the wrap of the underlying cloth vest free and started to work at freeing his arms. That pushed his pain up, and a grimace escaped.

Her hands took his as she stopped him. "Let me do that, Lucas."

She loosened the vest and helped him free his left arm. Then she leaned close again to guide the vest past his back and off his right arm without making him move it.

It was always a relief to take his armor off. The price of its protection was putting up with being too hot. Even more so today, but it had probably saved his life. The breeze blowing across his sweat-soaked tunic felt deliciously cool.

A sigh escaped. He was so ready to be out of the sun, out of the wadi, away from this place where death had stalked him...and failed.

He looked first at Simeon, now standing at his feet, and then at Rachel, kneeling so close he could hear her every breath. He owed them everything, and somehow he would repay.

Chapter 8

GETTING A ROMAN HOME

Rachel rocked back from her knees to her toes and reached for the bag she'd brought with her. She took Reuben's tunic out and held it against the Roman's chest. Reuben had been working with Abba as a blacksmith, and he'd been built like one—broad chest, muscled arms. The soldier was built the same. Reuben's tunic was the right size.

She stood, clutched it to her breast, and closed her eyes, hoping no one would see the tears trying to form in them. She remembered so well when she scolded Reuben about making the last tear in it because he and Asher were horsing around. After a single deep sigh, she handed it to Simeon.

"Here. Help him into this, and then I'll take him home."

She turned her back so she wouldn't see anything as Simeon helped him change. It also gave her a chance to wipe the tears away unseen.

"We're done, Rachel."

When she turned around, Simeon handed the Roman's tunic with the purple stripes to her, and she folded it before stuffing it into her bag.

◆

Lucius was glad to watch her hide it. That tunic proclaimed his high status as a member of the Roman equestrian class. Definitely not something to wear in a Galilean village so close to a garrison town. It was good that she'd thought to bring a plain, ordinary tunic that would help hide his identity.

42

He'd attached his dagger with the engraved brass handle and ivory-inlayed sheath and his ordinary purse to the leather belt she'd brought. The scabbard strap was slung across his chest. He was about to tuck the other two purses with the horse money inside his tunic. He would leave his helmet, his leather forearm guards, and his body armor behind.

Her eyes sobered as she stepped toward him. "That purse looks out of place on a laborer, and those other two jingle too much." She held out her hand. "And that's a Roman sword. We need to hide it and that dagger, too."

Lucius handed her the three purses right away, but with the *gladius*, he hesitated. He didn't want to give up the protection it afforded, even though he couldn't use it effectively at the moment. Then he looked into her eyes. Calm, steady, caring. Somehow he knew he could trust her completely. She was risking her own safety, too.

He drew a breath, held it, then released it slowly as he considered her demand. Perhaps she did know what was safest for them all. He would choose to rely on her to protect him until he healed.

He handed her the sheathed dagger. Then he slipped the strap over his head and handed the sword and its scabbard to her. She wrapped the strap around the scabbard and dropped the sword, the dagger, and the purses into her bag.

◆

Rachel stared at his armor lying on the ground. Someone might see it and decide to look for him. She glanced at her little brothers. What if a zealot tracked him to her house? He might kill them all for giving aid and comfort to the enemy.

She scanned the area. A cavity about two feet up the cliff looked big enough to hold it all.

"Asher, please hide his armor in there. Shove it in as far as it will go." She turned to Lucas. "You can come back to get it later."

The whole time she'd been helping the wounded man, Asher had been a statue, eyes glued to Roman. Her request pulled his eyes away, and he carried the armor over to the cliff face. He stuffed first the brass helmet with its stiff red crest, then the metal cuirass with its skirt of thick leather strips, and finally the arm guards deep into the hole. Then he came back to stare once more at the Roman.

Rachel knelt beside the Roman again. "Now comes the hard part, Lucas. You'll have to ride back to our house. Do you think you can?"

She wasn't sure he could. He'd seemed so weak when she first knelt beside him. He seemed a little stronger now, but not much.

"I can ride."

He looked like he thought he could. *Oh, Lord, please let him be right about riding.* At least his leg had broken below the knee. He would need his thighs to grip the donkey if he was going to ride.

She turned to her little brother. "Please bring the donkey to that rock."

Asher led the donkey over and stood holding its head so it wouldn't move away while the Roman mounted.

"Help me here, Simeon. Let's get you on your feet, Lucas."

Rachel and Simeon each supported an arm as he struggled up onto his unbroken leg, then acted as crutches as he hopped over to the rock. With the help of the rock, he got enough height to swing the broken leg across the donkey and settle in place. He wavered a little, then steadied.

Rachel rested her hand on the donkey's neck. "Do you think you can ride a couple of miles now?"

"Yes...Donkey's no worse...than the ground."

As she watched him set his jaw as he fought the pain, she wasn't so sure about that. "If you start to feel unsteady, tell me right away."

He nodded once.

Simeon rested his hand on the donkey's neck. Rachel caught his eye, and they both took stock of how well the Roman was sitting. He was slouched but not listing one way or the other.

Simeon raised his eyebrows and shrugged. "Can you get him home alone? I should stay with the sheep if you can."

She looked at Lucas for assurance, and the Roman nodded again. "You can stay. I'll manage."

Asher was still staring at the Roman. His lips were straight, his eyebrows dipping, his eyes unusually serious. She walked over to her little brother and tilted his face up until he was looking into her eyes.

"Asher, don't tell anyone about what happened here and what we're doing. It wouldn't be safe for Simeon and me." He nodded.

She knelt and hugged him before whispering in his ear so the Roman wouldn't hear. "Yeshua told us we should love our enemies. We're showing our love for Yeshua when we help this man."

Asher nodded, and then a fleeting smile appeared. The Romans soldiers had killed Reuben, so he hadn't understood why they were helping one. She stood and kissed him on the top of his head. He'd be fine now what she and Simeon were doing made sense.

She started off leading the donkey, then stepped back beside the Roman as the donkey headed for home. It knew the way. She kept a very close eye on him to see if he needed her to steady him. He was slumped and leaning forward slightly with his hands resting on the donkey's withers for balance. It was too obvious that he was hurting badly, but there was a determined set to his mouth. Still, determination often wasn't enough by itself.

Could he make it home? His eyes were only half open most of the time. *Oh, LORD, please take his pain and give him strength. If he falls, I'll never get him back on the donkey. Please give him enough strength to make it home.*

There was no way he would make it without the LORD's help.

Lucius was no more than minutes away from losing the battle between exhaustion and determination when the donkey finally walked up to a manger in a courtyard where some grass awaited it.

At last! Riding the donkey had proven a more painful ordeal than he expected. If it had been much farther, he couldn't have stayed mounted long enough to reach her home. He ran his fingers through his hair at that thought. She was such a petite woman she could never have gotten him back on the donkey by herself.

She stood beside him, looking up at him, biting her lip. It was the first time he saw worry in those brown eyes. "What's the best way for us to get you down?"

He looked down at her upturned face. She was so small. She wouldn't be able to stop him if he started to fall, and she clearly knew it. He had one chance to do this right.

"Get ready...on the right side...I may be shaky."

She moved around the donkey and prepared to catch him. He leaned back and swung his good left leg over the donkey's head before sliding off its back. When his foot hit the ground, it jarred his ribs, producing an explosion of pain.

He squeezed his eyes shut and clenched his teeth. Still, he managed to stay upright as he leaned back against the animal. His foot was barely on the ground before she slid under his left arm and wrapped her arm around his back to support him.

"Through that door, Lucas. Lean on me."

She was his crutch as he hopped toward the small house with a single door that opened into the courtyard. Each hop jarred his ribs, shooting more pain through his chest.

She lifted the latch and pushed the door open. The dark coolness inside wrapped around him. That was sheer pleasure after the long day baking in the sun. Along the wall was a wide mud-brick bench where several straw-filled mattress pads lay, and she guided him to one of them. They turned so he could sit on the ledge.

He gripped his leg just below the knee as he prepared to lift the splinted leg up onto the mattress.

"Don't try to do that yourself, Lucas. Let me help."

She slid one hand under his knee and took his ankle in the other.

"Turn as I lift, and we'll get you there." Together they got him sitting lengthwise on the mattress.

As he started to lower himself onto his back, she wrapped her arm around his shoulders and bore his weight as he lay down. It was amazing how much that reduced the pain from his ribs. As his head hit the pillow, she pulled her arm free. A deep sigh escaped as she helped him settle his broken leg into a more comfortable position before stepping back.

As he mentally dropped his guard for the first time since he was hurled over the cliff, the last of his strength drained away. It was all he could do to keep his eyes open.

"Did you want some food or water before you rest?"

"Water, please." He managed a weak smile.

She left him for a moment to fetch a cup of water from the large water jar in the storeroom that opened to the left of the door. When she returned, she also carried a bowl of water.

"Let me clean the blood from your face."

She dipped a rag in the bowl, wrung out most of the water, then began wiping his forehead. Each feather-light stroke of the cool, wet cloth washed away both blood and tension.

His eyelids kept drifting shut, but he struggled to keep them open. Watching her helped the pain somehow. His chapped lips parted to speak his thanks, but the pain of the deeper breath pulled a grimace from him.

She wet the cloth again and wiped the blood and sweat from his scarred cheek. "Don't try to talk if it hurts too much."

Good advice. He settled back and enjoyed the caressing dampness of the wet rag. Each time she shifted her eyes from the patches of dried blood to his own, that sweet smile appeared. She finished much too soon.

"There. That looks much better. Now for your drink."

Those gentle brown eyes moved close to his own as she slid her arm between the bed and his shoulders. As he let himself swim in their serene depths, she lifted and supported him until he drained the cup she held to his lips. When she lowered his head back onto the pillow, he closed his eyes completely.

"Thank you...for everything." His words were barely a whisper. Before she could even answer, he was asleep.

Chapter 9

ONLY FOR YESHUA

Rachel stood in the doorway, palms pressed against both cheeks as she watched the sleeping Roman. Following Yeshua's command to love her enemy had just created a huge problem for her whole family. She'd only planned to have him there for two or three hours until the soldiers came to get him. He should have been gone long before Abba returned from his visit with Uncle Samuel after delivering a wagon wheel. She wouldn't have had to tell her father what she and Simeon had done, at least not until it wouldn't upset him to hear it. And what if Nathaniel should return home to find a Roman soldier there?

She closed her eyes, ran her fingers through her hair, and bit her lip as she slowly shook her head. This Roman didn't seem to be a bad man like so many of the others. He'd stopped the ones that could have hurt Asher and gave Simeon money to pay for the lamb. So he was a generous man, but he was still a Roman soldier. It was only five months since someone from his garrison killed Reuben. This man might even have been part of that attack on the zealots Nathaniel ran with.

Now a Roman soldier would wear her dead brother's tunic and sleep in her dead brother's bed for the next seven or so weeks. What was Abba going to say when he got home? What was he going to do? She would have to tell him the truth about the man even if they were going to lie to the rest of the village.

One final shake of her head before she planted her hands on her hips. She knew what Yeshua wanted her to do, and she had done it. She had no regrets about that. Surely the LORD would help her deal with what her obedience might bring.

As she walked back to her loom, she began praying that Abba's love for Yeshua would overcome his grief and anger over Reuben's murder so he would let the poor Roman stay.

Joseph did not expect to find Rachel sitting under the canopy watching for him when he walked into the courtyard. She rose and strolled over to hug him as he approached the door. He placed his hand on her cheek, and his heart warmed as she leaned into it. His Rachel was a precious gift from the LORD, just like her mother before her.

"Abba, we had some excitement while you were gone. Simeon and Asher found a man who's badly hurt. His leg's broken and his ribs. Simeon came for me, and I brought him home. He's sleeping in Reuben's bed now. I hope you don't mind."

"That is as it should be. Yeshua told us to help anyone in need. He is welcome here for as long as he needs our help."

She took a deep breath. "There's more to it, Abba."

His head tilted. What more could there be? A man needed help. They would help him.

"Someone tried to kill him by throwing him off the cliff above the wadi. Simeon and Asher saw the vultures and found him just before a jackal got him."

"It is a good thing the boys found him in time. The LORD's hand must have been upon him."

Pride swelled Joseph's heart as he smiled at her. His children knew what was right and always tried to do it.

"There's still more to it, Abba." She swallowed hard. "He's a Roman soldier."

Joseph's smile flipped into a scowl. "You brought a Roman soldier here? And put him in your dead brother's bed? How could you, Rachel? Have you forgotten who murdered Reuben? How could you bring one of them here?"

She cringed as if his words were blows; then her imploring eyes locked on his. "I haven't forgotten, Abba, but I had to do it. Yeshua said we must love our enemies. I couldn't leave him there to die. I thought he'd be gone before you came home so you wouldn't have to meet him, but he can't go back to his garrison yet. It was another soldier who hired the men to kill him."

"What is that to me? Let the Romans kill their own instead of us. Send him back to his garrison. I do not want him here."

"Please, Abba. We have to let him stay. He's not like the others. He's the one who paid Simeon for the lamb."

"No." He crossed his arms, his brows and mouth drawn down as black anger filled his heart. What she was asking was too much. The Romans had cost him two sons. Nathaniel was lost to his hatred of Rome, and Reuben was dead because of it.

"Please, Abba. I told him we'd care for him. I know that's what Yeshua wants. You know it, too. Abba, please. If not for him, for Yeshua."

She placed both hands on his crossed arms and looked up at him with pleading eyes. "I know it's hard, but please let him stay...for Yeshua."

The tears that had been welling up trickled down her cheeks.

Joseph gazed into his precious daughter's eyes. The mixture of love and sadness there softened his resolve.

She was right. Yeshua wouldn't want him to reject the injured Roman in his time of great need. He uncrossed his arms, placed his hands on her cheeks, and swept the tears aside with his thumbs. He tightened his lips and shook his head slowly. Rachel had such a tender heart and such great love for Yeshua—just like her mother. Hannah would have done exactly the same and brought the Roman home.

He drew a deep breath and blew it out between pursed lips before he released her face. His heart ached for his dead son. It was so hard fighting the desire for revenge on the man who'd killed him, but what were the odds this Roman was the one who drove the sword into his boy's chest and left him lying in his own blood?

Yeshua had commanded him to love his enemy, and he would try. He could never help the man who had killed Reuben, but he could try to show Yeshua's love to this man who had been kind to Simeon and Asher.

"As you wish, Rachel. For Yeshua."

She threw her arms around him and pressed her cheek against his chest as she hugged him. "Thank you, Abba."

He wrapped her in his arms and kissed the top of her head.

She looked up at him. "There's still more, Abba."

He rolled his eyes. "What more could there possibly be?"

"I set his leg, but I don't know what to do for his broken ribs. He's in terrible pain from them. Can you help him?"

"When he wakes up, I will wrap his chest. His ribs will not move so much then, and they will hurt less."

"And can you make him a crutch?"

She was looking up at him, expecting a yes. Was there no end to what she would ask of him for this Roman? He sighed again.

"I will make one tomorrow morning."

"Thank you, Abba. Thank you for letting him stay and for helping him."

"I am doing it for you and Yeshua, not for him. The better we care for him, the sooner he will heal and leave. I do not want him here...but I will care for him in the name of Yeshua."

Her hug tightened and her eyes sparkled as she looked up at him.

Joseph kissed her forehead. "Now let us go in, and I will see to this Roman that you have made our guest for the next few weeks."

"I told him we'd have to pretend he's a Greek to keep him safe. I know we can't let anyone in the village know a Roman is here. We agreed he'd be Lucas of Corinth."

A crooked smile appeared as he shook his head. "Wise as a serpent, gentle as a dove. Let us go look at your Greek." He sighed and shook his head again. "I wish he really was a Greek and not a Roman."

A woman's voice penetrated Lucius's sleep, and a hand gently shook his shoulder.

"Lucas? Can you wake up now? Abba is here."

He was lying flat on his back, so Lucius turned his head to the side as he opened his eyes. Rachel stood there without her veil, her thick, long hair framing her gentle eyes and warm smile. He found himself smiling in return as the last traces of sleep left him.

It felt good to wake up to the smile of this kind woman who had come to his rescue. He felt welcome in her house. Then he looked past her shoulder to the face of the man towering behind her. The feeling of welcome instantly evaporated.

She turned her head toward the man and rested her hand on his arm before turning her gaze back on Lucius.

"This is my father, Joseph bar Jonah. He's going to wrap your chest before we have dinner."

"Can't thank you enough...for helping me." It hurt as much to speak as it had before he slept.

No gentle warmth filled the eyes contemplating him as if he were a bug. "Do not try until I finish with you."

Joseph's gaze swept over the rough job of splinting that Rachel had done with the firewood. He turned to Simeon, who stood watching at the door with Asher.

"Go to the workshop and bring me two wheel spokes."

"Yes, Abba." Simeon scurried off.

"Rachel, tear some cloth strips to tie the spokes to his leg. I need more cloth for pads so the splints will not cause sores. I will also need long strips to wrap his chest. You can prepare those while I resplint his leg."

"Yes, Abba." Rachel smiled at Lucius before leaving to do as her father ordered.

Joseph stood with his arms crossed, looking down at Lucius. He was an imposing man. Wide-set, dark brown eyes flanking a prominent nose. Wavy dark brown hair frosted at the temples. His full beard was frosted, too, and framed a pair of tightened lips. He was a big man—tall for a Jew, broad-chested, arms with bulging muscles like a gladiator, even in repose.

The coldness of his gaze chilled Lucius like an unexpected plunge into a mountain stream. It was blatantly obvious that her father was not as eager to help as she and Simeon had been. Rather than continue to meet that hostile stare, Lucius closed his eyes and waited for Simeon and Rachel to return.

Joseph untied the rope and lifted the firewood away. When the large hands felt where the break was, Lucius held his breath and gritted his teeth. She'd been much gentler when she touched him.

When he heard Rachel's footsteps, Lucius opened his eyes. Joseph turned to her as she stood beside him with the cloth strips. "You did well, Rachel. The bones are where they should be. I only need to give him smoother splints to make him more comfortable."

It hurt to raise his head, but Lucius wanted to watch Joseph work on his leg. Perhaps her father didn't want him there, but that wasn't keeping him from doing the best he could to help. His head dropped back onto the pillow as Joseph finished securing the splints. It did feel better not to have rough wood pressing directly into his flesh.

"Now the ribs." Joseph removed the belt and pulled his tunic up so it would be free when he was sitting. "Sit up and swing your legs off."

Joseph slid his arm under Lucius's shoulders and helped him into a sitting position. After Lucius swung his legs off the bed, Joseph pulled the tunic over his head, leaving his chest bare.

When Joseph first touched his horribly bruised side, Lucius jumped. Then he steeled himself so he wouldn't move. He held his breath when Joseph laid a hand on his right side and ran his fingers along each rib, checking to see how bad the breaks were. So much for thinking they couldn't possibly hurt any more.

Joseph nodded his head with apparent satisfaction. "The LORD has been merciful to you. The ribs are not broken in two, only cracked and maybe only bruised. They should heal well enough if you are careful what you do for a few weeks. I will wrap your chest for now so they cannot move too far when you breathe. They should hurt less when you use your arms as well."

Lucius nodded and smiled his appreciation, but no smile was returned. If anything, Joseph's scowl deepened.

He watched Joseph's face as he reached around him repeatedly to wrap the cloth strips snuggly around his chest. There was a penetrating coldness in his eyes—what a sharp contrast with the warmth in his daughter's. Not even the tiniest trace of welcome was evident.

Her father was not pleased that she'd brought him to their house. Would that cause problems for her? He'd be more worried if he hadn't seen the light shining in her father's eyes when he praised how she'd fixed his leg.

It was very odd that Joseph could be so unhappy about him being there yet still allow him to stay. Odder still since most Jews would consider his mere presence under their roof to be a defilement of their home. Maybe her father didn't care much about the laws of his religion.

But none of that mattered as long as he could stay.

◆

Rachel stood behind her father, watching him wrap Lucas. She had grown-up brothers who worked a forge, so the sight of a brawny male chest was nothing new to her. The poor Roman's muscular body was covered with bruises. It reminded her of the spotted oxen who pulled the Roman supply wagons from Legio to Sepphoris, except Lucas's spots were purple instead of brown.

The right side of his torso was almost entirely purple. He must have hit the ground tremendously hard when they threw him off the cliff. No wonder his ribs were cracked. It was truly a miracle that nothing else was broken except his right leg. The LORD had been so merciful to the Roman. Perhaps it was repayment for his kindness to Asher and Simeon. He should have died from that fall.

When Abba tucked in the end of the final wrapping to secure it, Rachel placed her hands on her father's shoulders and leaned over to kiss his cheek. He reached up and patted her hand.

"Thank you, Abba." She leaned into his ear and whispered, "For Yeshua." He turned to smile at her and nodded his head before turning cold eyes back on the Roman.

"That should help the pain...Lucas." He straightened up and walked away without another word.

Rachel picked up her brother's tunic. "Can you reach up, Lucas? So I can put your tunic back on."

He lifted his gaze from the floor at her words. She saw the pain and how quickly he tried to mask it. His weak smile wasn't enough to fool her.

"I'll try."

He grimaced as he raised his hands to a little more than shoulder height. *Poor man. Higher must be too much for him to manage right now.*

She stepped close and guided the tunic over his head and hands, letting it fall around him. Then she adjusted the shoulders of the tunic to lie properly on his own. She was ever so careful as she tried not to bump any of his many bruises.

◆

Lucius looked up at her face. She looked serious as she adjusted the tunic for him, then she gave him a quick, gentle smile. She truly was an attractive woman. If everything didn't hurt so much, he'd enjoy her standing so close, touching his shoulders and arms as she helped him dress.

He glanced at her father. Joseph was watching him with solemn eyes, his arms crossed, and the corners of his mouth turned slightly downward.

It would be a grave mistake to let her father suspect that attraction. Joseph bar Jonah was clearly a protective father who would guard his daughter from anyone he thought might harm her. He should be careful not to give Joseph any reason to tell him to leave.

"Thank you, Rachel." What a relief to be able to speak without it hurting so much. Joseph had known what he was doing when he wrapped his chest. "And thank you, Joseph bar Jonah."

Joseph nodded his response without smiling. "No thanks are needed. If it should feel too tight after a while, let me know, and I will fix it."

◆

Rachel was no longer beside the bed, so Joseph turned away from the sight of a Roman where Reuben should be. For Yeshua, the Roman could stay, and he would help him...but only for Yeshua.

Chapter 10

Always Good to Obey

For several minutes, Lucius remained sitting up where Joseph had left him. As long as he didn't move too much, the pain was tolerable...barely. He still felt drained and in need of more sleep, but what was the best way to get his leg back on the mattress and lie down without making his ribs hurt too much?

He hadn't figured it out when Rachel began carrying cushions out the door. He forgot about lying down as he watched her making final preparations for serving the evening meal.

She returned to his bedside after carrying out a tray of cups.

"It's almost time for dinner, Lucas. Are you feeling up to eating now? Would you like to join us or shall I bring you something here?"

"I'd like to eat with you."

He was more than a little surprised to be offered the choice. Many Jews wouldn't eat with a Gentile. His very presence in their house would be considered defilement by the ones who most rigidly followed the laws of Moses.

He'd seen a man who'd died of thirst by a well in the center of a village because the rabbi ordered the members of his synagogue to leave the "Gentile dog" alone and not defile the bucket by giving him a drink of water from it. How incredibly lucky to be brought to a Jewish home where a Gentile dog like himself was treated with kindness.

He still hurt more than she could possibly imagine, but it was nowhere near the level of pain in the wadi. He was hungry, and eating with her family should provide a welcome distraction.

Rachel turned toward Simeon, who was just walking into the room. "Simeon, would you please put some water in a bowl so Lucas can wash his hands before dinner?"

Simeon spun and headed out to do his sister's bidding.

"When the weather is this nice, we sit under the canopy around the mat where I serve, but I'm not sure how you're going to manage that by yourself, at least not this evening."

She stepped back to the doorway. "Abba?"

A deep voice penetrated the room. "Yes, Rachel?"

"Lucas would like to eat with us, but it's going to be hard for him to get down on a cushion. Can you help him?"

Joseph was just preparing to wash his hands, and now she wanted him to defile them more. The last thing he wanted to do was help this Roman with anything, but he had told her he would. His heart recoiled from it, but his head knew it was the right thing to do. He left the wash basin and returned to the room where her Lucas of Corinth awaited his help.

As he stepped through the doorway, he saw Rachel pick up the cushion that had been Reuben's. She smiled up at him as she slipped past to take the extra cushion out to the mat and shift the others to make room. Joseph's brow furrowed and the corners of his mouth turned down as he stared at Lucas. A Roman soldier wearing Reuben's tunic, resting in Reuben's bed, sitting at dinner on Reuben's cushion—it was a dagger into his heart to see it.

Lucius saw the hardening of his expression as Joseph walked toward him. Her father's dislike of him being there was clear with every crossing of his arms, every stern appraisal by that chilling stare, every downturn of his mouth. So why was Joseph willing to let him stay and even willing to help him?

"Stand up, Lucas."

Joseph helped Lucius to his feet. He was a brawny man with hard muscles from long hours working at the forge, but Lucius's eyebrows still popped up when her father simply scooped him up in his arms and carried him out to the canopy like a child. Lucius tried to straighten his expression so Joseph wouldn't laugh at him. Tried, that is, until he decided her father would find nothing about him amusing.

Joseph set Lucius's feet down by a cushion.

"Tomorrow morning, I will make a crutch so you can get around yourself. Take my wrists. I will help you sit."

As he held onto Joseph's wrists, Lucius lowered himself to the cushion using his good leg and stretched his broken leg out along the edge of the mat. Simeon brought the bowl of water over, and Lucius rinsed his hands in it. Joseph and Simeon then joined Asher at the wash basin to prepare for dinner.

Joseph's harsh voice softened as he spoke the blessing, "Blessed are You, LORD our God, King of the universe, Who has sanctified us with His commandments and commanded us concerning washing of hands.*"

Lucius's eyes snapped on Joseph. A prayer offered over so mundane a thing as washing before eating? This was a man who carefully observed Jewish law. So why was he going to let a man he thought to be Greek sit at table with them?

Rachel set the plates in front of each cushion. She placed the bread tray in front of the largest cushion and the large bowl, which contained the lentil stew made with onions, garlic, and leeks and flavored with cumin and coriander, in the center of the mat. The full-bodied aroma wrapped around him, and it smelled almost as good as the best of Jacob's stews. She finished by setting out a plate of sliced hard cheese, a bowl of raisins, a pitcher of watered wine, and five cups.

She took her seat to the right of Lucius as Joseph seated himself to his left. Asher settled in next to his sister, and Simeon sat opposite Lucius, next to his father.

Joseph first lifted the plate of bread. "Blessed are You, LORD our God, King of the universe, Who brings forth bread from the earth.*"

He lifted the wine pitcher and began to fill the cups. "Blessed are You, LORD our God, King of the universe, Who creates the fruit of the vine."

Then, in turn, he lifted the other serving containers," "Blessed are You, LORD our God, King of the universe, Who creates the fruit of the tree, Who creates the fruit of the ground, and through Whose word everything comes into being.*"

Then Joseph tore a large piece from the loaf of bread and passed the plate to Lucius, just as he would to a Jewish guest he welcomed. Lucius concentrated on keeping a straight face. It seemed wise to mask his amazement that he was being treated as the honored guest instead of getting the leftovers at the end.

He copied Joseph and passed the plate to Rachel. She took very little before passing the plate to Asher. As each serving bowl was passed, she continued to take less than anyone, even less than her little brother.

Her nearly empty plate triggered a flash of insight. She probably only prepared as much food as her family would need with little or nothing to spare. She was leaving most of her portion for him.

His eyebrows started down at the thought, but he forced them back to a neutral position. After all she'd done for him that day, the last thing he wanted was for her to go hungry so he could eat. His mouth started to open to tell her that, then he closed it. Saying something would only embarrass her. There was nothing he could do except eat what she sacrificed for him and find a way to thank her later.

Lucius watched how Joseph tore a small piece from his bread and dipped it into the stew pot. He began to reach with the bread in his right hand. Big mistake. Pain in the muscles on his right side told him not to do that again. He switched to his left hand so he wouldn't have to lean in as far.

As he placed the bread in his mouth, a sideways glance caught her watching him. He shifted his gaze from the stew pot to her face. A shadow of sadness had taken the sweet curve from her lips. Something glistened at the corners of her eyes. Was she trying not to cry? And then the shadow was gone. The friendly smile returned. She had masked the sadness the moment she realized he was watching her as well.

◆

Rachel had placed Reuben's cushion next to her father's, just as she would for any guest. When she set it there, she hadn't thought about that being the same place Reuben sat when no guest was present. To have the Roman sitting next to Abba, dressed in Reuben's tunic—she hadn't expected that to tear so cruelly at her wounded heart.

She glanced at Abba. He mustn't see her tears. It hurt him whenever he did. It was a good thing the Roman had looked at her. She didn't want to start crying in front of him, either. His scrutiny drew out the extra strength she needed to push back the tears. She would cry later when no one was watching.

◆

The meal was abnormally quiet. Joseph was accustomed to Simeon filling the silence with stories about the sheep or his friends. Perhaps his silence came from guilt over dragging the Roman home.

Asher's silence was normal. He would sometimes add something to a story his older brother was telling, but this evening there were no stories. He mostly just sat and watched the Roman.

Joseph had no desire to converse with his unintended guest. Initially, he said little, but the silence left him too aware of the Roman sitting where Reuben ought to be.

"Asher, what did you learn of Torah today?"

Asher's shyness vanished, and a grin split his face. Reciting at dinner what he'd learned in *bet sefer* always had that effect. He sat up straight and began. "The LORD said to Moses, 'Speak to the entire assembly of Israel and say to them: "Be holy because I, the LORD your God, am holy. Each of you must respect your mother and father, and you must observe my Sabbaths. I am the LORD your God. Do not turn to idols or...""'"

Joseph glanced at the Roman. Why was he watching Asher and listening so intently, as if he were trying to understand the Hebrew that Asher was reciting? He seemed to listen to every word all the time. It didn't matter whether they were speaking Greek or Aramaic. He watched them closely as well. Not surprising since he wouldn't understand the Aramaic they spoke most of the time. Probably did not trust them, but after what they had done for him, it was an insult for him not to.

Joseph's lips tightened. Then they relaxed as he thought no more about the Roman sitting next to him and simply focused on the word of God being spoken by his son.

"'Stand up in the presence of the aged, show respect for the elderly and revere your God. I am the LORD. When a foreigner resides among you in your land, do not mistreat them. The foreigner residing among you must be treated as your native-born. Love them as yourself, for you were foreigners in Egypt. I am the LORD your God. Do not use dishonest standards when measuring length, weight, or quantity. Use honest scales and honest weights, an honest ephah and an honest hin. I am the LORD your God, who brought you out of Egypt. Keep all my decrees and all my laws and follow them. I am the LORD.'"

Joseph nodded his approval of the recitation. "And what does this teach you, Asher?"

Asher looked first at the Roman, then back at his father. "That the LORD has always wanted us to treat foreigners like we treat each other. Maybe that's why Yeshua tells us we must love even the foreigners who are enemies, and that makes it a good thing that Simeon and Rachel helped Lucas."

Joseph didn't look at the Roman. Asher was speaking Aramaic, and a Roman soldier wouldn't understand any of what Asher just said. He only frowned slightly and nodded his head as his gaze remained fixed on his youngest son. He didn't like the conclusion Asher had reached, but he had to admit it was true.

"Yes. It is always a good thing to obey what the LORD has commanded."

Abba didn't look at the Roman, but Simeon did. He remembered how the Roman had spoken Aramaic when he paid for the lamb. Only Simeon saw the flash of understanding as the Roman tribune suddenly realized why Joseph had let him stay.

The evening meal had been served at the garrison. Marcus chose to eat the slop served by the army cook that night. The plan was more important than his dining pleasure. He made a show of asking several officers if they'd seen Lucius. He made sure each knew his brother had gone alone to look at a stallion. He feigned concern that Lucius hadn't returned when he'd told Marcus to expect him. The stage was set for him to take a couple of soldiers to search for his brother tomorrow.

The scavengers should have left enough of the body to prove his brother's death, assuring his rightful place as primary heir of the Claudius Drusus fortune. Then, in deepest grief, he would request a transfer back to Rome. Judaea would have fulfilled its promise as the ideal place to rectify his problem of being second-born, and he could return to civilized life away from the heat and dust of that hostile land.

Conversation had returned to normal after Joseph's words to Asher. The Roman's silence made it possible to mostly ignore his presence as Joseph talked with Simeon and Rachel.

However, Rachel glanced often at their guest. "Abba, we need to get Lucas to bed."

Joseph looked at the Roman. He was trying to bear the pain without letting it show, but as exhaustion crept up, his shoulders began to droop as if his spine were collapsing. The tightness at the corners of his mouth and the dullness of his eyes betrayed his true condition.

Joseph's lips tightened. He should have noticed Lucas was fading fast. He had taken the man under his protection as his guest, and even though he didn't want him there, he should still watch out for him while he was so weak. That he hadn't triggered a twinge of guilt. It was good that Rachel had.

"Simeon, some water for him to wash."

Simeon rose immediately and brought a bowl. After Lucas rinsed his hands, the rest of them washed and Joseph again spoke the blessing about God's command to wash one's hands.

While Rachel washed the cups and serving dishes, Joseph helped Lucas prepare for the night. Neither man chose to speak much, Lucas because he was too tired and sore to want to talk with anyone, Joseph because he didn't have anything to say to a Roman. Finally, he carried their guest back into the room and placed him again on Reuben's bed. He helped the Roman lie down and get as comfortable as possible with his injuries.

Then Joseph stood looking down at him. His lips tightened as his eyes chilled. A Roman in Reuben's bed. Not at all what he would have chosen, but there he was. For Rachel, he would let him stay. For Yeshua, he would care for his enemy. But it was still too hard to have him there.

Rachel entered the room. She opened a trunk and lifted out a light blanket.

"It can get chilly at night, and you should keep warm until you feel better." She came to his bedside and shook it out. Then she draped it over him and tucked it around him while Joseph stood beside her.

◆

Lucius gazed into her kind-hearted eyes as she patted his arm like she would a small child.

"May the LORD ease your pain and give you a restful night."

He shifted his gaze from her to her father. "I thank you both for taking me in. I owe you my life, and somehow I will repay you."

Joseph's eyes still chilled him. "You owe us nothing for doing what the LORD has commanded."

Lucius turned his gaze back on her to find a friendly smile and the warmth that was missing from her father's eyes. She patted his arm again and made one last adjustment of the blanket. Then she walked back outside, where her family was about to begin evening prayers.

◆

Without another word, Joseph spun and followed her. The LORD had commanded his people to love the foreigner. How could he ever bring himself to love a Roman soldier? That was too hard. He would care for his enemy until he healed...but only for Yeshua.

Chapter 11

LOOKING FOR LUCIUS

Morning came, and still no sign of Lucius. Marcus was increasingly worried that something had happened to his brother... or so his fellow officers thought. Right after breakfast, he went to the garrison commander and requested two men to accompany him as he traced the route his brother had supposedly taken.

Marcus led his men out of Sepphoris on the Nazareth road, but they soon turned onto the little-used track he'd sent Lucius down. He set the pace at a trot. It was best if his men thought him eager to find his brother, in case he was hurt.

The cliff should be two and a half miles from the turnoff. Another twenty minutes and he would prove he was Lucius Claudius Drusus Fidelis's oldest son.

The road climbed the back side of the hill and topped the crest. Only fifty more yards to the cliff. Marcus rode ahead of his men. Good thing since a self-satisfied smile kept leaking out. His lips twitched as he forced them to straighten. Thoughts of a brother's corpse should never bring a smile...on the surface.

His mind raced ahead to imagine that first glimpse. How best to feign distress? Leap from his horse and almost lean too far over the edge? Canter along the cliff, demanding the gods give him a way down?

He reached the edge, and his distress was intense and genuine.

There was no body. No body, no blood on the ground, no remnants of blood-stained clothing like a scavenger would leave—absolutely nothing to suggest his brother had ever been there, much less ended his mortal existence at the base of the cliff.

But it had to be down there somewhere. Lucius hadn't returned. If Marcus could search the wadi, maybe he could figure out what happened to the corpse, but it was a difficult and dangerous descent. To make that climb without any obvious reason would raise suspicions in the minds of the men he'd brought to witness his brother's demise.

He raised his hand to call a halt. Then he slid off his horse and pretended to be checking its right foreleg.

"Rest your horses."

The cavalrymen dismounted and stretched themselves. One gave the other a quizzical look.

Marcus stood at the edge and scanned the terrain. Below him stretched a wadi with some golden grass and small shrubs encroaching on the sand. The sand had been disturbed since the last flow of water... by someone driving a flock of sheep. No way to tell if that was before or after Lucius was supposed to have been hurled over the edge.

Looking over the edge made his own stomach flip, and he backed away. It was inconceivable that a man thrown from that cliff could have survived. It had been less than a day. No matter what scavengers had eaten their fill, at least his sword and helmet should have been there. Even hyenas didn't eat brass and steel.

Marcus pushed back the scowl provoked by the absence of his brother's body. Had the blacksmith taken his money, only to cheat him? Not likely since Lucius was missing, as requested. Something unexpected must have occurred when Lucius rode by the cliff. Maybe there had been too many people passing at the wrong time. Marcus nodded slightly. The blacksmith and his helper might have decided to kill him farther down the road where there were no witnesses. That must be it. Lucius hadn't returned, so the blacksmith must have done his job.

"Let's proceed. Watch carefully for any sign of him."

The two cavalrymen followed Marcus's lead and remounted. Marcus kicked his horse into a trot. Surely, somewhere down this road he would find what he was looking for.

Lucius awoke midmorning to find himself alone in the room. Without thinking, he tried to draw a deep breath. Big mistake. Even wrapped, a bolt of pain shot through his chest. A steady dull ache served as reminder that his leg was broken. He touched his head where the rock had hit. It was tender, but the lump was mostly gone. If he moved wrong and put any pressure on his other bruises, that hurt, too.

Still, he was alive, and none of his injuries were so severe that he wouldn't recover from them. He should be dead, but, as luck would have it, he'd ended up in a safe place with people who would take care of him until his leg healed.

The door was open, and he could see into the courtyard. With a great deal of effort and no small amount of pain, he raised himself to a sitting position and swung his legs off the bed.

"Is anyone there?"

Rachel stepped into his field of view, dusting flour off her hands. She must have been making the evening's bread. He was glad it was her and not her father.

"Good morning, Lucas. I hope you're feeling better."

"Some. It felt good to sleep."

She walked toward him, a friendly smile lighting her face. "Are you hungry now? I have some bread and goat's milk waiting for you."

"I am."

He was very hungry, but he paused as he remembered the tiny portions she took last night. They were alone. Now was the time to ask about that without the risk of embarrassing her or her father if they were too poor to add one more to their household.

"I saw what you did last night."

She tilted her head, a question ruffling the serenity of her eyes. "What did I do, Lucas?

"You let me eat your share. Are you doing that again? Is feeding me too much for your family?"

A slight flush covered her cheeks. Her eyes flitted away, then returned to him. He kicked himself for embarrassing her, but at least it was only the two of them.

"No. I'd only made enough for four yesterday. That was all. Today I've planned for all five of us, so you'll be eating your own share."

"Are you sure? It's more than enough just to let me stay here. I don't want to burden you or your family. I have money to pay for anything extra you need because of me."

"Obeying Yeshua's command is never a burden, Lucas. You're welcome to share bread with us as our guest."

"But if it becomes a burden, I want you to tell me."

He watched for any sign that she was concealing something, but the serenity of her eyes convinced him. It was unlikely that she was a skilled liar.

"Of course." She turned and walked to the corner of the room. "Abba made you a crutch so you can get around yourself." She brought it to the bedside and held it out to him. "Let's see if it's the right length. He'll trim it to make it right for you if it isn't."

He stood on his unbroken leg and placed the crutch under his right arm. It seemed like the right length, but when he took a step while leaning on it, the pain in his chest convinced him not to walk too far that day.

His teeth clenched as he tried to hide how much it still hurt to move. Rachel's smile dimmed as she watched him.

"Would you like me to bring your food here? I can if it would help, or you can join me under the canopy."

"The canopy with you sounds better."

"Then follow me." She headed back out the door with him trailing behind. As she walked under the canopy, she looked back over her shoulder.

"I thought that might be your choice if you felt up to it. I've moved the bench against the wall so you can sit more comfortably while you eat out here."

With the aid of the crutch, he hopped over to the bench. She'd already placed a cushion there. He lowered himself onto the bench and leaned back against the mud-brick wall. She picked up a second cushion.

"Lean forward, Lucas." She slid it between his shoulders and the wall, and he collapsed back on it. It was quite comfortable once he rested his head against it.

Rachel brought him a bowl of water for washing his hands and offered the same prayer about washing as Joseph had. This time it was no surprise. It appeared almost everything had a prayer about it. When she handed him a cup of goat's milk and a basket containing some bread, she blessed God for providing both, just as her father had the night before. A family of Jews who prayed all the time kept treating him like a Jewish guest instead of a Gentile defiler—what were the odds that such people would find him?

She moved a stool next to him for the bread and the cup of milk. "If you need anything, just tell me."

"Thank you, Rachel. For all of this."

With a gracious nod, she turned from him and returned to her baking.

Lucius tore off a piece of bread. Simple fare, but satisfying. He contemplated her as he took his first sip of goat's milk. She'd come to help a Roman soldier even though she knew her neighbors would hate her helping him. He didn't know exactly how dangerous that might be for her, but she was hiding his identity so the danger was real. Her father obviously didn't want him there. Joseph was obeying his god's command to treat the foreigner well, but the way she kept reminding him it was for Yeshua...she must have played a role in getting her father to let him stay.

He was still alive because of her brothers and her. That was a debt he could never repay. Such willingness to help a total stranger, and for Jews to help a Roman soldier like this...well, it was unimaginable. It would take seven weeks or so for his leg to heal enough for him to return to the garrison. Getting to know this unusual family would be the best part of spending that time here.

Getting to know her...that was especially appealing. He'd never met a woman with such a kind heart. She was pretty, too, in a way that had more to do with the serenity of her cinnamon eyes than with her actual facial features. He found her very attractive. As he sat looking at her, she felt his gaze.

"Did you need anything else, Lucas?"

"No. You've taken care of everything I need and more. I can't thank you enough for what you've done. For what you're doing."

"No thanks are needed, Lucas. I'm happy to do it. Be sure to tell me if you do need something."

She graced him with a warm smile before turning her attention back to the bread.

◆

At his workbench, Joseph drew the spokeshave along the rough-cut piece of wood, freeing the wheel spoke within as the curlicues of wood peeled away. He looked up when he heard Rachel talking with the Roman. Having that man so close to her made him uneasy, but with his broken bones, he wasn't much of a threat.

The crutch seemed to be working without any alterations. Joseph's lips tightened as he shook his head. In the time it took to make it that morning, he could have made a spoke or two for the wheel he was already late delivering. Still, helping a man in need, even a Roman, was what Yeshua asked of those who loved him, and he would do it to show his love for his Lord.

Marcus's jaw clenched as he oscillated between frustrated and furious. Lucius, living or dead, was nowhere to be found along the road. Finally, they entered a small village where the road ended. He spied an old man working in his garden and trotted over.

The rapid approach of a Roman officer and two cavalrymen would have unnerved any Jew in Galilee, and the old man was no exception. When Marcus threw his leg across his horse's neck and slid to the ground, the man stood erect and froze like a deer first spotting a pack of hunting dogs. His eyes began darting as if he would have loved to bolt were the two mounted soldiers not watching him as well.

Marcus walked up to him, his hand gripping the hilt of his sword.

"We're looking for a tribune. He came through here yesterday. Did you see him?"

"No, sir, but I wasn't here all day."

"He was coming to buy a horse from a breeder who lives around here. Tell me how to find that breeder."

The old man's brow furrowed before he shrugged. "No one breeds horses here, sir."

Marcus slid his gladius about two inches out of its scabbard, then rammed it down. The man's eyes widened, and he swallowed hard.

"No breeder? You lie, old man. I've seen his horses in Sepphoris."

The old man wiped at the sweat on his upper lip. "I don't know whose horses you saw, sir. I don't know any breeder. Maybe the man in Sepphoris lied?"

It would have been amusing to watch the old man tremble if only he had found the body. Or the horse.

"Has anyone brought a black stallion through here?"

The old man wiped his lip and swallowed again. "No, sir."

"Hmmph." Marcus's eyes kept boring into him. "Is there another road out of this village?"

"No, sir. Only one road, and we're at the end of it."

Marcus swung away from him and scanned the village, looking for someone else to question. He didn't see any other men, but two women stood under a canopy, working at their looms.

Marcus strode over to interrogate them. When they realized he was coming straight toward them, they dropped their shuttles and turned as if to scurry into the house and hide.

"You! Halt!"

The fear on their faces as they froze at his command would normally have made him laugh, but there was nothing funny about Lucius having vanished into thin air. He deliberately walked right up to them so they would feel him towering over them. Intimidation coupled with some pain was the quickest way to the truth.

"A tribune came here yesterday to buy a horse. Where is he?"

The younger woman clutched the arm of the older and hid half her face behind the older's shoulder, too frightened to say anything. Her mother glanced up at Marcus's angry face before turning her gaze quickly to the ground.

"We haven't seen any Roman soldiers here before you, sir. And I don't know anyone selling a horse."

Marcus gripped her chin and roughly tilted her face upwards to make her look into his eyes. He began to squeeze. He didn't mind if his fingers left a bruise or two. "Are you telling me the truth?"

She began to tremble. Her breath quickened as fear flooded her eyes. "I would never lie to you, sir. I don't know of anyone trying to sell a horse, and I haven't seen the tribune."

He continued to tighten his grip on her chin as he scowled at her. Tears wet her cheeks. He tightened his grip again.

"Please, sir. I'm telling the truth. I haven't seen him."

Marcus was convinced, and he released her with a sudden shove. She would have fallen, but her daughter clinging to her arm prevented it. He watched her touch her face where the marks of his fingers remained. There would be bruises. He spun on his heel and walked back to his horse. With a quick jump, he threw his leg across the horse's rump and settled into the saddle. He swung his horse to face his two men.

"I believe them. He hasn't been here. Someone lied about there being a stallion for sale up here. Someone who wanted the two of us on this road yesterday. Something happened to him before reaching here. Back to Sepphoris, but watch very carefully for any sign of him."

Marcus furrowed his brow and frowned, trying to look deeply worried that they hadn't found him. He nudged his horse into a walk and started back.

Something must have happened to Lucius, or he would have returned to the garrison yesterday. Whatever happened, it wasn't what he'd paid the blacksmith for.

If his brother was dead, where was the body? And if he wasn't dead, could he identify the blacksmith as the one who tried to kill him? And if he could, would the blacksmith reveal that he had been the one who hired him to murder his own brother? He would have a talk with the blacksmith to find out what really happened. Then he would make sure the blacksmith could never tell what he knew.

As they retraced their path along the road, something else began to chew at Marcus. Where was Lucius's horse? The blacksmith was supposed to have simply left it on the road. Even if they didn't find Lucius, they should have found his horse. That is, unless someone had stolen it. A superb horse like that, alone with no rider in sight—it would be a strong temptation for anyone who found it and was willing to ride it to one of the bigger towns like Sepphoris or Tiberias to sell it.

Maybe the blacksmith or his partner decided to make some extra money by taking the horse. It was worth at least three years' wages for most laborers. Or maybe Lucius hadn't been hurt that bad and had been able to ride off somewhere, and he would still show up at the garrison.

If only he had been able to find the horse. That might be enough proof that Lucius had met with foul play, making him the oldest brother. No body, no horse—no proof, and no proof meant it might be a long time before Father would decide Lucius was no longer first in the line of inheritance.

Chapter 12

THE RIGHT ASSIGNMENT

Lucius spent the morning sitting on the bench, alternating between watching her weave, watching Joseph at the forge, and napping. He awoke to the sounds of boys laughing as they returned from their lessons at the synagogue.

After washing with Joseph speaking the blessing, they gathered around the cushions. Lucius rose from the bench and hopped over where he sat the night before. With the crutch for balance, he managed to squat using his good leg and drop onto the cushion with his broken leg extended.

Rachel brought him a bowl of water. "I was going to bring yours to the bench like this morning, but you're welcome to sit with us. Please don't try to get down like that yourself yet. Abba or I will help you if you just ask. I don't want you getting hurt more."

"I didn't get hurt getting down, but I might need help getting up." His sheepish grin as he bent his head back to look up at her was meant to distract her from the scold. It would have been a better idea to let her help. Hitting the cushion hard shot pain through his chest.

His head swiveled downward so he could keep his eyes on her as she knelt on the cushion next to him. Those pretty eyes looked deep into his. One tight-lipped smile and a tiny shake of her head, and he knew she'd caught him in the lie. She saw the pain but was too kind to rub it in.

Joseph offered the blessing over the bread before passing it first to Lucius as the guest. Lucius watched Rachel as he passed it on to her.

If she didn't take a good-sized portion, he was going to insist that she take some money for his food. It was a relief to see she did.

After passing the bread to Lucius, Joseph mostly ignored him as he turned his attention to his sons.

"So, Simeon, what did you learn this morning?"

"It was a very good lesson, Abba. We were studying the prophet Isaiah. When it was my turn, I talked about how the prophesies were fulfilled by Yeshua. Rabbi Eliezer let me talk, but he wasn't very happy about what I said. He doesn't agree with how we understand the prophesies." He grinned at his father. "But that's what I expect. The leaders in Jerusalem weren't happy about what Yeshua said about the prophesies, either.

Joseph nodded his approval and smiled broadly at Simeon. His pleasure and pride as a father couldn't have been more obvious to Lucius. His own father had never looked at him that way.

Then Joseph focused on his youngest son. "And what did you learn, Asher?"

Asher grinned and recited the next portion of Leviticus that he had memorized.

Lucius listened with intense interest. These were the things his grandfather Publius had learned and decided to follow as a God-fearer. He'd been sixteen when Grandfather was killed. Mother always said Grandfather was the wisest man she'd ever known. Lucius remembered enough of him to think she was probably right.

Father had forbidden him to have contact with the God-fearers in Rome because he didn't want anyone to know about his son's interest in his grandfather's religion. But this was Judaea, not Rome, and at the age of twenty-four, Lucius no longer cared what a man like his father thought. It was good to have this chance to learn.

The boys had taken the sheep out to graze, and Joseph had returned to his workshop. Lucius expected Rachel to return to her weaving, so he was surprised when she walked over to Joseph at his workbench and returned with a bowstring drill and the felloe part of a wagon wheel. She placed two wedges to hold the felloe at the proper angle to drill a vertical hole. Then she positioned her feet to hold it firmly in place as she began drawing the bow back and forth to turn the twisted metal bit to drill the spoke hole. As she moved the felloe to position it for drilling the second hole, she glanced up and caught him watching her.

"Do you need me to get you something, Lucas?"

"I don't need anything. It's just that I've never seen a woman do what you're doing. I would have thought the weaving and cooking would take up all your time. Why are you doing that?"

She smiled at him before she responded, but was that sadness underneath her smile? When he tried to look into her eyes to confirm his suspicion, she looked away.

"My brothers used to help Abba with this, but Nathaniel moved away, and Reuben died a few months ago. Abba took on enough work for the three of them, and I'm trying to help him with some of what they would have done."

◆

Rachel pushed some hair that had fallen across her face behind her ear as she leaned forward over the bow and began moving it to turn the drill bit again. He couldn't see her eyes when she was leaning over. She wasn't good at hiding what she was thinking, and a Roman soldier was the last person she wanted reading her thoughts just then.

He'd just asked a dangerous question. Anything she might say about Nathaniel had to be chosen very carefully. He could be arrested and killed if this tribune learned that her oldest brother left the family to join the zealots. There had been too many attacks on Roman officials these last few months. The Romans had killed too many innocent people trying to stop them. People who'd never done anything wrong. People like Reuben.

Her eyes started to sting. She flipped the hair free from her ear. Then she kept her head down so her hair hid her face completely from his gaze.

He mustn't know a Roman soldier killed Reuben. It would be terrible if he said something about it where Abba could hear. It would be even more horrible if he tried to apologize. Nothing he could say could ever make it better. It would be salt rubbed into Abba's wounded heart for any Roman to think words could make any difference in their pain. It was already hard enough for Abba just having a Roman with them.

◆

Lucius watched her draw the bow back and forth, driving the drill deeper into the wood. He'd asked her a simple question, and it had upset her. He wasn't entirely sure he hadn't seen tears in her eyes before she hid her face from him.

Things must be worse for them than she was letting on. He turned his eyes on Joseph as he pumped the bellows at the forge. Her father stepped back from the heat and drew his forearm across his forehead before picking up his hammer and tongs again. A pause as he stared at the glowing metal, then a deep sigh before the ringing blows began. The work was hard, and her father's whole demeanor betrayed his fatigue.

Lucius turned his eyes back on Rachel and watched her spinning the drill bit with the bow. Joseph must be desperate for help if he was willing to let his daughter do that kind of work when she already had a full day's work simply as the woman of the house. Surely he could do some of it to pay for his keep. That would spare her from too much work while helping her father satisfy his customers. The debt he owed was more than he could ever repay, but at least he could do something.

As Marcus and the two soldiers returned to Sepphoris, they once more passed the cliff. He needed to go into the wadi and look, but the way down was treacherous. He couldn't think of a single good reason to give his men that would justify climbing down there without arousing suspicion. The most he could hope to do was ride slowly as he scanned it for any sign of life or, preferably, death.

When they finally reached the garrison, Marcus dismounted and dismissed his men. He then entered the main building and prepared to make his report to the commander.

As Marcus entered the room, the commander glanced up from the tablets on his desk.

"Drusus. What did you find?"

"Nothing, commander. I found no sign of him at all. I interrogated three in the village at the end of the road he was supposed to go down to reach the breeder. Each claimed not to have seen him and denied that anyone near there was selling a stallion." Marcus scowled, trying to look worried and even upset like a brother ought to be. "I'm afraid something bad has happened to him." He shook his head. "I was supposed to go with him, but my stomach was acting up. He went alone so I wouldn't miss out on a stallion I thought I wanted." He tightened his lips and shook his head again. "I shouldn't have let him do that for me."

The commander nodded sympathetically. "He should have been

safe enough on that road, Drusus. You had no way of knowing he might disappear."

His failure to find the body gnawed at Marcus. What if Lucius returned and claimed someone tried to kill him? That would lead to an investigation that might implicate him in the crime. But if the commander could be made to think Lucius ran away, then nothing he said would be believed. No crime—no risk of discovery. He furrowed his brow, tightened his lips, and looked intently at the floor for a few seconds before raising his eyes to the commander.

"Lucius knows this area well, and I can't believe he could have taken a different road by mistake...You don't suppose he decided to disappear on purpose? Maybe we need to expand the search and be looking for him hiding somewhere."

The commander's eyebrows shot up almost to his hairline.

"You can't be serious. Your brother disappear deliberately and abandon his duty? I can't think of any officer who's ever served with me who's less likely to do that. If anything, he's too scrupulous about following every requirement to the letter. Because of him, I've had to discipline some of my men for what I consider harmless pranks. Thankfully, the other officers usually ignore such things.

"Still, he's a fine officer, and I want him back in the garrison. We do need to expand the search. He might be injured somewhere. Since you're his brother, I'm putting you in charge of organizing that. Get it started."

"Yes, commander." Marcus saluted and turned on his heel to march from the room.

When the commander could no longer see, Marcus's jaw clenched. Organize the search for the man he wanted dead—what an assignment. He would have to make it look like he really wanted to find his brother.

His jaw relaxed, and a half-smile appeared. Actually, he did want to find his corpse more than anything else in the world right now. He needed that body to prove he was now the oldest son. Perhaps he really was the best man for the assignment after all.

Chapter 13

Unwanted Volunteer

Dinner was much as it had been the night before with Joseph speaking many blessings over washing their hands and each different type of food. Lucius still sat to Joseph's right in the position of a guest, but he felt more like an invisible observer. Much conversation flowed among the family, but almost none of it was Greek. In silence, he listened. Knowing Aramaic had revealed his mortal enemy at the garrison. It now allowed him to hear what each of these people truly thought and not just what they wanted him to know.

He liked what he heard.

Simeon had great intelligence. He talked with Joseph and Rachel more like an adult than a boy of twelve. He was quick with a smile, especially toward his younger brother.

Asher paid close attention to everything Simeon said and did. He didn't say much except to add something to whatever topic Simeon brought up. There wasn't even the slightest trace of the rivalry he'd always felt from Marcus.

His other brother, Tertius, was six years younger. That difference was enough that they weren't close. But maybe they could have been. Tertius had always seemed so pleased whenever he paid him special attention. They might have developed the kind of closeness that Simeon and Asher had. Too bad he'd been so focused on wanting Marcus to be his friend and never let them find out.

Rachel—his gaze drifted to her if he didn't stop it. Clearly a precious daughter to Joseph, but also the mother of the family. Joseph didn't treat her like a child. He respected her as the woman of the house. She'd been the one who wanted to let him stay, and Joseph had given in to what she wanted.

If there was one word to describe her, it was loving. Everything she did, every word she spoke revealed her love for the members of her family. Whenever Simeon or Asher talked about something, she asked some question that showed she cared. She made sure everyone, especially him, had plenty to eat and drink. She knew he was one of the hated Roman officers, but she took care of him like he was family. He'd never expected to meet a woman who could treat an enemy like the brothers and father she loved.

Joseph. He loved his family and took great pleasure in simply being with them. His smiles and nods encouraged the boys as they talked, but Lucius had no doubt Rachel was the apple of her father's eye. Watching Joseph with Rachel reminded him of Grandfather with his aunt Claudia, except Grandfather had treated Claudia like a child whereas Joseph clearly saw Rachel as a grown woman.

He fixed his gaze on the brawny man sitting beside him, then withdrew it before catching Joseph's eye. He took the breath but stopped before releasing the sigh. He didn't want to draw Joseph's attention. He definitely didn't want Joseph to realize he'd been analyzing him and his family.

Joseph was nothing like his own father. Father always focused on what was best for himself, not his family. His friends were more important than his sons, and he had virtually nothing to do with his daughter or wife.

Lucius had never doubted that Mother loved him and his brothers, and she doted on his little sister, who was now ten. But Father had never been what a father should be. He'd betrayed Grandfather to become head of the Drusus family, and Lucius had no doubt he'd betray any of his children if some personal threat or the right opportunity presented itself. He'd known Joseph bar Jonah less than two days, but he'd already bet this man would sacrifice anything for his family.

A pang of envy struck as Joseph asked each of the boys what they had learned that morning. To have a father who cared so much—that was the way it should be. He sighed.

As first-born son of a Roman family richer than many kings, why did watching this poor Jewish family punch small holes in his heart?

Were they so different because of the god they worshiped, the god Grandfather had chosen to die for? What was it about this god that made his followers so passionate about him? The whole family spent so much time talking about him. Maybe, if he listened to all they were saying, he'd learn enough to find an answer.

◆

As Joseph talked with his younger sons, Reuben's absence prodded him. His second son's love for Yeshua had made his contributions to their nightly discussions of God and Torah so satisfying to Joseph. He glanced at Lucas, sitting too close beside him, obviously watching them all but saying nothing. Again his chest tightened over the immense injustice of a Roman soldier sitting where his son should have been. Still, it was not showing Yeshua's love to the injured man to ignore him as completely as he had during dinner.

After that niggling prick of conscience, Joseph turned his attention to the Roman and addressed him in Greek. "I hope you are feeling better today, Lucas."

"I am. I want to thank you for all your family has done for me. I know there's no way I can repay you for saving my life yesterday, but I would like to ask something of you."

Joseph raised one eyebrow as he raised his chin. He had already done more than he wanted for this man...but probably not more than Yeshua wanted him to.

"And what is that?"

"Let me do something to earn my keep while my leg is healing. I don't want to be a burden by only being a guest in your household. I watched the work Rachel was doing this afternoon. I could do that, if you're willing to teach me."

Joseph's second eyebrow shot up at the request. He had not expected such an offer. In all he had ever seen, Romans only took from his people. And now a Roman asks permission to give?

His brow furrowed, and his mouth turned down as he considered the request. He didn't want to have any more to do with the Roman than was necessary. He would have to spend more time with him and talk with him more if he let him work.

He tightened his lips and shook his head slightly. He would rather work with anyone but this man, but the LORD knew he needed help. Maybe this was the LORD's way of providing. There was far too much work for him alone. For Rachel to do all her own work and help him, too—that was too heavy a burden, no matter what she might say. Perhaps the Roman could take over much of what she had been doing, even with his bruised ribs and broken leg.

His face relaxed, and he shrugged slightly. Perhaps it would be good to let the Roman work to earn his room and board since he wanted to.

◆

As Lucius watched the changing expressions on Joseph's face, he wasn't sure what to expect as his final response.

At last, Joseph spoke. "Very well, Lucas. I accept your offer. Tomorrow I will show you some of what I do when I make parts for the wagons and carts. I will find something you can do even with your broken bones."

Lucius glanced at Rachel. Her glowing eyes spoke her gratitude. She reached over and touched his hand where it rested on the mat.

"Thank you for doing this, Lucas. It will be a big help to Abba... and to me."

"It's nothing compared to what your family has done for me. I'll gladly do anything I can to partly repay my debt."

The tingling sensation of her fingertips on the back of his hand, the sparkle in her cinnamon eyes, and the smile that lit up her face at his words were payment enough for his offer. He liked it when she smiled. He especially liked it when her smile was meant only for him.

Tonight, Joseph watched him closer. The sagging shoulders, the tightness around the eyes and mouth, the slower blinks—he saw them all. Joseph offered the final blessing as they all washed their hands. Then he turned his attention to his Roman "guest." He stood up beside Lucas and offered his hands.

"Time for you to rest."

Lucas nodded. "I agree."

He held Joseph's wrists as he struggled up onto his good leg. Rachel was quick to get his crutch.

"After Abba helps you to bed, I'll come check on you."

"With the crutch, I can manage myself tonight."

Joseph nodded once. "As you wish."

It was a relief not to have to help the Roman again. Tomorrow he would have to spend more time with Lucas than he wanted since he had agreed to let him work. The corners of his mouth turned down at the thought.

◆

Lucius was relieved to avoid the cold gaze of Rachel's father as he helped. He'd seen the warmth in Joseph's eyes as he looked at each of his children. The contrast was striking, and he wasn't sure what he'd done that made Joseph so obviously dislike him. Maybe it was just him being there. Rachel had said her neighbors hated Romans. Maybe he did, too, or maybe he thought having a Roman there endangered his children.

He rubbed the scar on his cheek. No, that couldn't be the reason. She was telling everyone he was Lucas of Corinth. So why would a Jewish wagon maker be so hostile to a Greek he'd barely met? Maybe the reason would become clear in time, and then he could do something about it.

◆

Lucius was back inside and sitting on the edge of his bed when Rachel walked in.

She came to his bedside. "I'm glad you're getting around without help, but let me help you get comfortable for the night."

He was glad she'd come. He couldn't think of a better way to start the night than having a few words with her. Serenity and kindness... all wrapped up in one pretty woman. He could probably manage by himself if he had to, but he didn't want to.

"I want to thank you for everything you did for me today, Rachel."

He grasped his leg at the knee with both hands, lifted his broken leg, and swung it up as he turned on the mattress. He was trying to mask his pain from her, but a soft grunt escaped anyway.

"We're all glad to be able to help you, just as the LORD commanded. Let me help you with that leg."

She supported his knee and foot as she guided his lower leg into a more comfortable position. Then she supported his shoulders as he lowered himself onto the pillow. That helped the pain from his ribs, but even better, it put her cinnamon eyes close to his. They remained as peaceful as ever, but he had to consciously douse the fire kindling in his own. It was a good thing Joseph wasn't watching just then. She noticed nothing, but no protective father could have missed what was happening.

Finally, she drew the light blanket over him before resting her hand on his shoulder. "May the LORD ease your pain and grant you a peaceful rest."

He was savoring the warmth of her hand and the compassion in her eyes when he noticed her father standing in the doorway, staring at him with arms crossed, frowning.

"It's time for prayers, Rachel."

"Coming, Abba."

With one final pat on his arm, she turned to follow her father out the door. Lucius watched her swaying hips. Graceful, almost like a dancer.

He dragged his thumb along the scar, now partially hidden under thick stubble. Had Joseph seen his eyes kindle? Couldn't have. He would have done more than cross his arms and frown. Lucius would try to be more careful in the future. More careful about his thoughts as well as his eyes.

After he closed his eyelids, those cinnamon pools of peacefulness and her smiling lips filled his thoughts until he drifted off.

Chapter 14

THE NEW APPRENTICE

Lucius awoke when he heard the others rising. A dull ache radiated from his broken leg, and his ribs hurt more if he tried to take too deep a breath. Despite that, he felt much better than the day before. Good enough to start working for Joseph.

He rolled onto his right side and pushed up into a sitting position with his left arm as he swung his legs off the bed. Rachel turned immediately when she heard him moving.

"Good morning, Lucas. How are you feeling this morning?"

"Not bad. Much better than yesterday."

She handed him the crutch. "You can join the rest of us for breakfast." Her eyes sparkled as she smiled at him. "And today Abba will teach you some things so you can help us."

She rested her hand on his forearm and swept her fingers lightly across the hairs before lifting them. He fought the smile. She was only trying not to press on his bruises, but she had no idea how her fingertips triggered a wave of heat in their path.

Her smile broadened. "It's so good of you to help. It's been hard for Abba with Reuben...and Nathaniel gone."

Odd the way her eyes flitted away and then toward him when she hesitated before speaking Nathaniel's name.

"No thanks are needed. It's a debt of honor." He shrugged, and his breath caught. Shrugging and cracked ribs were a bad combination. "And it will be good to have something to do."

It was something he owed her family. He'd never liked too much

83

praise for anything he did. He didn't deserve any for helping the people who saved him.

He stood and placed the crutch under his arm. "Shall we join Joseph and your brothers for the blessings?"

She stepped back from him, clearing his path to the door. "After you."

As he hobbled out the door ahead of her, Rachel's head tilted. This Roman officer she'd rescued, he was nothing like what she'd expected. She'd gone to help him only because Yeshua said to love the enemy. Who would have thought a Roman would notice when she gave him her share of the food and want to help Abba because he saw they needed it? She'd been afraid of what bringing him home might cause. No more; it was good she'd agreed to let him stay.

After the final blessings and prayers that concluded breakfast, Joseph turned toward Lucas. "Time for your first lesson."

He stood and offered his hands to the seated Roman. As Lucas was struggling to his feet, Joseph shook his head slightly and tightened his lips. *Please let this Roman be a quick learner.* The less time it took to train him to do some of the simpler tasks, the better. Better because time spent teaching was time he wasn't working himself. Better still because he wanted as little talking as possible with the Roman, even if he might be part of the LORD's answer to his prayer for help.

Lucius clamped his jaw as Joseph pulled him up. Nothing hurt less, but that let him hide pain better. He got his balance, and then his attention focused on Rachel. Her eyes filled with a grateful glow that lit up her whole face. A fire that threw off light and warmed you up on a cold night—that's what her gaze and smile felt like.

She picked up his crutch and held it ready for him "Here. I hope it won't be too hard for you to work today."

"It won't. I'm ready to do something better than lying around."

With a quick smile and a nod, she turned away to clean up the remains of breakfast. He shifted his view to Joseph, and the warm feeling vanished. That grim mouth and stony gaze could douse any fire.

"Follow me." Joseph turned abruptly and strode toward his work area. Lucius took a deep breath and blew it out slowly. Joseph had agreed to let him help, but the next few hours were not likely to be pleasant for either of them.

◆

Joseph watched with arms crossed as Lucas hobbled from the canopy to the workbench. The Roman balanced on his good leg and leaned the crutch against the bench. With one hand resting on the work surface to steady himself, he turned expectant eyes on Joseph.

"You will not be able to stand for long, but you can sit after you have learned what to do." Joseph sized up the Roman. "How bad do your ribs hurt?"

"I can use my arms with no problem, if that's the question."

Joseph raised his eyebrows. "It was. In that case..." Joseph surveyed his tools before selecting the spokeshave. "I am making new wheels. They need eight spokes each. Let us see if you can make one."

He selected one of the short pieces of wood that he had roughed out. They needed final shaping with the spokeshave before they would fit into the holes in the hub he had made the day before. He placed one end in a clamp and tightened the screw.

"The spokeshave is held so." He positioned the tool against the wood. "Then it is drawn like this to make the curve in the wood." He drew the cutting edge along the wood twice, shaving off curlicues of wood.

Lucas's gaze followed Joseph's hands. "I see the angle of the tool and the length of the stroke, but how many cuts do you make before you have to turn the wood in the clamp?"

Joseph's eyes snapped to the Roman's face. Had this soldier worked with wood before? Or was he just a quick learner? He paid close attention to everything he saw and, for some things, maybe closer than Joseph would like.

When he didn't hear an answer, Lucas raised his eyes from the workpiece to Joseph's face.

Joseph nodded his approval of the question, but he didn't smile. "I will show you."

Joseph stepped back from the forge and wiped the sweat from his forehead. He stepped over to the bucket of water and filled the dipper. After swallowing several mouthfuls, he poured the rest on his head.

The lukewarm water felt cold after the heat of the forge. Then he turned his attention to the Roman sitting on the tall stool at the workbench.

He had to admit, although somewhat begrudgingly, that Lucas was a very quick learner and a careful worker. Even his first spoke was of reasonable quality, good enough that Joseph would not be ashamed to put it into a wheel for one of his regular customers. His newest apprentice was now making good progress on his second spoke.

It was good the Roman didn't talk much. Other than a few questions about the work, he'd been silent. When he wasn't looking toward the stool, Joseph could forget about Lucas being there. Allowing their guest to work had been a good decision. The LORD had indeed provided the help he desperately needed until Nathaniel should change his mind and return.

If he ever did return. Joseph tightened his lips and shook his head slowly. It tore his heart to remember Nathaniel's last visit—the hot words, his announcement that he would never return, the last view of his back as he turned north on the Sepphoris road. The ache lingered in Joseph's heart—one son dead, one son a zealot in danger of losing not only his life but his very soul.

He fixed his gaze on the Roman soldier he had promised Rachel he would help. Nathaniel was gone because his kind were in the land. Reuben was dead because the Romans kill the innocent when pursuing the guilty.

◆

Lucius sat up straight and arched his back to loosen his tired muscles. Mistake. It shot pain through his chest. Joseph had probably been right that his ribs were bruised instead of cracked, but they still hurt. He'd been rushing it when he told Joseph he was ready for this work today.

He glanced toward the forge. He wished he hadn't. Joseph was looking directly at him, and his face was dark as a storm cloud. The slight warming as Joseph demonstrated how to make the spokes and checked the quality of his work—no trace remained.

Joseph turned back to the forge, and Lucius sighed. Then he focused his attention once more on the unfinished spoke. He wasn't happy about Joseph's coldness, but it probably didn't matter what her father thought of him as long as he continued to let him stay.

A pleasanter sight entered his field of view when Rachel walked past him toward Joseph. She carried a tray holding two small bowls of dried dates. He suppressed a grin. He should have known she'd make sure they both had something for a midmorning break.

"Abba, I have some dates for you." There was a lilt in her voice that lifted Lucius's spirits even though it was directed at Joseph.

Joseph stepped back from the forge and turned toward his daughter. She placed her hand on his arm and stood on tiptoes to kiss his cheek. The corners of his lips inverted as a smile replace the serious expression he'd worn all morning.

"Thank you, Rachel. Your kiss is sweeter than the dates."

She flashed him a smile before turning to Lucius.

"I have some for you, too, Lucas."

Her bright eyes and cheery smile were as refreshing as the dates were going to be. It was no wonder the touch of her hand on her father's arm had been enough to flip his frown into a smile.

A thought flashed through his mind. A kiss on the cheek from her was something he'd like at least as much as her father did. He'd no sooner thought it than he kicked himself over that idea. The last thing he should be doing is thinking about what an attractive woman she was when her father was watching him.

"Thank you, Rachel."

Rachel studied Lucas as she placed the bowl on the workbench where he could reach it. He was trying to hide it, but he was tired and hurting. He shouldn't keep working, at least not that morning. It was time for him to come back to the bench under the canopy and rest.

"So, Lucas, what have you made this morning?"

"Not much yet." He picked up the finished spoke. "Just this one. And I'm working on my second."

She took the spoke from his hand and slid her hand along its smooth curve. "Nice. It's ready to go into the hub. You're going to be good at this. But one is plenty for your first morning working." She returned the spoke to the workbench and rested her hand on his arm. "You look like two would be too many so soon after your fall. Come back to the canopy and rest awhile."

He shook his head. "I'm not that tired. This isn't hard work, and this stack needs to be finished." He placed his hand on the pile of half a dozen roughed-out pieces.

So much for persuasion. She turned to her father. He'd see the pain and fatigue, too, once he bothered to look for them. "Abba, he really ought to stop now. At least for a while."

Abba stepped closer and focused on the Roman's eyes. "Rachel is right. You have worked too long with those ribs. Go back with her and rest."

"But I didn't even finish two, and—"

"And you can finish the second after you have rested. Now go." Abba crossed his arms and his lips tightened.

Lucas started to open his mouth, then stopped.

Rachel squeezed her lips to stop a grin. It was a good thing Lucas knew better than to resist Abba's command, but she wasn't about to reveal her thoughts that he should have done what she said right from the start. Men could be prickly about taking orders, especially from a woman.

She picked up his crutch and handed it to him. "You'll have time to make lots of spokes before your leg heals. You'll work better tomorrow if you don't do too much today. Come with me and rest."

◆

Lucius turned his gaze back on Rachel and saw the same compassionate eyes and kind smile that had comforted him in the wadi. He couldn't resist her request, especially since she was right. Besides, Joseph had ordered him to go. It would be unwise to disobey a direct command from her father. He was a brave man, but not foolhardy.

He placed the crutch under his arm. "Lead the way."

She set a slow pace, but it was almost too fast as he hobbled beside her. It had been less than two days since Simeon found him near death in the wadi. The work of the morning had made his ribs ache even without him moving much. It had been a painful mistake to try to work like he hadn't been hurt at all.

He glanced at her profile as they reached the canopy. Pretty in repose. Peaceful. Comforting. He wasn't sure why she cared, but it was gratifying that she'd been worried that he might do too much and then watched to be sure he didn't.

"I'll be grinding some flour. You can keep me company here, or even better, lie down inside and take a nap."

"I'd like to stay out here." He was tired but not sleepy, and he hurt enough he wanted a distraction.

"As you wish. You can nap on the bench, like yesterday."

"I'd like to talk awhile. I'd like to know more about you and your family."

◆

Rachel was moving a cushion from the mat to the bench as he

made that request. It made her more than a little nervous. There were things about her family she didn't want this Roman tribune to know.

"Sit down, Lucas, and you can tell me some things about yourself first. I'd find that more interesting."

She held the second cushion behind his shoulders as he lowered himself to the bench. "Why were you traveling that road? No one uses it much."

"I was doing a favor for my brother. We'd planned to go together to look at a stallion he thought he wanted, but he was sick that morning. He didn't want to lose the chance to buy the animal, so I was going to the breeder for him."

"You have a brother here in Judaea?"

"Yes. Marcus just arrived two months ago. He's two years younger than me, and he requested a posting out here so we could serve together."

"That must be nice for both of you. For him to want to come to Judaea, you must be close."

"Well, not before he came, but we've become so. He always preferred his friends when we were younger. When he sent the letter saying he wanted to come here, I was surprised. But I'm glad he came. A brother is someone you can rely on."

Her thoughts flew to Reuben. He'd always been someone to rely on, a brother with whom she could share anything that really mattered. They'd been true kindred spirits.

She pushed the thought back. She didn't want to start crying with the Roman watching. He'd ask why, and she didn't want to tell him anything about how Reuben died.

"So, I've met Simeon and Asher, but what about your other brothers?"

"Reuben was my twin. He died a few months ago. Simeon is a lot like him. Nathaniel is my oldest brother. He's working in Sepphoris now. He makes wheels and carts and wagons like Abba."

She'd answered his question, but was it enough to stop him asking more? It hurt to think about Reuben, and he must never know that Nathaniel was a zealot.

"I'm sorry about your brother."

She nodded, then changed the topic before the tears came. "Do you have any family beside Marcus?"

"Yes. My younger brother, Tertius, is eighteen and still lives in Rome. I have a little sister as well. Drusilla lives with my mother just east of Rome. She's only ten." One corner of his mouth twisted up, followed by one shake of his head. "She's really something. You'd like her. She's very smart and curious about everything. If she were a boy, she'd make a great engineer."

He seemed about to say something else, but he checked himself. Brothers, sister, mother—it seemed odd that he'd mentioned everyone except his father.

"Is your father dead?"

"No. He lives in Rome. We're not close like you and your father."

Was that a note of wistfulness as he spoke? She looked deeper into his eyes to see if they mirrored the regret she thought she heard. What she saw was fatigue and probably pain. It was time for him to rest.

❖

Lucius laid his head back against the cushion. There was no point in trying to hide his fatigue from her. She'd see it anyway.

Her head tilted like she was studying him. "We can talk more later. I need to start grinding the flour, and you need to rest before Simeon and Asher come from the synagogue. You look very tired. It would be best if you would sleep awhile. Are you sure you wouldn't like to lie down inside?"

Those serene, cinnamon eyes pulled Lucius in whenever he looked at her. For some reason he couldn't quite pin down, they made him feel better. "No, I'd rather stay here and watch you."

"Lying down would be better, you know." She wasn't giving up easily, but he was more determined. He wanted to watch her, and the choice really was his to make. No young woman could win a battle of wills with a tribune, even a broken one like him. His eyes held hers, and he saw her moment of capitulation.

"As you wish, Lucas." She turned from him and resumed her place by the hand mill. He watched her turning the upper millstone for a few minutes, swaying rhythmically as she hummed to herself, before his eyes drifted shut, but images of those eyes and those smiling lips persisted as sleep overtook him.

Chapter 15

THE SEARCH

Marcus assembled the troops early to begin the search. Lucius should have been dead for almost two days, and Marcus hoped his body hadn't been totally consumed by scavengers yet. He was counting on them to help the troops find the corpse if it wasn't visible to a search party riding down a road. He needed solid proof his brother was dead. Last night he'd formulated a plan for a thorough search that should turn up the evidence he sought.

Three main roads led out of Sepphoris. The most important one headed southwest toward Shimron and then to Legio and Caesarea. Marcus had ridden through several small towns and villages in the last twenty miles before they reached the garrison. There was no reason for Lucius to be anywhere along that road, but he would send search parties down it anyway.

Another headed north to intercept the road that ran between the coastal town of Ptolemais and Tiberias on the Sea of Galilee. He was positive Lucius hadn't gone that way, but he would send some troops as far north as the junction to make his search seem thorough.

The road that interested him was the one Lucius should have taken almost due south toward Nazareth and Jezreel. He would have the side road he'd sent Lucius down searched again. He would also have troops search each side road that went off the road between Sepphoris and Nazareth. Maybe Lucius missed the turnoff, and the blacksmith followed him to complete the attack on a different road. Maybe...

Marcus stood in front of his troops. "As you know, my brother, Lucius Drusus, left the garrison alone two days ago. He was supposed to have returned by evening, but he failed to do so. Today you are going to search for him. I will be sending most of you to search the roads to Shimron, Nazareth, or the Ptolemais junction. You are to question anyone who looks like they spend some time each day where they might see a passing Roman officer. He was in armor on a black stallion, and the scar on his left cheek might have drawn attention." Marcus traced the pattern of the scar on his own cheek.

"He was going to buy a horse on the first side road heading west from the Nazareth road. I searched that road yesterday and found nothing. You will search it again and also the other side roads between here and Nazareth." He paused, shifting his gaze to the ground, then back to the troops. Just like a deeply worried, affectionate brother. "Watch especially for any signs of scavengers, and check what they're feeding on."

Another quick casting of his eyes to the ground, another dramatic pause—that should do it.

"You twelve will stay here in Sepphoris. I have prepared a list of craftsmen and merchants who supply the garrison. You will go to them and ask if they have heard any rumors about a Roman officer who may have been killed."

Marcus paused once more to build dramatic tension. "I will personally pay 300 denarii as reward to the men who find my brother. You are dismissed to begin the search."

As the men mounted and headed off in their assigned directions, Marcus spun on his heel and strode back into the garrison headquarters. With so many searching, he should have the proof he needed by nightfall.

Nathaniel looked up from his workbench when the two Roman soldiers entered the wagonmaker's shop. He'd sought work at that particular shop because the garrison did a lot of business with his employer. He refocused his eyes on the spoke he was making while his ears tuned in to the conversation between the Romans and the shop foreman. Several times his attentive ears had gathered valuable intelligence about Roman activities that had proven useful to the zealot band that he and Daniel were now part of.

The foreman greeted the Romans with cool eyes and a formal smile.

"What can I do for you today?"

"A tribune is missing, and we're looking for information."

"Tell me more, and perhaps I can help you. I hear many things."

"Lucius Drusus went to buy a horse two days ago and never returned. Have you heard any rumors about someone killing an officer since then?"

"Drusus? Isn't he the one with the scar along his jaw?"

"Yes."

"I've met him. Missing, you say. Too bad. I haven't heard anything, but he's friendly with Jacob bar Asa. He practices Aramaic when he eats at Jacob's inn. You should ask there." The foreman shook his head. "I hope you find him alive. He's a good man."

After the soldiers left the shop, the foreman turned to Nathaniel with a grin. His voice dripped with sarcasm. "Yes, indeed, he's a good man...for a Roman."

Nathaniel nodded in agreement. Being good for a Roman wasn't saying anything at all.

Rachel kept her eye on the tribune as she worked at her loom. He'd insisted on returning to the workbench to finish the second spoke after the light midday meal.

One thing was clear. Roman men were just as stubborn as Jewish ones, and neither seemed to know what was good for them. She couldn't count on Lucas stopping when he should, and Abba didn't pay attention to how tired he was getting. He was just finishing the final cuts. That was enough...more than enough.

He'd started out sitting erect on the stool. Now he was making fewer cuts before pausing, and his shoulders slumped during those pauses. No matter how much he protested, she would make him rest before he started another one.

She parked the shuttle and headed toward the workshop.

Lucius had just released his second spoke from the clamp. He ran his hand along its smooth surface. Not too bad, if he did say so himself. Even Joseph had approved of the first spoke, and this one was better than the first.

He was leaning over to get the next rough-cut piece when she reached past him to place her hand on his outstretched arm. He startled and snapped his head around to look at her. She could move much quieter than he expected. She'd make a good spy in an enemy camp.

"Two really are enough for your first day, Lucas. I've been watching, and we both know it's time for you to rest."

He would have argued with her, but he glanced over at Joseph. Her father flicked his hand toward the house. "Go with her."

He'd been dismissed for the day. He hated to admit it, but that was a good thing. He hadn't expected using the spokeshave to make his ribs hurt as much as they did. His short rest during the morning had fooled him into trying again after the midday meal. He'd been able to complete the second spoke, but he was ready to hurt less.

He stood up on his good leg and reached for his crutch. Before he could touch it, she had it in her hand.

"Will you lie down for a good rest now you've finished two?"

She handed him the crutch. Before the first step, he set his mind to mask the pain. He'd found ten-mile marches easier than this short walk to the canopy with cracked ribs and a crutch.

"Maybe." She was one determined woman when it came to telling him he should get some sleep. He was tired, but he'd make his own decisions.

She matched his caterpillar pace. "So how did you like your first day as a wheelmaker? The spokes you made looked very good to me."

"Your father is a good teacher. I enjoyed the work."

She shook her head once. "Even though it hurt."

He glanced sharply at her. She was one perceptive woman as well.

She almost laughed. "It's plain you're hurting, Lucas. I see it in your eyes. I also see you need to sleep."

"In the wadi, you said the garrison physician would know what's best for a man like me. Do you think he'd make me sleep?"

"If he cared about you getting better as fast as you could, yes."

Cinnamon eyes sparkled as she smiled up at him. How could he have been so fortunate as to have someone like her find him?

"He's paid to get a man back to duty as quickly as possible, so maybe he would want me to sleep." One corner of his mouth twitched upward. "But I outrank him, so I'd only have to sleep if I wanted to."

"I hope you want to, at least for a little while." Warm concern replaced the sparkle. "If only to let me worry less about you doing too much today."

They'd almost reached the canopy. He looked first at the bench where he could watch her, then at the door. It was tempting to stay out with her, but deep fatigue was pointing him toward the bed inside.

"Since I don't want you to worry, I'll lie down for a while." He squeezed his lips together to keep his smile from turning into a too-playful grin. "This time, anyway."

The grin broke free, but he quickly turned it off. Joseph might be watching.

She followed him into the house. He sat down on his mattress, wrapped his hands around his knee, and swung his broken leg up onto the bed.

She helped him position it comfortably, then supported his shoulders as he lay down on his back. "There. That's much better for you."

Those smiling lips and cinnamon eyes so close to his...he had to agree that was much better. She patted his arm. "May the LORD ease your pain and give you a good rest."

"Thank you, Rachel. For everything."

After one more pat of his arm, she walked away from him and out the door to resume her weaving. His gaze remained fixed on her until she escaped his field of view. A gazelle—that's what she was, with gentle brown eyes and movements of infinite grace.

He closed his eyes. What good fortune to still be alive and to have come to this safe place where he could heal. Who would have thought a Drusus would end up hiding from the Roman army, sheltered by a poor Jewish family? How ironic that a Galilean woman and her father would risk caring for a Roman officer simply because they obeyed the Jesus his grandfather had died for.

Chapter 16

No Longer an Enemy

A pair of laughing brown eyes and an endearing smile adorned her as Rachel wiped his face with a damp cloth. He reached up to take her hand...and then he awoke. The real Rachel stood beside him with serious eyes, her hand resting on his shoulder and her finger held against her lips.

Before he could speak, she whispered her warning. "Shhh. Be very quiet, Lucas. There are soldiers in the village, and I think they're searching for you."

He sat up too quickly, and his jaw clamped as pain shot through his chest. He swung his legs off the bed.

Rachel move closer to the door. "They're riding toward Abba."

"Will he tell them I'm here?" He was too broken to face an enemy. "I can't go back yet."

"No. Abba will get rid of them. Just stay in here and be quiet." She turned as if to go back out to the canopy.

"Don't go out there, Rachel." She turned to face him, a question in her eyes. "It's safer for you in here, out of sight."

He was ashamed to admit it, but a young woman wasn't always safe near Roman troops. These men were on a mission, but some still might decide there was time for some entertainment if no officer was with them. With the wrong officer, it still might not be safe.

"I'm just going to peek out to see what I can. I won't go out. I understand the danger."

He grabbed his crutch and hobbled over to listen. Better if he was next to her if the soldiers came to the house. He wanted to stay, but he would reveal himself if he must to keep her and her father safe.

She stepped back into the shadows within the dark room after her quick scan of the road past the courtyard gate. She stood on tiptoes and whispered in his ear.

"There are four cavalrymen riding toward Abba. No officers."

◆

Joseph stood at the forge shaping a rim as the soldiers reined in at the entrance of the courtyard.

The one in charge separated from the column of twos and rode up very close. "You."

Joseph set down his tongs and hammer and turned to face him. "Can I help you?"

"We're looking for an officer who may have passed here two days ago."

"Many Roman officers pass on their way to Legio. Is there something special about the one you seek?"

"He was alone on a black stallion. If his helmet was off, you'd see a long scar on his left cheek."

Joseph slowly shook his head. "I've seen no Roman ride through here alone on a black horse."

The cavalryman nodded once before turning his horse to head down the road. The other three fell into formation with him. Joseph watched them until it was clear they were continuing down the road and would not be coming back. Then he strolled toward the room where Lucas was hiding.

When he entered, Rachel placed her hand on his arm. "Is it safe now, Abba? Have they gone?"

"Yes. They were looking for a Roman officer on a black horse. I told them I have not seen one. I do not expect them to return."

"Thank you for not telling them I was here, Joseph."

Joseph's head snapped toward Lucas. "Why would I tell them you were here? You are a guest in my house. The LORD has placed you under my protection. Of course I will protect you from anyone who would hurt you, Roman or otherwise." His eyes were cold, and his mouth tightened as he stood glaring at his unwanted guest.

"I meant no offense, Joseph. I never meant to imply you wouldn't protect me. I only want you to know how much I appreciate what you have done...what you are doing for me."

"I want no thanks for doing what Yeshua commands. You can

stop speaking them to me." With an irritated shake of his head, Joseph turned and headed back to the forge to continue his work.

◆

Lucius turned toward Rachel. "I meant no offense..."

She rested her hand against his arm and patted it. "I know." The warmth of her smile counteracted the icy anger in her father's eyes.

"Since you should stay inside until we're sure they won't return, will you lie down and rest again?"

After too much work and the stress from almost being found, he'd felt better at the end of a twenty-mile forced march. "I'll do whatever you think best, Rachel."

"Good. You'll get better much faster if you let me take care of you."

She escorted him back to his bed and helped him get comfortable again. "Try to sleep a while. I'll wake you in plenty of time to prepare for dinner."

◆

Lucas closed his eyes, and his deep, slow breathing told Rachel he'd fallen asleep almost immediately. She gazed at the cut that was mostly scabbed over and the purple bruises on his face and arms. Some were starting to mottle with a sickly greenish yellow as they began to heal.

So many bruises and broken bones. She hated to see him hurting. True, he was a Roman officer, a leader of the men who showed no mercy as they tried to crush the longing of the Jews to serve only God, not Rome. But he was still a man, precious to Yeshua, and he needed their help.

It was so hard for Abba to have him there. Pain and anger filled his eyes when he looked at Lucas in Reuben's clothes and especially when Lucas sat in Reuben's place at meals. Almost too hard, but at least Abba could find comfort in knowing he served Yeshua by caring for his enemy.

Lucas's breathing stopped; then the rhythmic rise and fall of his chest resumed.

She would lighten Abba's burden by caring for the Roman as much as she could herself. His cut, bruised face was no longer the face of an enemy to her.

The last of the search parties had returned, and Marcus was not happy. Lucius had not been found. Worse than that, not a single person was willing to tell the searchers they'd even seen him. Tomorrow he would go to the blacksmith to get his version of what happened to Lucius, but right now he had to report to the garrison commander.

When Marcus entered, the commander immediately suspended work on the report lying on his desk.

"Drusus. Has your brother been found?"

"No, commander. The last search party has returned. None found any trace of him or his horse. I also had the tradesmen who deal often with the garrison questioned. Nothing. I'm afraid we must conclude my brother has been murdered and his body secretly disposed of. It's time to let my father know my brother is gone."

First the commander's eyebrows rose, then his eyes narrowed. A frown appeared.

"Finding his body would prove he's dead. It might prove he's been murdered. Failing to find him only proves he's still missing. I know your brother. If he's somewhere hurt, he'll return as soon as he recovers. It's too soon to send your father a message that will cause him much grief when his son might still be alive. I know too well the effect of the letters I've had to send to my men's fathers. I won't send one until I'm sure."

The commander shook his head as he tightened his lips. "I'm surprised you've so quickly jumped to the conclusion that he must be dead, Drusus."

Marcus placed his hand over his mouth and drew it down across his chin. Stupid move. Much too soon with his request.

"You've given me hope that I might see my brother again. The people here hate us Romans so much. I didn't realize it would be this bad before I came. Too many would gladly kill one of us, given the chance, and no one would help if we needed it. He was carrying over a thousand denarii, so he could pay someone to help him, but they might just kill him for the money instead." Marcus shook his head. "I need to stop thinking the worst. You're right that missing is only missing, not necessarily dead."

The commander nodded. "You're new to Judaea. Men often underestimate or overestimate the danger of serving here. Your brother did neither. If anyone can survive going missing here, it's him. Don't lose hope, Drusus." He turned his attention back to his report, and Marcus left the room.

As he walked out into the courtyard, Marcus's eyes narrowed. The commander was right. Lucius might still be alive somewhere, injured but planning to return. He had no idea when that might happen or even if it would, but one thing was certain. The blacksmith needed to die before Lucius reappeared, and he knew just how to make sure that happened.

◆

It was almost time for dinner, but Marcus wasn't looking forward to it. He'd decided it would look odd for him to enjoy a good dinner at an inn when his brother was missing. It would take no acting ability at all to look like he was not enjoying any dinner made by the garrison cook.

But first, it was time for another letter to Father. The commander might be unwilling to send a letter, but it would seem odd even to Father if he didn't write about his brother's disappearance right away. There was time before he had to gag down the vile stew that awaited him in the dining hall.

He withdrew a papyrus sheet from his writing desk, dipped the pen into the ink, and began.

> Marcus Claudius Drusus to Lucius Claudius Drusus Fidelis, my father, greetings. If you are well, then I am glad. I write to tell you what I fear may be very bad news.
>
> I have been unable to keep Lucius from taking foolish risks here. He wanted to buy a stallion from a breeder south of Sepphoris. He and I were to go there two days ago, but I was sick that morning. Rather than waiting until I could go with him, he went to the breeder alone. I asked him to wait for me, but he was afraid the horse would be sold.
>
> I regret to tell you that he has disappeared without a trace. I searched for him myself yesterday without success and sent out many search parties today. I greatly fear that he has been murdered. The commander here tells me that I should not yet assume the worst, that he may only be injured and will return. If this were not Judaea, I would have reason to hope the commander was correct. But this is Judaea, and an injured Roman with no one to protect him will almost certainly become a dead one as soon as a Jew finds him.

I will write you as soon as I know my brother's fate. The commander tells me not to despair, and we must try. May the gods guard your safety.

Marcus struggled to suppress a smirk as he sealed the rolled papyrus with wax and addressed it. Tomorrow it would leave with the military dispatches to Rome. As soon as he could prove Lucius was dead, he would follow it home.

Chapter 17

FAITH OF HIS GRANDFATHER

The gentle pushes of her fingertips on his left shoulder pulled Lucius out of deep slumber.

"Lucas? Are you ready to wake up now?"

His eyelids drifted open, and a slow, sleepy smile appeared. "You were right about me needing to rest."

"And now it's time for dinner. I hope you're hungry." A playful smile lifted the corners of her mouth. "I made you your very own share."

As he started to raise himself into a sitting position, she slid her arm beneath his shoulders and lifted to protect his ribs. Her arm on his back, her hand on his shoulder, the warmth of her body nearby, her eyes so close to his. She only meant to spare him pain, but that small gesture of kindness did much more than take the stress off his ribs. It would be pure pleasure...if only everything didn't still hurt so much.

"A good rest followed by a good dinner...a man can't ask for better care."

She patted his arm before she turned away from him and stepped toward the door.

He sat on the edge of the bed with his shoulders slumped, eyes closed, head hanging as he ran his hand slowly through his hair. When she wasn't looking at him, he didn't mask how much he hurt.

"Lucas?" Footsteps came closer. She was almost at his bedside.

He opened his eyes and put the mask back on. "Sorry. I'm coming."

She rested her hand on his arm where there wasn't a bruise. "I wish I could stop all the pain right now. The LORD spared you, and He'll heal you, but that's going to take some time."

He looked up into those eyes softened by sympathy. They glistened with unshed tears. He had never known anyone who cared about the pain of a stranger the way she did. Most didn't even care that much about the pain of their friends.

"It's not so bad. It's much better than yesterday, and it will get better every day. Don't cry." He stood up to show the pain was not too severe.

"Forgive me, Lucas." She wiped her eyes. "I should be comforting you, not the other way."

"Another good dinner is all the comforting I need this evening, and I'm sure it's waiting for me...after I wash my hands and bless God for telling me to."

Rachel drew back. Her spine straightened as her smile fled.

Lucius watched her eyes cool toward him. What a foolish choice of words, and not at all what he meant.

"I'm not mocking you or your god, Rachel. My grandfather was a God-fearer in Rome. Father didn't want his friends to know I was interested in Grandfather's religion, so he ordered me to have nothing to do with the God-fearers there. He has the right to do that, and I obey him when I'm at home. But this is Judaea, not Rome. I used to wonder about Grandfather's beliefs. I'm glad of the chance to learn about them here with you."

The warmth returned to her eyes, and a smile brightened her whole face. "Now I know why the LORD had Simeon find you. He wants you to learn more about Himself and about what Yeshua did. You can get to know someone really well in six or seven weeks. You'll be amazed by what you'll find as you get to know Him."

His head tilted, and his eyes narrowed. "Get to know him? Like a person?" Then he nodded once as his face relaxed. "Sounds like what Grandfather used to say."

"Of course it would, Lucas. God is the same in Rome or Judaea."

As he stood in silence, Joseph stepped into the doorway.

"Rachel, is anything wrong?" His glowering eyes were riveted on Lucius as he spoke.

"No, Abba. We're coming." She followed her father out the door.

Lucius was right behind her, but his mind was still turning over her words. The way she had treated him from the first moment she saw him still amazed him. She'd told him in the wadi she was doing it to obey Yeshua. Her father could barely stand the sight of him, but he'd let him stay for the same reason. Now she was claiming that she didn't just obey her god, that she actually knew him, and that he could know her god, too. He could know Grandfather's god, the one he died for. Know him like one man knows another.

He could hardly wait to see what she thought he was going to learn.

The family seated themselves around the mat. The cushion between Joseph and Rachel had become Lucius's regular assigned seat. Warm on one side, cool on the other—it was what he expected now. After the blessings, the conversation began.

Joseph began by asking his sons in Aramaic what they learned that day. Before the boys could respond, Rachel spoke in Greek.

"I'm sure Lucas would like to hear what you learned as well. Let's use Greek so he can." She patted Asher's arm as he sat beside her. "It will be good for you to get more practice speaking Greek as well."

Simeon glanced at Lucius and flipped to Greek. "Tomorrow *bet talmud* will be listening to Torah study with you, Abba. Rabbi Eliezer will be leading, so we'll all sit at the back to hear his teaching."

Joseph's head dipped. In deference to Rachel's request, he also spoke Greek. "I am glad to hear that, Simeon. It is always good when Rabbi Eliezer teaches."

Rachel turned to Lucius. "We go to synagogue to hear and learn more about Torah and the prophets early on Monday and Thursday mornings. We go twice on Shabbat, before dinner and again in the morning."

Joseph lowered his eyebrows as he looked at his daughter. In Aramaic he spoke, "I do not think Lucas is interested in our worship, Rachel."

Joseph's mouth curved down when he turned his gaze on Lucius, then up when he looked once more at Rachel.

Lucius took a deeper breath, steeling himself to address her father after that wordless rebuff. Asking something of Joseph made him nervous, but this was even more important than working to help out. Joseph's words had just made it harder, but the worst Joseph would do is say no. He cleared his throat and charged ahead.

"Joseph, I would like to join your family tomorrow when you go to synagogue." Joseph's head twitched backward before his eyebrows scrunched. "That is, if you don't mind me joining you."

"Why would you want to do that, Lucas?"

"My grandfather was a God-fearer. I never got to learn about his religion when he was alive. I would like to now."

◆

Taking the Roman to synagogue was the last thing Joseph wanted to do. Questions would be asked, and they would need a story that would satisfy all the men of the village. It could be very bad for his family if any of his neighbors realized they were harboring a Roman officer. He rubbed the back of his neck as his mouth turned downward.

Could the Roman pull off the deception that he was a Greek laborer? He had that confident expression and bearing of an officer, even with his broken leg. His nose was just like Emperor Hadrian's on the coins. His hair was too straight and too short. Even though his beard had grown fast and thick, it was still short. Joseph could see a hint of the scar on his jaw, although that might be because he knew it was there. But anyone the Roman troops spoke with might guess it was there as well.

Joseph shook his head. "The synagogue is uphill about an eighth of a mile—too far for a man with a broken leg."

"That's a very short walk. The crutch you made me works well. I'm sure I can do it."

Joseph's lips tightened. Romans were persistent when they wanted something. "It would do you no good to come with us. Torah is read in Hebrew, then retold in Aramaic. All of the teaching and discussions are in Aramaic. There is nothing there for a Greek-speaking man to learn."

Lucas switched into Aramaic. "That won't be a problem for me, Joseph. I don't know Hebrew, but I've learned some Aramaic during my time in Judaea. I think it will be enough for me to understand most of what is said."

Joseph's eyes saucered, and he sat up very straight. Then a scowl pulled his mouth down. "It would have been good for you to tell me this earlier, Lucas."

"Perhaps I should have. It didn't seem important. We've had no problem understanding each other using Greek."

Joseph continued frowning as he stared at the Roman. An uncomfortable silence stretched out between them as Joseph considered Lucas's hopeful eyes. Then he sighed.

Of course he would take him to synagogue. The LORD always welcomed those who wanted to know him. The prophets had foretold that

Yeshua would come and be the light to the Gentiles as well as the Jews. Yeshua himself had praised a centurion's faith before healing his servant, and the LORD told Apostle Peter in a dream that he should go to the God-fearing centurion Cornelius to teach him about Yeshua. This Roman wouldn't be asking if the LORD hadn't placed that desire in his heart.

"As you wish, Lucas. You can come. I will introduce you and explain why you are with us, and there should be no problem."

Lucas's broad smile told Joseph he had made the right choice. "Thank you, Joseph."

"He can sit at the back with me, Abba." Simeon grinned at the Roman. "Then if he has questions, he can ask me without interrupting the teaching."

"I appreciate that, Simeon. I'll probably need your help." Lucius looked back at Joseph. "Sitting at the back with Simeon sounds good. I don't want to disturb anyone by my presence."

Joseph tightened his lips and nodded. The Roman's presence was a constant disturbance to him. Still, the LORD had brought him to them for his healing. Maybe He had brought the Roman to them so he would learn about the LORD as well.

Asher looked first at Lucas, then at Rachel, and finally at Abba. "So, should I tell you what I learned today in Greek or Aramaic?"

Rachel leaned sideways and hugged him. "Whatever you want to do is fine, Asher. Just fine."

Chapter 18

LIGHT FOR THE GENTILES

For Lucius, standing in the courtyard the next morning waiting for the others was like standing near the top a hill, feeling the energy in the air just before a lightning strike. It would be his first time listening to the teaching of the Jewish scriptures that Grandfather had loved. Rachel had given him one of Reuben's clean, unmended tunics to wear in honor of the occasion.

Joseph emerged from the house with his prayer shawl. Then he led his assembled family plus one through the gate and up the street. Simeon and Asher were right beside him. Rachel stayed back and walked beside Lucius.

For a man using a crutch with bruised ribs, the eighth of a mile from their house to the synagogue was a very long distance. He started off at a good pace, but he soon had to slow down. As he leaned on the crutch and swung his good leg forward slower and slower, he sensed her gaze upon him.

He turned his eyes away from her. He wanted no questions about the wisdom of what he was doing. His jaw clenched against the pain, but no amount of pain was going to keep him from getting his long-felt questions answered.

"Are you going to be able to walk so far, Lucas?"

He consciously relaxed his jaw. "Yes. It will just take me a while." Joseph and the boys were getting some distance ahead of them. "I'm not keeping up, but I'm sure you won't let me get lost on the way."

The twinkle in his eye drew a smile to her face.

"The LORD helped us find you, Lucas. He'll keep us from losing you now we have you."

◆

Joseph reached the synagogue and turned to speak to Lucas before they entered. The Roman was walking much slower than he expected. It was obvious that each step was hurting him, but his determination to get to the synagogue was just as obvious. Joseph crossed his arms and waited patiently.

"I think it hurts him a lot to walk, Abba." Simeon shook his head in sympathy. "He must really want to learn about the LORD. It's a good thing he knows more Aramaic than I thought he might."

Joseph's eyes snapped onto his son. "You knew he understood what we were saying?"

"Yes, Abba. At least some. He spoke Aramaic when he gave me the money for the lamb."

Joseph frowned. "You should have told me, Simeon. We might have said something that put Nathaniel in danger. This Roman must not know your brother is a zealot." He looked down at Asher. "We all need to be careful what we say in front of him. Understand, Asher?"

"Yes, Abba. Can I go to *bet sefer* now?"

Joseph smiled down at his youngest and flicked his hand. "Go."

He turned his attention back to Simeon. "Is there anything else I should know about him?"

"No, Abba. Nothing I can think of."

"Watch over him at synagogue today. Let me know if there is a problem."

"Yes, Abba."

The two stood watching until Lucas and Rachel finally reached them.

Joseph appraised the Roman. He was a study in contradictions. Already physically tired and hurting, but still brimming with energy. "Walking here today was not a good idea, Lucas. It was too far."

"But I'll only have twenty-five or so chances to come. I didn't want to miss one."

Simeon grinned at his enthusiasm, but Joseph remained cool.

◆

Rachel touched Lucius's arm. "I'm going to sit with the women. Can you manage now?"

"Yes." He fought a grin. "Thank you for making sure I didn't get lost."

Her eyes warmed at his joke. "Abba and Simeon will watch over you now so you don't."

He watched her as she walked away. She was one special woman. He started to smile at the thought, then checked himself. Her father was watching.

Joseph's mouth curved down when he saw the direction of Lucius's gaze. "Lucas." Lucius flipped his eyes to Joseph's. "We will go in now, and I will introduce you. Listen carefully to what I say so you remember in case someone asks you about it later."

"I will, Joseph." He had no idea what story Rachel had told her father about him. It was vitally important for his safety that no one discover what he truly was. It might be just as important for all of them, whether Joseph realized it or not.

As he hobbled into the building behind Joseph, all eyes turned toward him. All were curious. Some were welcoming. Some, but not those of an older man seated in the front row. He looked furious that Joseph had brought an obviously Gentile man into the synagogue. The anger in his eyes and blackness of his scowl made Joseph's usual expression seem positively friendly.

Rabbi Eliezer spoke first. "Joseph. I see you have brought a stranger to joins us."

"Yes, Eliezer. This is Lucas of Corinth. Simeon and Asher found him where he had been left by robbers. It is the LORD's special timing that they should find him just as Asher has learned Torah about how to treat foreigners who reside among us."

Joseph paused and squared his shoulders before reciting, "When a foreigner resides among you in your land, do not mistreat them. The foreigner residing among you must be treated as your native-born. Love them as yourself, for you were foreigners in Egypt. I am the LORD your God."

Joseph paused again and scanned the room. Several of the men were nodding in response to the Scripture. "Lucas will be with us until his leg heals. He has spoken his desire to learn more about the God of Abraham, Isaac, and Jacob. He will be sitting with Simeon today where he can listen and learn the word of God."

Eliezer turned his focus on Lucius as he opened his arms in a gesture of welcome. "We are glad to have you with us, Lucas of Corinth."

"I thank you for your welcome, Rabbi Eliezer, and I look forward to learning from you today." His Aramaic was accented but otherwise perfect. Eliezer smiled at him once more and then began.

Lucius sat at the back with Simeon, enthralled by what he heard. There had been a reading from Leviticus in Hebrew, which he partially understood from the similarity to Aramaic. He was glad when the translation was given because he'd missed part the first time. The teaching from the rabbi on how the commands went beyond the simple words was enlightening.

The rabbi put away the first scroll and took out another. As he unrolled it to the place where he was to read, he looked up. Lucius met his gaze, totally focused on what Eliezer was doing.

Rabbi Eliezer pronounced the blessing before beginning to read God's word. "And now the LORD says—he who formed me in the womb to be his servant to bring Jacob back to him and gather Israel to himself for I am honored in the eyes of the LORD and my God has been my strength—he says: 'It is too small a thing for you to be my servant to restore the tribes of Jacob and bring back those of Israel I have kept. I will also make you a light for the Gentiles that you may bring my salvation to the ends of the earth.'"

Eliezer read on, and Lucius was hanging on every word. Who was the servant who was the light for the Gentiles? And how would he bring salvation to the ends of the earth? An excitement was building that he couldn't explain. It was as if the God of Israel was speaking to him personally through these writings, just as Grandfather had once told him. The God of the Jews had planned to be the God of the Gentiles like him, too.

Simeon leaned over and whispered in his ear, "The prophet Isaiah was writing more than 700 years ago about Yeshua of Nazareth. Yeshua is the servant."

Lucius's eyes widened at Simeon's words. His grandfather had died for his faith in Jesus of Nazareth. Then a satisfied smile spread across his face. He would learn more about the faith of his grandfather than he had ever expected as he came to synagogue with them.

◆

Eliezer saw the focused eyes and happy smile of Joseph's guest. God must have planned for him to be with them that day since the reading from the prophet Isaiah was perfect for a Gentile visitor. It was good that Joseph had brought Lucas of Corinth. He was a Gentile wanting to look for the light of God. It was gratifying to be the one to speak God's words to him.

◆

As Eliezer read, several of the men glanced over at Lucas and either smiled or nodded. Relief flooded Joseph at their acceptance of him being there. The Roman should be able to come and learn as he wanted without causing a problem. A Roman tribune pretending to be a Greek laborer being allowed and even welcomed into the fellowship of the Jewish synagogue. Surely God had a sense of humor in all that. If they only knew what Rachel and Simeon had brought among them, there would not be the smiles on all their faces that he was seeing. All except for Benjamin's, that is.

Benjamin did not look happy that he had brought the Greek, but then Benjamin was never happy about anything Joseph did. He hated how Joseph and his children regarded Yeshua of Nazareth as not only a prophet, but as the long-expected Messiah, the Anointed One, who claimed to be the Son of God.

Chapter 19

PAYMENT IN FULL

The short street that ended at the blacksmith's shop was deserted. Marcus had chosen to come early before the other shops opened. He had business with the blacksmith that was best left unobserved.

The blacksmith was at the forge, working on the new sword, when Marcus entered his shop. The ring of hammer blows masked the sound of his approach. When Marcus cleared his throat, the smith spun around.

"Didn't hear you come in." The smith set aside his hammer and turned back to face his customer. "So, you've come for the second part of what you ordered. I should have the sword finished by tomorrow."

"I've come to discuss a problem with the first part."

The blacksmith's bushy eyebrows scrunched to form a single hairy line. He wiped some sweat off his furrowed forehead with the back of his hand. "What do you mean? The first part went exactly as ordered. I got him off his horse with a rock to the head. Then we threw him off the cliff."

"Then why didn't I find a body when I rode along that road two days ago? I rode to the end, and there was nothing like what we agreed to along the road. I had a search party ride that road again yesterday, and they found nothing."

"That can't be. He couldn't be alive after a fall like that. He looked dead as can be down in the wadi. If he wasn't dead then, he was close enough to it that he was dead before we got back to Sepphoris."

"He wasn't there."

"I know his leg broke. There was blood all over his face, and he wasn't moving at all. He couldn't have gotten out of the wadi by himself. Someone would have had to help him, but that can't be. No one around here would help a Roman officer...no offense."

"None taken. I know you're right, but his body wasn't below the cliff."

"It must be there somewhere. A hyena might have dragged it off. Did you look for vultures?"

"There weren't any. I had men with me, so I couldn't go down into the wadi to search myself. I can't go there now without raising suspicion. I need you to go back and find out what happened to his corpse. I need to have it found so the commander will be convinced he had an accident there. Some of the other officers know about our rivalry. I'll be a suspect if he just disappears."

"I can go this afternoon, but it will cost extra." The blacksmith's oily smile started to narrow Marcus's eyes until he forced them to relax.

"I made payment in full for a completed job. This is part of completing it."

"I don't think so. I heard that the brother of a missing officer has offered a 300-denarii reward for finding him. For so much, many will be looking for him, and that makes it much more dangerous for me. More will be required for me to take the risk of being found with his body."

"How much more?"

"Fifty denarii." The blacksmith's smirk betrayed his expectation of his greedy demand being met.

Marcus hesitated before answering. The smith needed to think he was considering the deal. "That's acceptable. I'll be back tomorrow to check on the sword, and you can tell me then what you find. You'll get your extra money then. I need to get back to the garrison now."

The expanding smirk that signaled the blacksmith's satisfaction with making Marcus pay again irritated him, but it wouldn't serve his purpose to let it show.

As Marcus started to walk away, the smith turned back to his forge. He gripped the bellows handle and began to pump air onto the coals that had cooled while they talked. The whooshing sound masked the soft footsteps behind him.

With one swift slash of his dagger, Marcus opened the smith's throat from ear to ear. He jumped back to avoid getting any of the spurting blood on him. As the big man collapsed, Marcus calmly looked on.

He believed the blacksmith had tried to kill Lucius, as planned. He also believed the smith had botched the job. Lucius hadn't died instantly or even slowly below the cliff. Somehow he'd managed to get away from where he fell. If he was dead now, fine. No body meant a delay, but even the commander would decide he was dead at some point. If he was still alive and going to return, the only person who could connect him to the attempted murder was now dead himself. It wasn't as tidy as he'd hoped, but at least there were no loose ends now.

No loose ends—except for a dead blacksmith. Marcus wiped every trace of blood off his dagger with the blacksmith's tunic and slid it back into its ivory-inlaid sheath.

As he stepped out into the street, the shutters on the shop next door suddenly swung open. The shopkeeper was looking directly at him.

Marcus first startled, then stopped the smile that started to leak out as he considered this unexpected good fortune. In battle, the best defense was often a good offense. The same should be true for concealing a murder.

He strode up to the shopkeeper like a man with a purpose. As usual, he was greeted by a fake smile.

"How may I serve you, tribune?"

Marcus focused icy eyes on the man. "You can tell me who was the last one to go into the blacksmith's shop before me."

"I don't know, tribune. I just opened, so I wasn't watching the street."

Marcus stepped closer to the man and rested his hand on his sword. Intimidation and pain, or at least the threat of it, should do the trick. The fake smile was replaced by twitching lips as the shopkeeper stepped back.

"Tell me what you do know. I came to check on a sword I'm having made, and I find the blacksmith lying in there dead. Whoever was in there just before me murdered him." He moved in close again, partially drawing his sword from its scabbard. "Who would have wanted to kill him?"

"That would be a long list, tribune. There are many people with grudges against him. He had many gambling debts. I have heard that he would hurt someone he owed if they kept pressing him to pay. He was always picking fights, too, and he didn't just fight. He liked to hurt people."

Marcus deepened his scowl. "Rome does not tolerate murder. I want a list of those you think most likely to want him dead." The shop-keeper hesitated. "I want that list now unless you want your name at the top of it."

The man's hands shook as he drew a wax tablet and stylus from below his counter. He was poised to write, but then he stopped. "I don't want to accuse anyone without knowing. In the Law of Moses, two witnesses must swear for a man to be condemned."

"I don't care about your law of Moses. Only the law of Rome matters. Write, or you'll be charged with the murder yourself."

As the shopkeeper began to write, Marcus tightened his lips to hide a satisfied smile. The dead blacksmith wasn't going to be a loose end after all.

Chapter 20

WELCOME AMONG THEM

The final blessing in synagogue came much too soon for Lucius. He reluctantly pulled his thoughts away from the teaching to the village men who were about to scrutinize him. Rachel had warned him that the village would question him being there. As the first elderly man approached, his heart rate began to ratchet up until he willed it to slow down. Mustn't seem nervous or suspicions would be aroused.

As he'd heard in Asher's recitation of Torah, he rose to show proper respect, balancing on his good leg with the crutch to steady him. That brought a smile to the old man's lips. A good start to the interrogation.

"Welcome, Lucas. I am Mattathias bar Amon. It is good to meet a young man seeking to know the LORD. I will be teaching in a few days, and I hope you will be with us then."

"I hope to come every time, and I will look forward to learning from you, Mattathias bar Amon." The tension that had stiffened his spine ebbed with Mattathias's smile and nod before he turned away.

As the men filed out of the synagogue, several others paused to welcome him. As the last one turned away, he released the breath he'd been half holding during each examination. None had been excessively curious about either who he was or where he was coming from when he was robbed. Joseph's explanation of him had been enough.

◆

As Joseph conversed with Eliezer, he kept one eye on his "Greek" guest to make sure he didn't say or do anything that would reveal who he was. He soon decided he needn't have worried. Lucas of Corinth was a man who listened instead of talking as much as possible. He even managed to conceal any visible sign of the arrogance so typical of the Romans.

Joseph finished his conversation with the rabbi and walked toward the door.

"Simeon, Lucas, come."

Simeon fell in beside his father. "I like it when we join you in synagogue, Abba."

"Eliezer wants to serve the LORD well. You have a good teacher for *bet talmud*."

"I think so, too." Simeon grinned. "I like to show him where Yeshua is in the writings of the prophets, like what he read from the prophet Isaiah today. He doesn't agree yet, but he listens."

Joseph nodded. "To listen is the first step toward knowing." He glanced back to be sure Lucas was following. The Roman was a listener. Perhaps before he left, he would hear enough to begin to know God.

◆

Rachel left the two young women with whom she was talking and joined Lucas walking behind Joseph.

"Was synagogue like what you expected?"

"It was much better." A broad smile confirmed his words. "And to think this happens four times a week. It's very much worth the effort of getting here."

She nodded her head as she focused on how he was walking. He seemed genuinely happy, but he was hurting. Their pace was much too fast for him, even going downhill.

"Abba."

Joseph looked across his shoulder. "Yes, Rachel?"

"We're walking too fast for Lucas. You can go ahead. I'll stay with him until he gets home."

Joseph turned around. As he stared at Lucas, his mouth turned down. "Take your time, Lucas. I do not want this to set back your healing."

As Joseph and Simeon increased their pace, Lucas slowed his to less than half of what it had been.

His sigh of relief confirmed she had read him correctly.

"Thank you for doing that, Rachel. It was getting hard to walk that fast."

"If you need to stop to rest, we can do that, too."

"Maybe when we get half way. I don't want to take too long. I should be making spokes."

She shook her head. "I think you should rest a while after we get back. You look tired."

"I sit at the workbench. That's resting."

"It isn't when you have bruised ribs, too. I know they hurt when you're using the spokeshave. Walking so far on a crutch is harder on your ribs than on your leg."

They had reached the halfway point. He would have kept walking, but she touched his elbow. "We're going to rest a little."

"I can keep going." He took another step.

She wrapped her hand around the post of his crutch. "Don't make me take your crutch away to make you rest. I will, you know."

She lowered her eyebrows as she made the threat, but her gentle eyes and smiling lips neutralized any effect of the eyebrows.

His mouth twitched upwards. "I might fall over if you did, and what would Joseph say to that? I might hurt myself more and have to stay even longer." His smile turned ironic. "I'm sure nothing would make him happier than having me here longer."

Rachel's gaze darted to his eyes. She'd seen how cold her father was to him. Lucas was joking about it, but it bothered him. It was so hard for Abba to have a Roman there instead of Reuben. He really was trying to show Yeshua's love to his enemy, even though it hurt to do it.

"Abba doesn't want you to leave before you're healed. You really are welcome in our house for as long as you need to be here."

His eyebrows rose at her serious tone, but quickly settled back in place.

"I know. Don't think I meant otherwise. You and Simeon have made me feel welcome from the first moment I met you in the wadi. I do appreciate your father letting me stay and helping me so much. That's more than I have any right to expect. I appreciate him letting me come to synagogue with him, too. Having more people know I'm at your house makes it more dangerous for you. I don't want any of you to get hurt because you helped me."

"It's Yeshua's command that we help you, and Abba is as glad to do it as I am."

She didn't want him asking why it was so hard for Abba to have him there. She didn't want to tell him Abba blamed Rome and her soldiers for the loss of two sons. It was time to change the subject.

"Now, doesn't it feel better to have rested? Ready to walk some more?"

Her cheery smile as she asked drew one from him in return. "I'm ready to try whatever you think I'm ready for."

"I think you're ready to keep me company under the canopy as I grind some wheat. Then maybe after midday break, you can help Abba in the shop again."

"I really am ready to help now."

"Maybe so, but I'll get Abba to tell you not to, and then you'll have to rest like you should."

"I just can't win against you, can I." He grinned at her.

She glanced sideways at him as she took the first step. "Almost no one can."

As they slowly made their way back to the house, Lucius glanced at her often. She truly was a winner in every way that mattered.

After the midday break, Lucius followed Joseph back to the workbench to start shaping his third spoke. As Rachel stood by her loom, guiding the shuttle back and forth through the warp threads, she kept a careful eye on him to see if he was overdoing it. He wouldn't stop even if he should, and Abba didn't watch him closely enough to stop him, either.

As he was finishing the final cut with the spokeshave, she strolled over to put an end to his workday.

He began speaking while she was still behind him. "Are you coming only to check my work or to stop me from doing any more today?"

Her lips twitched at his understanding of her. "The first, of course, and maybe the second if I think you need me to."

He freed the finished spoke from the clamp and handed it to her. "So what do you think? Does it meet with your approval?"

She slid her hand along the curve. Each spoke he made was better than the one before. "You're very good at this, Lucas. To make one that's so smooth and uniform on your third try...did you work with wood before?"

He shook his head. "No. All I know of woodworking, your father taught me."

"What did your father teach you?"

He shook his head again. Was that regret that clouded his eyes? "Nothing worth learning."

She rested her hand on his arm and squeezed it sympathetically. He had said before that he and his father weren't close. She changed the subject.

"So, do you think you need to come rest awhile?"

Lucius looked up at her and grinned rather sheepishly. "No..."

His ribs were hurting again. It was more from walking to synagogue than from using the spokeshave, but he didn't want to tell her, no matter what caused it.

"So that means yes." She placed her hand on his forearm. First contact sent a tingling shock through him, and his muscles that were already firm contracted and bulged. She must have thought she'd hurt a bruise because she lightened the pressure and swept her fingers back and forth instead of giving him a pat. That feather-light caress was more than he could stand where Joseph might see his response, so he placed his other hand on hers to stop her moving fingers.

"This afternoon no means no. It might feel good to rest, but I can make one more before dinner. I appreciate your concern, but I'd rather keep working."

She was looking into his eyes, like she was trying to gauge his determination. She should know he was not going to be persuaded.

"Can I at least bring you something to drink?"

He saw what she was doing, but he managed to suppress the big grin that her persistence brought. "I'd like a drink of water. You take better care of me than I need, but I'm not going to complain." The grin escaped as he continued to look into her eyes.

"Yeshua wants us to care for each other the very best we can, Lucas."

"And you do that better than anyone I've ever known."

He squeezed her hand before lifting it away. She gave him a dazzling smile before turning to fetch him some water mixed with a little wine from the house.

Joseph was shaping metal at the forge, but the ring of his hammer had not completely drowned out their quiet conversation. He always paid attention when the Roman was near her. It was good that Lucas chose to work with him rather than sit under the canopy with her. No

Roman should find his daughter too interesting. He heard their words and was satisfied.

He might not have been so satisfied if he had seen their eyes and smiles.

Chapter 21

SHABBAT

After breakfast, Lucius followed Joseph to the workshop. While Joseph was rough-cutting some wood pieces for spokes, he sat on the stool and watched Rachel.

She was singing to herself as she added a handful of grain to the opening in the top of the quern. As she turned the upper quernstone to grind the grain into flour, she swayed in rhythm with the turning stone. Fluid grace marked her movements, and her voice was enchanting. To sit under the canopy and watch would be pleasurable, but unwise since her father kept scrutinizing him. Besides, Joseph needed his help.

When Joseph dumped the armful of roughed-out spokes on his workbench, he turned at once to begin his morning's work. No delight for his eyes, but his ears found pleasure in the lilting melodies with Hebrew words he sometimes understood.

It took many cuts to make a spoke, and his ribs complained with each one. He released the clamp and turned the spoke for the last time. He blew out a long breath. Not even one finished, and he was already sore and tired.

At least the music distracted him, and it helped that she was grinding much longer than yesterday. She'd barely finished when it was time to bring the midmorning refreshments.

The sight of her swaying hips as she passed him was like a dipper of cool water scooped from a mountain stream after a long march. First to her father, but she would be coming to him next. He could use some care from the most caring woman he'd known. A grin tried to break free, but he held it in check. Her father still watched him too closely when she was beside him.

◆

As Rachel stood by Joseph, she admired the hub rings he'd just completed.

"I like working with wood, Abba, but I wish I could work with metal, too. You make such beautiful things, so perfectly round and smooth."

"It is more than you should do even helping me with the wood." Joseph glanced over at the Roman. "It is good that Lucas wanted to spare you."

She placed his dates and drink on the brick shelf by the forge. Then she stood on tiptoes to kiss his cheek. "The LORD blessed both him and us when Simeon found him."

Joseph snorted. Lucas was no blessing. He saw a Roman soldier every time he looked at Lucas, and it took no small effort to keep from thinking how it would be Reuben working at the bench were it not for the soldiers from his houseguest's garrison.

"The LORD blessed me with you, Rachel." He kissed her on her forehead and turned back to the forge.

◆

As Rachel carried Lucius's share of dates and water to his workbench, a lovely smile lit her face. "So, have you been overworking again this morning?"

She set the tray on the bench and rested her hand on his forearm. Lucius saw it coming and braced himself to conceal the effect of her fingers on his skin. There was something about her simple touch that both comforted and excited him. He'd often been in the company of women, but none had ever had that confusing effect on him. He'd expected fleeting contact, but even after he laid the spokeshave on the bench, her hand remained. He was in no hurry for her to remove it.

"Not at all. You've taken such good care of me the past few days that I can work a morning without it being too much for me."

He glanced at Joseph. Her father was facing the forge, so he let himself bask in the warmth of her smiling eyes. The heat of her fingers warmed more than his skin where they rested. Even after she lifted her hand, it was impossible not to smile himself.

His smile drifted toward a full grin. "It sounded to me like you were the one overworking this morning. Your songs were lovely, but I thought you were never going to finish grinding."

"I'm baking for two days today. Tomorrow is Shabbat."

She offered him the cup, but he didn't take it right away. He wanted to prolong their conversation.

"You'll like Shabbat. We go to synagogue both evening and morning."

"I can manage that, as long as you stay with me to keep me from getting lost."

"The LORD will find you and keep you from ever getting lost again."

His head tilted. What did she mean by that?

Her eyes lit as her lips curved. "You don't understand now, Lucas, but you will."

"Will you teach me, Rachel?"

"I won't have to. The LORD will teach you himself."

She set the cup down on the bench and patted his arm. "Shabbat is coming, and I still have much to do."

She resumed singing as she walked back to the canopy to finish the baking.

As he ate the first date, he watched her mix the flour and water to make the dough. He'd be glad when everything stopped hurting so much, but he didn't mind that it would take at least six more weeks for his bones to mend. He certainly wouldn't miss the coldness of her father, but he was in no hurry to say goodbye to her.

The sun was low in the sky when Joseph's family gathered inside their house to begin their Sabbath observance. Joseph wore his prayer shawl. Lucius stood behind Simeon as Rachel draped her veil over her hair and lit the Shabbat lamp. She waved her hands over the flame three times and covered her eyes with her hands, blocking her view of the lamp before she spoke.

"Blessed are You, LORD our God, King of the universe, Who sanctified us with his commandments, and commanded us to be a light to the nations and Who gave to us Yeshua our Messiah, the Light of the world.*"

As the flame of the lamp cast dancing shadows on the wall, Joseph turned to Lucius.

"Now we go to synagogue for Kabbalat Shabbat. You can sit at the back again with Simeon and Asher."

Rachel stepped over beside Lucius. "The boys will need to save Lucas a seat since he walks so slowly. I'll stay with him to make sure he gets there without harm."

"As you wish, Rachel." Joseph and the boys headed out the door.

She turned to Lucius. "Well, shall we go? I know you don't want to miss anything."

It had been a long day. He'd worked longer than he should have. His ribs already hurt more than yesterday, but she was right that he didn't want to miss any chance to learn.

"Since I'm so slow, we'd better. I don't want to make you miss anything. I'll try to keep up."

"Don't concern yourself about me. We'll walk just fast enough for you to stay comfortable, but no faster."

"Still taking good care of me at your own expense." He was pulled once more into those smiling cinnamon eyes.

"Yeshua wants us to care for you, and you can be sure we will. Now, let's go."

Service was over. Even as tired and sore as he was after walking so far on a crutch with bruised ribs, he wouldn't have missed the prayers and readings of Kabbalat Shabbat for anything. Joseph and the boys had walked on ahead, and once more Rachel was keeping him company as he made his way home.

Home. It was funny, but that was the word that first came to mind when he thought of Joseph's house. It wasn't that Joseph was any friendlier. Her father more or less tolerated his presence. It was the way they included him in the rhythm of the day as if he were part of the family.

The way Rachel included him. She couldn't have made him more welcome if she'd tried. It was as if she'd completely forgotten he was an officer in the hated Roman army. She kept close watch to make sure he had everything he needed. She tried to keep him from doing more than he should so soon after his fall. Best of all, she'd opened the door for him going to synagogue with them to learn some of what Grandfather had loved.

He glanced down at her as she strolled beside him. She changed this walk of pain into a walk of pleasure.

Rachel felt his eyes and turned her face toward him. "Is something wrong, Lucas? Are we walking too fast?"

"No. I'm fine, Rachel. I'm more than fine. It was very good to be there tonight."

"I'm glad. And when we get home, we'll have Shabbat dinner after Kiddush. I think you'll enjoy that, too."

More than fine? He couldn't fool her. Not even his contented eyes could hide the fatigue that dragged him down. The food and wine should help, but he still needed watching. He was even worse than Nathaniel and Reuben when it came to trying to hide something hurting from her.

She turned her eyes to the darkened ground ahead of her. Sometimes Lucas looked at her like he read her emotions too well, and she didn't want him to see the mistiness in her eyes. Reuben would never hide anything from her again.

Lucius wasn't sure what to expect as they gathered around the mat. Every meal was accompanied by many blessings of God for providing, but even he, a Gentile unfamiliar with many Jewish ways, knew that Sabbath dinner might be something special.

Joseph began the blessings, "Blessed are You, LORD our God, King of the universe, who has given to us holidays, customs, and seasons of happiness, for the glory of our Lord Yeshua the Messiah, the light of the world.*"

Lucius focused on those last words. Simeon's comment and Eliezer's reading from the prophet Isaiah last Thursday sprang to mind. Yeshua, the light of the world. He looked over at Rachel. Her eyes glowed as she listened to Joseph's blessing. Her love for Yeshua had brought him to this place of safety. He was still here because her father loved Yeshua, too.

Joseph continued, "The sixth day. Thus the heavens and the earth were finished, and all the host of them. And on the seventh day, God ended His work which He had made, and He rested on the seventh day from all His work which He had made. And God blessed the seventh day and sanctified it because in it He had rested from all his work which God created and made.*"

Joseph poured his cup of wine and lifted it. "Blessed are You, LORD our God, King of the universe, Who creates the fruit of the vine.*" The others said, "Amen."

"Blessed are You, LORD our God, King of the Universe, who made us holy with His commandments and favored us, and gave us His holy Sabbath, in love and favor, to be our heritage, as a reminder of the Creation. It is the foremost day of the holy festivals marking the Exodus from Egypt. For out of all the nations You chose us and made us holy, and You gave us Your holy Sabbath, in love and favor, as our heritage. Blessed are you LORD, Who sanctifies the Sabbath.*"

Again the chorus, "Amen."

"Where two or three are gathered in My name, there am I among them. We acknowledge Your presence, Yeshua, at our Sabbath table. We welcome Your Presence in by asking for the Shekhinah Glory of God to fill our hearts and to give us a sense of communion. Before we drink from this cup, we acknowledge that You, Yeshua, are the vine and we are branches and that our lives are dependent upon You as our Lord and Savior. We sanctify this cup symbolizing the Cup of Salvation that You offer to those who trust in You.*"

As he finished the prayers, Joseph passed the cup to each of his children in turn. As he received it back from Rachel, he looked at Lucas. He hesitated as he scanned the Roman's face, then handed the cup to him as well.

The LORD had brought this Roman to his house and put great hunger to learn in him. Although his heart still recoiled from it, his head knew the LORD had chosen him to instruct this Gentile in His ways. Yeshua would want him to share the cup.

Lucius took the cup from Joseph's hand and held it. He looked at the rich ruby color of the fragrant liquid and then at Joseph with a question in his eyes. There was something very special about what they were doing, and Joseph's hesitation in offering it made him pause. Joseph's eyes were cool, but he nodded his permission. Lucius took his sip, then handed the cup back to Joseph.

The meal continued with their handwashing before they took their seats around the mat. Joseph raised the two loaves of bread that Rachel had placed on a special plate that Lucius had never seen her use before.

"Blessed are you, LORD our God, King of the Universe, Who brings forth bread from the earth.*"

All spoke, "Amen."

After Joseph took a piece of bread himself, he distributed the bread to the others, and their relaxed time of conversation began.

Lucius wasn't sure why, but there was something so satisfying about sitting among them, listening to their conversation. The past five days had been unbelievably painful, and tonight he was exhausted, but it hadn't been all bad. Rachel's eyes were radiant as she talked with her brothers and father, and they occasionally sparkled at him as well.

The kindest woman in the world had found him and brought him to this place that now felt almost like home. He was a lucky man.

As the family began to share the highlights from their week, Rachel turned to smile at him. "For me, the highlight of this week was finding Lucas. I give thanks to the LORD that Simeon found him before the jackal killed him. I give thanks that the LORD is healing him and he's feeling so much better." Her smile broadened. "And I especially give thanks that he wants to learn about the LORD."

Simeon grinned and nodded his head vigorously, and Asher copied Simeon's nods. Lucius glanced at Joseph to see his response. He half expected to see a frown while Joseph's head shook in disagreement. But while Joseph's eyes were serious and there was no trace of a smile, he was nodding slowly as he gazed at Rachel.

Joseph's eyes turned on Lucas. The arrival of the Roman had certainly not been the highlight of his week. It still pained him to see Lucas in Reuben's tunic, on Reuben's cushion, in Reuben's bed. But he was no longer angry that Rachel had brought him home. In caring for his enemy, he was serving Yeshua. Every opportunity to serve Yeshua was a blessing, even if it came in the form of a wounded Roman soldier.

Chapter 22

SABBATH REST

After the morning Shabbat service, Lucius hobbled down the hill. Rachel strolled beside him, her conversation distracting him from the pain. To walk that eighth mile a fourth time in two days was hard, but definitely worth it. More readings from Torah, another reading from the prophet Isaiah, more teaching on what it all meant—he couldn't think of a better way to start the Sabbath morning.

Joseph and his two boys turned into the courtyard even before Lucius and Rachel reached the halfway point. Walking so slow had one advantage. It gave him a few minutes with the warmth of Rachel's eyes without the coolness of Joseph's serving as the unpleasant counterpoint.

"I think you may be walking a little better."

"It's not so hard as long as we don't move too fast." He grinned at her. "If I try to rush, you'll probably take my crutch away."

Rachel eyed him as he took another halting step. "I might, but only if I have to because you won't rest when you should." They walked a few more steps. "I'm glad today is Shabbat for you." Her head tilted. "Have you ever kept it before?"

He shook his head. "No, but Saturday is always a good day in the garrison. The zealots mostly keep your Sabbath."

◆

Rachel's spine twitched at his mention of the zealots. Nathaniel. Was he keeping Shabbat at Uncle Samuel's?

Her lips tightened, even though she tried to stop them. No, not really. He was probably only going through the motions since he turned away from Yeshua. What if he got himself killed right now? He was estranged from God. He wasn't prepared for death. Not like Reuben had been.

She might never be with him again if the Romans killed him. She swallowed hard as she tried to push that worry out of her thoughts.

◆

Lucius read the tension in her shoulders, and that triggered suspicion. "Are there any zealots here that I should watch? They mustn't find out I'm Roman. Helping me could put you in danger from them."

An unexpected delay in her answer drew his eyes to her face.

She swallowed again. "No one here likes the Romans, but that's all. I don't know anyone living here now who fights with the zealots." She forced a smile.

Her eyes flicked away, then toward him. Was that fear before her eyes turned calm again? Calm, but not serene. His question had unnerved her. Clearly she either knew some or suspected some, but it was no surprise that even someone like her, willing to help a Roman tribune, wouldn't betray anyone to him.

"I don't want to hurt anybody, Rachel, but I don't want them to hurt you, either. If you think I need to know who they are later, I hope you'll tell me in time."

She gripped a handful of her tunic, and her eyes broke away from his. "I don't want anyone to get hurt."

He smiled to reassure her, but the serenity didn't return to her face. "You don't have to worry. Lucas of Corinth will do his best to make sure no one does."

In the silence that followed, he wanted to change the subject as much as she obviously did. She wasn't smiling at him. "So, what next? Is there more to Shabbat celebration?"

Her soft sigh of relief accompanied the relaxing of her shoulders. "Yes. Next we eat, then we rest, like God did on the seventh day." There was that smile he liked again. "It will be good for you, Lucas. It's hard to get you to rest when you should, but Shabbat will make it easy."

They had reached the gate, and as they headed toward the canopy, he was looking forward to an afternoon spent resting. An eighth of a mile was a short distance only if you had two good legs. He wouldn't admit it to her, but a day doing nothing was about all he could handle.

Lucius lounged on the bench under the canopy, waiting and watching. Sepphoris was always quiet on the Jewish Sabbath, but he'd never given much thought to what everyone was doing before. With so much to do and so little help to do it, it seemed odd when Joseph didn't work at the forge as he had after synagogue on Thursday. Instead, the family ate a leisurely meal, and now her father sat under the canopy, talking with a man close to his own age about many different things and nothing of great importance.

He reached down and tugged at one of the splints, trying to relieve the discomfort where it was pressing against his leg a little too hard.

Joseph's eyes turned on him, and a frown appeared. "Lucas." Lucius squared his shoulders. "Go lie down and rest with the splints off so you don't get sores like a mule with a bad pack saddle. I want no delay in your healing."

Lucius would have bet a week's wages at any odds that Joseph wanted no delay in his healing. He was no gambler, but he couldn't think of a safer bet. Still, regardless of his motive, Joseph was right about relieving the pressure for a while. He placed his crutch under his arm and hobbled into the house.

Rachel broke off her conversation with Simeon and Asher. "He'll need help with that, Abba. I'll help him today so you and Eli can enjoy Shabbat together."

Joseph pulled in a deep breath. He wasn't eager to help the Roman himself, but he was even less eager for her to spend too much time with him.

Eli took the decision out of his hands. "You have a good daughter, Joseph. So kind and helpful to anyone who needs her, just like her mother before her."

"Rachel is truly a blessing from the LORD, Eli." Joseph twisted toward Rachel and nodded once. "Make him lie on his back and take the splints off until we are ready to eat. That should keep him from getting sores."

Eli's eyes warmed as he watched her follow Lucas inside. "I have been watching your houseguest in synagogue these last three times. He tries not to miss a single word. It is so rare to see such burning interest in the LORD and Torah among our own people. To see it in a

Gentile? I never thought that could be. It is good that Simeon found him so he can learn while he heals in your house."

Joseph shrugged as he spread his hands. "I do not understand the ways of the LORD, Eli. It may well be that He put Lucas with us for that reason. I would not have expected a man like him to want so much to learn about our faith. With those ribs, he suffers much pain just to get to synagogue, but he is eager for the next time and never complains."

Eli stroked his beard. "He is a quiet young man. He has hardly said a word since I came today."

Joseph shrugged again. "Quiet is good." *And the safest thing for a Roman among Jews.* He glanced at the doorway. *And for the Jews who choose to shelter one.*

"So true, Joseph. It is good for a young man to listen instead of talk. He will learn much more that way."

Joseph was tired of speaking of the Roman resting inside on Reuben's bed. He was only twenty feet away through an open door, but at least he was out of sight for a while. "So, Eli, you were telling me of your newest grandson..."

Lucius sat on the edge of the bed and swung his good leg up. Then he grabbed his knee and lifted his broken leg onto the mattress. As he stared at the splinted leg lying on the bed in front of him, he ran his hand though his hair and sighed. Joseph was right; he'd get sores if he didn't release the pressure for a while, but how should he do that?

He bent at the waist and reached for the cloth tie nearest his knee. How could he manage to take the splints off himself and lie down without shifting the alignment of his broken bones?

The answer stepped through the doorway. "Don't try to do that yourself, Lucas. I'll help you."

Rachel came to his bedside and wrapped one arm around his shoulders for support as he lay back on the pillow. Serene eyes so close, soft tresses brushing against his cheek, lips almost close enough to kiss, the warmth of her body next to his—it was good Joseph wasn't watching because it was impossible for a man not to respond to a woman like her.

With his head on the pillow, he gazed up into her doe-like eyes. She was only looking at him like she would a child or a brother, but those eyes still lit the fire. Her smile drew one from him. "I'm glad you came. I wasn't sure how to manage it alone."

"You don't have to. I'll take care of you." She pulled the pillow up a little to make his neck more comfortable.

"You're very good at that." The touch of her fingers at the nape of his neck as she positioned his head was heating his blood again.

"It pleases Yeshua when we care for each other, as He commanded." A playful grin brightened her eyes. "You've given me lots of opportunity to please Yeshua since Simeon found you. Now, you'll need to lie very still after I remove the splints. We don't want your bones to slide apart again."

"Whatever you say, Rachel." Her grin triggered one in return. "You take much better care of me than any garrison physician would. I'm glad your father let me stay."

She rested her hand on his shoulder and patted it. "You've given Abba an opportunity to please Yeshua, too."

He could safely bet another week's wages that was the only reason Joseph hadn't sent him to the garrison that first evening.

"Now let's get your leg comfortable, and I'll loosen the splints for a while."

He lifted his head to watch her release the splints.

She placed her fingertips on his forehead where there wasn't a bruise and pressed his head back to the pillow. "You don't need to watch. Lie back and relax."

He watched her face as she loosened the cloth strips and let the spokes fall away. Always so calm and capable. She wasn't smiling as she worked. But the moment she looked back at his face, that smile reappeared, and a pulse of warmth spread through him.

"There. Does that feel better?"

"Some."

"I can make it feel even better. There are some spots where the splints have rubbed, but I can soothe those with oil."

From the storeroom, she fetched a small jar of olive oil. She poured a little onto a plate, then carried it over to the bed. After dipping her fingertips into the oil, she rested them on the red area where the spoke had been pressing. As her fingers traced soft, slow circles, she began to hum.

His head settled into the pillow as his gaze drifted from her fingers to her face. His eyelids felt heavy, but watching her beat resting them. "That does feel better. Simeon was right in the wadi about you knowing what to do. The garrison physician would never do what you're doing. Even if he thought about using oil, he'd just slap it on."

"I'm glad it's helping. Since you're resting your leg, why don't you close your eyes and rest everything while I do this?"

"As you wish, Rachel. No arguments from me today."

He hadn't fully realized how tired he was until he obeyed her. Then the fatigue he'd been holding off came crashing down. He let all his muscles relax until he was like a rag doll. As she continued rubbing oil into his skin and humming one of her grinding songs, he drifted off.

◆

As Rachel finished, her gaze settled on his face. It was only five days since his fall, so it was still mostly purple where the rock and helmet hit him. So many bruises on his whole body—he must hurt so much, but he almost never let it show when he thought she was watching. She'd seen the truth sneak through when he didn't. And then he would try to convince her it was nothing so she wouldn't worry. Who would have thought a soldier could be so considerate of her feelings or so grateful for the littlest thing she did for him?

His breathing had become slow and deep. Moving slowly so she wouldn't awaken him, she pushed back his hair to look at the two-inch scabbed-over cut at his hairline. It might leave a scar to match the one on his jaw. She ran her fingers lightly through his hair. He didn't stir.

Even if he was a Roman, he was still a good man—generous, appreciative, helpful, a man with a hunger for God. A man like him should live, not be killed by some unknown enemy at the garrison. *Yeshua, thank you for telling me to bring him home. Thank you for making Abba let him stay.*

She left him and walked out to the courtyard.

"He fell asleep, Abba. I'm afraid to leave him. If he wakes up alone with the splints off, he might hurt his leg again before he realizes he shouldn't move. I'm going to sit in there and watch over him until he wakes up."

Eli's face lit with a smile before he turned to Abba. "Kind and unselfish, just like your Hannah was."

Abba nodded his approval. She bent over and kissed his cheek before walking back into the house.

◆

As Joseph watched her pass through the door to take up her vigil over the Roman, his mind turned to Hannah. They had truly been one flesh, as God declared, and her death had ripped the heart out of him.

It had been five years, but he still longed for her company every day. Rachel was just like her. Hannah would have watched over her enemy with Yeshua's love, too.

Marcus was in full uniform as he strode through the garrison gate. Even off duty, he was afraid to mingle with the Jews without it.

He was sick of Judaea and disgusted by the delay in finding his brother, dead or alive. He wanted to go back to Rome, and he wasn't willing to simply wait. It was time to find out where Lucius might be hiding if he was still alive. No one had been willing to tell the searching Roman soldiers anything. He needed a friendly Jew to find out, and he knew exactly whom to ask for help.

Lucius had taken Marcus to eat at his friend's inn more than three dozen times in the two months since he'd arrived. Why Lucius would have wanted to form a friendship with some Jewish innkeeper like Jacob bar Asa was beyond comprehension, but it might prove useful now. The Jew actually liked his brother and might be eager to help find him.

Marcus was preparing his false face to present to Jacob as he approached the inn. He gripped the handle on the gate to the courtyard and tugged. What the...it was locked. Then he remembered.

Sabbath. The garrison commander liked Sabbath because most of the Jews just sat around doing nothing that day. Even the zealots took the day off, so the Romans had a day of relaxation as well.

He shook his head in disgust. He would have to wait another day before asking Lucius's friend to help him find his brother so he could try to kill him again.

Lucius drifted up from the soft darkness to find her fingertips slowly moving his hair back from his right temple. There were no bruises there, so the tingling sensations from her stroking fingers weren't diminished by the pain of her touching bruises. He'd seen her awaken Asher like this, and now he understood that relaxed smile it brought to her little brother's lips.

But for him, the caresses weren't relaxing. As her fingers slipped through his hair, he concentrated on keeping his breathing from speeding up and betraying the excitement he felt building. He delayed opening his eyes, hoping she would think he was still asleep and continue.

"Lucas? Time to wake up for dinner. Three stars are out, and Shabbat is over. It's time for me to splint your leg again."

She stopped stroking his temple and rested her hand on his shoulder to gently shake him. Too bad she did that. He couldn't pretend to be asleep anymore, so he opened his eyelids to be greeted by cinnamon eyes and smiling lips the color of ripening plums.

"I hope you feel rested now. You slept most of the afternoon." She patted his shoulder. "It was very good for you."

"I can tell."

She replaced the pads and held the spokes against them. Then she bound the spokes to his leg once more with the cloth strips.

"There. Now you can get up and join us under the canopy." As he began to raise his chest, she slid her arm under his shoulders and helped. Her eyes, her lips—everything so close again, and she had no idea how they affected him. He was glad. The moment she did, she'd stop helping him that way.

She reached for his crutch and stood waiting for him to take it from her.

He swung his legs off and stood. With his crutch in place, he grinned at her. "An afternoon in your special care is enough to make any man feel better."

"Since all I did was release the splints and watch to make sure you didn't hurt yourself while they were off, I wouldn't say I gave you much care, Lucas." She graced him with another smile. "But I was glad to do it. Now, let's join Abba and my brothers for dinner."

She turned to walk out the door ahead of him. A crooked grin broke free as he shook his head. He remembered much more care than that. The massage with oil to sooth his leg, the gentle stroking of his temple to awaken him—the touch of her fingertips would be what he'd remember about this afternoon that had been his first Sabbath rest.

Chapter 23

A Brother's Affection

As Marcus wove his way through the streets on Sunday to the inn of Jacob bar Asa, he wanted to punch someone. He kept chewing on the response of the garrison commander a few minutes earlier. When he'd suggested again that his brother was either dead or hiding or he would have sent a message to the garrison, the commander had simply responded, "Perhaps, but you shouldn't lose hope yet. Broken bones take at least six weeks to heal, and he may be someplace where he can't safely send a message."

The commander was still unwilling to send the letter of condolence to Father. It had been six days. Six days! Surely that was long enough to decide a missing Roman was dead in this hate-filled land. Why must the commander wait eight weeks?

That meant two more months in this provincial armpit since he couldn't ask for a transfer until Lucius was officially dead.

Marcus's hand fisted until he forced it to relax. Officially and truly dead—it was still possible that Lucius would show up at the garrison, and he'd have to try to kill him again.

When he entered the inn, he walked to the table in the rear that he usually shared with Lucius. Jacob saw him and approached with a friendly smile.

"It is good to see you, Drusus. Is your brother with you?" He glanced back toward the entrance.

Marcus put on his concerned-brother face. "No, that's the problem I hope you can help me with."

"Problem?" Jacob's eyebrows lifted, but his smile remained.

"Yes, Lucius has disappeared, and we can't find any trace of him."

Jacob's eyebrows slammed down. Had the news actually upset him?

"Disappeared? When?"

"He went to buy a horse last Monday and never came back."

Jacob pulled air through his teeth as he shook his head. His brow furrowed as his eyes clouded. "That is very bad. Six days is a long time missing."

"That's what I think. I looked for him Tuesday and sent search parties down all the main roads and side roads last Wednesday. Nothing. I asked most of the tradesmen who work for the garrison if they'd heard any rumors about him, but no one is willing to tell what they know, if they know anything."

Marcus ran his hand through his hair and slowly shook his head as he tightened his lips. Perfect to convey his deep brotherly concern.

"Help me, Jacob. I know you're his friend, and if anyone might know something useful, it's you. Where would Lucius have gone if he was hurt? Who might have helped him if he was in trouble and needed to disappear?"

"He would have been welcome to ask my help anytime for anything, but I have not seen him since you both ate here ten days ago."

"Is there someone else he might go to? Maybe in one of the nearby towns?"

"I never heard him speak of a friend in any of the villages, but that does not mean he might not have one. He has a reputation for being a fair man, not an arrogant tyrant like many officers." Jacob's eyes flitted to a pair of centurions seated at a table near the door before returning to Marcus. A nervous smile lifted his lips as his eyes veiled. "No offense—I do not mean you, Drusus. I am sure any brother of Lucius would be a good man like himself."

What could a Jew like you know about good men? Marcus directed his gaze at the officers so Jacob wouldn't see his irritation. "No offense taken. I've seen what you mean."

Jacob visibly relaxed, then sighed. "I wish I could help you."

"Did Lucius have any men he spoke with a lot here at your inn?"

"He knows several tradesmen and merchants who deal a lot with the garrison. He spoke with them to practice. Sometimes he ate with them, but I do not think they were friends. They would let him sit with them to talk, but they never sought his company when he arrived here first."

Marcus tightened his lips once more and shook his head to dramatize his concern. "I was hoping you might have some idea where he might be." He looked up at Jacob and tried to force a shaky smile beneath worried eyes. "If you hear something, anything, will you let me know immediately?"

Jacob rested his hand on Marcus's shoulder and nodded. "I will ask around and see what I can learn. Lucius is a good friend, and I want him back here at my table. Now, let me feed you some of my stew. On me today."

Marcus faked a grateful smile. "Thank you, Jacob. I'm not very hungry with Lucius missing, but he wouldn't want me to say no to any stew of yours."

Jacob squeezed Marcus's shoulder before striding toward his kitchen. Missing six days probably meant missing forever. His shoulders slumped at that thought. He flexed his fingers to summon his servant to tell him to take dinner to his good friend's brother. Feeding Marcus was the least he could do to honor the memory of the only Roman he would gladly call friend.

After the food had been delivered, Jacob glanced over to see if Marcus was able to eat. What he saw was eye-opening. Marcus was wolfing down the stew, and a smirk appeared several times on his lips. That was not what he expected from a man concerned about the loss of a dear brother.

He shook his head as a frown appeared. He had come to know Lucius well as he helped him learn Aramaic. He had grown fond of the young Roman with a heart for understanding his country and his fellow Jews. He would be asking the LORD to protect his friend if he was still alive, to let him be safe somewhere so that he might soon return.

He glanced at Marcus again. No grieving brother could look so satisfied, even when eating the best stew in Sepphoris.

If the LORD answered his prayers, he would have to warn Lucius that his brother's affection was not all it might seem to be.

Chapter 24

ALMOST A SMILE

It was Monday, and once more Lucius was hobbling uphill to synagogue. Hard to believe it was only a week since Simeon found him near death in the wadi. His broken leg still ached, and his ribs hurt when he used the crutch or worked too long with the spokeshave, but otherwise he felt surprisingly good. His bruises were only slightly tender, and the least severe were fading away. Another week and all the purple blotches would be gone.

He didn't need to look at Rachel to know a smile played on her lips as she walked beside him. One almost always did. He glanced sideways, and there it was.

She felt his eyes, and turned hers upon his. "Are we going too fast, Lucas?"

"No." Another step, another swing of the crutch. Almost too fast, but it would be easier going home. "I hope there will be more reading today from the prophet Isaiah."

She nodded. "I like that, too. He foretells so much about the Messiah. Did you know he was writing about Yeshua of Nazareth?"

"Simeon told me, but not everyone in synagogue seems to understand him that way. Why is that?"

"So many want a Messiah who will lead an army to drive out the Romans, not one who suffered as the final sacrifice for all our sins."

He nodded slowly. The people of Judaea hated him being there. He felt the daggers in their eyes every time he passed near a crowd of men.

He became silent and somber, his eyes fixed on the street ahead of them. Welcome and Roman were not words used together in that land. One more step, one more swing of the crutch.

He turned his eyes on hers when she rested her fingertips on his elbow for a few seconds. "There is one Roman I'm glad to have in Judaea, Lucas."

"I'm glad there's one Judaean woman willing to care for a Roman like me."

"It pleases Yeshua, but it makes me happy when I can help you, too."

They had reached the synagogue, and she rested her hand on his arm before they parted.

"Enjoy synagogue, Lucas. I'll see you after."

As he watched her walk away to join the women, he fought a grin. Seeing her after would be a pleasure he would look forward to.

Lucius took his accustomed seat at the back of the room. Simeon wasn't there today to help him understand what might be confusing, but he'd been there enough that everyone seemed to take his presence for granted. He felt comfortable among them now.

Eliezer wasn't teaching today. Instead, Mattathias, one of the older men who'd greeted him the first time, removed a scroll from the ornamental closet at the front of the room and unrolled it to read.

As Mattathias read from the prophet Jeremiah about the siege of Jerusalem by the Babylonians and its destruction, Lucius tried to remember the history he'd studied almost ten years earlier. His tutor in Rome had taught him how Babylon had conquered Assyria and was later conquered by Persia, but he'd made no mention of what he considered an unimportant event in a small vassal country remote from the great seats of power of the mighty emperors.

The history of Judah's conquest was as he expected. The prophet had been shockingly brave to tell the people of Jerusalem to surrender to the Babylonian army because it was God's will that they go into captivity. Of course the rulers wanted to kill Jeremiah for delivering that message.

Nebuchadnezzar's commander of the imperial guard set fire to the temple and all the important buildings in Jerusalem and dragged the important people captive into Babylon. That was exactly what he expected of an emperor who wanted to crush a country enough to ensure no future rebellion. Rome often did the same, except they took the conquered king and his nobles to drag through the streets of Rome in a general's triumph before their public execution and the conquered people to sell as slaves or kill in the arena.

What he did not expect was the discussion that followed about the destruction of the temple and the Jewish captivity being the will of God rather than a defeat due only to the greater power of the king of Babylon. Jeremiah had even prophesied that the God of Israel would leave the captives in Babylon for only seventy years, and that was exactly what had happened.

Mattathias spoke what he obviously considered words of encouragement. "It was the LORD's will that His temple would be destroyed by pagan Babylon, but He promised it would be rebuilt when Babylon fell to Cyrus, as it most surely was. All happened exactly as He promised it would. It is fifty-two years since Titus's armies destroyed the temple built by Herod. As Babylon was destroyed seventy years after it destroyed Solomon's temple, perhaps it will be only another eighteen years until Rome, too, is destroyed, and Israel is again free to rebuild her temple."

Benjamin sprang to his feet, chest heaving like he'd run five miles. "No! I do not believe we must suffer eighteen more years under the Roman yoke. The people of Israel in those days had turned to idol worship from worship of the one true God. The seventy years were for their purification. We were faithful in our worship of the LORD alone when the Romans came. We are faithful now. Israel does not need seventy years of purification. It was not the LORD's will for the temple to be destroyed, and it is not His will for us to wait to regain our freedom."

Joseph shook his head. "No, Benjamin. It was the LORD's will. Yeshua prophesied the destruction of the temple the week he was killed, almost forty years before it came to pass. When Titus's legion was through, it was exactly as Yeshua had prophesied that not one stone would be left on another. Go to Jerusalem, and you will see every stone was thrown down as Yeshua said. They pried them apart to get at the gold that flowed between when it melted off the burning roof."

Benjamin turned on Joseph, sparks snapping in his eyes. "Yeshua, Yeshua! That is all we hear from you. You say he was a prophet and even Messiah, but the Romans killed him, so what you say cannot be true. Next thing you will be telling us that garbage about him commanding us to love our enemies. Love the Romans? No! I do not want to hear any more about what your Yeshua said today."

"As you wish, Benjamin." Joseph smiled and raised his hands in a peaceful gesture. "No more discussion of Yeshua today."

◆

Benjamin was not content to let it drop. Joseph had been a blasphemer for years, always bringing up that Yeshua and his teaching, insisting he was the long-awaited Messiah. The true Messiah would drive the hated Romans from the land and restore the mighty kingdom of David and Solomon. Justice without mercy, that is what Messiah would give the Romans. He would lead an army of true Israelites and throw off Caesar's yoke forever. Love the Romans? Even the thought of it was so vile it made Benjamin want to spit.

How could Joseph not want to fight the occupation now? The Romans had murdered his own son, and still he refused to support the zealots. He was no true son of Israel.

Benjamin glanced over at Lucas. Joseph even kept bringing that Greek dog to defile the synagogue, and Eliezer let him.

A malicious sneer twisted his lips. What better way to strike at Joseph than to embarrass this man so much he wouldn't want to come again? No Gentile defiler had any right to be sitting among them anyway.

◆

"What do you think, Greek?" Benjamin swung around on Lucius. "Was it the LORD's will?"

The last thing Lucius was expecting was a full-on frontal assault by Benjamin. His head snapped up and back as he locked eyes with his attacker. The hatred there was as intense as any he'd seen from a zealot lunging at him with a real sword.

He'd never intended to take part in any discussions. He'd planned to be as inconspicuous as possible, sitting silently at the back while he learned about God. But now they were all looking at him, expecting a response.

He cleared his throat. "I haven't much knowledge of what happened, but it seems to me that the god who created the sun and the stars and the earth and everything on it could have easily stopped a Roman army from destroying his temple if he wanted to. That makes me think it must have been God's will."

Benjamin snorted and turned his beet-red face away when Lucius's reply was so logical there was no way to counter it. Lucius had made one confirmed enemy with his answer, but several of the other men nodded thoughtfully and looked at him with approval.

◆

Joseph looked at Lucas as well. Benjamin had meant to make the Roman feel stupid and out of place among them. Joseph expected a soldier to respond with anger. That was not what he saw. Lucas treated Benjamin's taunting like a genuine question, and that reply had answered the question perfectly. He could not have explained it better himself. Benjamin would certainly not agree, but it was a good thing that he had brought Lucas to synagogue today.

◆

Lucius glanced at Joseph, expecting glowering eyebrows and a plunging mouth for making Benjamin mad with his answer. Displeasing Joseph in synagogue was the last thing he wanted to do. He might not let him come next time.

What he saw surprised him. Joseph was nodding his approval with a slight smile on his lips. Lucius drew a deep breath and blew it out slowly. It was gratifying to have finally done something that Joseph would smile at, even if it were ever-so-small a smile.

Rachel was once more at his side as Lucius limped home from synagogue. Despite Benjamin's ill-natured attack, he'd found it fascinating and enjoyable. Now he was enjoying the company of the only woman in Judaea who would be genuinely glad to have him walking beside her.

"I'm sorry Benjamin was so unfriendly to you, Lucas. You shouldn't take it personally. He doesn't like anyone in my family because we follow Yeshua."

"What Benjamin thinks of me doesn't matter. A Roman in Judaea gets used to hostility. At least he wasn't trying to put a dagger in my side."

Her eyes widened as her fingers flew up to cover her mouth. "Oh! Has that happened before?"

He hadn't expected that response to his flippant statement. He was sorry he'd said it.

"Not recently." He grinned at her, hoping she'd think his careless words were spoken in jest.

She didn't need to know he was always on guard when walking

in Sepphoris since one of the other officers was knifed in a crowd. The tribune in command of the troops stationed there had ordered his men not to leave the garrison without body armor since the stabbing. Lucius owed his life to that. His body armor was the main reason his ribs only bruised instead of breaking in two and puncturing his lung.

"Well, we'll be careful to keep everyone thinking you're Greek so it won't happen here." Her happy eyes revealed his success.

They walked a few steps in silence before she spoke again.

"I thought your answer to Benjamin couldn't have been better. It was just like what Abba would have said. I could see that he appreciated you saying that."

One corner of his mouth turned up. "I noticed. Your father almost smiled at me after I said it."

She first looked away, then trained her gaze on his eyes. "I know Abba hasn't been friendly, but that doesn't mean you're not welcome with us as you heal. He's happy to please Yeshua by having you here."

"No man could ever feel unwelcome with you taking care of him."

They had almost reached the gate. He was sorry. Having her at his side, talking with her for that eighth of a mile when it was just the two of them—it was the perfect ending to a trip to synagogue. He would be looking forward to it again in only three days.

Chapter 25

NOT GOOD FOR RACHEL

The next day, Joseph glanced up from the wheel that he was preparing to fit with its iron rim. Coming up the road were his brother-in-law, Samuel, and Samuel's son, Daniel. Joseph's brow furrowed deeply as a frown tugged his mouth down.

Samuel was more than the brother of his dead wife. He was a good friend, and Joseph was always glad to see him, even if he did have strong zealot leanings. Daniel he was not glad to see. Daniel—the nephew who had led Nathaniel into the zealot camp and had thereby caused Reuben's death.

Why did they have to come while the Roman was there? The visit could end in catastrophe. Although Samuel sympathized with the zealots, he would never do something that would hurt Joseph's family, even if he found out they were harboring the officer.

Daniel might. He was a hothead who was just as likely to try to kill the Roman as to talk to him, and Joseph would have to try to stop him. No matter which way it turned, someone would end up hurt...or dead.

◆

Lucius released the clamp and turned the spoke for the next cut. When he glanced at her father, he saw the frown. What had he done now? Nothing he could think of. He ran his fingers through his hair and sighed as Joseph's glare swept over him. Then he saw that Joseph was looking past him at two approaching riders, one about Joseph's age and the other near his own.

Relief drew another sigh from him. At least it wasn't him upsetting

Joseph today. That thought almost brought a smile to his lips, but he stopped it before it escaped. Smiling while Joseph frowned probably wouldn't be the wisest thing to do.

Joseph set down his tongs, and a warm smile appeared as he walked toward the older man.

"Shalom, Samuel. It is good to see you."

Samuel swung his leg over his horse's neck and slid to the ground. The two men embraced.

"Shalom, Joseph. I am riding south for business and did not want to miss this chance for a short visit."

With eyebrows raised, Samuel looked at Lucas, then back at Joseph. He obviously wanted an introduction to the strange man at the workbench, so Joseph made one in Greek before any questions could be asked.

"Samuel, this is Lucas of Corinth. Simeon and Asher found him after robbers attacked him. He is staying with us until his broken leg heals. He wanted to work to repay me, so he is my apprentice for now. Lucas, this is my brother-in-law and his son, Daniel."

Samuel's eyes were friendly as he spoke to the stranger in Greek. "God has blessed you by placing you in Joseph's household to heal."

Lucas nodded his agreement. "To be in the house of Joseph bar Jonah would be a blessing for anyone. I am honored to meet you, Samuel."

Joseph was not eager for them to converse beyond formalities. "Come, Samuel, Daniel. Rachel will have some fruit and wine to refresh you before you go on your way."

Joseph turned and began walking toward the canopy. The sooner he got Samuel and Daniel away from the Roman, the better.

Daniel dismounted and took his father's reins as Samuel walked away at Joseph's side. He led both horses over to the post holding up the workshop roof. As he tied them, he sized up this Lucas of Corinth, who had returned to shaping a wheel spoke.

He did not like what he saw.

Joseph's apprentice was tall and broad-shouldered. With each pull on the spokeshave, his arm muscles flexed. Even with the many purple bruises and his splinted leg, he projected an aura of masculine power. His face was rugged and what a woman would consider handsome.

147

Such a man should not be living in this household with his Rachel.

◆

Rachel parked the shuttle and came from her loom when Uncle Samuel and Abba stepped under the canopy. A bright smile lit her eyes.

"Uncle Samuel. It's so good to see you again. It's been too long."

"That it has, Rachel, and I am afraid our visit will only be a short one. We have far to ride today."

"But there must be a few minutes for me to get something to refresh you."

Samuel rested his hand on her cheek. "Of course. You are so like Hannah, child. My sister never let me leave without feeding me something, no matter how great my hurry."

She flashed a smile and disappeared into the house.

Joseph and Samuel had already settled on the cushions when Rachel emerged with a tray holding a bowl of dates, a pitcher of watered wine, and three cups to set before them. Daniel walked under the canopy and took a cup from the tray. Then he remained standing.

Rachel's smile stiffened. That was not a good sign. It meant he might follow her when she went back to her weaving, and talking with Daniel was the last thing she wanted to do today. Or any day, for that matter.

She knelt and set the tray between Abba and Uncle Samuel. *Please make him sit and stay with Uncle and Abba.* Keeping her eyes deliberately turned away from Daniel, she rose and stepped back to the loom.

◆

Rachel had already started weaving the shuttle between the warp threads when Daniel walked over to stand with one hand on the loom frame.

"It's good to see you again, Rachel. You look happier than at my last visit."

"Nothing has changed, Daniel."

He wasn't sure what she meant by that comment, so he let it pass. "Nathaniel is doing well. He asked me to tell you."

"I'm glad to hear it. Tell him we miss him terribly and wish he would come home."

Her voice was cool, controlled. He didn't like that. Nothing did seem to have changed since he came a few weeks ago when she was so deep in grief.

"I was hoping you would be feeling better."

"Better?"

"You know. Less sad. I'd like to see you happy again."

"In time, I'm sure I will be. The LORD heals our grief with time."

She kept her eyes on the shuttle as she wove it from left to right through the long threads. When she pushed the yarn tight against the row above it, she still didn't look at him.

He cleared his throat. "I would like to speak to your father about us when your grief is passed."

She sucked in her breath. Her eyes that had widened when he said "us" quickly narrowed. She shook her head. "There is no 'us,' Daniel. There will be no 'us,' not ever."

It was as if she had slapped him. Flat out rejection? From her? "What do you mean?"

Rachel fixed her eyes on his, and her voice turned icy. "I'll never want to be your wife. You're filled with hatred. You're proud that you kill. I could never marry a zealot who cares more about killing Romans than about loving the LORD."

She drew a deep breath and paused. He froze, his anger rising as he waited for her next words. "I will not marry a man who doesn't follow Yeshua. There's no point in you speaking to Abba. He knows how I feel, and he will not say yes to you."

She set the shuttle down. "You may as well join Abba and your father now. I need to take some dates and water to Lucas. He can't come get them easily with his broken leg."

She left him standing there as she entered the house to get another tray. He felt stupid the way she'd left him alone, but he sauntered over and sat beside his father to join their conversation as if that had been his own decision, not hers.

When she emerged carrying a tray with a bowl of dates and a cup of water mixed with a little wine, he fixed his eyes on her. He took a sip of wine and watched her over the cup to conceal his focus should her father choose to look at him. A glance at his uncle told him he needn't have worried. Joseph was only looking at Samuel as they talked.

Daniel kept his gaze upon her as she approached the workbench. His free hand clenched when she smiled warmly at the Greek as she handed him the cup and set the bowl where he could reach it easily. She picked up one of his finished spokes and ran her hand along it. Daniel couldn't hear her words clearly, but they were spoken with a smile and warmth in her eyes. Even worse, he saw the Greek turn on his stool to look up at her. There was a broad smile on his handsome face, and his eyes mirrored hers.

Daniel's stomach knotted. Rachel, the woman he wanted to marry, was nicer to some Greek nobody with a broken leg that her brothers had dragged home than she was to him.

He half-listened in silence as Samuel and Joseph finished their conversation and his father rose to leave. Rachel was still standing at the workbench beside the Greek. He was still smiling up at her.

Daniel's heart pounded faster as his mouth went dry. She wasn't just taking refreshments to that Gentile dog. She enjoyed his company—more than she enjoyed his. That was not to be tolerated.

"Uncle."

"Yes, Daniel?" Joseph's eyes weren't any warmer than hers had been.

"I see a problem, Uncle. A problem for Rachel."

Joseph frowned. "What problem are you talking about?"

"It's not good for a strange man to live in the same house with her. People will talk, and who will want to marry her then? You should send him away."

Joseph's frown plunged into a scowl. "It is not your business if I have a houseguest. It is between me and Yeshua that I am helping this man. The LORD has put him under my protection, and he is welcome to stay in my house until he is healed."

Flinty eyes over flaring nostrils triggered Daniel's hard swallow as Joseph continued. "It is my job to protect Rachel, not yours. Lucas of Corinth is not a problem where Rachel is concerned, and you had better not go around suggesting otherwise if you do not want your cousin's reputation hurt."

Joseph took a step toward his nephew, fists clenched. "If I find that you have led anyone to question her purity, you will answer to me."

Samuel placed his hand on his brawny brother-in-law's forearm. The tight-flexed muscles relaxed as Joseph's fist slowly opened.

"Daniel meant no harm, Joseph. His fondness for his cousin led him to speak. I know there is no problem here." He frowned at his son. "And Daniel would never say anything to hurt his cousin."

Daniel cast his eyes down. "No, Abba. I would never hurt Rachel. I meant no offense by my words, Uncle. Forgive me."

◆

Joseph stepped back and turned toward Samuel. "It has been good having you visit, Samuel. I know you need to be on your way, and I have too much work to do to visit for long with Nathaniel gone and

Reuben dead. The help that Lucas is giving me has been a true blessing from the LORD."

He focused icy eyes on Daniel. It was as hard to welcome this nephew who had led his son astray as it was to welcome the Roman. Maybe harder.

His eyes warmed after he turned them back to his friend. He rested his hand on Samuel's shoulder. "I hope you will stop in on your way back home, if you have time."

Samuel's smile and nod told Joseph that all was still well between them, despite him threatening Daniel over his ill-conceived comments.

Joseph escorted Samuel and Daniel toward their horses. Rachel passed them on her way back with the empty tray.

"It was good to see you again, Uncle. May the LORD bless and protect you on your journey."

Samuel beamed at her. "You are so much like your mother, Rachel. My sister would have been so proud to see the woman you have become."

Lucas glanced at them as they passed him, then focused again on his work. Daniel glared at him. Joseph saw the daggers, but the Roman didn't. It was good they were not staying for dinner.

Samuel and Joseph embraced before Samuel mounted. "Shalom, Joseph."

Joseph raised his hand in farewell. "Shalom, Samuel."

He stood watching his friend and his nephew ride away. Then he turned back to the forge. As he pumped the bellows to bring the coals back to yellow heat, his lips tightened.

He had only defended Lucas because Daniel had insulted Rachel. His houseguest was, in fact, a problem for him, but not because of her. It still hurt to have a Roman soldier wearing Reuben's tunic, sitting on Reuben's cushion, sleeping in Reuben's bed. The Roman was welcome to stay in his house until he was healed, but only because Yeshua would want him there.

Chapter 26

MAYBE A ROMAN?

When Nathaniel rode into his uncle's courtyard after his day's work in Sepphoris, he found Daniel waiting for him by the stable. His cousin and Uncle Samuel had planned to visit his family yesterday, and Daniel had promised to bring him news about them all. Since his fight with Abba the day he brought Reuben home, he'd missed them more than he cared to admit. Especially Rachel, but how could he go home to see her, to see any of them, when he'd told his father he wouldn't?

"How was my family, Daniel?" He swung his leg over the horse's neck and slid off.

"I didn't see Simeon or Asher, but your father seemed well."

"And Rachel?"

Daniel rubbed the back of his neck and shook his head. "I don't know."

"What do you mean, you don't know?" Nathaniel's voice took on a sharp edge.

"I'm worried about her. Your father has a Greek staying at the house. Simeon and Asher found him after someone robbed him. He still looks pretty beat up, and he has a broken leg."

Nathaniel shrugged, and his voice returned to normal. "Taking someone like that in and caring for him sounds like something Abba would do. What's the problem?"

"I don't think it's wise for Joseph to let him stay there with Rachel. He's about my age and really handsome. He's got splints on his leg, but that doesn't mean he can't do something to her."

Nathaniel shrugged again. "I don't see a problem. Abba is there all the time, and Rachel can easily defend herself against any man with a broken leg."

Daniel kicked at the dirt. He watched the little swirl of dust settle before he looked up at Nathaniel. "I'm not sure she would want to defend herself. He's been helping your father, and I watched her take him some dates and water at the workbench. She was much too nice to him. He seemed much too appreciative of her bringing them to him, too. You know what I mean—smiling too much, looking at each other."

Nathaniel shook his head. "Rachel wouldn't do anything she shouldn't. She's always nice to everyone. There's nobody kinder than her. That's all it sounds like to me."

Daniel's mouth twitched. "You didn't see what I saw. Maybe she was only being kind to him, like you say, but he was looking at her like he thought it was something more. I'm worried about her being safe or people getting the wrong idea about what's going on there."

Nathaniel's brow furrowed. Gossip could be a dangerous thing for a woman, even when there was no basis for the accusations. "Tell me more about him."

"His name is Lucas of Corinth. He's built like he's done heavy labor or trained to fight. Some women really like muscles like his."

Nathaniel suppressed a smirk at the jealous glint in Daniel's eyes. His cousin was sensitive about being on the scrawny side. Samuel was a successful merchant, and his son had lived an easy life, free of manual labor. Even though Daniel envied his own broad shoulders and muscled arms and torso, he always tried to avoid the kind of work that produced them.

Daniel ran his fingers though his hair as his mouth turned down. "He's got brown hair that's shorter than most and straight. His beard is thick but really short, like it hasn't been growing too long. His nose looks just like Hadrian's on the coins. Actually, he looks much more Roman than Greek to me."

When Daniel said Roman, Nathaniel's eyes narrowed. "Roman?" His lips tightened. "How long has he been there?"

"Less than two weeks. He wasn't there last time your father dropped in to visit Abba."

"Does he have a scar on his jaw?"

"I don't know. His beard was really thick. There might be one underneath it. Why?"

"The Romans were searching all over Sepphoris for a missing tribune with a scar on the left side of his jaw. I never heard they found him. The timing is about right."

Daniel scrunched his eyebrows. "If he is a Roman, that would be very dangerous for her. You know how they treat our women."

Nathaniel nodded as his mouth set to a grim line.

"I'm going to check this out myself. He'd better be a Greek and not that Roman."

◆

Daniel nodded and tried not to smile. "Good. Who knows what kind of lies he's told your father. If Joseph doesn't watch him closely..." Daniel drew his breath through his teeth.

Nathaniel's face darkened like a thundercloud. "Abba's too soft-hearted when someone needs help. He'd throw a rope to Hadrian himself before he'd let that pagan son of Satan drown."

One curt nod by Nathaniel, and Daniel knew he'd accomplished his goal.

"I'll go home tomorrow right after work. If it is that tribune, there will be one less Roman defiling our land before I come back."

Daniel suppressed a grin. He couldn't get Joseph to do anything about that Greek rival for Rachel's affection, but Nathaniel would take care of the problem. After the Greek was gone, maybe Rachel would be more willing to consider him as a husband.

The next day, Nathaniel left the wagon maker's shop in Sepphoris early so he would have time to ride to his home village before dinnertime. His stomach began to churn as he turned off the main road and approached the entrance to his father's courtyard. It had been more than five months since he'd last been there. The hot words of anger he'd yelled at Abba rang again in his ears. He wasn't sure of the reception that awaited him, but his concern for Rachel overrode any concern he had about getting into another fight with Abba.

His father's back was toward him as he worked the forge. Seated on a stool by the workbench was the Greek that had Daniel so concerned. Nathaniel's first view of the man's face in profile supported Daniel's opinion that he might, in fact, be Roman. It was a Roman nose if he'd ever seen one. The man was muscular, ruggedly handsome, intensely masculine—just the sort that could turn even a sensible girl's head to mush. Daniel was right to be worried. It was a good thing he'd come to investigate.

He dismounted and stood fingering the reins. His father's back was still toward him. He took a deep breath and blew it out. Whatever awaited him, he would face it for Rachel.

The stranger glanced out the gate, then fixed his gaze on him. Nathaniel squared his shoulders. Time to face whatever Abba was going to do.

The stranger looked toward Abba. "Joseph. I think someone wants to speak with you."

Abba plunged the metal band he had just shaped to encircle a hub into the bucket of water. He held it there with his tongs until the sizzle subsided. After he lifted the still-hot metal from the bucket, he nodded in satisfaction as he inspected its smooth curves. Then he placed it on the brick bench beside the forge. He was still holding the tongs and hammer when he turned.

"Nathaniel!" A beaming smile split his face. He dropped the tools where he stood and strode toward Nathaniel with his arms outstretched. "Welcome home!"

As father wrapped son in a crushing hug of welcome, Nathaniel dropped the reins and embraced his father as well.

"It's good to see you, Abba. I hope everyone is well." He stepped back from the embrace, unspeakably relieved by his father's joy at seeing him. "I've missed you all."

Abba was still beaming. "As we've missed you. The boys should be back soon with the sheep, and Rachel is in the house. Come, she'll want to see you right away."

With one arm around his son's shoulders, Abba reached out for the horse's reins. He led the two of them into the courtyard. Then he tossed the reins across the horse's withers and slapped its rump to head it toward the manger where the donkey often fed.

"Rachel! Nathaniel has come home."

Rachel burst through the doorway and flew to her brother. He caught her as she jumped into his arms and swung her around. She rested her hand on his cheek and devoured him with loving eyes before wrapping her arms around him again and burying her cheek in his chest.

"I'm so glad you've come home. I've asked the LORD to bring you back every day since you left. It will be so good to have you home with us again."

"I'm only here for a visit, little one. I'm working for a wagon maker in Sepphoris now, and I need to be back there tomorrow."

Rachel's smile dimmed, then brightened. "Even just a visit is so much better than not seeing you at all. You'll stay for dinner?"

He couldn't say no to those bright eyes. "Of course."

◆

Lucius listened and watched the ecstatic reunion with great curiosity. So this was the Nathaniel they mentioned often by name but seemed careful to avoid telling him anything about. It seemed odd that he would be working in Sepphoris when his father needed him here. Even odder that he was greeted like someone who'd just returned from the farthest reaches of the Empire. There was some family history here that made him very curious, indeed.

◆

Nathaniel looked over at the Greek sitting at the workbench, watching them. "Abba, let me do some work for you until dinner. Daniel said you rescued a Greek who was helping you, but a man with a broken leg can't help with everything."

Joseph caught Nathaniel sizing up the Roman, and a revelation hit. Lucas was the reason for the return of his son. Nathaniel had come because Daniel told him he was worried about his Greek houseguest.

The left corner of his mouth twitched up. Well, the Lord accomplished His purposes in ways beyond man's understanding, and if it took an injured Roman to get his son to change his mind about coming to see him, then he would thank the Lord for bringing him the Roman.

He rested his hand on Nathaniel's back. "Come, my son. Rachel has been helping me with a few things that require four good legs. We can spare her some of what she would have done tomorrow." He lowered his voice so Lucas couldn't hear. "Say nothing about your zealot friends. Who knows what a Greek might say later and to whom. This one speaks Aramaic."

Nathaniel nodded. "I understand, Abba. I'll be careful."

◆

Nathaniel would be very careful. If this man was the missing tribune, revealing he was a zealot could endanger them all. He hated how Rome too often punished all the members of a family for the actions of only one. The Lord had commanded that parents were not to be put to death for their children, nor children for their parents. Each would die for their own sin. There was no sin in his fighting to drive the conqueror from the Holy Land, but he would never kill women and children just because they were Roman.

Abba left his hand resting on his back as they walked up to the Greek.

"Nathaniel, this is Lucas of Corinth. Simeon and Asher found him near death in the wadi after robbers attacked him. Your sister brought him home for his broken leg to heal. He wanted to pay for his care by helping me with what he can."

"It's my pleasure to meet you, Nathaniel." Lucas straightened up and offered him a friendly smile.

Nathaniel's lips curved into a stiff smile, but as he gazed at Lucas, his eyes cooled from lukewarm to icy.

"Lucas." Nathaniel paused, locking his eyes on Lucas's. "It's good for Abba to have your help while you remain with him. I trust that won't be too long."

The nose, the hair, the short beard, his military bearing in the way he squared his shoulders as they met—the more he looked at Lucas of Corinth, the more suspicious he became that this might be the missing tribune.

His eyebrows scrunched and the corners of his mouth dipped lower. His jaw jutted forward as he tipped his head to look down his nose at this Lucas. A Greek? Not likely.

Nathaniel's transformation from stiff to blatantly hostile was not at all what Lucius expected from a man he'd barely met. He'd grown accustomed to the coolness in Joseph's eyes, but why the icy coldness in his son's? With a nod and another friendly smile, he turned back to his work. Sitting at dinner tonight with the two of them was likely to be a chilly experience. Maybe he could sit by Rachel or Simeon so he'd have at least one friendly neighbor while they ate.

Chapter 27

THE WORRISOME GREEK

Lucius took his turn washing his hands as he listened to Joseph's blessing and thanks for the commandment to wash. He wasn't entirely sure what to do next. The presence of Joseph's oldest son would change the seating arrangements. Rachel had brought a sixth cushion from the house and rearranged all the others to make room for it, but who would sit on which remained unclear. He wasn't sure where Joseph would want to put him.

He glanced at her father. He had little doubt that Joseph would have preferred to put him anywhere but with them at any of their dinners. Her father still spoke to him as little as possible and always with a coolness that was rather disconcerting at times. If it weren't for the friendly eyes and gracious attentiveness of Rachel and the amiable and entertaining chatter of Simeon, he would have rather not eaten with them himself.

When they gathered under the canopy, Joseph motioned toward his accustomed cushion before offering his hands to help Lucius lower himself to the ground. Nathaniel's nostrils flared and his mouth turned down before he seated himself on the other side of Joseph.

After Joseph blessed God for giving them bread, he started to hand it first to Nathaniel. To offer first to Nathaniel would have made him the honored guest. Lucius eyes flicked between the two. Was Joseph going to treat his son like a guest in his own home?

Nathaniel's back straightened and his mouth twitched. Joseph stopped midway. When his father passed the plate to Lucius instead,

Nathaniel relaxed. The smile that was offered by the father and then returned along with a nod by the son told Lucius this visit might be the first after some breach between them. His curiosity that was piqued by the excited greetings upon Nathaniel's first arrival was further aroused.

Lucius caught Rachel's eye as he prepared to tear off his portion of bread. As she watched him, he tore off half his usual amount. She'd prepared for five; she now had six. He didn't want her to go without for her brother, as she had for him the first night he'd been with them. He would gladly forego half so she would eat as well. Understanding and appreciation shone in her grateful smile and warm eyes.

As Joseph continued blessing God for their food and drink, Lucius glanced over at Nathaniel. He was being scrutinized as if he were some loathsome bug to squash. But why?

His eyebrows started to rise, but he forced them back into a neutral position as Nathaniel's eyes swept over him. They exuded a coldness that bordered on hatred. Lucius had found some possible explanations for Joseph's lack of warmth, but there was absolutely no reason for Joseph's son to look at him that way when they'd exchanged all of twenty words that were mere formalities.

Tonight would be a good time to say as little as possible...at least as long as her brother was looking at him like a cobra ready to strike.

◆

Nathaniel saw their silent exchange, and it stoked the fire of his anger. Daniel's suggestion that Rachel could find some stranger irresistibly attractive had seemed absurd, but seeing her receive wordless messages like that made him wonder.

As they ate, Nathaniel's gaze was most often directed toward Lucas. He'd seen enough Roman soldiers in Sepphoris to know how different they were from the Greeks, Jews, Syrians, and Arabs that made up much of the population.

This man—too much about him seemed Roman. That easy self-assurance just like the Roman officers when they were relaxing. His nose classic Roman. His hair medium brown and too straight, not curly like the Greeks he knew. Too short as well, like a soldier who needed a haircut.

His eyes a shade of brown that could be Roman or Greek, but there was a watchfulness about them like a soldier on patrol. The thick, short beard might be as little as a week old for a man whose beard grew fast. Left and right sides not quite matching. There might be a scar hiding under the beard on the left side.

◆

Lucius wasn't paying close attention to Nathaniel. He was mostly enjoying the happiness radiating from Rachel's face every time she looked at her brother. He'd never seen her more beautiful. Her eyes sparkled and a delighted smile appeared every time her brother glanced her way. The smiles Nathaniel gave her in return made very plain how much he loved his little sister.

He watched Joseph, too. The shadow of sadness was absent as he sat conversing with his oldest son. Whatever had been keeping Nathaniel away, it was not because Joseph didn't want him there.

◆

If Lucius had been watching Nathaniel more closely, he would not have looked at Rachel as much.

Nathaniel was observing much more than the injured man's facial features. He was watching how he looked at Rachel, and he didn't like it. He saw exactly what Daniel had seen. The supposed Greek looked at her too often, and he obviously enjoyed the view. It was time to find out who Abba's guest really was.

Nathaniel's eyes narrowed, and he began the attack. "So, Lucas, where are you from?"

◆

Lucius straightened and flipped his gaze onto Nathaniel. He hadn't expected to be pulled so directly into the conversation that swirled around him. Nathaniel's eyes bored into him. It wasn't because her brother was trying to make him feel part of the family circle.

"I left Corinth when I was seventeen."

"And then?"

An interrogation? He snapped to battle alertness. "I've lived many places since then."

"Such as?" Her brother was circling, too much like the jackal in the wadi.

"I've been in Judaea about three years."

"Have you ever lived in Rome?" Nathaniel stared straight at him, obviously watching for any sign of falsehood. It was time to tell him the truth, appropriately framed.

"I lived there for a while after leaving Corinth." Time to go on the offensive before there was a question too risky to answer. "Rachel told me you were working in Sepphoris now. Do you like that town?"

Nathaniel blinked twice in quick succession. Lucius suppressed a smile. Her brother hadn't expected to be questioned himself.

"Well enough."

"Is making wagons there better than doing it here with your father?"

Lucius saw his barb strike home. Nathaniel glanced at his father. Joseph's face radiated only affection, not condemnation for leaving him in the lurch.

Rachel eyes widened as they flicked back and forth between Nathaniel and Lucius before settling on her brother. "Nathaniel, I've been learning how to work with wood. I can see why you always enjoyed it so much. Lucas is learning, too." She turned her smile on Lucius. "I think he enjoys it as much as I do."

Lucius's appreciation of her redirection pulled a smile. "I'm glad there's something I can do to show my gratitude for everything I've received here." He turned his eyes back on Nathaniel. "You are fortunate to have such a kind family, Nathaniel. Your God has blessed you."

◆

Rachel had tried to distract him, but Nathaniel had come to find out who this man really was. She was not going to deflect him from his goal.

That focus even blocked out his father's warning to be careful what he said in the presence of this stranger. His words would only upset a Roman, and a Roman corpse couldn't report him.

His eyes narrowed as he prepared to detect every nuance of Lucas's response to the assault he was about to launch. No Roman officer would be able to sit passively while the honor of Rome was attacked. It was time to push the supposed Greek into revealing his true identity.

"We would be more blessed if the Romans would leave this land. They are brutal tyrants who have no right to live among us and rule over us. They steal from us with their taxes and make our women and children into their slaves. Their presence here with their false gods and worship of their emperor defiles our land. Their emperor Hadrian is a filthy lover of the murder of the innocent and the depravity of the Greeks. Their officers are the arrogant scum of the earth, unfit to walk our streets and leer at our women."

Joseph frowned. "Nathaniel..."

◆

At first, Rachel couldn't tear her eyes away from Nathaniel. What was he thinking, spouting his hatred for Rome in Abba's house in front

of a stranger? Especially this stranger. It was dangerous...too dangerous for them all.

Her eyes saucered as she swung them onto Lucas. He was sitting
so calmly, just watching her brother as if he were in a friendly conversation. But for how long? How could Lucas resist rising to the bait her
brother was tossing before him? How could any Roman just sit there?

Her breaths came more quickly. Lucas was her friend now. If Nathaniel knew he was a Roman tribune, he'd kill him right before her
eyes. Lucas was too badly hurt to defend himself. Watching her brother
kill her friend...that would be the most horrible thing she could imagine.

It was all she could do to keep from burying her face in her hands,
but she must. She tried to shove the images of them fighting, of Lucas
dying from her mind. She fought to get her fear under control, to keep
her face from betraying her thoughts. Nathaniel would know Lucas
was not who he claimed if she couldn't control herself.

Then a glance at her brother told her he wouldn't notice. Nathaniel's eyes were locked on his prey, like a lion crouching with every
muscle tense, vibrating before the pounce. He ignored Abba and leaned
toward Lucas.

"You've been in Judaea long enough to see all this, Lucas. Long
enough to learn to hate Rome for her brutality and lust for power. Long
enough to see why true Jews will do anything to free Judaea from the
yoke of the oppressor. You've seen her cruelty to anyone who wants
freedom. Haven't you? Don't you agree the Romans must be fought
until Rome is driven from our land?"

An angry retort surged through Lucius's mind, but he stuffed it
down. He knew exactly what Nathaniel was doing. Now all the questions about where he came from made sense. So did the scarcely veiled
hostility from the moment Nathaniel arrived. No matter what her
brother did to provoke him into revealing he was Roman, he would act
the Greek. To do otherwise would be too dangerous for them all.

With his broken leg and no weapon, he'd be unable to keep her
brother from killing him. Even if he had a weapon, he wouldn't want
to kill Rachel's brother while she watched him, and simply wounding
him would never be enough to end it.

If Nathaniel killed him in Joseph's house, the Roman troops would
come to kill her father and enslave her and her little brothers as retri-
bution for the killing of one of their own. There was no way he would

put her and the rest of her family in such grave danger by responding as Nathaniel expected.

He glanced at Rachel. She looked like a rabbit cornered by a pack of hunting dogs as her eyes flitted between her brother and him. Her fear was understandable. Any other Roman soldier discovering her brother was a zealot would be deadly for him and maybe for her whole family.

Joseph scowled at his son. "Stop this, Nathaniel." Nathaniel flicked his hand as if to shoo away his father's command.

As Lucius juggled how best to respond, Nathaniel spat out his challenge. "Answer me, Greek, or are you afraid to?"

Lucius donned his mental armor and prepared to engage. Time to speak the truth, just not the truth about himself. Many of the accusations Nathaniel was making were totally justified. He'd seen enough unwarranted cruelty by his fellow soldiers to make him question the way Rome was governing Judaea himself.

"Much of what you say is true. Rome has no patience with anything that might challenge her authority. Anyone can suffer when Rome exerts her power. My own grandfather never did anything wrong, but he was killed when he became a Christian. The Jews are not the only ones who've suffered at the hands of Rome. They only suffer more because they refuse to look to the future instead of back to the past."

His lips tightened as he shook his head slowly. "I wish Judaea wasn't suffering, but Rome is too strong for the zealots to change that. They will only bring more pain and destruction down on the Jewish people by their attacks. There's already been more than enough. Too many innocent people die when Roman troops respond, as they must, to the zealot violence."

Too many innocent die...the haunting smile of the dying youth he'd killed five months ago resurfaced. He shook his head to erase the image and focus again on the present.

He locked his eyes on Nathaniel as he spoke his heart. "Judaea is not unique. The other provinces were conquered lands, but they've made peace with the conqueror, and their people don't suffer because they have. Corinth is prosperous and at peace now because Achaia became content under Roman rule. She shares in the great benefits of the Pax Romana. It no longer matters how brutally Rome treated Corinth when she was first conquered. Judaea should follow her example. It's time for the Jews to set aside their swords and learn to live peacefully under Roman rule. The Jews will never win, and continuing to fight will only force Rome to crush them."

Nathaniel grew red-faced and his eyes bulged as he listened to Lucius's calm response. His breath came faster and faster. He began to rise. "A Greek has no business telling a Jew not to defend his land from tyrants!"

Lucius raised his hands in a peaceful gesture. "That's true, but you insisted on hearing what I thought, Nathaniel. Don't get so upset because I've told you."

◆

Joseph kept his eyes trained on the Roman as Nathaniel pressed the attack. Why did he listen without anger? When Lucas said Rome was often wrong and fighting only caused suffering and more fighting—that was the last thing he expected from a Roman tribune. He glanced at Simeon. His younger son liked this Roman. It was good for him to hear the warrior speak with regret of the innocents who suffered in war.

But it was time to end this conversation before it went too far and turned into the fight that Nathaniel seemed determined to provoke. He placed his hand on Nathaniel's shoulder and applied enough pressure to keep him seated. "Enough of discussing the Romans. Time to eat and enjoy each other's company instead."

Nathaniel scowled at Lucas, who ignored the scowl and turned his attention to Simeon as he began a story about one of the ewes. Joseph's own scowl relaxed. It was good the Roman had enough sense to obey him and drop that topic immediately. His own son certainly didn't.

◆

Nathaniel felt Rachel's fingers touch his hand. As soon as he turned his gaze toward her, she drew him into conversation. His breathing slowed, and his scowl was soon replaced by a smile. It was so good to be with her again. What he'd missed most while he was staying away were the love in her eyes as she looked at each member of her family and the music of her laughter. He would make it a habit to visit home much more often.

He glanced over at Lucas. There was more than her laughter that would bring him back soon. It was a good thing Daniel had told him about this worrisome Greek.

Rachel really was very nice to him—much too nice. She made sure they were all getting enough food, but she seemed especially concerned that he was. His broken leg got in the way of him sitting facing the center of the mat. That made it hard for him to reach everything.

She kept an eye on him and made sure to move whatever he seemed to want within his reach before he even asked for help.

She was definitely too attentive for Nathaniel's peace of mind. This Lucas seemed to truly appreciate even the smallest thing she did for him, and she sparkled when he smiled as he thanked her. His cousin may have been right to worry about the Greek staying here.

The supposed Greek. He was almost certain there was more to this man than what he claimed to be.

Abba wasn't acting normally toward him. His father was one of the friendliest men he'd ever known, but he hadn't seen him smile at his guest even once. Abba didn't even look at Lucas very often, and when he did, there was coolness in his gaze. He made no attempt to converse with his guest or include him in his other conversations.

No, there was something not quite right about Lucas of Corinth, if that really was his name, and something strange was going on. He would come back often until he found out what it was and put a stop to it.

For Joseph, dinner ended much too soon. The pleasure of having his son come home would have been complete if Nathaniel had come to stay. Still, even just having him return after his avowal that he never would was enough to make Joseph pour his thanks out to God.

After Joseph pronounced the blessing over their after-dinner hand-washing, Nathaniel turned to him. "I need to leave you now. I have to get to work early tomorrow since I left early today. It's been so good to be with you again, Abba. I'll be back soon."

Joseph beamed at him as he rested his hands on his oldest son's shoulders. "This will always be your home, my son. Come often."

Nathaniel cast a glance at Lucas that Joseph didn't miss. "I intend to, Abba."

Rachel hurried over to wrap her arms tightly around her brother. She tilted her head upward to gaze into his eyes. "It hasn't been the same without you, Nathaniel. I'm so glad you've come back to us."

He stroked his sister's cheek with his knuckle. "I'll be back soon to check on you, little one."

She laughed. "You can come back so I can check on you. I don't need checking on."

Lucas was balanced on his good leg, silent in the background, smiling at their obvious pleasure in the reconciliation this visit had brought. Nathaniel fixed an icy stare on him.

"You can check on me while I'm checking on everyone else."

Simeon and Asher joined them to escort Nathaniel to his horse. After embracing his little brothers, he mounted. With a loving smile at them all and one more chilling stare at Lucas, he turned his horse and rode out of the courtyard.

Joseph stood watching his son until he was out of sight. As he turned back toward the canopy where they would soon say evening prayers, his gaze fell upon Lucas. Yeshua had already blessed him for his faithfulness in letting the Roman stay. Who knew how long it might have been before Nathaniel returned if he hadn't needed to check on their houseguest?

As he walked past Lucas, he paused. "So your grandfather died for his faith in Yeshua? How?"

"Lions in the arena in Rome."

"To understand the faith of your grandfather, it will not be enough for you to learn all you can in synagogue. The LORD taught His people how to live with Torah, and He spoke to us for hundreds of years through His prophets, but He made us righteous before Him through the sacrifice of Yeshua." He fixed serious eyes on Lucas's face. "As Yeshua has commanded, before you leave here, I will make sure you understand it all."

Joseph didn't smile at him, but Lucius was still stunned when Joseph rested his hand on his arm and squeezed as he passed.

Chapter 28

RESPONSE OF THE ROMAN

aniel was waiting for Nathaniel when he rode into his uncle's courtyard. When he threw his leg over the horse's neck and slid to the ground, Daniel was immediately at his side.

"So, what did you think?"

Nathaniel grinned at his cousin. "It was good to see my father again. I'm glad I went tonight."

Daniel's lips tightened at Nathaniel's playful avoidance of his question. "That's not what I'm asking. What did you think of that Greek?"

The grin faded from Nathaniel's face. "I'm not sure."

"What do you mean, not sure? Didn't you see the way he looks at Rachel?"

"I did. I think you're right that he admires her. I don't think she wants him to do anything about it."

"But she's so nice to him. Much too nice."

Nathaniel wasn't about to add to Daniel's suspicions about Rachel liking his father's houseguest, even if he thought there might be something to them. He shook his head.

"You know Rachel. She's always nice to everybody. She'd be just as nice to a Roman soldier as she'd be to her own brother. She did take really good care of him, but he's got a broken leg and can't do a lot for himself. She'd do the same for you if you were there with a broken leg." He grinned at his cousin and gave him a shove.

◆

Daniel wasn't expecting that and had to step sideways quickly to

167

catch himself. His mouth tightened at the off-target comment about her taking care of him. He'd seen how cold her eyes were as she told him in no uncertain terms that she wanted nothing to do with him.

Nathaniel grinned again. "That's an idea. If you want to get Rachel to pay you a lot of special attention, we can go there, and I'll break your leg. I bet she'd be just as sweet to you then as she is to the Greek."

Daniel clenched his teeth as he tried to mask the sting of that remark. After his last visit, he wasn't so sure.

Nathaniel's grin faded, and he turned serious. "I agree he looks more Roman than Greek. There were too many things that make me think he might be that missing tribune. He's got the nose and the hair. There might be a scar under that beard. There's something about him that seems more like a soldier than any ordinary Greek I've met."

Nathaniel rubbed the back of his neck as his brow furrowed. "I tried to get a rise out of him, calling Roman officers scum, insulting the emperor, telling him why we hate Rome for its cruelty, why Rome has no business in Judaea. It didn't work. He went off on how Corinth suffered when it was conquered, but now it's prosperous under the Roman yoke because it goes along with whatever Rome wants." Nathaniel's frown deepened. "He had the gall to tell me we Jews should be a bunch of submissive sheep like the Greeks."

Daniel mirrored his frown. "What did you say?"

"I told him no Greek had the right to tell a Jew not to defend his land."

"What did he do then?"

"He agreed with me! I couldn't get any fight out of him no matter what I said. I let it drop then because he is Abba's guest. I could tell Abba didn't want me pressing it further, so I didn't. Not this time, anyway. I plan to go back in a few days to see if I can find out who he really is." Nathaniel's eyes narrowed. "I'd stake my life on it that Lucas of Corinth hasn't told Abba the truth about himself. I still think he might be that missing Roman."

He looked at Daniel. "Maybe you'd like to come, too." He grinned. "You could talk to Rachel while I talk with Abba's Greek."

"Maybe."

Daniel wasn't so eager to talk with Rachel when her brother might see just how little she wanted to have to do with him, at least not while that Greek was there. It only took seven or eight weeks for a broken leg to heal. Maybe then things would be different.

Everyone else was asleep, but Rachel lay awake, staring at what she could see of the ceiling in the dim moonlight. The more she thought about the argument between Nathaniel and Lucas, the faster her heart beat. In the heat of the moment, she'd been afraid that Nathaniel would hurt Lucas, maybe even kill him. Now, in the cool quiet of the night, she was terrified because Nathaniel had revealed himself as a zealot to a Roman officer.

When Lucas's leg healed and he returned to his garrison, what was to keep him from looking for Nathaniel the next time the Romans were hunting zealots? He knew her brother worked for a wagon maker in Sepphoris. How many of those could there be? Had Nathaniel's taunting words, spoken in anger without thinking of the consequences, started something that would lead to his death by a Roman sword?

A sudden thought wrapped her in horror. It might mean his death on a Roman cross.

Her bed was in an alcove closed off by a thin curtain, but she could still hear Lucas's slow, deep breathing across the room. His ribs were only bruised, and Abba had unwrapped him so he could breathe normally. Before tonight, she'd liked listening to his rhythmic breathing. It meant he wasn't in too much pain. Did each deep breath now mean it was only a matter of time before she lost another brother?

Teardrops began escaping, trickling across her temples and into her ears. Her eyelids shut, but that didn't stop the rivulets as more tears flowed, wetting her hair. Her chest heaved with the sobs she struggled to keep silent so no one would awaken.

Until surging emotion drove her to exhaustion and sleep, she lay in the darkness, pouring her heart out to God, begging Him to protect Nathaniel from the vengeance of Rome.

At breakfast, Lucius noticed Rachel was unusually quiet. Her eyes were puffy, like she'd been crying, and they darted away every time he looked at her. It was as if she was afraid of him but trying to hide her fear.

At first he couldn't think of anything he'd done that could possibly have made her afraid. Then it struck him. She wasn't afraid of him for her sake. She was afraid of him for her zealot brother. As they'd walked home from the morning Shabbat service, she'd told him she didn't know anyone living in the village now who fought with the zealots, but Nathaniel didn't live in their village...now. She'd been very careful to tell him the truth while protecting her brother as well.

He'd seen how much she loved Nathaniel. She must know that his foolish talk had betrayed what he was. No wonder she was afraid.

But she didn't need to be. He had no intention of doing anything that would hurt her or her family. As soon as he could, he would let her know that. Maybe then he would see the warmth in her eyes that had become so important to him.

No singing drifted across the courtyard as Rachel ground the extra flour for Shabbat, and Lucius regretted being the reason. He was tired of listening to the silence when Eli came mid-morning to ask Joseph's help. The two of them walked down to Eli's house for a few minutes. Would Joseph be gone long enough for him to hobble over and explain to her? What if Joseph came back to find him with Rachel instead of at the workbench?

As he weighed the risk, the grating sound of one stone grinding against the other stopped. There was a short silence, and then he heard her coming.

He turned to watch her. How could she do it? Even though he frightened her now, she was still bringing dates and water to make him take a break to rest his ribs. She was also bringing him the perfect opportunity to allay her fears about her brother's foolish talk the night before without Joseph overhearing. The last thing he wanted was for her to be afraid because of him.

When she reached him, she offered a tenuous smile before turning her eyes from his. As she offered the cup to him with her eyes downcast, he trapped her hand with his own. He couldn't let her leave before he spoke what she needed to hear. Her eyes snapped up to his. He locked his eyes upon hers.

"That was an interesting dinner last night. Meeting your brother Nathaniel was a little more exciting than I'd expected. He's very passionate about Judaea's position in the Empire."

He watched the fear flit across her face even though she tried to hide it. Nathaniel had said so many things last night that he should never have said to a Roman officer.

"I know your brother's a zealot, Rachel. He suspects what I really am. I saw how hard he tried to make me mad enough to say or do something that would reveal I'm Roman."

Her eyes saucered, and her breathing became fast and shallow as fear wrapped tighter around her heart. He'd seen the same fear the night before when her brother started on his tirade. She was no fool. She knew what Nathaniel exposing himself as a zealot to a Roman might mean.

"I see how that frightens you. I want you to know that you don't have to worry about me knowing. I won't do anything that would hurt your family. Remember on Shabbat I told you that Lucas of Corinth would do his best to keep anyone from getting hurt?" He smiled to reassure her. "There's nothing your brother can say or do that will provoke me into revealing I'm Roman.

"Your brother's a hothead, but I'm not. I know the next time he comes he'll probably try to goad me into a fight again, but I won't let any arguments turn into the fight he's spoiling for. You also don't have to worry about me hunting him as a zealot after I leave. Getting your brother killed is the last thing I would ever want to be part of."

She had been trembling as he held her hand. She stilled as his words sunk in. He watched the tension drain away as her eyes, her lips, her whole body relaxed. He felt the barrier between them crumble.

"Oh, Lucas! I'm so glad to hear you say that. We worry about him all the time. He used to follow Yeshua, but now...I keep praying that he'll realize he should follow Him again and come home before it's too late. I don't want to lose him, too."

Lose him, too. The glimmer of fresh tears at the corner of those gentle eyes told him she was missing Reuben again. Could she ever bear losing Nathaniel as well?

"You'll never lose a brother because of me if I can help it."

He squeezed her hand before letting it go. His words had dispelled the cloud of worry, and her bright, grateful smile was exactly what he'd hoped for.

"I was so worried about you knowing I hardly slept. I should have known better. You're not like the others." She rested her hand on his arm and squeezed. "You're a good man, Lucas of Corinth, and I'm very glad we rescued you."

"I am, too. You bringing me here has changed my life. You kept me from dying, and I'm learning about God. No man could ask for more. I owe you everything, and I'll never be able to repay you all."

"Helping Abba is payment enough." A playful smile appeared. "And you'll even leave here trained in a trade if you ever want to stop being a soldier. You really do make beautiful spokes. I'm sure a wagon maker would hire you. You won't ever have to worry about having enough money to live on again."

He grinned at her plans for him. She had no idea she was helping a man from one of the wealthiest families in the Empire, but she wouldn't have cared even if she'd known. She was the only person he knew who wouldn't treat a beggar any different than a king.

However, there was one distinction she would make that he regretted more each day. He knew enough of the Jews to know that a good one like Joseph would only want his daughter to marry another good Jew, and a daughter like Rachel would never marry against her father's will.

Each time she focused those kind eyes upon him, each time she smiled that gracious smile—his heart was drawn more powerfully to her. She was the most extraordinary woman he'd ever met, the kind of woman he would love to make his wife. But that was an impossible dream. Her father would never let her marry a Gentile like him. A Greek would never be acceptable, and a Roman would be beyond the pale.

◆

Joseph was returning from Eli's, and he saw Lucas holding onto Rachel's hand. He was too far away to hear their words, but he could see Rachel's fear. He clenched his teeth and lengthened his stride. He had assumed it was safe to leave her alone with the Roman for a few minutes, but maybe he had been wrong. Then he saw the Roman release her hand, and a happy smile appeared. When she rested her hand on his arm, she was beaming, and the Roman was grinning at her.

That was a good thing. If the Roman ever tried to hurt her, he would gladly snap his neck.

Rachel turned at his footsteps. "I put your dates and water on the brick bench, Abba." She walked over to him, stood on tiptoes, and planted a kiss on his cheek. As she stepped back, a delighted sparkle lit her eyes.

"You look happy this morning, Rachel."

He glanced over at Lucas. What had the Roman said or done that frightened her? Why was she so happy now?

"I am, Abba. Nathaniel came back to us, even if it was only for a visit." She turned her head to smile at Lucas. "And I think Lucas is feeling so much better today."

Joseph eyed the Roman. There was more to their conversation than she was telling him, of that he was sure. But whatever it was, it didn't appear to pose any danger to Rachel.

"Don't let him work too hard, Abba. I can't trust him not to if I'm not watching."

Her father nodded but said nothing. He would help the Roman for Yeshua, but he wasn't his nursemaid.

Lucius's heart warmed at the smile Rachel flashed toward both of them before she returned to the canopy. Joseph watched her for a moment. Then he shifted his gaze to Lucius, and Lucius felt the chill. Her father's lips tightened before he turned back to the forge.

As Lucius watched her walk away from him, a sigh escaped. He should work at reconciling himself to the way things were destined to be. Joseph could barely stand his presence. Even if Joseph liked him, there was no chance a good Jew would ever consider a Gentile a suitable husband for his precious daughter. Marrying Rachel was as impossible as plucking a star from the night sky.

Chapter 29

BETTER THAN THE FIRST TIME

The sun was almost down, and the family gathered for Rachel to light the lamp before they all walked to Kabbalat Shabbat. As she waved her hands over the flame and recited the blessing about Yeshua being the light of the world, Lucius couldn't take his eyes off her. She seemed to almost glow as she began their Sabbath worship with that prayer. Yeshua was so important to her, like a real person she knew and loved. His grandfather had felt that way, too—enough to die for him. Joseph had promised to explain it all to him before he left. Would that be soon?

As the family headed out the door, Simeon turned and grinned at him.

"Asher and I will save you a seat so Rachel won't have to make you walk too fast."

Lucius grinned back. "She threatens to take my crutch away if I do, so I don't think you have to worry."

Joseph was almost to the gate, so Simeon scurried to catch up with him and Asher. Lucius was glad using the crutch slowed him down. These leisurely walks to and from synagogue with Rachel had become his favorite times of the week, even if using the crutch did make his ribs hurt. A few minutes basking in the warmth of her smiles without the chilling effect of Joseph's eyes and a chance for a real conversation with her were about as good as any man could want.

"It's hard to believe I've only been with you for eleven days, Rachel. Being with your family feels like I'm home." He fixed grateful eyes on her. "The way you took a Roman in and treat me like a friend... there's no way I can thank you enough for that."

"The LORD led my brothers to you in the wadi. He wanted you here with us while you heal." She briefly rested her hand on his arm as her eyes sparkled at him. "I'm very glad he did."

"I'm glad your father loves Yeshua enough to let me stay."

"Abba is glad to do anything to please Yeshua."

◆

Rachel wished she could say Abba was glad he was there, too, but they both knew that wasn't so. Abba couldn't bring himself to welcome Lucas because he was Roman, but at least he'd let Lucas stay so she could care for him like she'd promised.

"Going to synagogue, learning about the LORD is one of the best parts of being here. He told me yesterday he would make sure I understood everything about Yeshua before I leave."

Rachel's heart warmed as she heard him speak his desire to know God. She would never have believed a Roman would be more eager to know about Yeshua than the young Jewish men in her village. If only he were a man of her village and not a Roman officer destined to return to his garrison...then he might be someone Abba could betroth her to.

She glanced sideways at his face. He was looking straight ahead as he hobbled along, trying to ignore the pain in his ribs that using the crutch caused. The purple bruises on his face and arms had become mottled with greenish yellow. In a few more days, he would look like he'd never had them, but even with them, he was a handsome man.

A very handsome man. It wasn't just his facial features. Maybe those weren't so handsome when you came right down to it. He did have that Roman nose that looked like it might have been broken at least once, and there was that long scar on his jaw that made him look dangerous until the beard covered it. No, it was something else. It was those light brown eyes that could go from serious to laughing before she could take a deep breath. And his mouth, the way it curved into a smile whenever he looked at her.

He must have felt her contemplating him because he turned to look at her, too. The heat spread from her cheeks to her ears as she watched those lips curve. It was that smile he seemed to reserve just for her. She was glad it was getting dark enough that he couldn't see her blush.

They had reached the synagogue.

"I'll see you after synagogue, Lucas. I hope you enjoy it."

His smile turned into a grin. "I always do. Not even Benjamin can take the pleasure out of synagogue."

He headed in to find the seat Simeon was saving for him. She stood looking at him as he disappeared through the door. A very handsome man with a heart for God. Too bad he would leave in five or six weeks. She sighed as she headed in to join the other women.

The next morning, Lucius and Rachel made their way slowly back to the house after the second Shabbat service. He turned his gaze on her as she strolled beside him. It had been a wonderful morning so far. It was fascinating when Rabbi Eliezer taught, and now he was walking home beside the woman who was well on her way to owning his heart, even though he'd never intended her to. Even though he knew nothing could ever come of it.

She felt his gaze, and turned her head to return it. Her eyes sparkled like she was enjoying the slow walk home as much as he was.

"You look happy, Rachel."

"I am."

He would love to think walking beside him was part of the reason. She seemed to like being close to him, but maybe that was just wishful thinking on his part. Having her next to him made him feel warm and content inside. Was there any chance she felt the same?

Her eyes were glowing. "I love Shabbat. The LORD truly blessed us with this day of rest together. To be with my family all day, not working but just being together...the only thing that would make it better would be if Reuben and Nathaniel were here." A shadow of sadness flickered across her face as she spoke Reuben's name.

Lucius was not at all sorry Nathaniel was absent, but he was curious about Reuben. Almost everything he wore or used had once been her brother's. For some strange reason, he felt a strong connection to him.

"If you don't mind, I'd like to know more about Reuben. You said you were twins. Was he a lot like you or more like Nathaniel?"

Rachel's eyes warmed. "He was a lot like me, only better. He was always looking out for everyone."

"That sounds just like you, but I can't imagine that anyone could do it better."

"He was my best friend. We were always close, even when we were little children, but we grew closer as we got older."

The sadness started to build in her eyes. That wasn't what he wanted. Then she pushed it back before the tears came.

"I think you know what I mean, Lucas. You have your brother Marcus."

"Marcus and I weren't really close until he came to Judaea. I always wanted to be, but he never seemed interested in that. Maybe because he's two years younger. Now we're both men, those two years don't seem to matter. I hadn't seen him for more than three years, not since I posted out here. It surprised me when he wrote that he wanted to come to Judaea just to serve with me. He left a posting near Rome where most of his friends are. Now we've become good friends like I always hoped we would."

They turned in at the gate. He was sorry their walk was ending, but he would be sitting by her as they ate, and maybe there would be time for more conversation as they all rested this afternoon. He expected it to be a very good day.

The midday meal was over, and the boys had already left the canopy. Joseph turned his eyes on Lucas as he sat next to him. There was time now to fulfil his promise.

"Lucas, it's time."

Lucas turned his eyes from Rachel to Joseph. Joseph could tell the Roman wasn't quite sure what it was time for, but whenever Joseph spoke, Lucas gave him his full attention.

"Now we have time for me to tell you what you need to know about Yeshua."

Lucius shifted on his cushion to face Joseph more directly. "I'm ready."

Joseph knew Lucas was deeply interested in the things of God, but he had not expected the intensity of the Roman's eyes as they locked on him. There was an eagerness, an ardent hunger like he had never seen before, even in his own children who loved learning about God and talking about Him. *Today, LORD, give me the words to make this conversation tell this Roman all he needs to know.* He took a deep breath and began.

"When the LORD created the whole world, He finished by creating man in His own image, man and woman both. The LORD said it was very good, and so He ended the sixth day of creation. When He had finished, He blessed the seventh day and made it holy. We remember this with Shabbat. We do all our work the other six days, and we rest this day set aside as holy to the LORD, as He commanded.

"The LORD had fellowship with man and woman in the Garden of Eden and gave them all they needed, but they chose to disobey and eat of the fruit that He had forbidden them, the fruit that gave them knowledge of good and evil. Their disobedience was sin. This sin made them unfit to be in the presence of the LORD because He is holy and cannot tolerate sin. Because of it, He drove them from His presence, telling them they would suffer and labor their whole lives and finally die. They and their children had many children, but too many decided to do what they wanted and not seek to please the LORD. Their sin made the earth corrupt and full of violence, so the LORD decided to end them and their evil ways. He took Noah, a man who walked with the LORD, and his sons and their wives and saved them on an ark while he purged the earth of evil men. Again, there were generations born, and many decided not to worship and love the LORD and obey as they should.

"But the LORD came to Abraham, the father of us Jews, and told him to leave everything and follow Him. The LORD promised that all people on earth would be blessed through him. His offspring, Isaac, Jacob, and Joseph, followed the LORD, too. The LORD made Joseph a great ruler in Egypt, and the children of Jacob, whom the LORD renamed Israel, moved there. The Pharaohs after Joseph died made the people of Israel into slaves, but the LORD sent a deliverer, Moses, to lead them from Egypt and back to this land that the LORD had promised to Abraham forever. We sacrifice the lambs each Passover to remember how the blood of the first Passover lambs told the angel of the LORD which houses held the people who trusted the LORD while he killed the firstborn of Egypt so Pharaoh would let Israel go. It was to Moses that the LORD gave Torah to tell us how we must live to please Him. To disobey any of the laws given through Moses is to sin against the LORD, just as man has always done. No man can keep all the laws perfectly, no matter how hard he tries, so no one is holy enough before the LORD to be worthy to be in His presence.

"The LORD made provision in Torah to cover our sins with the sacrifice of an animal free of blemish so that we can approach Him to worship. Only blood can pay for sin, but the blood of an animal only covers for a while. It does not remove our sins for good. So the sacrifices had to be made again and again in the temple so we could approach the LORD.

"But it was the LORD's plan to come Himself to be the perfect sacrifice that could pay for a man's sins, to erase them instead of just covering them up. He told us through His prophets that He would do this. You have heard some of the prophesies He gave through Isaiah, but there are many more."

Lucius nodded. "Simeon tells me when those are read in synagogue."

"A little over a hundred years ago, the Spirit of God came to the virgin Miriam in Nazareth, and the LORD came to earth as a perfect man as Yeshua. He lived without sin, and He sacrificed Himself on a Roman cross to pay for the sins of all who choose to believe in Him as the true Deliverer. Yeshua promised that anyone who believes in Him would never die but would have eternal life with the LORD.

"My own sins were taken by Yeshua and paid for, not just covered. Now I can approach the LORD, not because I am perfect at keeping His laws, but because Yeshua was perfect and God the Father looks at me as having His perfection, even though I am still a sinner. As the LORD is my judge, I am guilty, but Yeshua has taken my punishment so I do not have to.

"Lucas, this was the faith of your grandfather. When he died in that arena, he knew he was not really dying, only his earthly body. He is now with Yeshua in Paradise, and he will be forever, just as Reuben is, just as Rachel and I and the boys will be someday.

"With Kiddush at Shabbat dinner, we remember Yeshua is at our table. We ask the Shekhinah Glory of God to fill our heart. We acknowledge that Yeshua is the vine and we are the branches. We know our lives depend on Him as our Lord and Savior. We drink from the cup as a symbol of the cup of salvation that Yeshua offers. He gives salvation to all those who trust in Him as the Messiah who paid for our sins so we can be with the LORD."

Lucius sat transfixed as he listened to Joseph's words. As he heard how all men were sinners, unfit to be with a holy god, his heart was pierced by thoughts of the things he had done that would be considered sin. He tried to be a good and honorable man, but he failed so often. He thought of the many things Asher had recited that were part of Torah, the things he should do to please God, and even more so, the things he should not do. What he'd thought honorable as a Roman—he now knew some was sin before God.

He took a deep breath and blew it out before speaking. "I'm a sinner, unfit to approach the LORD. I need what Yeshua did for me. I want his sacrifice to remove my sins. What should I do so it will?"

◆

Joseph almost smiled at this Roman who was so eager to accept what the Messiah offered. The LORD had surely brought him to them so he could receive Yeshua as savior.

"You have done it. You have confessed you are a sinner, and you have asked Yeshua to save you from your sin. You need nothing more to save you, Lucas, but it is good now to learn what is pleasing to the LORD and to try to live that way. When you do, you are showing Him how grateful you are for what Yeshua has done for you. As the LORD has loved us and forgiven us through Yeshua, we are to love and forgive others. We are to care for each other, as Yeshua commands, and we are to show our love for the LORD by trying to obey Him even when it is hard for us."

"As you have in letting me stay." The broadest smile Joseph had ever seen lit up Lucas's face. "Thank you, Joseph. There was no way I could repay your family for saving my life, but that was nothing compared to what you've just given me."

Joseph nodded once. "No thanks are necessary, Lucas. I have only given you what the LORD wanted you to receive. Give all your thanks to Him."

Joseph stood. "I'm going now to visit a while with Eli. If you have more questions as you think about all this, I will answer them later."

◆

Lucas watched Abba for a moment as he walked toward the gate. Then he turned his face toward Rachel.

The light in his eyes, the joyful grin—Rachel had never seen a happier person than he was at that moment. She leaned forward and rested her hand on his.

"I'm so glad I was with you for this, Lucas. Nothing is more wonderful than the joy that comes from knowing the LORD's forgiveness."

He turned his hand to lace his fingers with hers. "I never thought I would say this, but I'm glad someone tried to kill me. If they hadn't, I wouldn't be here. You saved my life, Rachel, and then you brought me here where Yeshua would save my soul."

She gave his hand a gentle squeeze before pulling her hand away as she settled back on her cushion. "The LORD works in ways we often don't understand. You were already my friend, Lucas, but now you're my brother, too."

He placed his hands behind him and leaned back as he gazed up at the clear azure sky. She didn't see even the tiniest hint of pain when he took a deep breath before releasing it in a slow, contented sigh. "I enjoyed Shabbat last week, but that was nothing compared to today. Today was so much better than the first one. I just can't put it into words."

She stood. "Being with the LORD will do that to you, Lucas, and this is only the beginning."

She held out her hands. "Time for you to rest a while without your splints. Come inside."

He gripped her wrists and struggled up on his one good leg. "One more thing I like about Shabbat. Will you watch over me like last week?"

"Of course. Yeshua always wants us to watch over each other." She handed him his crutch. "Lead the way."

He hobbled through the door ahead of her. *I'll watch over you, Lucas, for as long as you need me to.*

Her heart was overflowing with thanksgiving that this man was now a follower of Yeshua. Who knew what that might mean for the future?

Only God.

Chapter 30

DINNER WITH NATHANIEL...AGAIN

It was late Sunday afternoon when Nathaniel turned off the Legio road and rode toward his father's house again. It had been three days since he first saw the Greek, and the more he thought about it, the less he liked him living in the same house as his sister. Rachel seemed too friendly toward him, and there was something about Lucas of Corinth that reeked of Roman no matter what he might claim to be.

He'd asked a soldier who came in to pick up a wheel whether the missing tribune had been found. Still missing without a trace. He almost told the soldier where to look, but then he decided it was too risky. Roman soldiers couldn't be trusted, and he didn't want a troop of them showing up at Abba's house, especially if Rachel happened to be home alone.

No, he'd just have to figure out the puzzle that was Lucas of Corinth and then take care of him if the answer turned out Roman.

◆

Lucius was working at the bench when Nathaniel came through the gate. He sighed as he anticipated sitting through another dinner with her zealot brother.

Nathaniel rode up close and frowned down at him. "You still here, Greek?"

Lucius looked up and offered a friendly smile. "Still here."

He hadn't expected a simple smile to be like oil on a fire. Her brother's frown deepened. Nathaniel nudged the horse to crowd Lucius even more.

Lucius leaned an elbow on the bench and rested his hand against his cheek. He moved his fingers to cover his mouth. He didn't want Nathaniel to see the grin that was trying to break out. Her brother reminded him of a silly youth puffing out his chest, trying to impress his friends with his bravado. He hadn't promised Rachel he wouldn't laugh at her brother, but that would start a fight faster than anything. He had promised he wouldn't be the one to start anything.

Joseph set aside his tools and walked over to push against the horse's neck to move Nathaniel away.

"It is good to see you again, son. Stay for dinner?"

"I'd like to, Abba. It's good to spend the time with you all." He swung his leg over the horse's neck and slid off.

Joseph wrapped his arm around his son as he turned toward the house. "Rachel! Nathaniel is here again."

Rachel instantly appeared in the doorway and hurried over to hug her brother. The beaming smile that lit up her face made those brown eyes sparkle. That more than made up for Nathaniel's frown as far as Lucius was concerned. Putting up with her zealot brother at dinner was a small price to pay to watch her enjoy herself.

She wrapped her arm around her brother's and leaned her head against his shoulder as she escorted him and Joseph back toward the canopy.

Lucius felt forgotten at the workbench, but that was fine with him. Being forgotten was better than being the target for Nathaniel's ill-humored attacks. He stood, placed his crutch under his arm, and hobbled toward the canopy where the whole family was gathering to eat. Maybe Nathaniel would ignore him for the rest of the evening. He'd promised her he wouldn't let her zealot brother rile him enough to betray he was Roman. That would be much easier if her brother would pretend he wasn't there like her father used to.

Lucas may have felt forgotten when Nathaniel first arrived, but it was much too obvious to a protective brother that she was very aware of the Greek as they sat at dinner. Just like last time, she paid too close attention to what he might want and made certain it was within his easy reach. The Greek seemed to be just as aware of her. It was a good thing Daniel wasn't there to see how much they looked at each other and how brightly her eyes sparkled when he smiled.

Nathaniel tore off a piece of bread and dipped it in the stew. His jaw tightened when Rachel slid the pot a little closer to Lucas so he could do the same.

Greek or Roman, he had no business there. Even if he posed no physical threat to Rachel, he was a threat to her heart.

◆

Joseph glanced at Nathaniel sitting once more at his left hand, and he was almost content. For five months, Nathaniel had stayed away. It had begun to look like he meant it when he said he would never return. Now at least he was visiting, so there was hope he might return for good.

Nathaniel had been watching Simeon as he talked about one of the ewes. Then Joseph saw his eyes flick over to the Roman at his right hand. The kind look of a brother was replaced by the fierceness of a warrior. Nathaniel was visiting, but he wasn't back. He was still lost to Yeshua.

Joseph glanced at the Roman. Lucas was nodding and smiling as he listened to Simeon. He seemed oblivious to the hostility seething across the mat from him. Then Joseph saw Lucas glance at Nathaniel. He must have seen the anger, but he gave no sign and kept smiling as he focused back on Simeon.

Joseph took a sip of wine. He glanced once more at Lucas. He hadn't wanted him there. He still didn't, but the LORD had used him to make Daniel jealous so he would complain to Nathaniel and Nathaniel would come home to protect Rachel. The LORD's ways sometimes took unexpected directions, but they were always good.

Joseph took another sip. "So, Asher, what did you learn of Torah today?"

"We learned about the Year of Jubilee, Abba." Asher squared his shoulders and closed his eyes as he began drawing the scripture from his memory.

"The land must not be sold permanently, because the land is mine and you are but aliens and my tenants...If one of your countrymen becomes poor and sells some of his property...it will be returned in the Jubilee and he can then go back to his property...If one of your countrymen becomes poor among you and sells himself to you, do not make him work as a slave...He is to be treated as a man hired from year to year; you must see to it that his owner does not rule over him ruthlessly. Even if he is not redeemed in any of these ways, he and his children are to be released in the Year of Jubilee, for the Israelites belong to me as servants. They are my servants whom I brought out of Egypt. I am the LORD your God."

A huge grin broke free as Asher finished his perfect recitation of God's word.

Joseph nodded his approval as he beamed at his youngest son. Seeing Asher and Simeon grow in their knowledge and love of the LORD was one of his greatest pleasures. He glanced at the Roman sitting beside him. Even though Reuben would be sitting there were it not for Romans like him, it was still good that this particular Roman wanted to learn about the LORD and had decided to follow Yeshua. Surely that was the reason the LORD had the boys find him. Now that Lucas had made that decision, he could leave any time. *The sooner the better, LORD.* His smile faded. It was still too hard to have a Roman where Reuben should be, and perhaps it always would be.

◆

Lucius glanced over at Nathaniel and caught angry eyes fixed upon himself. Her brother wasn't listening to the recitation to hear the word of God. He was planning his next attempt to trap a Roman.

Inwardly Lucius sighed. Not again. He'd hoped to avoid verbal sparring with Nathaniel tonight since it upset Rachel, but that was not to be.

The moment Asher finished, Nathanial began the attack. "We will never be able to observe the Year of Jubilee as the LORD commands until we drive the foreign conquerors from Judaea. First the filthy Greeks took our land and enslaved our people so we couldn't observe Jubilee. Judas Maccabeus led the LORD's warriors to victory and threw off the Greek yoke. Israel was free to follow Torah for a hundred years until the Romans came, and again we have Gentile dogs who take our land and give it to foreigners who won't return it. They make our women and children slaves, never to be freed. We need another Maccabeus to rid us of the Romans."

Joseph scowled at his son. "Nathaniel..."

Nathaniel leaned forward and glared at Lucius. "Were your people part of those Greeks? Or in league with the Romans? The Romans are the worst of all. They plunder and rape the whole world."

Rachel's eyes darted from Lucius to Nathaniel and back again. Fear flared in them. He caught her eye and offered a tight-lipped smile to calm her. She could count on his promise that he wouldn't let Nathaniel bait him into saying something. He held her eyes just long enough to see his silent message to trust him douse the fear. Then he focused on Nathaniel.

Lucius's eyes and voice were calm "The Greeks who conquered under Alexander were from Macedonia, not Achaia where Corinth is. No, my ancestors were not part of those Greeks."

"And what of the Romans? Are you one of them? You took their part the last time I was here." Nathaniel eyes gleamed as he set the trap.

"No, I didn't. I only told you what would happen if you choose to keep fighting them. It happened after Vespasian and Titus crushed the first Jewish rebellion. What came of the zealot uprising? The temple destroyed, thousands of women and children taken to suffer and die as slaves, and the men who survived the battles taken to die in the areas. Rome is no weaker than it was then, and it is certainly no more patient. If the zealots insist on starting another war, Rome will finish it this time in a way that makes the last war look like nothing."

Nathaniel was red-faced and breathing hard by the time Lucius finished.

"The LORD will fight with us, and Rome cannot win. The Messiah will appear and lead us to victory."

"The LORD could remove Rome from Israel himself without your zealot swords, Nathaniel. Since He hasn't, it must be His will for Rome to be here, at least for now."

Nathaniel started to lean in, but Joseph put his hand on his son's shoulder and firmly pushed him back where he had been.

Lucius saw Joseph scowling. Was it at him or Nathaniel or both? Didn't matter. Even if Joseph was mad at him, something was driving him to speak.

"The Messiah you're waiting for isn't coming as a military leader. Rachel told me that he's Yeshua, and he already came to conquer sin, not Rome. What does he think of all your hatred and your desire for war, Nathaniel? You used to follow him, so you must know."

Nathaniel's jaw dropped. It snapped shut into a scowl as his eyes darkened. "What do you know of Yeshua, Greek?"

Lucius looked first at Joseph. His slight nod gave permission, and Lucius flipped his gaze back on the angry young zealot. "Joseph told me about what Yeshua did for sinners from every land, not just Judaea, and I've decided to follow him like the rest of your family."

Before Nathaniel could respond, Joseph stepped in. "Enough discussion between you two. You will not agree tonight. Time to talk of other things."

Rachel leaped into the tense silence to change the subject. "I was talking with Elizabeth today, and her baby is going to be here very soon. Her first was a son, but she's hoping the second will be a daughter. She was saying..."

As everyone turned their focus on Rachel, Nathaniel wasn't sorry. Lucas of Corinth was too adept at avoiding his snares. Anyone that smooth must be hiding something.

He still didn't know who Abba's houseguest really was, but the two things he'd learned that night he didn't like. First, Lucas looked at Rachel much more than he should, and any man with eyes in his head could see the admiration in those looks. The second was even more worrisome. Above all else, Rachel wanted a man who followed Yeshua, and there were very few of those around. That decision by the Greek was a much greater threat to Daniel's interest than his handsome face and muscled body ever could be.

Joseph took his attention off Rachel and turned it momentarily on Lucas. The corner of his mouth twitched upward. In the exchange between his zealot son and this Roman soldier, Lucas had said exactly what he wanted to say himself. Of those two men, who would have expected that only the Gentile warrior would understand what God's Messiah really came to do?

The next morning, Lucius and Rachel began their slow walk to synagogue. His ribs didn't hurt as much as they had, but he didn't speed up their pace. The goal of walking slowly was no longer less pain but more time alone with her.

"I'm sorry Nathaniel had to go after you again last night."

"I expected it. I can tell from his eyes when he's planning to attack." He grinned at her. "It's almost turning into a sport between us."

"I still want to thank you for your patience with him. It isn't fun to watch, and I'm sure it's not fun for you."

The left corner of his mouth turned up. "It keeps me in practice for Benjamin. He's left me alone the past few times when he's argued with Joseph, but I expect that can't last. The way he looks at me, I know something's coming."

"Well, I know Abba was as glad as I was that you reminded Nathaniel of what Yeshua taught. He turned away from Yeshua to take up the sword. He's become so angry, just like my cousin who got him mixed up with the zealots in the first place. I was afraid he was going to try to hurt you last night."

"You don't have to worry about that. I won't lose my temper to give him an excuse, and Joseph will keep him from going too far, just like he did the last two times."

He didn't want to keep talking about her zealot brother. There were more pleasant things to think about.

"I wonder what the readings will be at synagogue today. I hope it's Rabbi Eliezer teaching again. Simeon is right about him being worth listening to, and it helps to have Simeon beside me to explain some of it."

"It's so good that you love the word of God, Lucas. It's even better that you decided to follow Yeshua, like us. I'm sure that's why the LORD had Simeon find you." Her lips curved up as she gently squeezed his arm.

The glow in her eyes drove the last thoughts of Nathaniel away. "I think so, too. I'll never look at life the same again."

As they continued their slow progress up the street, Rachel kept glancing at him. How wonderful it would be to have a husband like him, a man who could understand the deepest feelings of her heart, a man who followed Yeshua and loved the LORD like she did.

Lucius caught her glances and smiled in return. To have a wife like her, a woman so filled with love that she even had enough to give to a Roman enemy who'd been left to die—nothing could be better. If he were a Jew, he could imagine himself asking Joseph for her hand and Joseph agreeing to let them marry.

Then his smile faded away. If he were a Jew. . . but he was a Roman, and as a Roman, he didn't need much imagination to know the response he'd get if he ever were to ask.

Chapter 31

ONLY A BLACK HORSE

Marcus had managed to control his mouth in the commander's office, but as he walked back to his quarters, it was all he could do to keep his frown from morphing into the blackest scowl. Lucius had been missing for fifteen days—fifteen days! What Roman soldier could possibly be missing for fifteen days in Judaea and still be alive? Why on earth would the commander insist that no missing man would be declared dead until he'd been missing at least a full two months? That meant it would be another month and a half before he could even request a transfer out of Judaea, and who knew how long it would take to get it.

Marcus rubbed his lips with the back of his hand. The commander looked at him funny each time he asked about sending the condolence letter. He'd better stop asking after today. There might have been a trace of suspicion in the commander's eyes this morning. The sympathy he'd seen there before was certainly gone.

He massaged the back of his neck as his eyebrows dipped. He'd made a big show of wanting a new horse as the excuse to get Lucius down that road where he should have died. If he didn't keep up the pretense of needing a horse, someone might say something that made the commander get more suspicious than he might be already. Buying a horse should help with that. Definitely time to visit the horse traders to keep up the ruse.

Marcus had just finished looking at a gray mare that some fawning Arab was trying to convince him to buy. She was a pretty animal, but he preferred stallions. He liked the power and the unpredictability of a really spirited animal between his legs. Lucius had, too.

As he worked his way through the market, his head snapped to the right as he spied something he never expected to see. There, being curried by a middle-aged man who looked like he was probably Syrian, was his brother's black stallion.

He was almost sure it was Lucius's horse. It was totally black—no stockings, no blaze with a distinctive shape. That made it harder to prove it was his stallion, but there was something unusual about how it looked at you, like it was working something out. It had this tendency to flick its ears a certain way, and it shook its mane when it tossed its head more than most horses did. He was almost certain he would know that horse if he saw it, and he was almost certain he was seeing it now.

He approached the horse and ran his hand across its shoulder and down its foreleg.

The Syrian stepped close with a smarmy smile. "Ah, tribune! I see you are drawn to fine horseflesh. This stallion is the finest in the market today."

Marcus reached up and stroked the animal's cheek. It turned its face toward him. There was that look he'd seen many times.

"He's a nice animal. Where did you get him?"

"In Tiberias." The Syrian shook his head. "So few men there appreciate a truly fine animal. That is not a problem here in Sepphoris, where noble Romans like yourself know superior horseflesh when they see it." He slapped the horse on the shoulder. "And this is a truly superior horse. It would be a shame for a man who did not know that to own him."

"Where in Tiberias did you get him and when?"

"There was a Jew in the horse market. He did not deserve such a horse, so it is good he was selling him. I can see you are a man who would appreciate this horse's value."

"When did you buy it from the Jew?"

"Ten, maybe twelve days ago. I have cared for the stallion like it was my own child since then."

Marcus nodded. Three to five days after Lucius went missing—that was plenty of time for someone to take it cross-country to Tiberias to sell it. Anyone who found it wandering near the road where Lucius disappeared would know it would be risky to sell a "found" horse in the town where the owner probably lived.

Marcus untied the horse and began to lead it away. The Syrian moved in front of him.

"What are you doing, tribune? We have not negotiated the price yet."

"And we're not going to. This animal belonged to a tribune who went missing fifteen days ago. I'm taking it to the garrison, and you're coming with me. When we get there, you can try to convince me you didn't kill him and take his horse." Marcus drew his sword. "Walk in front of me. If you try to run, I'll kill you."

The Syrian blanched and started to tremble as if he would collapse on the spot. Then he collected himself. "But I have two more horses I cannot leave. I beg you to let me get them. Too many would steal them, and my children would starve. I did not kill your tribune. I only bought the horse from a Jew in Tiberias. I will tell you everything I can about that man, but please let me bring my horses."

Marcus scowled at the quivering man. He was probably telling the truth since some Jew who lived along that deserted road should have found Lucius's stallion, not some Syrian horse dealer. The man would be more likely to tell all he knew if he let him bring the animals.

"Bring your horses, but don't try anything. I will kill you if you do."

Marcus's interrogation of the Syrian had been singularly uninformative. He had bought the horse from a Jew who was about 30 years old, give or take a few years, who had a beard and short-to-medium-length dark-brown hair (which Jew didn't?), who had only the one horse to sell, who led it instead of riding it because it was so spirited, and who didn't know how much it was worth. The Jew had volunteered nothing about where the horse came from, and the Syrian hadn't bothered to ask since he was getting such a good deal. The Syrian bought it wearing a rope halter and without a saddle, so he hadn't seen the metal faceplate of a military bridle or any of the distinctive medallions that formed part of the special harness the military horses wore. He could honestly say he had no reason to suspect it might belong to a Roman military man. Marcus was no closer to knowing where Lucius had gone than he was before he found the stallion.

He did, however, now have proof that Lucius had met with foul play.

The soldier who normally looked after the officers' horses was examining the stallion to see if he recognized it. He ran his hands along the stallion's legs and back, stroked its neck, and watched its mannerisms.

He glanced over at Marcus Drusus, so openly impatient for him to pronounce this animal to be Lucius Drusus's horse.

It probably was, but the animal was all black, so there really were no markings distinctive enough to make him completely certain.

He held the halter on both sides of the stallion's head and stared at its face.

Lucius Drusus was a good man who always appreciated how well he'd cared for his horse. He was sorry Lucius had gone missing. Marcus Drusus was an arrogant man who took his hard work for granted and complained if he didn't do something as fast as Marcus thought it ought to be done. The coldness in Drusus's eyes made it seem he was more interested in finding his brother's horse than in finding his brother.

"No, I can't be sure. An all-black horse looks like every other all-black horse."

Drusus's eyes nearly popped. "But this horse has all the right mannerisms."

"I'm sorry, tribune. I can't tell if this is your brother's horse or not."

As Marcus stared at the soldier, the man's facial muscles didn't reveal a thing, but he was sure he saw smug satisfaction lurking in his eyes. It was Lucius's horse, and the soldier was deliberately lying.

The commander had come to hear the verdict. Finding Lucius's horse...surely that would prove Lucius was most likely dead, even though that wasn't what the commander wanted to believe. Marcus might have convinced him if only the soldier had told the truth.

The Syrian was also standing by, nervously waiting for the verdict. He would be out the price he'd paid if it did turn out to be a stolen horse. When the soldier made his pronouncement, his body slumped in relief.

The commander nodded in satisfaction. "Good. Don't lose hope,

Drusus. Your brother might return yet." He turned and headed back to his office where too many reports awaited him.

The Syrian moved closer to Marcus. "So, you can see this is a beautiful animal. Were you interested in buying it today?"

It was all Marcus could do not to punch him in the face before he turned and stalked away.

Chapter 32

LONGING

Rachel carried the tray of dates and water out to the workshop. Abba stepped back from the forge as she set his share down on the brick bench beside him. He lifted the cup and drained it before taking a date from the bowl.

"Just what I needed, Rachel."

"I'm glad, Abba. I don't want you to work too hard."

He had seemed so tired sometimes before Lucas came. He was better now. Having Lucas's help had taken away some of the pressure of too much work, and having Nathaniel visit had taken away much of his sadness. She stood on tiptoes and kissed his cheek before turning to Lucas.

She placed the dates on the workbench and held the cup for him to take from her hand. She liked the way his fingers always touched hers before he took hold of the cup. She liked the teasing twinkle that often appeared in his eyes as he drew his fingertips across her hand. She also liked the way the corners of his lips turned up into that special smile that he saved just for her.

He was a very handsome man now the last of the bruises had faded away. To see him now, you would never know he was so close to death only sixteen days ago. The only obvious sign left was his broken leg. His ribs weren't completely healed, but they didn't seem to be much of a problem. She could tell it still hurt him some to use the crutch, but he didn't seem to be hurting when he worked with the spokeshave anymore. At least he didn't hurt any more than he could hide from her, and she watched him closely enough that he couldn't hide much.

"So, Lucas, how much have you done this morning?"

He handed her the spoke he'd already made. "Enough to earn some dates and a smile from you. Does this one pass inspection?" He grinned at her.

She ran her hand slowly along the smooth, curved surface. "I think so, but you can work on making the next one better."

He didn't need to improve anything, and she knew he knew she knew it. His grin got a little broader. "If that's what you think, I'll try to do better."

She tucked the tray under her arm and flashed him a happy smile before heading back to the canopy where the loom awaited her.

Lucius watched her for several seconds as she walked away. Then he turned back to his work with a quiet sigh. She would be the perfect wife for him...if only he were a Jew.

Lucius was thoroughly enjoying Thursday dinner. Nathaniel had come, but he hadn't tried to start a fight tonight. That was unexpected, but he welcomed the peace for a change. He didn't really mind arguing with Nathaniel, but it distressed Rachel. It was good to have a dinner where she could simply enjoy her brother's company without watching the two of them spar.

Nathaniel had decided to leave the Greek alone for a while after their argument about following Yeshua. He wasn't able to get Lucas mad with his own attacks, and he didn't like the counterattacks that Lucas fired back at him. Not exactly counterattacks, but statements and questions that made him squirm if he thought about them later.

He wasn't saying anything directly to the Greek tonight, but he was watching him closely. He didn't like anything he was seeing. He didn't like the way Simeon seemed to really enjoy Lucas talking with him. It was almost like the Greek was another big brother. He especially didn't like the way Lucas looked at Rachel when Abba wasn't watching him, and Abba spent so little time watching Lucas that he could spend most of his time watching Rachel. He didn't like that earnest gaze with the occasional hint of longing that he masked the second she looked directly at him. The Greek might be in love with her. At the very least, he wanted her.

Even worse, he could see that Rachel liked Lucas. That was totally unacceptable even if Lucas was a Greek instead of the Roman he suspected him to be. His sister should only marry a fellow Jew, not some Gentile dog. His cousin Daniel had liked her for a very long time, and Nathaniel expected a proposal to be coming from him soon. Lucas of Corinth had no business with Rachel, and he would find an opportunity soon to tell him so in no uncertain terms.

It was Lucius's third Shabbat in Joseph's house, and he didn't want to think about his time there being almost half over. The rhythm of life with them—with her—was something that felt second nature to him now. The trips to synagogue to hear God's word, the blessings and prayers at meals and other times, knowing Yeshua had made the sacrifice for his sins—all felt so right. He would gladly trade his former life of luxury in Rome for the life he was living right now.

As he walked slowly back from Kabbalat Shabbat with her at his side, he wished he could freeze time. He glanced at her. She was so beautiful, so kind...so beyond his reach. Once more he regretted being the wealthy Roman tribune instead a Jewish wagon maker. A sigh escaped.

"Are you all right, Lucas? We're not going too fast, are we?"

He masked his regret and forced a smile. "No, it's fine. I'm just tired today."

She flashed him that beautiful smile again. "It's a good thing it's Shabbat. We'll get you all rested up before three stars tomorrow."

He nodded so she wouldn't realize his true thoughts. Rest was good, but no amount of rest would solve his real problem.

Joseph began the blessings for the Sabbath meal. Lucius had enjoyed the previous two, but since Joseph had explained what Yeshua had done, every word meant so much more to him.

Joseph was almost to the most important part. "For out of all the nations You chose us and made us holy, and You gave us Your holy Sabbath, in love and favor, as our heritage. Blessed are you LORD, Who sanctifies the Sabbath.*"

Lucius joined them all in the "amen."

"Where two or three are gathered in my name, there am I among them. We acknowledge Your presence, Yeshua, at our Sabbath table. We welcome Your Presence in by asking for the Shekhinah Glory of God to fill our hearts and to give us a sense of communion. Before we drink from this cup, we acknowledge that You, Yeshua, are the vine and we are branches and that our lives are dependent upon You as our Lord and Savior. We sanctify this cup symbolizing the Cup of Salvation that You offer to those who trust in You.*"

As Joseph passed the cup to each of his children in turn, Lucius couldn't take his eyes off it. When it finally reached him, he cradled the cup as he gazed into the ruby liquid. As he lifted it to his lips, he was thanking Yeshua for loving him enough to be the sacrifice for his sins. As the sweet wine flowed across his tongue, he felt the heat and light of God's presence surrounding him. He closed his eyes and drank it all in. When he opened them to hand the cup back to Joseph, the warmth of God's presence remained.

Joseph saw the glow in Lucas's eyes. He was glad he had told this Roman all he needed to know about the faith of his grandfather. The LORD had surely brought him to them for that purpose, and Joseph thanked Him for giving the young man the gift of his own faith.

The LORD had truly been with the Roman, as he had said to Rachel that first day. First the boys found him before the jackal killed him. Then Rachel brought him home where he could heal. Lastly, he found his own faith in Yeshua. Surely the LORD's purpose for him coming to them had now been fulfilled. As soon as the splints came off his leg, he could leave.

Rachel saw his beaming smile, and it filled her heart with even greater love for Lucas. To see him so filled with joy because of his love for God...her heart was almost bursting with happiness for him. The deepest desire of her heart was to marry a man who would share her great love for Yeshua. Now one was standing right there before her. If only Lucas would decide he loved her...like she already loved him.

Lucius was alone at the workbench when Nathaniel rode in to join them for dinner the following Thursday. He glanced up at her brother, then fixed his attention back on the spoke in his clamp. Nathaniel had adopted the habit of mostly ignoring him except when he particularly wanted to pick a fight. That usually didn't happen until sometime during dinner, so Lucius's head jerked up when Nathaniel spoke.

Nathaniel sat leaning on his horse's withers, looking down with a sneer twisting his lip. "I have something to say to you, Greek."

"What would that be, Nathaniel?"

"I don't like you living in this house with my sister. I don't like the way you look at her. I don't like the way you talk to her. I don't like the way you assume you're good enough to be around her."

"Well, since I'm Joseph's guest, not yours, it really doesn't matter what you like."

Lucius had spoken calmly, but his anger began to rise like never before. He fought to push it back down. A fight with her brother when Joseph wasn't there to stop it would be a very bad idea, and it might come to that if he couldn't control his own temper.

Nathaniel sat upright and nudged his horse closer. He loomed over Lucius where he sat on the stool. "Don't start thinking you have any kind of future here. You know that Abba will only let Rachel marry a good Jew. No Greek...or Roman...can ever be worthy of my sister, so you can forget anything you might be hoping for with her."

Lucius pushed on the horse's chest to back him up a little.

"Do you think I'm a fool, Nathaniel? I've lived in Judaea long enough to know what to expect. No lecture from you is needed."

He almost kept the sharp edge off his voice...almost, but not quite. That was more kindling on the coals smoldering in her brother's eyes. Joseph wasn't there to douse any flame, so he'd better not be striking a spark or adding logs to the fire.

Better try to calm the hothead down. "Besides, Rachel doesn't care for me that way, so you don't need to be worried about what I might want."

He watched the red move up Nathaniel's neck and the fire blaze in his eyes. Her brother was still spoiling for a fight, but Lucius was determined to disappoint him. "I want to finish this spoke before dinner. I'm sure you'll enjoy talking to Rachel much more than to me."

He turned his back on Nathaniel and picked up the spokeshave. As he drew it toward himself and watched the curlicue of wood lift away from the half-formed spoke, he heard Nathaniel's horse moving away.

A deep sigh escaped once Nathaniel was out of earshot. He did, indeed, know what to expect. He needed no lecture from Nathaniel to know that the dearest desire of his heart was forever beyond his reach.

It was Shabbat again, and Eli had come to visit after the morning at synagogue. Lucius was sitting on the bench where his leg was more comfortable as Joseph and Eli relaxed on cushions.

Lucius could see why Joseph liked Eli so much. He had yet to hear him say an unkind thing about anyone, just as her father never did. Since the first time he went to synagogue, Eli always made a friendly inquiry about how he was doing whenever he saw him. More than once, he'd imagined how totally pleasant his stay might have been if she were Rachel bat Eli instead.

Joseph glanced at Lucas relaxing as he listened to them talk. Even now, after almost four weeks, he still saw a Roman, and that reminded him that Reuben was dead because of a Roman soldier. He was glad he had let Lucas stay when he was so badly hurt, and he was glad he had told the young Roman about Yeshua, but he still didn't want him sitting there where he would see him the whole afternoon.

"Rachel."

"Yes, Abba?"

"Take Lucas in to rest with his splints off for a while."

Rachel left Asher and Simeon and walked over to Lucas. She offered him her hands to hold for balance as he stood up on his good leg.

"Let's go take care of you, like Abba says."

"You do that better than anyone I've ever known, Rachel. It does feel good to get the splints off for a while."

"I'll rub some oil where they press too hard, like before. You can sleep if you want, and I'll make sure you're safe until you awaken."

"That sounds good to me. Lead the way."

Eli watched him disappear through the doorway, and his eyes warmed. "He is a fine young man, Joseph. It is good that he has been here with you and become a God-fearer. Many of us could see the wisdom of his answer when Benjamin asked if it was the LORD's will that Rome destroyed the temple. For a Greek like him to recognize the power of the LORD so clearly from the beginning—that is an amazing thing."

Joseph nodded. "The LORD probably brought him to us just so he could learn to follow Him. There is even more to it than you know. Lucas has decided to follow Yeshua like you and I do."

Eli grinned. "I rejoice to hear that, but I am not surprised. His hunger for God opened his heart to the gift of salvation that Yeshua brought. The broken leg that brought him here must have been the LORD's will." He shook his head as a wry smile appeared. "It amazes me how often the LORD works his will in our lives through the bad things that happen. It is hard for me sometimes to give thanks in all things, even the bad ones, but who am I to question the LORD's ways?"

Joseph nodded, but he didn't speak. It was hard to see how it could have been the LORD's will for Reuben to be murdered or for Nathaniel to abandon his faith in Yeshua and become a zealot. Surely not everything that was bad could be in accordance with God's will.

Chapter 33

GOOD IN JOSEPH'S EYES

Rabbi Eliezer usually led the synagogue service on Monday, so Lucius was sitting at the back with Simeon again. The reading was about what God had told the Israelites to do when they entered the Promised Land to possess it. There were commands about making no treaties, not intermarrying with the locals, and destroying the altars and idols of the people being driven out before them. All were to make sure God's people didn't turn from Him to the gods of the people already in the land.

Lucius found himself ignoring the discussion that followed as he considered intermarriage. Maybe here was the explanation for why so many of the Jews refused to let their daughters marry someone who wasn't a Jew. But it seemed clear to him that God's reason for that command was only so the sons and daughters of Israel wouldn't turn to the gods of the foreign ones they married rather than staying true to God himself.

He wouldn't lead Rachel away from God. She loved Yeshua so much that she would help him grow stronger in his faith as they enjoyed married life together. Surely that would be pleasing to God, and such an intermarriage would be something that would honor God and be everything He wanted a marriage to be. Was there a possibility that Joseph might understand the command the way he did? If so, maybe it wasn't totally impossible for her father to let Rachel become his wife.

His thoughts were jerked back to the discussion. Or more accurately, the absence of it. A deathly stillness permeated the room. Simeon sat rigid beside him. Benjamin was standing there, glowering at Joseph.

Lucius had missed what had just been said. Benjamin's teeth clenched and his eyes bulged as they spit flames toward Joseph, who had his hands raised in that peaceful gesture he often used toward Benjamin when he wanted to end an argument.

Lucius wasn't expecting what happened next.

Benjamin swung around, and the flames licked at him instead. Benjamin's teeth unclenched as he chomped onto his new target. "The people of God are the descendants of Abraham, Isaac, and Jacob. There is no place among us for people like this Greek." He was shaking an accusing finger at Lucius, whose head snapped back before he froze. "He says he follows the LORD now, but he never kept Torah before he came among us. He has years of sin that cannot be covered without temple sacrifice, and there can be no such sacrifice until the temple is rebuilt."

Benjamin stood glaring at Lucius, his utter disgust with Joseph's guest clear in the flaring of his nostrils and the sneer on his lips.

Lucius didn't intend to respond, but something stirred within. Remaining silent would be wrong. Words sprang up in his mind, and he heard himself speaking.

"The temple will never be rebuilt, Benjamin. The LORD wanted the Roman legions to destroy it, and there's no reason for it ever to be rebuilt. There's no more need for your animal sacrifices to cover sin. The final sacrifice for all sins for all time was Yeshua. It was the LORD's will for Rome to destroy the temple so people would realize the sacrifices would never be needed again."

"Yeshua was nobody, and he did nothing!" Benjamin's eyes bulged again like his head was about to burst. "You've been listening too much to Joseph."

Lucius shook his head. "No. I've listened to what Torah says about sin and to the readings from the prophet Isaiah about what the Messiah would do, and I've thought about why the LORD let Rome destroy the temple. He never would have allowed it if the sacrifices were still needed. Torah teaches that sin is covered only by blood, and Yeshua was the last blood sacrifice that would ever be needed."

Benjamin's face turned redder, and his breathing came fast. He would have answered, but he had no idea what to say. Most of the men were staring at Lucius, and some were obviously considering what he said. Even Rabbi Eliezer was nodding slowly.

Lucius glanced at Joseph and saw something he'd never expected to see—warm eyes and a smile of approval as he nodded in agreement.

Eliezer also smiled at him. "Not quite what we were discussing, Lucas, but an interesting thought anyway." He turned his eyes back on the older men near the front of the room. "Now, as Torah commands us, we—"

◆

As the service ended and the men filed out, Lucius sat very quietly at the back. Some frowned at him, some smiled at him, and some simply looked thoughtful. Joseph was among the last to leave. Simeon rose and handed Lucius his crutch before heading out the door. Joseph stopped and contemplated him.

"You surprised me today, Lucas. I think you surprised everyone."

"I hadn't planned to speak, Joseph. It just came out."

"It was good, Lucas. It was good. Now let's go home." That approving smile flitted across Joseph's face once more before he turned and walked out.

Lucius shook his head in amazement as he followed. He had finally done something good in Joseph's eyes.

Marcus lifted his body armor and slipped it over his head. As he fastened the clasps at the side, his eyebrows dipped and his mouth arched downward. Judaea was a miserably hot place to serve when he had to wear a metal cuirass every time he stepped outside the garrison walls.

It had been four weeks since Marcus had ridden down the road looking for his brother's corpse that wasn't there. It had been two weeks since he'd found Lucius's horse, but no one would believe him. It would be four more weeks until the commander would finally admit Lucius was dead and send the condolence letter to his father that would open the door for him to leave this hostile land.

In the meantime, he needed to buy a horse. He'd overheard the paymaster talking with one of the other officers who was withdrawing money for that purpose. Their snide remarks about him getting his brother killed just so he could get a good horse angered him.

Then he started to think about the three hundred denarii he'd withdrawn to pay the blacksmith. There was nothing to explain why he'd withdrawn it or how he'd spent it. If his brother should return knowing about the hired assassins, he needed something to show for it if the commander should decide to ask.

He'd missed his best opportunity already. Lucius's stallion had been the best horse in the garrison. He could have bought it from the Syrian, but he was too angry to think clearly when the man made the offer. He could have offered much less than the stallion was worth and scared the Syrian into taking it. Then he could have told everyone he'd paid the true value of the horse, and there would have been no money unaccounted for.

He headed toward the paymaster's office. Time to withdraw five hundred denarii and find a decent horse, one that he could claim he'd paid eight hundred for. It galled him to think of the sport others would make of him being overcharged. Still, it was worth being thought a poor judge of horseflesh to avoid being thought a murderer.

The night sky was clear, and the stars seemed to shine with unusual brilliance as Lucius hobbled home from Kabbalat Shabbat beside Rachel. He noticed her gazing upward.

"What are you thinking, Rachel?"

"I was just thinking what a wonderful world it is that the LORD has given us. The stars are so beautiful. Nights like this I just feel so... so content with all the blessings I have." Her eyes were radiant as she graced him with that gentle smile that he so loved to see, but there was too little moonlight for him to see them as clearly as he wished. "Having you here with us has been one of them. You're part of our family now."

If only he could tell her she should become his wife and make her family his for the rest of their lives. An almost overpowering urge to take her in his arms swept through him. It took every bit of self-control he had to keep the crutch under his arm and take that next step instead.

"I can't tell you how many times I've thanked the LORD for Simeon and Asher appearing just when they did. They're like little brothers to me now."

He stopped and faced her. That might be a dangerous thing to do, but he knew his own strength, and it would be enough.

"But that's nothing compared to how I've thanked Him for you."

◆

Rachel held her breath. Was he about to tell her he loved her? That he wanted to marry her as much as she wanted to marry him? To really be family for the rest of their lives?

◆

Lucius felt her looking at him, but in the dark he couldn't see the deep love of a woman for a man that shone in her eyes. If he had, his next words might have been different.

"You're the very best friend I've ever had. You've shown me so much love from the first moment I saw you. I thought I was a dead man, but when I looked into your eyes in the wadi, I saw my future again."

If only he could tell her how much he wanted that future to include her by his side. He started to open his lips, then pressed them together. That was an impossible dream. He was a Roman, Joseph wanted a Jewish son-in-law, and she'd never shown any sign that she loved him as a man rather than a brother, anyway.

He turned and took another step. It was too dangerous to just stand there with her. Once again, he'd almost reached out to pull her into his arms. He wasn't as strong as he thought he was. For her sake and for his, he had to control himself.

He glanced up at the sky. "The stars are beautiful, but God put them beyond our reach."

He was glad it was dark enough that she couldn't see the regret in his eyes. The stars were beyond his reach...just like she was.

Chapter 34

DINNER WITH DANIEL

It was late afternoon Tuesday when Lucius glanced out the gate to see two men turn off the Legio road. A substantial older man in expensive garb and a scrawny young one dressed equally well were riding a pair of fine horses toward the courtyard gate.

"Joseph, Samuel and Daniel are coming."

Joseph struck the red-hot metal twice more before plunging it into the water bucket. The sizzle subsided, and he withdrew the hub ring to place it on the brick bench. He set his tongs and hammer on the bench as well and turned to greet his friend.

He walked toward Samuel with his arms spread. "Shalom, Samuel. It is good to see you again so soon. Can you stay a while?"

"I am headed home, so yes. I have been looking forward to breaking bread with you since we left Caesarea. It is too long since we had time to talk."

Samuel dismounted and tossed his reins to Daniel. Joseph put his arm around his brother-in-law's shoulders as they walked past the workshop. As they were passing, Samuel's eyes settled on Lucius.

"Ah, Lucas. It is good to see you looking so much better." Samuel's smile was warm and friendly.

"It is a pleasure to see you as well, Samuel." A greeting in Greek drew a Greek response.

Joseph's eyebrows dipped. "Aramaic, Lucas."

Samuel turned questioning eyes on Joseph.

Joseph's brows relaxed when his gaze shifted to his friend. "Lucas knows Aramaic well enough to go to synagogue. He has become a God-fearer who follows Yeshua."

Samuel beamed at Lucius and switched their conversation to Aramaic. "So being brought to Joseph's house has been a double blessing to you, Lucas."

"It has, Samuel, and I thank the LORD many times each day."

Daniel finished tying the horses to the post and fixed his eyes on Lucas. The bruises were gone, and the Greek was even more handsome than he remembered. Rugged good looks, broad shoulders, arms like a gladiator—those were bad enough, but for him to follow Yeshua? Nothing was more important to Rachel, so nothing could possibly be worse.

Lucas had turned back to his work without looking at Daniel, and that irked him, too. He should have received the same kind of respectful greeting his father had from some low-class Greek laborer. His eyes threw daggers at the Greek's back before he followed Joseph and Samuel across the courtyard to the canopy. Then his eyes fixed on Rachel as she walked over to greet his father with the warm smile he would have loved to receive himself.

This time he wouldn't make the mistake of giving her the chance to snub him like she had last time. Joseph and his father had seated themselves, so he joined them. Rachel shouldn't think he was desperate to get her to talk with him like she had with the Greek...even though he was.

He'd chosen the cushion that let him look past Joseph and see the Greek without it looking like he was deliberately watching him. With each flex of the Greek's shoulders as he sliced another curlicue off the roughed-out spoke, Daniel's hatred grew.

How could Joseph have taken this Gentile dog into his family the way he had? How could he let a man like that be around Rachel for weeks? Nathaniel had been coming often for dinner. Why hadn't her brother done something about him by now?

Rachel directed a gracious smile at his father, but she seemed to be avoiding eye contact with him.

"I'm so glad you'll be sharing bread with us, Uncle. It won't be long until dinner, but I'll fetch something for you to drink right away."

His father's affection for his niece shone in his eyes and curved his lips. "That would be good, Rachel. It has been a dusty ride."

A quick flash of a smile at his father, and she disappeared into the house. Not once had she looked him in the eye. She avoided looking at him like she was embarrassed. Well, she should be embarrassed by the way she'd treated him last time, but he was willing to overlook that. She was only a weak-headed woman under the spell of the virile Greek, and she would appreciate how lucky she was that he wanted her as his wife as soon as the temptation of that handsome man was gone.

The presence of Samuel and Daniel changed the seating arrangement but not quite the way Lucius expected. Samuel sat, of course, as the most-honored guest to Joseph's right. He'd expected Daniel to take the second-best place to Joseph's left. After the handwashing and blessing God for that commandment, Lucius began heading toward the cushion between Samuel and Rachel. He didn't plan to lower himself to sit until Joseph approved his guess. He didn't want to be presumptuous and, besides, getting down and up was still hard. He didn't want to do it twice. As a Gentile among Jews, he might even be excluded from eating with them entirely, depending on what Samuel thought of Gentiles.

"Lucas." Lucius turned his eyes on Joseph as soon as he spoke. "To my left. Daniel will sit by Samuel."

He would have preferred the less honored place right next to Rachel, but he hobbled obediently to the place Joseph assigned. To be seated just behind Samuel in importance was an honor he hadn't expected. But perhaps it was less an honor for him than a deliberate message to Daniel that he wasn't particularly wanted there. Joseph looked at Daniel the same way he looked at him.

◆

Daniel would have been more upset about being regarded below the Greek if his assigned seat hadn't put him next to Rachel. Joseph's slight lost most of its sting as he watched the Greek struggle to lower himself to the cushion between Joseph and Simeon. He had to angle his broken leg past Joseph, and that put his left shoulder facing her. He would have to twist around even to look directly at her. The Greek wasn't likely to be keeping most of her attention on himself when he couldn't even face her easily.

Everyone settled into their assigned places, and Joseph began the blessings by lifting the plate of bread. "Blessed are You, LORD our God, King of the universe, Who brings forth bread from the earth.*"

Daniel watched Lucas. His eyes were fixed on the wine pitcher as Joseph began to fill the cups. "Blessed are You, LORD our God, King of the universe, Who creates the fruit of the vine.*"

For Daniel, the blessings were mere formalities. The Greek's expression mirrored that of Joseph. Daniel glanced at Rachel. The three of them and Simeon...all looked like the words were spoken to someone who was there with them and listening.

Joseph finished speaking the blessings over the rest of the food. After tearing his own piece from the loaf, he passed the bread plate to Samuel, who took his share. When the plate came to Daniel, he tore off his piece and then offered it to Rachel with his left hand to make it easy for her to brush his hand with hers as she took it.

He watched her face as he offered, hoping for a smile and a blush as she let her fingers brush his. What he got was cool eyes as she reached for the plate with her left hand to avoid touching him. She tore only a tiny portion from the bread and was about to pass the plate to Asher.

Daniel caught the twisting of the Greek in his peripheral vision. Rachel immediately looked toward him. He smiled at her with tightened lips and shook his head once. The warmest smile he'd seen on her all evening lit her eyes as well. She took more bread, about half a portion, before passing the plate to Asher. The Greek's eyes met hers again as he nodded once.

Daniel's lips almost disappeared as he squeezed them together. Cold to him, warm to the Greek. Speaking to each other without a single word. It was enough to kill a man's appetite.

It was enough to make him want to kill the Greek who was stealing Rachel's affection, but killing her favorite wouldn't win her back to him. No, Nathaniel would have to get rid of this rival for him, and then Rachel would come to her senses and decide she wanted him after all.

It was early morning before Daniel had a chance to speak to Nathaniel alone. After following his cousin out to the stable, he stood stroking the horse's neck as Nathaniel tossed the saddle on his back and cinched it in place. Nathaniel was about to mount to ride to Sepphoris when he finally spoke.

"You know we stopped at your house on the way up from Caesarea." He tightened his lips and shook his head. "I'm really worried about Rachel. That Greek. He spent the whole meal looking at her like she was going to belong to him. He'd look; she'd blush. Teasing her the whole meal with those smiles. It was embarrassing to watch her act like he interested her. I don't know why your father doesn't see the danger. He's almost well, and I think he's more of a threat to her every day."

Nathaniel turned from the horse. "I don't like him there, either, but Abba watches him."

Daniel's mouth curved down as he shook his head. "No, I don't think he does. Not close enough. I think he has your father fooled. He seated him on his left last night, like he was a good friend. Let him be part of his conversation with Abba. If she were my sister, I wouldn't put up with him being there. Not with the way he looks at her."

"I've told him before that Rachel's not for him. He knows I'm watching out for her. He's afraid of what I might do to him. Every time we almost get into a fight, he backs down."

"But what if you're not there when he gets a chance to do something? I don't trust him."

Daniel watched the lighting and thunder build in Nathaniel's eyes. "I'm going for dinner tomorrow. I'll make sure he knows what will happen if he does anything."

A slow smile twisted Daniel's lips as he watched Nathaniel ride away. Mission accomplished.

Chapter 35

A LIMIT TO HIS PATIENCE

It was Thursday, one of Nathaniel's usual days for coming to dinner. Lucius expected to be ignored. That had become Nathaniel's usual response to his presence, and that was just fine with him.

He was alone in the workshop when Nathaniel rode through the gate. He glanced at her brother for a quick gauge of what the mood was likely to be at dinner. What he saw dragged a sigh from him.

Nathaniel's eyes were drilling into him as he rode directly toward the workbench. A black scowl pulled his mouth in a downward arc and made his two eyebrows almost merge into a single one.

Nathaniel reined in just short of the workbench and turned his horse so Lucius had a full view of his muscled chest and arms as big as some men's thighs. He rested his left fist on his hip as his right hand fingered the reins.

"Abba's not here now to protect you, Greek, and it's time for you to understand something. Understand it clearly. You're going to leave here the moment you're healed enough to walk. Don't think you'll do anything with Rachel before you go. Daniel saw even more than what you've let me see. I swear, if you do anything to hurt her...anything...I'll break your neck."

Lucius had planned to never lose his temper with this arrogant, angry man-child, but suddenly...suddenly that required more self-control than even he had. His breath came fast and his nostrils flared.

"Your cousin is a fool or a liar. He didn't see anything because there was nothing to see. I would never do anything to hurt Rachel...

or her brothers or Joseph, for that matter. As far as you breaking my neck, you could only do that if I choose to let you." The knife edge on his voice sharpened still more as he rose to his feet. "And I won't let you, Nathaniel."

Nathaniel's eyebrows rose and his back straightened as the mild-mannered Greek assumed the stance of a warrior. Chest out, arms flexed at his side, hands fisting then flexing. Even with the splints, he looked ready for battle.

Lucius watched anger replace shock as a scowling Nathaniel prepared to dismount. Her brother was ready to engage. Could he stop him without hurting him? Or getting hurt himself? The rank stupidity of the challenge he'd just issued struck him full force.

He settled back onto the stool and raised his hands in the pacifying gesture Joseph always used with Benjamin. Calmness coated his joking tone. "On second thought, we probably shouldn't get into a wrestling match. You might rebreak my leg, and then I'd be here for another eight weeks. That doesn't sound bad to me, but you might feel different about it."

Nathaniel hesitated. His jaw clenched, but he remained mounted.

"Nathaniel!" Both heads turned to see her trotting toward them.

◆

Rachel stepped out of the house to find a terrifying sight. Lucas was standing up, tensed and ready to fight. Nathaniel sat bolt-upright on his horse, hackles up like an angry dog, glaring down at Lucas. Abba was nowhere to be seen.

Her breath stopped. Then Lucas sat down on his stool, raised both hands, and looked as relaxed as ever.

"Nathaniel!" She started toward them. *Oh, LORD! Don't let them fight. Please protect Lucas.*

Both men looked when she called, but it was Nathaniel who held her gaze. The fury burning in his eyes faded as she got closer. By the time she reached him, he was smiling at her.

Lucas turned back to the bench. Nathaniel threw one last set of dagger-eyes at him before dismounting to let Rachel hug him.

She wrapped her arm around his. "I'm so glad you're here. I've missed you. Come keep me company until Abba returns from Eli's."

"All right, little one. You can tell me what you've been doing since Sunday."

Without even a quick glance back at Lucas, she led Nathaniel away.

Lucius picked up the spokeshave and drew it along the wood, releasing another curlicue.

He frowned as he slowly shook his head. *LORD, give me patience with him.*

He'd almost broken his word to her. He almost let her zealot brother push him past his limits of control. He would not let that happen again.

He glanced out the gate. Joseph was almost back from Eli's house. With Joseph there, their evening conversation should be cooler...or at least safer. Her father might be needed to control them both.

It had been a quiet week at the garrison. Sabbath would start at sundown, promising another quiet day tomorrow. The commander placed his hands behind his head and arched his back. The reports were finished, and he expected an evening of relaxation with his wife and children.

The click of hobnail sandals trotting down the hallway drew his attention.

"Commander." The soldier slapped his chest with his fist. "A convoy has been attacked on the road to Ptolemais near Hannathon."

"What happened?"

"Not a robbery. A quick hit-and-run with the wagons left alone. Zealots after the escorts."

"Any casualties?"

"Two injured. They're with the physician now. One dead. Lucilius Barbatus. The attackers were mounted and got away."

The commander's jaw twitched. The dead soldier was the only son of a centurion who was a good friend. He'd been a young man himself when they served together in the Parthian campaign, and he would have been killed were it not for Sextus Barbatus.

The commander stood. "You're dismissed."

The soldier struck his chest again, turned on his heels, and strode from the room.

The commander lowered his head. His hand fisted and slammed down on the table top. *May the flaming wrath of the gods consume every single zealot in this accursed province! May the fires of Hades consume that Jew who's made me have to write one more condolence letter to a father who's lost his son...to my friend.*

Marcus entered the commander's office in time to see him raise his fist to strike the table again. The fist froze in midair as the commander fixed burning eyes on him.

"What do you want, Drusus?"

Marcus's head jerked back. The blackest scowl twisted the commander's lips down as his eyes flamed. "I can wait."

"All you ever do is wait, Drusus. You're supposed to be figuring out what will cool down the rebellion. What have you done? Nothing. Not one single thing since your brother disappeared. You need to be out there with the people like Lucius was if you expect to figure out how to get this endless cycle of attack and reprisal to stop."

Marcus squared his shoulders as his eyes smoldered at the attack. "Lucius didn't do anything either, other than getting himself killed by being out with the Jews."

"Your brother was a brave man. He took risks to do what needed to be done, and maybe it got him killed, but at least he was man enough to take the risk. If you don't have the courage to do the same, there's no point in you being here. A tribune of Rome should be a man of courage in everything he does, no matter how difficult or dangerous the assignment. If you can't do that, then you should go back and be a political lapdog to the governor in Caesarea. There's no place for cowards in my garrison."

Marcus bristled as the commander's eyes bored into him. "I won't leave until my brother returns or I'm sure he's dead. I report to the governor, not you."

The commander's lips disappeared as his eyebrows plunged down. "No, you don't report to me, so get out of here. I have too much to do to waste my time with you today."

Marcus turned and strode from the room.

The commander sat down and drew a papyrus sheet from the table drawer. He ran his hand through his hair before picking up a pen. As he dipped it into the ink bottle, the deepest sigh escaped. It was time to write the letter.

Marcus's anger cooled almost as soon as he stepped out the door. The commander had just given him the perfect excuse for leaving Sepphoris as soon as Lucius was declared dead. He certainly would corroborate Marcus's claim that he was upset and unable to forget what had happened to his brother. When he wrote Father, he would find the perfect way to use the commander's words to protect himself from suspicion. What did it matter if the commander thought him a coward as long as he made it easy to withdraw first to Caesarea and then back to Rome?

Chapter 36

WORST DAY OF HIS LIFE

It was Tuesday, and Joseph had gone midmorning to make a delivery. Lucius was alone in the workshop. He'd healed enough to stand while he worked today. In another week or so, he would be leaving.

His mouth turned down at the thought. He was going to miss many things when he left, and helping Joseph was one of them. He'd grown to really enjoy working with wood. There was deep satisfaction in seeing a rough piece of wood turn into something useful that even had a certain beauty to it.

Something was crawling on the back of his neck. He reached up with his left hand and brushed it. Nothing there. When he took his hand down, the feeling was still there. Then he heard a faint rustle behind him.

He turned from the workbench to find Rachel standing about eight feet behind him, tears trickling down her cheeks as she silently gazed at him. Deep pain clouded her cinnamon eyes.

"Rachel? What's wrong?" He placed the crutch under his arm and took a step toward her. "Did I do something?"

She held up her hand to stop him. "No, it's nothing you've done. It's just...well, I was thinking about Reuben, and you looked too much like him for a moment. You standing there in his tunic, using the tools he used." She paused to wipe the tears from her cheeks. "I miss him so much...we were twins, and we were always like this." She clasped her hands. "We could talk about anything, and he always made me laugh." She wiped away more tears and gave him a watery smile.

216

He took another step toward her. Her whole family was still grieving the death of her brother. They often spoke of Reuben but never about how he died. Was there something odd about it? Sometime they even changed the subject so quickly if he was listening, like there was something they were hiding from him. "How long has it been?"

"It was exactly six months ago today."

That was the same day he killed the unarmed youth in the action against the zealots. His stomach began to knot.

"Did he die here at home?" *Oh, LORD, let the answer be yes.*

"No, he was in Gath-Hepher."

The knot in his stomach tightened. It was the same town. He was afraid to ask the next question, but he was unable to stop himself.

"How did he die?"

She was silent for a moment. "You don't want to know. You won't like the answer."

His chest tightened, and his heart recoiled like metal under the blows of Joseph's hammer. Why didn't she want to tell him? Was it because she suspected he might be to blame? No, that couldn't be. She couldn't know he'd been there. She turned her face to the ground. What didn't she want him to see in her eyes?

"But I do want to know. Really. Tell me." He had taken another step toward her and now he placed his hands on her arms. His crutch rested precariously against his side.

She turned her face upward to look into his eyes. She took a deep breath before answering. "He was trying to get Nathaniel to come back home when the Roman troops came. One of them killed him."

The knot was replaced by a sinking, twisting feeling. He was spiraling down into a black pit. The feeling of wanting to vomit slammed into him just as it had that day as he watched the youth die. The bed he slept in, the clothes he wore—all had belonged to the teenage boy he'd killed by mistake. The boy who smiled and forgave him as he died.

He alone was the cause of all the pain and grief for these people who'd only shown him kindness and mercy. The sword in the sack at the foot of his bed had sliced open the hearts of this family he'd grown to love.

She lowered her face as the tears began to roll down her cheeks again.

"I should have told you before, but I didn't want you to feel we might blame you for what another soldier did." She looked up into his eyes. "I don't blame you at all. But sometimes it just hurts too much to remember..."

The rivulet of tears was turning into a river, and he was drowning in the flood. She'd never let herself cry like that in front of him before.

Piercing guilt ripped through him. How could that not show on his face? To keep her from seeing, he pulled her into his arms and held her. His crutch slipped from his side and fell to the ground.

She wrapped her arms around him and clung to him like a tree trunk in a wadi during a flash flood. She let the tears flow, and he fought to keep his head above that torrent before he drowned in it. How he had longed to hold her like this, to feel her soft body pressed against his and her arms wrapped around his chest, but today they only felt like iron bands that constricted his ribs and kept him from breathing. Each catch of her breath as she wept was like a knife thrust into his gut.

If only he could undo that day. If only he had seen the boy didn't have a sword before he drove his own into the boy's chest.

He rested his cheek on the top of her head. "I'm sorry, Rachel. I am so sorry. I'd give anything to bring your brother back." His voice caught. *Oh, God! I'm the one who broke her heart.*

◆

Rachel pulled back and looked up at him. Anguish filled his eyes as he looked into hers. Then he tore them away to look past her, but the pain in them remained.

She rested her head against his chest again. She could hear his heartbeat, and something about that steady rhythm was so comforting. He understood her grief, and he shared it with her. If only he would understand she loved him and share that with her, too.

◆

She pulled back again and smiled up at Lucius. Her eyes were warm, and that warmth was enough to sear his very soul. He couldn't bear to have her looking at him with eyes of affection when he deserved a look of hatred. She didn't know she was in the arms of the one who'd killed the brother she loved so dearly. He placed his hand on the back of her head and guided her cheek back onto his chest so he couldn't see her eyes.

He would gladly embrace all the pain in the wadi again to drag his thoughts away from this anguish in his soul. She should know he was the one who killed Reuben. He should tell her, but how was he ever going to do that? He should tell her...but not today. Today he just couldn't bear having her know.

The tears finally stopped, so Rachel stepped back. She leaned over, picked up his crutch, and handed it to him. She managed a trembling smile as she flicked the last of the tears from her cheeks with her fingertips.

"I got your chest wet. I'm sorry. I don't want you to feel bad about Reuben's death. It wasn't your fault. Besides, Reuben loved Yeshua as much as any of us, and we know his death was just the beginning of eternal life with Him in Paradise." She sniffed and gave a small shrug. "It's just that we loved having him here with us so much."

Tears started to form in her eyes again. She gave him a watery smile. Then she raised her hand to keep him from following her as she spun to go back to the house.

He made no effort to follow. It would be a dagger twisting in his heart to watch the new flood of tears that she didn't want him to see.

As she walked away with her head down, he tipped his head back and rolled his eyes at the sky. *Oh, God! Why did he have to be Reuben?*

He would have sworn the day he killed the unarmed boy was the worst day of his life. He was wrong. This one was so much worse.

Asher was kicking up the dust as he and Simeon strolled down the street after their lessons at the synagogue. Simeon stopped at the sheep pen to check one of the ewes that had been favoring her rear leg, but Asher was in a hurry to get something to eat. He entered the courtyard just in time to see Rachel with her arms wrapped around Lucas, her cheek pressed against his chest as he held her close. He froze by the gate, his eyes riveted on the pair. Rachel had obviously been crying, and Lucas looked like Abba did when Nathaniel brought Reuben home. Then Rachel had walked away with her head down, and Lucas was staring up at the sky.

Simeon came around the corner and almost ran over his little brother. "Don't just stop by the gate like that without warning me."

"But I just saw something, Simeon."

"What?"

"Lucas. He had his arms around Rachel, and she was crying."

Simeon's eyes focused first on Rachel as she entered the house, then on Lucas as he slowly shook his head while he hobbled back to the workbench.

"Should I tell Abba?" Asher looked up at his older, wiser brother for guidance.

"No, don't say anything about it to Abba. It's nothing for him to worry about. Lucas was just hugging Rachel to comfort her. You know how Rachel always hugs you when you're crying."

Asher nodded. Everything was fine if Simeon thought nothing was wrong. Simeon was twelve. He understood things better.

"Let's go eat." Asher started toward the door where Rachel had disappeared.

"You go on. I want to ask Lucas a question. I'll catch up with you."

◆

Lucius turned from the bench when he heard Simeon walking up behind him. His breath caught when saw Simeon's grim look. He tried to mask the alarm those straight lips triggered. Simeon smiled even more than Rachel did. What if the boys had seen Rachel in his arms?

"How was *bet talmud* today?"

"Good." Simeon paused, which did nothing to ease Lucius's anxiety. "Lucas, Asher just saw you. I told him not to tell Abba, but I want to know what's going on." He paused again. "Do you like Rachel?"

Lucius took a deep breath before speaking what was true yet deceptive. "Your sister is the kindest person I've ever known. I think everyone who knows her must like her." He was hoping against hope that he wouldn't have to answer Simeon's real question.

"I mean do you really like her, you know, like a man likes a woman?"

Simeon's eyes were drilling into him. If he wasn't honest with Simeon right then, Joseph would know about the embrace before dinner. That would be the end of his sanctuary there, the end of his time with these people who'd become so important to him, the end of his time with the woman he loved.

"Yes. I think she's the most amazing woman I've ever known. But you don't have to worry about me doing anything about that. I would never do anything to hurt her. I don't plan to ever tell her how I feel. It would be pointless. Joseph would never allow her to marry me, even if she wanted to. He'll only let her marry a good Jew. I can't hope for anything else."

The serious look disappeared from Simeon's face and was replace with a sly smile. "Abba will try to do what would please Yeshua, no matter how hard it is for him. Maybe it isn't as hopeless as you think."

Lucius shook his head. "He'd never let me anywhere near her if he knew I was Roman instead of Greek."

Simeon grinned. "He already knows. He's known from the beginning. Rachel would never lie to Abba."

Simeon's words were like a gut punch. So that was why her father acted so strangely, treating him well but never quite welcoming him. Several times the first week he was with them, he'd overheard her reminding her father that he was doing it for Yeshua. Rachel and Joseph and the two younger boys would do anything for Yeshua. Even so, how could Joseph stand to have him there at all after Reuben's death, him just being a Roman soldier? And what would Joseph do if he knew he'd been helping the Roman who actually killed his son?

"Don't worry about Abba hearing about today. I told Asher that you were only comforting Rachel like she comforts him. I told him Abba doesn't need to know, and he'll follow my lead." Simeon slapped Lucius on his upper arm. "Hope is always a good thing. You should give it a chance. I think Rachel likes you, too."

He patted his stomach. "I'm starving, so I'd better go get something to eat before Asher gobbles down everything."

Lucius watched Simeon's back until he disappeared into the house. He ran his fingers through his hair as the deepest sigh drained his lungs.

Simeon could think what he wanted, but it probably was hopeless. It wasn't entirely what Joseph thought that would determine their fate. Rachel could never love him if she knew he was the one who killed Reuben, and he didn't think he could ask her to. It was too much to ask anyone to forgive. Before there could be a future for them, he would have to tell her, but after he told her, she'd want no future with him at all.

Chapter 37

Not Much Longer

Wednesday was a big day for Simeon, and he could hardly contain his excitement as they ate the midday meal. Today was the day he would begin training at the forge with Joseph. His eyes were glowing, and Lucius could see how proud he was that his father had finally decided he was ready to take on the work of a man.

Simeon was almost bouncing as he and Lucius walked out to the workshop together.

"I've been looking forward to this for so long. I was a little younger than Asher then, but I still I remember when Abba started Reuben at the forge. It's the sign that Abba thinks I'm becoming a man."

Simeon was grinning ear to ear. Regret tinged Lucius's smile as he thought back to what his own father had thought was the proper transition from childhood. It hadn't been graduating to the work of a man. It was his father complaining that he couldn't take him to the orgies that would make him a man because his grandfather had forbidden such things.

"Your ribs are probably healed enough now. Is Abba going to have you learn the forge, too?" Simeon's eyes perked up at the possibility of them learning together.

Lucius hadn't considered that before. As he gazed at Simeon's eager face, the prospect of the coming goodbye began to punch a hole through his heart. How little time he had left with this boy he'd grown to love like a brother.

"No. There's not enough time left before I have to leave for it to be worth Joseph's effort to train me."

Some of the excitement drained from Simeon's face as he spoke. "I hadn't thought of that."

Joseph turned from the forge and stood with his hands on his hips. "There is work to be done, Simeon. Time to begin."

Simeon's eyes regained their sparkle. "Coming, Abba."

As he turned and hurried toward his father, Lucius's chest tightened a little more. His final goodbye to Rachel wasn't the only one that would rend his heart.

As Lucius and Rachel began their slow walk home from synagogue Thursday morning, he was very quiet. He was trying to mask the sadness in his eyes, but he wasn't sure he was succeeding. They were most of the way home when she finally spoke.

"What are you thinking about, Lucas?"

"Forgiveness."

"Forgiveness? What about it?"

"How hard it is. Hard to forgive others. Harder to forgive yourself. I wondered for a long time why Joseph didn't want me here. Since you told me about Reuben, I think I know. A Roman soldier killed Reuben. How does a father forgive something like that? Every time he looks at me, he sees the man responsible."

"In the beginning, maybe that was so. But you're not the man who killed Reuben. I don't think Abba sees you the same way he did before he got to know you. You haven't done anything he needs to forgive."

Lucas gazed into those eyes that looked at him with such trust. She didn't realize he'd spoken the absolute truth. The knowledge that he was that very man tore into him. He ought to tell her. He almost started to, but she was looking at him as if he were a dear friend, and he just couldn't. He couldn't bear seeing the pain in her eyes that confession would bring.

Even worse, that gentle acceptance of him that she'd shown from the very beginning would surely be replaced by her wanting to have nothing to do with him. He wasn't strong enough to face that. He had so little time left with her, anyway. He couldn't bear to ruin the last few days of this best time of his life.

"Every man does things that need to be forgiven. I know I have. I know God has forgiven me for what I've done. I've even been forgiven by the person I hurt most, but I can't forgive myself." He looked into those beautiful eyes that shone with sympathy. "Even you would be unable to forgive me if you knew everything I've done."

◆

Rachel longed to take away the sadness in his eyes. "I could forgive you anything, Lucas." *Anything...because I love you.*

She almost spoke her love for him, but she stopped herself at the last moment. He'd given her no reason to think he loved her like that, and he was leaving so soon. Too soon. How had seven weeks together passed so swiftly, capturing her heart and leaving his still free? "Yeshua told us we're forgiven only as much as we forgive others."

◆

Lucius saw once more that gentle smile that had comforted him in the wadi. How he would have loved to see a smile that bespoke the love of a woman for a man, but maybe it was better he didn't. Joseph would never let her marry him. It was best if only his heart was broken when it was time to leave.

They reached the gate. It was time for work, and he was glad of it. These quiet walks with her were precious things, but sometimes the most precious things were what can hurt the most.

Lucius braced himself when Nathaniel rode into the courtyard for Thursday dinner. Her brother's mouth tightened and his eyebrows dipped until they almost merged. Joseph wasn't working at the forge, so he rode over so close that his horse was almost pushing Lucius off his stool.

"So, Greek, that leg of yours must be almost healed. As soon as those splints come off, it's time for you to leave."

Lucius was in no mood for discussing his health with Nathaniel at that moment. He stood and placed the crutch under his arm. Then he patted the horse's neck before he pushed steadily to move the animal away from him. He wasn't going to let her zealot brother rile him this time. He'd promised her, and he intended to keep that promise.

"I'll leave when Joseph and I think it's time. We can make that decision without your help." He punctuated his statement with a tolerant smile.

Nathaniel's blood started to heat. There was nothing that made him angry quicker than the calm way Lucas disregarded his attempts to pick a fight. Treating him like an indulgent uncle would treat a child—the Greek dog had no right to do that.

He still couldn't get a rise out of him using insults to Rome. Maybe he was that tribune, maybe not. The way Lucas had challenged him last Thursday made him think he might be, but then he backed away from the fight, like always. Could a Roman tribune be that much of a coward? Or was it all an act? Either way, he had no business near Rachel. Just thinking about that threw fuel on the fire.

Lucius saw Nathaniel's temper rising. As much as he might like to tell her brother what he really thought of him, at least one of them needed to act like an adult if he was to prevent a fight like he'd promised her. He'd lost his temper once before, and it almost turned into one. Today would not be a repeat.

Rachel came out of the house and saw her brother crowding Lucius with his horse.

"Nathaniel! Welcome. Come talk to me."

She started walking over to break it up. With a final glare at Lucius, Nathaniel swung his horse away. "I'll be right there, little one, as soon as I take care of my horse."

Lucius sighed. There'd be a heaping serving of hostility at dinner if the start of Nathaniel's visit was any indication.

The first part of dinner was calm, and Lucius began to think their short skirmish would be the whole battle. Then Nathaniel began talking about what was going on with Samuel's family.

"I think Samuel is going to be coming this way soon. Daniel, too, if he doesn't have something else more important going on." Nathaniel grinned at Rachel. "There's someone here he really wants to see, but he's been very busy with...some of his friends."

Joseph frowned. "I don't want to hear about your zealot cousin and what he is doing."

"I know you don't agree with me, Abba, but the zealots are serving the LORD, and their swords are making a fitting sacrifice to Him. I'm proud to say I agree with them."

Nathaniel glared at Lucius, as if daring him to finally betray himself as Roman. Lucius glanced at Joseph and saw the pain in his eyes as he heard his son's words.

This dinner might be his last with Nathaniel. He drew a deep breath as his lips tightened. For Joseph's sake, he would speak the truth that would drive Nathaniel from his father again if Joseph were to say it. He'd gladly risk the son's wrath for the sake of the father. *God, please help this lost son see the truth before it's too late.*

Lucius squared his shoulders and leaned in. "You think they're serving the LORD? Have you ever driven a sword into someone and watched the life fade from their eyes? It can haunt you, Nathaniel. Sometimes it feels like a part of you dies, too. It's bad enough when you do it to protect yourself or someone else. That's only killing. But then there's murder. When the Jews in the Kitos rebellion killed hundreds of thousands of men, women, and children just because they weren't Jews, that was murder. When the zealots kill the family of a Roman soldier or a tax collector, that's murder. That's not just killing as a soldier in a holy war to free Israel from a conqueror."

He watched Nathaniel getting angrier with each word he spoke, but he didn't care. What he was telling him had to be spoken before Nathaniel went past the point of no return.

"If you think these zealot murders are pleasing to the LORD, you're a fool. You think the Romans are evil because they try to maintain the peace and hunt the zealots that are committing murder. Sometimes they end up killing innocent people, too, but they don't know the LORD and what He commanded. You do, and so do your zealot friends. What do you think the LORD thinks about them deliberately spilling innocent blood? About you if you approve of the murders? You know what the LORD wants. You know what Yeshua commanded. Don't break your father's heart by abandoning everything the LORD has taught you and dying in your sin."

Nathaniel's nostrils were flared, and he had to unclench his jaw to speak. "How dare you lecture me? No Greek has a right to tell a Jew what would please the LORD!"

Nathaniel started to rise, but Joseph pushed him back down.

"Enough. We will talk of this no more tonight."

Rachel reached over and touched Nathaniel's hand. When he turned to look at her, tears filled her eyes. "Please, Nathaniel. No more."

He took a deep breath and blew it out to calm himself. "All right, little one. No more tonight."

Joseph turned toward Asher, eager to start a different conversation before Lucius and his son started to fight again. "So, we are ready to hear what you learned in *bet sefer* today."

As Asher began his recitation, Lucius looked at Rachel. She wiped away the tears and her lips quivered as she smiled at him. Tears because of his fight with her brother. Even though he wasn't sorry about saying anything he'd said, he was sorry he'd made her cry.

◆

But the fight hadn't brought forth Rachel's tears. They were for Lucas. He was about to return to that world where he must kill or be killed, where what he had to do would haunt him, and where he would struggle with forgiving himself.

She longed to draw his hand to her cheek and tell him he didn't have to live that way. There was a choice. He could live a life free of all that pain. If only he would choose to stay with them...with her...and live in peace.

Lucius sat in silence on the bench. This might be his last Shabbat with this family he'd grown to love. Even if it wasn't the last, there couldn't be more than one or two more. He didn't want to think about that, but it kept popping back into his mind. Soon there would be no more of Rachel lighting the lamp, no more hearing Torah and the prophets in synagogue, no more slow walks home in the dark with her, no more drinking of the wine of remembrance of what Yeshua had done. He sighed.

◆

Joseph appraised Lucas as he sat on the bench. In two days, it would be seven weeks since he came to them. He was a young, healthy man. His leg should be healed enough to remove the splints. It was time to start building back muscle so he could leave.

His mouth curved up at the corners. Not much, but some as he thought of what that would mean.

Lucas had been brought to them by the LORD's will. He had no doubt of that. The Roman's hunger for God's word and his eager acceptance of Yeshua as Messiah proved it. Perhaps the LORD had also meant his coming to be the means for bringing Nathaniel home, at least to visit.

But even after seven weeks, Joseph saw a Roman soldier every time he looked at Lucas. The Romans had killed Reuben. They might some-day kill Nathaniel, if he didn't come to his senses in time. He'd been obedient to Yeshua's commands, but he'd had his Roman houseguest long enough.

♦

"Lucas, how is your leg feeling?"

Lucius's eyebrows rose then settled at the question. "Good."

"Do you think it is ready for the splits to come off?"

Lucius didn't like the direction of the conversation but only be-cause he knew what the splits coming off would mean—the end of his time with her.

"Maybe. I'm not sure."

"Today when you rest without them, don't put them back on. You should be fine with just the crutch."

Lucius nodded his agreement. He had no basis to argue with Jo-seph other than his desire to prolong his stay.

"Rachel, take care of Lucas and his splints."

"Yes, Abba." Lucius had already risen when she walked to his side. "Let's go in, Lucas."

Once more he sat on the bed and swung his leg up. She stepped close as he lay back on the pillow. He watched her face as she loosened the cloth strips and lifted the spokes away for the last time.

"I guess I won't need to stay with you to make sure you don't hurt yourself with these off." A wistful look filled her eyes.

"No, but I wouldn't mind if you kept me company anyway. We can just talk."

"What would you like to talk about?"

His heart warmed as her eyes lit up. She was glad he'd asked her to stay.

"Oh, anything. Maybe about what it was like growing up in your family with Joseph as a father." He sighed. "I wish I'd had what you had...what you have."

"I can do that, but you'll probably find it boring. I'll try to think of some funny stories from when we were little." She patted his arm like she had so many times before. "Then you can tell me some of your sto-ries, too."

As he listened to her voice and watched her eyes, he tried to push back the thought that this would probably be the last Sabbath he would ever spend with her. A week from now he would once more be the Roman tribune relaxing in the garrison in Sepphoris, and Sabbath would have been reduced to a day when the zealots mostly left the Roman soldiers in peace.

Chapter 38

DUTY

On Sunday right after the midday break, Joseph harnessed the donkey and hooked it up to the cart he'd just finished. He'd promised immediate delivery upon completion, and he was eager to keep that promise like he always had before his two sons were gone.

Rachel waved goodbye as Joseph drove away. As she turned back into the courtyard, her eyes fell on Lucas at the workbench. She fought a sigh as she contemplated him standing there.

It had been seven weeks since Simeon found him in the wadi. The splints were off, and he was no longer using the crutch to walk around the courtyard. He did still limp because he favored his bad leg, and he still wasn't walking very far before resting. His broken bones might be completely healed even now, but it was certain that he would be healed enough to leave within the week. A choking tightness surrounded her heart again as that thought darkened the future.

That special smile greeted her when she walked over to stand beside him.

He released the finished spoke from the clamp and handed it to her. "Ready for your inspection." A big grin made his eyes twinkle.

She slid her hand up and down the spoke, caressing its smooth curves. He was so good at this. It really was a thing of beauty. She kept sliding her hand, trying to decide what to say to him.

His twinkle faded. "Rachel? Is there something wrong?"

"No...well...yes."

"What is it? Can I help?" His eyes had turned solemn, and she heard it in his voice even as she kept her eyes off his.

"What are we going to do when you leave?" She kept looking at the spoke. She was afraid she might cry if she looked into his eyes. "You've become like family, to me and Simeon at least. And I don't know what Abba is going to do when you leave and he has to do all the work by himself again."

She kept running her hand up and down the spoke. "You could stay, you know. Everyone at your garrison must think you're dead by now. They won't be expecting you to come back. You could stay on with us and work with Abba. It may not seem so to you, but I'm sure he would be glad if you did. So would Simeon...and so would I."

◆

Just having her standing so close was all it took to make Lucius want to wrap her in his arms and hold her forever, but he'd trained himself to only smile. That was all a Roman would ever be allowed. At that moment, he would have gladly traded his Roman birthright, the Drusus fortune, anything and everything to be a simple Jewish wagon maker.

If she had looked at his eyes, she would have seen how much he longed to do exactly what she was suggesting. Her words had broken through his defenses, and his true feelings were momentarily exposed. He loved her so deeply it ripped at his guts to even think about leaving. He would give anything to have her by his side as his wife for the rest of their lives.

But he knew Joseph would never let him marry her. He was now a God-fearer who followed Yeshua, just like them, but he was also the Roman soldier who'd killed Reuben. Joseph would never let her marry a Roman...never, and if her father ever learned he was the Roman who killed his son, he'd be lucky if he only banished him from this house forever.

It would kill him to watch her marry another man, and that was exactly what she would do someday. She was so kind and loving toward him, but she'd never given him any reason to believe she was in love with him. None at all. If she ever found out he'd killed Reuben, she might not hate him, but she'd have every right to. He couldn't bear that, either.

All things considered, it was best for him to leave as soon as he could. It took all the strength he had to once more mask the love his eyes revealed and speak the words he must.

"I can't stay, Rachel. It's my duty to return to the garrison. I'm going to miss you all, but I need to leave soon."

◆

Rachel nodded. Then, without ever looking at his face, she turned and walked back into the house. She managed to hold herself together until she was in the darkened room. Then she sat on her bed and buried her face in her hands. She rocked and rocked as she fought to keep the sobs convulsing her whole body silent. He mustn't hear and come to investigate. He mustn't know how much his decision hurt her. She didn't want him to feel guilty for causing her pain.

Tear after tear dropped to the floor until their separate circles merged. The man she loved with every fiber of her being didn't love her enough to want to stay. He would leave, and she would never see him again.

After a few minutes, she straightened up and wiped the last of the tears away. Abba mustn't think she'd been crying when he returned. He'd want to know why, and she didn't want to tell him she'd given her heart to the Roman he'd never wanted there in the first place. The Roman who didn't love her like she loved him. The Roman who chose duty to Rome over staying with her.

Nathaniel joined them for Sunday dinner, as had become his custom since he started checking up on Lucas of Corinth. Something was very different that night. He wasn't sure what had caused it, but he was very glad to see it.

Each visit, he'd become more worried about how Rachel treated the Greek when they were eating. He'd told Daniel she was so attentive to him because his splinted leg made it hard for him to reach things as he sat on the cushion, but he'd known that wasn't the only reason since the first time he watched them. He didn't like the way the Greek responded to her attentions, and he hated how his every thank-you drew such happy smiles and sparkles to her eyes. He couldn't stand the way they talked together with him smiling so much and her rapt attention to whatever he was saying.

Tonight was different. The splints were off, and Lucas had no more difficulty than any of the rest of them. Rachel was leaving him to fend for himself. Lucas had spoken very little to anybody, and he and Rachel hadn't talked one-on-one about anything. He still saw the Greek looking at her when she wasn't looking at him. What he was thinking was mostly masked, but there was an occasional glimmer of longing that was immediately hidden if she happened to look back at him.

Nathaniel was decidedly pleased with what he was seeing. With his leg healed, the Greek or Roman or whatever he was would be leaving very soon. Rachel would be safe from the attentions of the man who had no business with her anyway.

Chapter 39

GOODBYES

Lucius had managed the walk to synagogue without his leg hurting Monday morning. He could have kept up with Joseph and the boys, if he'd wanted to, but he had walked slowly to have one more time alone with her.

It hadn't been what he'd hoped for. Usually they talked, but she was silent. She looked sad, and he was afraid to ask why. After he'd told her he couldn't stay the day before, she'd spoken to him very little. Maybe she was just trying to make it easier for him to leave, but it still hurt more than she had any way of knowing.

Since he couldn't stay, it was clearly time to go.

He wasn't sure how he was going to manage to say goodbye to her without revealing his heart. He wanted to avoid that at all costs. She would think it was her fault that he was hurting, and he didn't want that. It was his own fault that he'd let himself fall in love with her. She'd never encouraged him to do it. She couldn't help being so wonderful that he couldn't resist.

If only he'd been born a Jew, if only he hadn't killed her brother, if only he could stay and marry her, if only...He sighed deeply. So much of the pain in life was wrapped up in the "if onlys."

They were just finishing the midday meal on Wednesday when Rachel's friend Leah came running down to tell her that Elizabeth had delivered her baby during the night. She'd gone back with her to Elizabeth's house to see the new baby girl.

It was as if God had opened the door for Lucius to leave without her sad goodbyes driving a dagger into his heart. He would leave before she returned.

Joseph had gone back to the forge, and Simeon had gone with him. Asher was still eating the last of his bread when Lucius rose. "Come with me, Asher. I need you to do something for me."

Asher followed him into the house and stood near the door as Lucius walked over to Reuben's bed. At its foot was the bag she'd brought to the wadi. In it was everything she'd taken from him to hide his Roman identity. It was safer to walk back to the garrison as a Greek laborer, so he would take it all in the bag.

Soon enough he would don his uniform and be the Roman tribune once more. This interlude of happiness was over, but life must go on.

"I'm leaving now, Asher."

Asher blinked twice. "Why?"

"I have to go back to the garrison now my leg is healed."

Lucius reached into the bag and lifted out the first of the two heavy purses. He lifted the corner of Reuben's mattress and slid it underneath. Then he lifted out the second and bounced it in his hand so it jingled a little before hiding it under the mattress, too.

"I'm leaving these for your father. Don't tell him they're here until you're going to bed tonight. I don't want him to try to give them back to me. I want you to make sure Joseph understands that they are a gift from a friend who thanks him for caring for him like family. They are not payment for room and board like I would give an innkeeper. No amount of money could ever repay your father and sister for what they've done for me."

Asher stood staring at him.

"Do you understand what I'm saying?"

"A gift from a friend, not payment for an innkeeper, and I don't tell Abba it's there until bedtime."

Lucius hung the bag on his shoulder. "I'm going back to Sepphoris now. Time to say goodbye to Joseph and Simeon."

"And Rachel?"

He swallowed hard as he looked down at Asher. It felt as if Joseph had wrapped his chest again, but much too tightly. "I'd like you to say goodbye to her for me."

Asher nodded his head without speaking. Lucius tousled his hair as he walked past and headed out the door. Asher followed.

Simeon was watching closely as Joseph showed him how to heat the metal to the right shade of orange before pulling it out to shape with the hammer. Lucius watched in silence until Simeon sensed someone was behind them and turned.

"Lucas?"

Joseph turned as well. When he saw the bag hanging from Lucius's shoulder, he locked his eyes on Lucius's and his lips tightened.

"It's time for me to leave, Joseph. I want to tell you how grateful I am for you letting me stay with you while my leg healed. I also want to thank you for letting me work for you. It meant a great deal to me to show my gratitude by helping you. I especially want to thank you for letting me go to synagogue with you and, most of all, for telling me about Yeshua. I might never have known the LORD without your help. This time with you has changed me forever. I have no words to tell you how much all this has meant to me." He paused as his eyes swept across the three of them. "I will miss you all."

Joseph nodded once. "Helping you was what Yeshua wanted us to do, Lucas, and the LORD wanted you to come to Him. It is a good thing the boys found you and Rachel brought you home."

Joseph's words were spoken without a smile, but they still warmed Lucius. He saw neither sadness nor satisfaction in Joseph's eyes. Her father was not sorry to see him go, but he was no longer sorry he'd let him stay.

Lucius turned his eyes on Simeon. "Simeon, I'd be dead without you. I'll never forget you." He offered his arm to Simeon as he would to a man.

Simeon took it like a man, but his eyes were moist. "I'll miss you, Lucas."

Lucius nodded in response. This was much harder than he'd expected. "I'll miss you and Asher, too."

"Will you come visit?"

"No. It would be too dangerous for you if anyone found out you'd saved a Roman officer."

Asher had been standing perfectly still, staring at him just like the first day in the wadi. Without warning, he threw his arms around Lucius and clung to him. Lucius wrapped his arms around Asher and stood looking down on his tousled hair. He held him close until Asher finally wanted to let go. That hug tore at Lucius's heart more than any words could.

He shifted the bag on his right shoulder and stepped back. He took a deep breath and blew it out before lifting his head and squaring his shoulders.

Joseph rested his hand on his left shoulder. "Go in peace, Lucas, and know that Yeshua loves you." The corners of his mouth twitched up in the closest thing to a smile he'd ever given his guest.

Lucius nodded without speaking. He wasn't sure his voice wouldn't break. With one final tight-lipped smile, he turned and walked away. Behind him, the sound of hammer striking metal resumed, then faded away as each step carried him farther from what had become home.

Each blow of that hammer drove another nail into his heart.

It was good that he'd left when she wasn't home. Saying goodbye to the boys was hard enough. Saying goodbye to the woman he loved, the woman he would never see again, would have been more than he could bear.

Lucius had walked about a mile, and his leg was hurting. It wasn't so bad that he couldn't keep walking, but he would be very glad to get back to the garrison and rest it. He had another four miles to go, so he slowed his pace, hoping that would help his weakened muscles.

The sight of Nathaniel riding south to visit his family and check on him was not a welcome one. It was no surprise when Nathaniel reined in beside him and sat glaring down at him with a smirk.

"It's about time you left, Greek. You didn't belong there with my family, even if you were helping out in the workshop. I don't think Abba ever wanted you there. I know I didn't."

"Joseph still needs help, Nathaniel. I hope you'll go home and help your father again. Joseph is the finest man I've ever met, and you would do well to become more like him."

Nathaniel sat up straighter, and the anger began to build in his eyes. How predictable. How could Joseph's oldest son have ended up so different from the rest of his family? If he didn't abandon his present course, Rachel was sure to lose another brother.

The memory of her tears tore into him again. He had killed Reuben. Could he save Nathaniel? Her brother had never listened to him yet, but maybe it was worth one final try. What he was about to say was sure to upset the young zealot, but he was going to say it anyway...for Rachel.

"I know you aren't going to like what I'm about to say, but I care too much about Joseph, Rachel, and the boys not to say it. She told me about Reuben, and I've seen up close how much losing him still hurts them all. I don't want to see Rachel's heart broken again. I don't want to see Joseph or Simeon or Asher suffer like that again. I know Reuben died when the Romans were hunting zealots and he got caught in the battle. He was only there because of you."

Lucius shifted his weight to relieve the pressure on his weak leg.

"Choosing the zealot path like you've done will only get you killed and maybe the rest of your family as well. You might deserve to die, but I don't want to see Joseph killed and Rachel and the boys sold as slaves. That's what happens to a zealot's family when Rome decides to make an example of them. I care too much for Rachel, for all of them, to let you drag them down with you."

Nathaniel's brow furrowed as he scowled at Lucius. "The fate of my family is none of your business, and you better never come back again to see any of them if you know what's good for you. I know you've had your eye on Rachel, but she's not for Gentile scum like you. You better hope I never see you again."

He reached where his sword should be, but it wasn't there. He'd left it at Samuel's because Joseph didn't want him to wear it to his house.

Lucius read his intention. Perhaps Nathaniel was a lost cause after all. "I hope we never meet again because it might be over swords, and I don't want to take another of Joseph's sons from him."

Nathaniel's nostrils flared like an angry bull's. "What makes you think a cowardly Greek like you would ever be able to match swords with me?"

Lucius fixed his stare on the brash young zealot and sighed. Nathaniel was a fool, and that foolishness would end up getting him killed. "Do you really think I'm a Greek, Nathaniel?" He shook his head again. "I hope you never have to find out...If you love them, turn from this zealot madness and return to your father before he loses another son and Rachel loses another brother."

Lucius turned away and continued to limp north up the road.

◆

Nathaniel's anger still burned as he glowered at Lucas's back. Then he swung his horse to head south. It would be good to visit his family without having the Greek sitting next to Rachel. He'd never liked the way her eyes glowed every time she looked at him.

Rachel was beaming as she walked back down the street from Elizabeth's house. Her new baby, Anna, was so beautiful. She'd never seen a more radiant smile on her friend's face than the one she directed at her new-born daughter.

Her smile dimmed when she saw Asher slumped against the wall of the sheep pen, kicking up dust as he stared at the ground. She hurried over and knelt in front of him. She tipped his chin up to look into his eyes. He'd been crying.

"Asher! What's wrong?"

"He told me to tell you goodbye."

Her brother's face blurred before she closed her eyes.

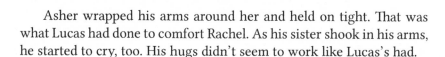

Asher wrapped his arms around her and held on tight. That was what Lucas had done to comfort Rachel. As his sister shook in his arms, he started to cry, too. His hugs didn't seem to work like Lucas's had.

Chapter 40

THE RETURN

Lucius had been walking for more than an hour. The muscles of his right leg ached more with every step. He'd probably left too soon, but he'd been afraid not to seize what might be his only chance to leave without watching her eyes as he told her goodbye.

He'd only gone a couple of miles. With at least three more miles to Sepphoris, would his leg give out before he got there? He sat down on a rock beside the road and massaged the cramping muscles that had weakened while he wasn't using them.

He gazed back toward the south. Was she home yet? Had Asher delivered his message? He shook his head slightly. *Stop thinking about her. It's over.*

He hadn't rested his leg enough, but it was time to move on anyway. He was about to rise when he spied the cloud of dust being stirred up by a Roman convoy. A deep sigh of relief escaped. A centurion and two dozen troops would be escorting the caravan of wagons up from Legio. A ride was at hand.

He stood as the centurion reached hailing distance. He knew the man well. They had frequently sparred together since Celsus would also rather hone his fighting skills than gamble or get drunk during his leisure time.

"Celsus!"

The centurion looked at him, then did a double-take. "Drusus? Lucius Drusus?"

"The same." Lucius grinned at him.

Celsus swung his leg over his horse's neck and slid to the ground. He strode up to Lucius and slapped him on the shoulder. "No offense, but dressed like that and with that beard, I took you for a Jew. It's good to see you. It's been so long that even the commander was about to decide you must be dead."

"I could use a ride back to the garrison." Lucius slapped his right thigh. "The leg that broke isn't quite up to a five mile walk."

"Horse or wagon?"

"Wagon. It will take a while until my leg's strong again."

The first wagon that reached him paused while he climbed up onto the seat by the driver. The whip cracked and the oxen resumed their slow, steady pull toward Sepphoris.

The pain of leaving her family still tore at his heart, but he tried to force it from his mind. Marcus would be waiting at the garrison. It would be good to be with his own brother again, and in time, the pain of leaving his almost-brothers would fade.

As the wagons rumbled into the garrison courtyard, all eyes turned toward the bearded man on the first wagon. As he passed through the gate at the head of the column, Celsus had sent word to the commander that he had found Lucius Drusus, and the word of his return rebounded through the troops.

Lucius watched their eyes as he climbed down. Some were friendly, some were neutral, but none seemed hostile. Somewhere among those surrounding him was the man who wanted him dead. It was doubtful that his enemy had changed his mind.

He proceeded immediately to the commander's office. As he walked through the door, the commander stood, a broad smile spreading across his face.

"Drusus. Good to have you back. I was about to give up and write that letter to your father that your brother thought was needed the second day you were missing. It's good to see I was right about you being injured but destined to return. Where were you?"

"With the family of the boys who found me where a hired assassin left me to die. I was ambushed on the way to buy Marcus's stallion and thrown off a cliff."

The astonishment on the commander's face looked almost comical. "Hired assassin?"

"As he was throwing me off the cliff, he said another soldier hired him."

"Who?"

"That I don't know. That's why I didn't come back right away. With a broken leg, I wouldn't have been able to stop a second attempt."

The commander placed both palms down on his desk. "As your first duty back, find out who tried to kill you. There are enough Jews who would send us to the Underworld. I can't have murder within our own ranks."

The commander sat down and pulled a report back in front of him. "Keep me informed on your progress."

Lucius saluted and headed toward the officers' quarters. He needed a bath, a shave, and a change of clothes. Then he would begin the hunt for the man who wanted him dead.

Marcus's spine relaxed as he led his troop through the gate. It had been an uneventful ride to Legio and back, but he always felt uneasy until he was safe inside the garrison again. How he hated this land! He would have been back in Rome by now if the blacksmith hadn't been such an incompetent. Less than a week and it would be the two months the commander always waited before declaring a missing man dead. Then he would return to Caesarea and request his transfer back to Rome. It was about time.

As he prepared to dismount, Crassus trotted toward him.

"Drusus! You'll never guess who just showed up."

Marcus looked down at the officer who was his "best friend" in Sepphoris. He'd decided it might seem suspicious if he didn't try to make some friends, even though he'd only planned on being there for less than three months. He needed someone to drink and gamble with since Lucius didn't want to, and Crassus had been as good as any to pick.

"Who?"

"Your brother. He came in with the wagons a little while ago. Celsus found him about three miles south of town on the Legio road and gave him a lift."

Marcus was dumbstruck. Lucius had returned from the dead!

Crassus laughed at his stunned look. "I wanted to be the first to tell you. You should have seen him when he got here. Even you might not have recognized him with that beard. He looked like some Jew who'd been working in the fields."

Marcus collected himself and aimed his expression at thrilled amazement. At least the amazement was real. "Lucius? Back alive? I'd given up all hope for that. Where is he now?"

"Don't know. I'm sure he'll find you."

Marcus tossed his leg over his horse's neck and slid off. "As soon as I take care of my horse, I'll find him if he hasn't found me first." He pasted on a smile that he hoped looked thoroughly delighted. "I can't believe he's still alive." He slapped Crassus's shoulder before leading his horse toward the stable.

The smile remained, but his eyes cooled. Lucius was still alive now, but he would try to rectify that as soon as he could. He was sick of Judaea, and he wanted to go home.

Lucius sat with Marcus at a table in the dining hall. He had positioned himself where he could see the faces of the men as they entered. The food wasn't as good as he would get at Jacob's inn, but he wanted to watch the reactions of the soldiers as they first saw him. He was hoping for some response that would provide a clue to who wanted him dead.

"I can't get over it being someone here in the garrison who wants to kill you. Maybe he wants to kill us both. I should have been with you that morning."

Lucius nodded, but he didn't look at his brother. He was keeping his eyes fixed on each face as they saw him. So far, none had reacted with anything more than normal surprise.

"You thought learning Aramaic was a waste of my time, but that's why I'm still alive. Right before he tossed me off the cliff, I heard one assassin say it was a soldier who hired him. A couple of shepherd boys found me a few hours later. I would have let them bring me back to the garrison if I hadn't understood Aramaic, and I'd probably be dead now. As it was, I hid out with the boys' family until my leg healed and lived to tell the tale."

Marcus blinked twice at the comment about the assassin's careless talk. "Did he say who it was?"

"No. That's the problem. I know I have an enemy here, but I have no idea who that might be."

Marcus placed his hand over his mouth and rubbed his jaw. "Maybe someone you got in trouble with the commander? You got more than one man disciplined for upsetting Jews." His eyes scanned the soldiers sitting at the tables. "You know, there were those three who were jumping over the sheep."

Lucius shifted his gaze to look at them. When one looked at him, the soldier quickly dropped his eyes and said something to his companions. The other two glanced at him quickly, then just as quickly focused back on their food.

"I didn't think much of it at the time, but I did overhear that tall one saying it was funny that the officer who kept taking the Jews' side would be the one that got killed by them. Then they all laughed."

Lucius's brow furrowed as he stared at them, and Marcus was pleased with the effect of his comment. The beauty of what he'd just said was that it was true.

Lucius blew his breath out through pursed lips as he nodded slowly. "I think I'll have a talk with them tomorrow. Each one separately. I'll soon know if one of them is responsible."

Marcus suppressed a grin as he stirred the disgusting stew that the garrison cook was passing off as their dinner that night. Of course they would deny involvement, but that didn't mean they might not be tried and executed for it anyway. Lucius couldn't prove they'd done it, but they couldn't prove they hadn't.

Joseph and Nathaniel were thoroughly enjoying dinner together, but they were the only ones. Rachel was sitting next to Joseph where Reuben once sat, but that was no longer Reuben's place in her own mind. That spot belonged to Lucas now, and her heart ached because he wasn't sitting there. She was trying to put on a cheerful face for Abba and Nathaniel, but she wasn't totally successful. She managed to keep the tears from forming, but she had to work at smiling. Even with a smile on her lips, there was no sparkle in her eyes.

Simeon hardly said anything, and Asher looked like his pet lamb had just died. It started to irritate Nathaniel that the departure of the Greek should be upsetting everyone except Abba so much. Abba had always been cold to the Greek, so at least he would share the satisfaction that Lucas of Corinth was gone.

"I passed that Greek you had here on my way from Sepphoris." He didn't like the way Rachel perked up at the mention of him. "I'm glad he's gone and never coming back. I didn't like him living here with Rachel. You never know what a man like that might do."

Abba's smile vanished. "You shouldn't listen to your cousin Daniel. Not about anything. There was never any danger to Rachel from him being here. Lucas of Corinth is an honorable man. He only showed Rachel respect and appreciation for her kindness to him."

Nathaniel frowned. "An honorable man? I think he was lying to you the whole time he was here, Abba. He showed up just when a Roman tribune went missing. I've seen enough Romans in Sepphoris to know one when I see one, and I still think he's that tribune."

◆

Joseph shook his head. Nathaniel was right, of course, but he was not going to tell his hotheaded son that he had willingly taken a Roman under his protection. It would lead to a fight, and a fight with Nathaniel was the last thing he wanted right now.

"Do you think a Roman tribune would have been so patient with you, Nathaniel? Or been so interested in the things of God? He wanted to go to synagogue every time he could. I told him about Yeshua myself, and he follows Him now like we do. It was a good thing the boys found him. We cared for him as Yeshua commands, and I am glad we did. But Lucas is gone now, and there is no reason for us to keep talking about him."

Nathaniel was as willing as Joseph to think about something other than Lucas of Corinth, so their conversation moved on to other things.

◆

Rachel was not so eager to stop thinking about Lucas. When she let herself, she could still see that broad grin and those laughing eyes as they strolled home from synagogue. She could see him looking up at her with that teasing smile as he waited for her to pronounce her approval of the latest spoke he made. She could see the intense feeling in his eyes as he drank the cup of remembrance of Yeshua's sacrifice at Shabbat dinner.

If only he had looked at her with the same love in his eyes that burned within her. If he had, she would have let him know he should ask for her hand because he already owned her heart. He was exactly the kind of man she wanted to marry—a man with a heart for Yeshua, a man who appreciated the smallest thing done for him and who wanted to help whenever he could, a man who could see the good in his enemies and the flaws in his own countrymen. It took every ounce of self-control she possessed not to cry as she thought of him being gone forever. If he'd stayed, maybe he would have grown to love her, too. Maybe...

Simeon looked at his sister. She was clearly struggling to act like everything was fine. Lucas had really loved her. She'd liked Lucas from the first day they brought him home. Did she love him, too? It sure looked like she might. It was too bad that Lucas wouldn't be asking Abba for her hand. He would have been a really good brother.

He wasn't as sure as Lucas had been that Abba would reject his request because he wasn't a Jew. He'd become a God-fearer and follower of Yeshua, and that should have been enough to make up for him being a Roman. If Rachel had asked Abba to let her marry him, he would have said yes. Rachel could get Abba to agree to almost anything.

Rachel was glad when dinner was finally over. It was becoming harder not to cry. While Joseph spoke the final blessing as they washed their hands, she closed her eyes. Maybe tomorrow would be better. Maybe she wouldn't miss him quite as much. Maybe...

Nathaniel had left for Samuel's house, and Asher was ready for bed. He walked over to Reuben's mattress and pulled out the two purses.

"Abba, Lucas told me to give you these tonight. He said to tell you it's a gift from a friend, not payment to an innkeeper."

Asher held the purses out to Joseph, one in each hand, and shook them just enough to make them jingle.

Rachel stared at the purses, her hand over her mouth, as Joseph took them from Asher. "That's Lucas's horse money. He was going to buy one when he was attacked."

When Joseph loosened the drawstring on the first purse and reached in, his fingers felt the cool metal of many coins. When he dumped the contents on Reuben's mattress, nineteen gold coins and

25 silver ones glittered in the lamplight. His brow furrowed as he considered what lay before him. When he dumped out the second purse to find the same, he stood silent and motionless, staring at the pile. He had never seen so much money in one place before.

A thousand denarii. That was a fortune in his village. No one else had even a quarter as much.

Rachel picked up a gold aureus and stared at it in her palm before wrapping her fingers tightly around it and clutching it to her chest. "Oh, Abba. Look at what Lucas left us. In the wadi, he offered me 500 denarii to let him stay with us, but I told him I wouldn't take money for doing what Yeshua wanted."

"It would seem he paid you anyway. We can't take this much. I should return most of it to him."

Asher shook his head. "No, Abba. He told me to tell you it wasn't a payment. It's a gift to a friend to thank you for treating him like family. He told me to give it to you tonight so you wouldn't try to give it back."

Rachel picked up a second aureus. "You can't try to give it back to him, Abba. It would hurt him to know you don't think of him as a friend and won't accept his gift." She covered Hadrian's head with her thumb, leaving only the nose that was shaped just like Lucas's visible. "I think he would want you to use some to hire a helper. He was so happy when you let him help you. He hated seeing you work so hard with only me to help. You have to let him do this."

Abba nodded slowly as he stared at the money.

"I never expected this." He picked up some coins and let them run through his fingers. Lucas of Corinth, whoever he really was, had ended all his financial worries. "It is far too much, but I must accept it. It would be wrong to reject the gift of a friend."

Chapter 41

SUSPICIONS

Lucius tightened his lips and shook his head as the last of the three soldiers who'd harassed Simeon's sheep and broken the lamb's leg left the room. He'd expected one of them to be the soldier who hired the men to kill him. No such luck. Marcus had been right about the tall one commenting on the irony of a Jew killing him when he was the closest thing to a friend the Jews had in the garrison. After some questioning, the man admitted making the statement, but Lucius had finally believed his adamant denials that he had ever hired anyone to kill him.

He'd frightened the men into being his eager allies in trying to find the man who was really out to get him. Perhaps they would come to him in a day or two with the information he needed. Right now, he was no closer to identifying his enemy than he had been when he rode through the garrison gate. He had no other clues to follow and no other soldiers who made him suspicious. He would just have to keep his guard up and watch everyone to see if his enemy was about to strike again. Everyone except Celsus, the commander, and Marcus. Those were the only three he could be completely sure of.

He sat down and massaged his leg. He needed to start working to rebuild those muscles. A walk with Marcus to Jacob's inn for dinner would be an enjoyable way to do that. There was another advantage in eating at Jacob's tonight. Many of the officers ate there since Jacob served some of the best food in town, and he even treated Romans like they were welcome. Maybe his friend had overheard a conversation that would prove helpful in tracking down the man who wanted him dead.

Marcus followed Lucius through the narrow passage into Jacob's inn and over to his customary table. Jacob was across the courtyard talking to two of the officers who often ate there. When he turned and saw Lucius, he spread his arms and strode toward his young friend.

"Lucius! You have returned!" He wrapped Lucius in a crushing hug and slapped him on the back before stepping back to place his hands on Lucius's shoulders. "It is so good to see you. I thought you must be dead by now."

"It's good to see you, too, Jacob. I've missed your stew...and your conversation." Lucius beamed at his friend.

Marcus kept his pleasant mask in place, even though he was irritated by their obvious pleasure at seeing each other. It was this Jew's fault that Lucius understood the blacksmith and stayed away when he would have been easy to kill. Two months wasted in Judaea because of that...two months of bad food and dust and danger.

"Today you can have some of both. I will be back with stew for you and your brother, and then you can tell me what happened to you."

The brothers settled in at the table to wait for Jacob. Marcus glanced around the room. "I came to Jacob while you were missing to ask him if he could find out what happened to you. I never heard anything from him."

"Given what happened and where I hid while I recovered, I'm not surprised. Whoever hired the men who tossed me off the cliff wasn't going to be talking about it where Jacob might hear. Anyone who eats here regularly would know he's my friend."

Marcus nodded. The food at Jacob's inn was the best in Sepphoris, but watching Lucius talk with Jacob like he was a friend left a bad taste even with the finest food. He especially didn't like it when they conversed in Aramaic. He didn't like not knowing exactly what was being said.

◆

Jacob brought the tray with two bowls of stew to the table himself. He joined them in the third chair. "So, what happened and where were you for so long?"

Jacob asked in Greek to include Marcus in their conversation. He had seen the poorly veiled look of anger in Marcus's eyes before when they talked for too long in Aramaic.

He rested both arms on the table and leaned forward to hear his friend's tale of adventure that had fortunately turned out well. This would be an opportunity to watch the brother as well. Before he said anything to Lucius, he needed to be more certain that his suspicions were well founded. After tonight, he should know.

◆

Lucius recounted his tale of being unhorsed by the assassins, hurled off the cliff, and almost killed by the jackal before two shepherd boys found him. Then it got more difficult. How was he ever going to describe the first time he saw those brown eyes that comforted him with their genuine concern and those lips that curved into that kind smile that gave him hope when he had decided he was going to die? He simply couldn't without reliving the pain of knowing he would never see them again, so he shortened seven weeks into one sentence.

"So I stayed with the boys' family until my leg healed. Now I need to find out who wants me dead before he tries again."

◆

Jacob first nodded slowly, then shook his head. "Well, I am glad he failed, and I hope you find him soon." He rested his hand on Lucius's shoulder. "It is good to have my favorite Roman back here at my table. I missed you."

Marcus's irritation at Jacob's expression of affection for his brother was fleetingly displayed in his eyes and at the corner of his mouth before he masked it. He was quick, but Jacob was watching like he never had before. This time he saw. He also got momentary glimpses of cold calculation in Marcus's eyes as he looked at Lucius while he told the tale.

"I'm hoping you might help me, Jacob."

"If I can. Just ask."

"Have you heard any of the officers who eat here say anything that might be suspicious?"

Jacob slowly shook his head. "No...nothing. Now that you are back, maybe someone will say something. My servants and I will listen, and I will let you know if we hear anything." He glanced at Marcus. There was that cold, reptilian look in his eyes that was quickly masked when Marcus realized he was being observed. "Your stew is getting cold. You should eat, so I will leave you to enjoy." He rested his hand on Lucius's arm again. "I look forward to seeing you often in the future."

Lucius flipped into Aramaic. "Thank you, Jacob. It's good to see you again, and I'll be back soon."

As Jacob walked away from their table, he made a decision. As soon as he had the opportunity to speak with Lucius alone, he would warn him that his brother's affection was not all it seemed. He should be watching his back.

It had been four days since Lucius returned. Marcus was almost back to the garrison after an uneventful ride to legion headquarters. The trip had given him time alone to analyze his failure and regroup for success.

His first plan for removing Lucius had failed because he entrusted its execution to someone else. That seemed like a good idea at the time, but hiring someone was risky. Even if they succeeded, that left someone knowing he planned the murder. Clearly, it was better to do something this important himself while somehow placing the blame on someone else.

All he needed was an armed Jew that he could claim was a zealot. Kill the Jew, kill Lucius, and blame the Jew for killing him. Simple. Clean. Untraceable. Now he just had to wait for the right Jew in the right place at the right time.

Lucius had given Marcus's 500 denarii to Joseph, and it was time to repay him.

The paymaster looked up from the accounts when he heard Lucius enter. A smile curved his lips.

"Drusus. Good to see you back. What do you need?"

"I'd like to transfer 500 denarii from my account to Marcus. It's the money for that stallion I never got to buy for him."

"If he's going to be buying horses, he'd be smarter to take you with him."

Lucius's left eyebrow cocked. "Why is that?"

"You've seen that horse he's riding now. He pulled out 300 denarii only three days before you both pulled 500 that day you disappeared. Then he got 500 a couple of weeks later just before he bought his stallion. He claims he paid 800 for it, but it's not worth than much. It might be worth 400, maybe 500, but it isn't an 800-denarii horse. Either he's a poor judge of horseflesh, or he's been spending money on something else." He grinned. "Maybe he's been hiring assassins. I'd be transferring your whole account to him if you end up dead. If he's going to keep paying too much for horses, he might need it."

Lucius's eyebrows slammed down. "That isn't funny. I still haven't figured out who tried to have me killed, but for certain it wasn't my own brother."

The paymaster raised his hands in a pacifying gesture. "No offense meant, Drusus. You know him better than I do."

"Yes, I do, and I'd appreciate it if you didn't even joke about it." His head tilted. "But that does raise a question. Did anyone else pull out an unusual amount just before I was attacked?"

The paymaster shook his head. "No. Only the usual amounts the men spend gambling and drinking." His mouth turned up in a half-smile. "Not much else to do here. Not everyone wants to spend their free time sparring like you and Celsus or talking with Jews like you do."

"If anyone does ask for more than usual, let me know right away. Just in case they decide to try again."

"Of course, tribune."

The paymaster watched Lucius as he left the office. Then he shook his head. Lucius Drusus was one of the friendliest young officers who had passed through the garrison, and he genuinely liked him. He didn't like Marcus. That one acted like he was more important than he really was, and the paymaster didn't like arrogant young fools.

How could two brothers be so different? He'd trust Lucius Drusus with anything. Marcus Drusus, now that was a different story.

That evening, Marcus once more took a sheet of papyrus from his writing desk. Time for another letter to Father. He sighed. He had hoped this would be the letter announcing Lucius's death and his request for a transfer back to Rome. No such luck, but Lucius had returned without suspecting his role in the first attack. He merely had to watch for the right opportunity, and his gullible brother would be only a memory.

He dipped his pen into the ink bottle and began writing.

Marcus Claudius Drusus to Lucius Claudius Drusus Fidelis, my father, greetings. If you are well, then I am glad. I have excellent news that I am sure will bring you great gladness.

Lucius has returned, and he is well. He was thrown from a cliff by two Jews who wanted to kill a Roman. He did not die in the fall but only suffered a broken leg. He has recovered and is now back with me at the garrison.

I can only hope that he will be more careful in the future. I will do my best to keep him from taking foolish risks, but this is still Judaea. Men seek to kill us whenever an opportunity presents itself. It is my sincerest hope that we can keep each other safe.

I hope all will continue to be well with you. May the gods guard your safety.

He rolled the papyrus and sealed it with wax. It was not the letter he had hoped to be sending, but it would do to cover his next move against Lucius.

Chapter 42

WANTING THE IMPOSSIBLE

It had been a week since Nathaniel told him the Greek had left Joseph's house, so Daniel decided to pay Rachel a visit. He might not have the muscles and rugged good looks of the Greek, but he had plenty of money since his father was a successful merchant. A smart woman should consider him a much better husband than some Greek whose clothes revealed he was only a laborer. What could a Greek laborer, even a handsome one, have to offer a wife? Nothing.

He wanted Rachel, and today he would convince her she wanted him, too. When she'd told him she wasn't interested in being his wife the last time he visited, the Greek was still there. A girl can be foolish when a handsome man is around. Now that his rival was gone for good, she should be ready to be more sensible.

She couldn't afford to be picky. Joseph wasn't a wealthy man, so she wouldn't have much of a dowry. She was almost eighteen, well past the age when most girls were betrothed. She said she only wanted a man who followed Yeshua, but there were so few of those around and none of the right age. She couldn't expect to find one. No, Rachel was not the kind of woman that men would be lining up for, so she should be more receptive to his proposal today.

Joseph was not to be seen when Daniel rode into the courtyard. Rachel was alone, working at her loom.

Daniel rubbed his hands together, then wiped them on his thighs. It would be easier to talk with her when Joseph wasn't listening. It would be enjoyable to talk a while after he proposed and she accepted.

The left corner of his mouth rose at the thought.

When Joseph returned, he would tell his uncle that Rachel wanted her cousin to be her husband as well. As soon as he confirmed their betrothal with Joseph, he would tell his own father. He didn't expect any problem there. They were rich enough that her pathetic dowry wouldn't matter. His father already loved Rachel and would want her as his daughter-in-law.

◆

When Rachel heard the hoofbeats and looked up, she sighed.

Daniel, of all people. There wasn't anyone she would rather not see. What was it going to take to finally convince him to give up asking her to marry him?

He dismounted and slapped his horse to send it over to the manger. He sauntered over and leaned his hand against the loom's support post. "You look pretty today, Rachel."

She didn't like his smirk. She chose to ignore the compliment.

"I hope Uncle Samuel is well. How is Nathaniel?"

"Everyone is well at my house."

She said nothing more. Maybe her silence would discourage him. Abba had gone to help Eli for a few minutes. If only he would hurry back, she could suggest Daniel go talk with him.

◆

Her silence should have served as a warning, but Daniel was never one to pick up on subtle messages.

"Having Nathaniel live with us has been good. We've become almost like brothers."

Rachel nodded her head but didn't reply. She just kept weaving the shuttle between the warp threads.

"It would be good if we really were brothers." He grinned at her, anticipating the cleverness of his next comment. "Or at least brothers-in-law."

Rachel shook her head. "We already discussed this, Daniel. Nothing has changed." She stopped weaving and fixed her eyes on his. "I don't want to marry you...ever...so unless Nathaniel marries your sister, he will never be your brother-in-law."

He hadn't expected so blunt a rejection a second time, and blood surged to his face. "What's wrong with you, Rachel? You're almost eighteen. Your father can't give you much of a dowry. You're not so pretty that being older and poor won't make you unattractive to most men. They'd have to overlook you following Yeshua, too. You should feel honored that I want you."

"But I don't want you, Daniel. It will be your fault if Nathaniel ends up dead in some zealot attack. It's your fault that Reuben's dead already. I'd rather remain unmarried in my father's house than marry a man like you."

The coldness in her eyes stoked his anger. "So what do you want? Someone like that Greek that was here? I saw how you looked at him, how he looked at you."

"He's a better man than you'll ever be. He follows Yeshua now. You don't follow the LORD at all."

◆

Simeon and Asher came through the gate and froze at the sight of Daniel and Rachel staring each other down.

"Stay here." Simeon started walking toward them.

Fury fired Daniel's eyes. "I told your father he shouldn't let that Greek stay here. What has he done to you? What have you done with him?"

Rachel's fists rammed into her hips. "Nothing. He's a good man. I would have married him if he'd asked me. I'll never want to marry someone like you. Go away and stop asking me."

Daniel grabbed Rachel's arm and twisted it down. She cried out in pain as she dropped to her knees.

"You'll be sorry you talked to me like this. I'll make you pay for it."

Simeon broke into a run. "Get away from her!"

He barreled into Daniel, knocking him sideways so he let go of Rachel's arm. Then he stood between his sister and their cousin. Rachel stood up behind him, rubbing her arm where Daniel had grabbed her.

"You stay away from my sister."

Daniel shoved Simeon to the ground before stalking over to his horse. Simeon scrambled back to his feet and stood in front of his sister again.

Daniel mounted, rode over close, and glared down at the two of them. "You'll be sorry you chose that Gentile dog over me."

He swung his horse and cantered out the gate, almost knocking Asher over. Her little brother ran to her and wrapped his arms around her, burying his face in her tunic. Rachel tilted his chin up to look into his frightened eyes. She ran her fingers through his hair and managed a smile, trying to look calm even though she was still shaking inside.

"It's all right, Asher. He's gone, and I don't expect he'll be back."

Simeon stepped close and wrapped his arms around his sister. "I'm sorry he came when I wasn't here to protect you."

She hugged her brother. "You did protect me." She took a deep breath. "Now I want you both to promise me you won't say anything to Abba about any of this."

Simeon's eyes widened. "But he should know. He can get Uncle Samuel to tell Daniel to never come here again."

"No. We mustn't say anything. I'm afraid Abba might kill Daniel for what he just did. Promise me you won't tell him. Ever. Promise?"

Asher and Simeon both nodded. Rachel breathed a sigh of relief. It was best if Abba never knew.

As they ate dinner around the table inside Samuel's house, Daniel was unusually quiet. He wasn't just quiet; the corners of his mouth stayed turned down and sometimes his brow was furrowed. What Rachel had said kept eating at him. His father had asked him if anything was wrong, and he'd said no. Nathaniel kept looking at him like he didn't believe him.

When Daniel finally left the family table to walk outside, Nathaniel followed him.

"What's the problem, Daniel?"

He considered saying nothing, then decided it would be better if Nathaniel heard his version before Rachel had a chance to talk to him. "I went to see Rachel today."

"You did? Why?"

Daniel kicked at the ground. "I wanted to ask her to marry me."

Nathaniel's head tilted. "So what's wrong tonight? Wasn't she home?" A huge grin split his face. "I wondered when you were finally going to ask her. She'd make any man a fine wife. You'll just have to go back again when she's there."

Daniel did not appreciate his cousin's grin. "She was there."

"So, when do you become my brother-in-law?"

"I won't." He wasn't about to tell Nathaniel what really happened. "I don't want her anymore."

It was Nathaniel's turn to frown. "Why?"

"I knew it wasn't a good idea for your father to let that Greek stay. I'm not sure she didn't let him do things with her that she shouldn't have."

Nathaniel's frown turned into a scowl. "Rachel would never do anything she shouldn't." He stared into Daniel's eyes and saw the lies within. "She turned you down. That's your problem, isn't it."

"No! When I asked her about him, she told me she wanted him, and I think she's done something about that. I don't want that kind of woman."

Fast as a striking snake, Nathaniel grabbed Daniel by the throat and slammed him up against the wall, lifting his scrawny body until his feet were flailing in midair. Years at the forge and the adrenaline rush of a protective brother made it easy to hold Daniel there as he tugged at Nathaniel's hands and kicked at him, trying to break free so he could breathe.

"That's a filthy lie, and you know it. If I ever hear you've lied to anyone else about my sister like this, I'll kill you. Understand?"

Daniel couldn't speak with Nathaniel's hand gripping his throat, so he tried to nod as he hung there. Then Nathaniel tossed him aside like a doll and stood glaring down at him. "Never, ever say that about my sister again."

Daniel nodded vigorously before he scrambled to his feet and scurried away. Striking back at Rachel wasn't worth getting himself killed.

Rachel carried Abba's midmorning drink and dates out to him and set them on the bench. Joseph set down his tools and turned to face her.

"Thank you, Rachel." He smiled down at her. "So like your mother."

She stood on tiptoes and kissed his cheek, but she didn't say anything. She was too aware of the empty stool.

Furrows formed in Joseph's forehead. "You seem sad."

"I miss Lucas. He'd become like part of the family. It hurts like when Nathaniel went away." She tried to offer Abba a smile, but it was very weak. "But maybe he'll come visit us sometime, like Nathaniel does now."

Joseph shook his head. "Simeon asked. He said he wouldn't because of the danger to us if a Roman came."

Her eyes brimmed with tears. "So it's like Reuben—gone from us forever."

She covered her mouth as the tears began trickling down her cheeks. Then she turned and walked away.

Joseph watched her as he slowly shook his head. He had never expected it, but he missed the Roman, too.

Lucius had been back at the garrison for ten days, and every day his leg felt stronger. It was strong enough for the ride to Legio and back to brief the legate in command of the II Traiana. There was only one problem. That road went through Rachel's village. His leg was strong enough to stand the ride, but was his heart strong enough to stand being so close without yielding to his desire to be with her again?

As the troop rode into the village, he could hear the distant sound of a hammer striking metal. As they rode past her side street, he could see Joseph's back through the gate as he swung the hammer. Simeon was standing beside him, watching. Right now, Rachel would be grinding grain, gracefully swaying as she sang, or maybe standing at her loom, weaving the shuttle back and forth through the threads.

He longed to turn up that street, to ride through the gate and over to the canopy, to take her in his arms and hold her close. But that would put her in danger, and he would never choose to do that. He was a man who always did what he ought to do, not what he wanted to do. As his horse kept walking, his view into the courtyard grew smaller and smaller until it was gone. Soon the sound of the hammer would fade into silence as well.

He turned his eyes back on the road to Legio. He forced himself to focus back on what had to be, not what he wished could be. Only pain came from dreaming about the impossible.

Chapter 43

WARNINGS

Jacob was relieved to see Lucius enter the courtyard alone. He was increasingly worried about him. Each time he saw the brothers together, he picked up more hints of Marcus's dislike. He wasn't certain whether the animosity was growing or whether Marcus was just being more careless about it being seen. Either way, Lucius needed to be warned.

He walked over and sat down by his young friend. "It is good to see you. No Marcus?"

"He's drinking with his friend Crassus tonight. Why he'd choose that over your stew is beyond me. But that gives us a chance for a longer conversation. We haven't done that often since Marcus got here."

"Your brother speaks no Aramaic. He wants us to speak Greek so he will know what I am saying. He thinks things he does not want others to know. He suspects I do, too."

Jacob's eyes turned serious, and his brow furrowed. "There is something I have been wanting to tell you when he was not here with you. Something that has me worried."

Lucius arched his eyebrows. "Worried? What is it?"

"I know you are very fond of your brother. I see it every time in how you treat him." Jacob paused, fully aware that his next words might cause trouble between them. "I have been watching your brother since you disappeared and then returned. There is something...I am not sure he is fond of you. There is a coldness in how he looks at you... like a stalking lion looking at prey."

Lucius was thunderstruck. "What are you talking about?"

"I started to worry when he came here for information when you were first missing. When we talked, he acted like he was upset and would do anything to find you. When he did not think I was watching, he acted like he did not care you were missing at all. Since you have come back, I have watched him closely. He may seem to care for you, but when you are not watching, there is that look again, like the lion. I do not see the love of a brother in his eyes."

Lucius was staring hard at him, his eyebrows pulling downward. "Marcus is my brother. He only came here to be closer to me. He wanted us to serve together."

Lucius's eyes had chilled. Their friendship was teetering at the cliff's edge, but Jacob cared too much for the young Roman not to forge ahead.

"So he says. I do not believe him. Your brother is nothing like you, Lucius. You are a good man, much better than him. I think he resents that. In him, I see a man who cares about no one but himself. I see no sign of the love for you that you have for him. You should be careful where Marcus is concerned. I do not think you can trust him...I think he may be the one who is trying to kill you."

First Lucius simply stared at Jacob in silence. Then incredulity was replaced by anger. His eyes flamed as he pushed back his chair and stood up. Jacob had never seen Lucius angry before. How much more he looked like Marcus when he was.

"Marcus is my brother. You have no right to accuse him of anything. He's never been someone to show his affection for anyone, even the members of our family. That's all you're seeing. He would never try to kill me—his own brother. For you to even suggest that...to try to drive a wedge between us...that's not what I expect from a friend. Maybe I was wrong to consider you one. I'll find someplace else to eat where my brother is welcome, too."

Lucius turned and strode out of the inn. Jacob stood and watched him go.

A deep sigh escaped as he shook his head. He had only spoken because he truly cared about Lucius. He did not want to see him dead by his brother's hand. As the gate closed behind the young Roman, a sense of loss enveloped him. Even if Marcus did not kill him, he had lost his friend. Lucius was so angry. He could not expect him to ever return.

Lucius had the next morning off, and he was sitting on his bed reading the Septuagint he'd just bought in the marketplace. He longed to go to synagogue or listen to the evening discussions of Torah between Joseph and his boys, but that would never happen again. Reading the word of God alone was all he could do now he was back at the garrison.

A knock on the door interrupted the depressing thoughts about what he was missing.

"Enter."

The door opened. A young soldier strode over to him and slammed his fist against his chest. "A letter for you, tribune."

Lucius took the rolled papyrus from the soldier, who saluted again and left immediately.

His eyebrows rose as he read the name of the sender. Why would his uncle Titus be writing him? He hadn't seen his uncle since he left for military service in Thracia thirteen years ago. Titus had chosen to remain near Perinthus rather than return to live at his estate north of Rome. Lucius had been Simeon's age when Titus left, and he'd missed his uncle. He was like Grandfather—a kind, honorable man. How Grandfather could have raised two sons who were so opposite was hard to fathom.

He broke the seal and unrolled two sheets. What first met his eyes was a short note from Titus.

> Titus Claudius Drusus to Lucius Claudius Drusus, my nephew, greetings. Be warned not to let your brother Marcus know that you have received the enclosed letter. Secrecy is imperative if those you love are to remain safe. May God guard your safety.

With some trepidation, Lucius lifted the sheet away and began to read the secret missive. The real letter was from his mother. His eyebrows shot up as his hand covered his mouth. Mother and his little sister Drusilla were supposed to be at the estate east of Rome. Why Titus would be forwarding a letter from her to him was beyond his ability to guess.

Cornelia Scipia to Lucius Claudius Drusus, my dear son, greetings. If you are well, then I am glad. I write to tell you what your father is trying to do and what I have done to protect your sister from him.

I have divorced Lucius Fidelis, and I am now living in Perinthus with your uncle Titus. Tertius learned of your father's plans to marry Drusilla to the younger son of his best friend, Marcus Corvinus. There is something very wrong with that boy. He tortures and kills animals and slaves for pleasure. Tertius warned me when he could not persuade your father to spare Drusilla certain suffering and maybe death at his hands. Without your father's knowledge, I have brought Drusilla to Thracia, where your uncle and your aunt Claudia have welcomed us.

Do not tell Marcus any of what I have written you. Destroy this letter after you read it so he won't find it, and do not even tell him that I have written. I can't trust him not to tell your father where we are. I have also written Tertius. He loves his sister, and he is the reason I even knew what Fidelis was planning in the first place. Marcus loves no one but himself. I am sorry to say it of my own son, but I want to warn you about Marcus as well. He is too much like his father. Be careful of him.

I love you, Lucius, and I hope I will see you again. I wish you were serving in Perinthus instead of Judaea. I worry about your safety in that dangerous place. I am sure Titus could help arrange your transfer here if you want to be closer to your sister and me. He is a friend of the governor of Thracia, and he is sure the governor of Judaea would agree to your transfer if asked.

Now that we are safe with your uncle and aunt, all is well with Drusilla and me. Both Titus and Claudia worship the god of your grandfather Publius. I always thought Publius was the wisest of men until he died for that god. I begin to think he may have been wise in that choice as well. May the god of your grandfather guard your safety.

Lucius was shocked, but not by the report that his father would risk Drusilla's life to make his friend happy. He already knew his father's good friends were more important to him than his children were. He was stunned that Mother would be afraid that Marcus would betray her to Father. Her letter warned him against Marcus as well. The words of warning from Jacob and the joke by the paymaster— they wouldn't have surprised her at all.

He shook his head. No. She was wrong. Marcus would never deliberately hurt Drusilla. When she was little, he used to play hide and seek with her whenever she wanted. She loved being tickled, and her squeals of delight when he found her echoed through the villa. He gave Drusilla her first pony when she was five and taught her to ride.

Marcus had spent so little time at the eastern estate in the last few years that Mother didn't really know him. Marcus wasn't any closer to their father than he was. For years his brother had made comments that proved Marcus didn't like or respect Father any more than he did. She was wrong to think he would betray her to him.

He would destroy the letter as she asked and say nothing out of respect for her wishes, but he couldn't believe that his own brother would have any part in Drusilla being hurt that way. No brother would.

Chapter 44

THE REAL ENEMY

As Lucius walked past the commander's office the next afternoon, he glanced in. What he saw, he'd never seen before. The commander was sitting with his elbows resting on the table, his shoulders slumped, and his face buried in his hands.

Lucius stepped into the room and closed the door. "Commander?"

The commander leaned back in his chair and ran one hand through his hair.

"You know, Drusus, there are days I'd rather be serving anywhere but Judaea. This is one of them."

Lucius walked over to the desk. "What happened?"

"You know Josiah bar Azor?"

"The tax collector? The one who brags about overtaxing so much he's the biggest thief in the province?"

"The same. He was moving his family down to Caesarea, and they were ambushed." He closed his eyes and ran his fingers through his hair again. "Dead. All dead, and they didn't die easy. He had three girls, the youngest only three. They played with my children. His wife was a kind woman. My wife knew her well. She used to take the money Josiah gave her for jewels and clothes and give it to the widows and orphans."

The commander leaned forward to rest his forearms on the table. "My wife's scared to death that our children might be next. Maybe I should send my family down to Caesarea, maybe even back to Italia."

Lucius jumped when the commander slammed his fist down.

265

"I'm sick of it, Drusus. The zealots murder, and I send out my troops to punish them. For a little while there's peace. Then it starts all over again."

Lucius nodded. "I asked for this assignment to try to break the cycle, but after more than two years, I still have no idea what might work."

The commander frowned as he shook his head. "Nothing's going to work unless one of their own gets them to change. Someone they'll listen to needs to be urging submission instead of pouring more oil on the flames of hatred." The commander tipped his head back, stared at the ceiling, then lowered his eyes to Lucius's. "It might have happened ninety years ago if Pontius Pilate hadn't given in to the Sanhedrin and had Jesus of Nazareth crucified."

Lucas head popped back. The commander talking about Yeshua?

The commander uttered one short laugh. "You look surprised. Well, the Nazarene taught that the Jews should love their enemies and give Caesar what he was due. Sounds like a recipe for peace to me. Too bad there aren't more of his followers now. Things would be different if there were enough Jews who love their enemies for the province to be peaceful, like Macedonia or Thracia."

Lucius stood silent with his eyes locked on the commander.

"Don't misunderstand me, Drusus. I'm not a Christian, don't intend to become one. My loyalty is to Rome and Caesar, not a dead Jewish rabbi. Still, if Pliny had the rebellion in Bithynia and Pontus like we've got in Judaea, he wouldn't have been in such a hurry to gather up his Christians and execute them. No governor of Judaea would make that mistake if he thought about it. I'd choose a Christian over a zealot any day. At least they don't think the murder of the children of those serving Rome is a noble act."

The commander shook his head. "Too bad you were missing for two months. Nothing happened to forward your assignment while you were gone. Your brother was too afraid to spend much time outside the garrison working on the problem. I'm still hoping you can figure out how to cool the hatred and stop these attacks. I don't expect the Jews to love us, but surely they can learn to live with us so we can live with them."

The commander stood. "What I just said...it's just between you and me."

Lucius nodded. "Of course."

A deep sigh escaped the commander. "I really don't mind killing rebel Jews, but I don't like having my men killed when they're only trying to keep the peace. Murder, reprisal, murder—the cycle never ends here." He squared his shoulders. "Time to plan the counterattack to hunt down and kill Josiah's murderers. I need to speak with my centurions."

The commander walked past Lucius and out the door.

Lucius stared at his retreating back. He was right that the province would be more peaceful, but he'd misunderstood what Yeshua really did. He didn't mainly come to bring peace between men, even though he did do that. The way Rachel and Joseph had treated him was proof of it. No, he came to bring peace between God and men by his death, and nothing Pilate could have done would have stopped a sacrifice God himself had planned.

Perhaps he'd find a time to explain it all to the commander before he left the province. A time when the commander wasn't focused on the next battle. Maybe then he would listen to the words and hear them, the words that could bring him peace forever, no matter what the zealots might do. He would pray for that chance.

Nathaniel's frown and troubled eyes reflected the turmoil in his mind as he rode into Samuel's courtyard. When he learned that the wagon they'd just completed was being delivered to a Roman tax collector who was moving down to Caesarea, he'd been happy to pass on the news. That was, after all, the main reason he was working at that particular shop. Its trade with the garrison allowed him to overhear useful information about troop movements and money shipments, information that enabled the zealots Daniel ran with to plan what they should do.

That particular tax collector was notorious for taking so much more than the actual taxes that his name had become slang for extortion and robbery. Nathaniel thought the zealots had planned to waylay him and take back what he'd stolen. Something much worse had happened.

Even thinking about it made Nathaniel's stomach churn. The man's wife and three young daughters were traveling with him. Word had spread through Sepphoris that the zealots had forced him and his wife to watch his children be brutally murdered, starting with the youngest girl who was only three. Finally they had murdered his wife and then killed him.

One reason he hated Rome was the way it punished a whole family when a single member broke Roman law. The LORD had forbidden punishing a child for his father's sins. How could men claiming to serve the LORD in fighting Rome do such a horrible thing?

He had to talk with Daniel. They needed to break with the group that had murdered innocent children and find another one that fought the invader while still honoring the LORD and following His commandments. Tonight after dinner, they could make their plans for what to do next.

Right after dinner, Nathaniel led Daniel out to the stables, where they could talk without being overheard.

Daniel leaned against the wall. "So, what's the problem?"

"We need to break with Eliakim's group."

Daniel's eyebrows rose. "Why?"

Nathaniel furrowed his brow as he tightened his lips. "They did something terrible today, something totally against what the LORD has commanded."

Daniel spread his hands. "I have no idea what you're talking about. All they did today was kill that tax-collecting dog, Josiah bar Azor."

"I heard that's not all they did. His wife and children were with him. They murdered them all."

Daniel shrugged. "So? It does no good to kill the dog if you don't kill the pups as well. He was worse than a Gentile, and his wife was even Greek. It's time we rid Israel of his kind...and her kind as well. The Greeks bring their corruption with them, just like the Romans. Lukuas in Cyrenaica and Egypt, Artemion in Cyprus—they had the right idea when they killed anyone who wasn't Jewish. It's time to purge Judaea of the Greeks and Romans and their corrupting influence. We should kill them all, too."

Nathaniel's jaw dropped as he stared at his cousin. He couldn't have actually said what he'd just heard. "Daniel! The LORD commanded that we shouldn't murder. To kill the Roman soldiers, the tax collectors, that's holy war. To kill their women and children, that's murder."

Daniel shrugged again. "Eliakim doesn't think so, and neither do I. You've listened too much to your father about the teachings of that Yeshua."

Nathaniel's chest constricted, making it hard to breathe. He thought he knew his cousin. "It is murder, Daniel, and murder like that doesn't honor the LORD."

A sickening flash of understanding chilled him to the core when Daniel simply shrugged once more. This cousin, the one he had looked up to for so many years, was condoning murder of the innocents. He didn't care what God had commanded at all. He was worse than the Romans because he should have known what was right and wrong in the eyes of God.

It was as if scales fell from his eyes. The path he was on himself was not rebellion against Rome...It was rebellion against God.

"I should have listened to my father. If I hadn't been such a fool listening to you, Reuben would still be alive. May the LORD forgive me for being part of all this." He raised both hands and took a step back. "I can't do this anymore."

Nathaniel turned to leave. Daniel grabbed his tunic. "Don't go. We need you to spy on the Romans. I need you to fight beside me as my brother."

Nathaniel pulled free of his grip. "No. I'm through. I want to serve the LORD, not Eliakim. Tomorrow I'm quitting my job in Sepphoris, and I'm going home."

Chapter 45

The Cost of a Life

Marcus glanced at his brother walking beside him. Lucius looked too serious, like something was gnawing at his insides. He, on the other hand, was having a hard time not grinning. Today might be the day he got another shot at becoming the oldest son.

It was the day after the zealots ambushed Josiah bar Azor. Sepphoris was on edge, waiting for the second sandal to drop. As soon as the commander heard from the paid informants where the murderers had taken shelter, the troops would be launching the reprisal attack.

If Lucius didn't accidentally get killed by a real zealot, it would be the perfect occasion for killing any Jew that was handy and blaming him for Lucius's death. That didn't even have to wait for the troops to move. Anyone would believe that another zealot might be inspired by the first murder to kill the first Roman that was handy.

A young Jew emerged from the wagon maker's shop just ahead of them and headed toward his horse. A sword hung at his side.

Marcus's heart rate ramped up. This was the one he'd been waiting for. No one else was around. Kill this one, kill Lucius, blame the Jew for killing his brother. Not as easy as the ambush should have been, but more certain.

"See that sword? He's one of the zealots. This one's not going to get away."

◆

Lucius turned to look and froze. It was Nathaniel.

"Leave him alone, Marcus. Not everyone with a sword is a zealot. He's not doing anything wrong."

Marcus took a step toward Nathaniel. Lucius put his hand on Marcus's arm to stop him, but Marcus shrugged it off as he glared at his brother. He shoved Lucius away and strode toward his first target.

◆

Nathaniel had just told the foreman that his father needed his help and he was going home to help him. As he walked toward his horse, his heart was buoyant for the first time in months. The last tie to his old zealot life was severed.

Home and family were only a few miles away. He'd have to confess to Abba that he'd been wrong and ask forgiveness, but he knew he'd have it even before he asked. It was good to truly be at peace with God again. He'd made that confession last night, and he was as sure of his forgiveness through Yeshua as he was of Abba's.

As he was preparing to mount, someone jerked his sword from its scabbard. He stumbled back and spun in time to see the tribune toss it away.

The Roman held his own sword ready to stab Nathaniel. As he began the thrust toward his target's chest, Nathaniel swung his arm up and knocked it away. The blade sliced into his forearm, but he managed to scramble away from the horse to get room to maneuver.

As the tribune was about to strike again, a second officer seized his arm and twisted him away from Nathaniel.

"Stop it, Marcus. He wasn't doing anything."

Marcus jerked free from the other's hand. "Get your hand off me, big brother."

Nathaniel kept backing up as he stared at the Roman brothers, the one snarling, the other tight-lipped. They looked like twins, except for a scar on the more muscular one's cheek.

"Get out of here, Nathaniel."

Nathaniel's jaw dropped. He knew that voice. It was the accented Aramaic of the Greek who'd stayed at Abba's house.

He'd always suspected Lucas was the missing Roman officer, but why would he step in to help him when the other Roman was his own brother? Holding his bleeding arm against his chest, Nathaniel stumbled to his horse.

◆

Marcus's lip curled into a snarl as Lucius planted himself between him and his target. The Jew was going to get away before Marcus could kill him, but maybe he didn't have to kill him. Cutting him was enough to be able to claim he'd fought with Lucius. Time to move to the next step in the plan.

"You keep getting in my way, big brother. Time for that to end."

"What?" Lucius stared at Marcus, jaw dropped, brows gathered.

"I ought to have killed you myself. The two I hired bungled it. It's time to correct that mistake."

Time stopped moving as Lucius stared at his brother. Not even for the briefest moment had he suspected his own brother, despite what Jacob had said, despite the warning from their own mother.

Marcus lunged at Lucius, who jumped out of the way as he drew his own sword. His hours of practice with Celsus had increased his response speed well beyond anything Marcus expected. Marcus tried to stab Lucius again, and the sound of metal on metal echoed off the wall of the wagon maker's shop as Lucius deftly deflected his blade.

Nathaniel was struggling to mount. The smell of blood was spooking his horse, and it was hard to control the animal and still get into the saddle with one good arm. He finally made it. He swung the horse to look at the fighting brothers. The Roman was attacking Lucas, but Lucas appeared only to be defending. Then Nathaniel drove his heels into the horse and galloped away.

Marcus thrust his blade toward Lucius's chest, cursing as he did.

Lucius parried. "Why do you want me dead?"

"Stupid question. The inheritance. What else matters? If I get rid of Tertius, too, it will all be mine."

Marcus slashed at Lucius. Lucius caught the sword with his own and turned the blow aside. "Stop! We can work this out."

"Too late for that. You know I want you dead."

Another strike and Lucius parried it easily. "I forgive you for trying to kill me."

"I don't want your forgiveness. I want your death."

Marcus rained several strikes and thrusts on Lucius in rapid succession. Lucius deflected each one with ease. "You don't have to do this."

Marcus lunged at his brother; Lucius sidestepped and swatted the sword aside with his own. "I'll ask Father to give you a larger share."

Two more thrusts and parries. "Marcus, stop! There's more than enough for all of us."

"I don't think so. I want it all."

Lucius deflected Marcus's thrust. He smoothly turned aside the quick slash that followed. "Stop, Marcus! I don't want to kill you."

"What makes you think you can?"

The conversation ended as Marcus began thrusting and slashing as fast as he could. Lucius had always been the better swordsman, and months of practice with Celsus had honed his skill until he was one of the best in the garrison. It was easy to keep deflecting each of Marcus's strikes. He would have had no trouble getting a thrust past Marcus's defenses, but he didn't want his brother dead or even hurt.

He was trapped in a nightmare of flashing metal and ringing blows—unable to get Marcus to stop attacking, unwilling to end the fight by killing him.

A cough exploded behind Lucius. The sound drew his attention for a split second, but that was enough. He was too slow responding to Marcus's next strike, and the sword sliced into his thigh. The leather skirt of his armor kept the blade from cutting to the bone, but the gash was deep enough that he began to bleed freely.

He was in trouble.

The foreman and two of the workers from the shop had heard the fight and come to the doorway. They stood there for a while watching the two officers fighting—one attacking, one defending and trying to talk him out of it. When the foreman coughed, that changed. It had been rich entertainment to see the Romans fighting each other. It would be even better if one of them ended up dead. That looked likely now. Blood was dripping down the leg of the defender, and he was starting to stumble.

Celsus was patrolling that sector of the town with a squad of eight men. He heard the ring of sword-on-sword in the distance, and he started toward it to investigate.

Lucius was struggling to keep his balance. Marcus paused and grinned at his wounded brother. A rivulet of blood was dribbling down his leg. His sandal was already soaked, and the blood made red footprints where his foot rested too long. Lucius was bleeding out, and the kill would soon be easy.

"Looks like I won't be the one dying, big brother. I'll blame that Jew you saved. No one will suspect me. I cut him. I'll claim you did that before he killed you. It will be easy enough to find him. I'll kill him and his family so no one will ever know the truth. First you, then Tertius. Maybe Father, too, and then I'll have it all." His twisted grin grew broader.

◆

Lucius's jaw clenched against the pain and the horrible prospect of his own brother murdering all the people he loved. He couldn't let that happen, not to Rachel's family, not to his own. As the hatred in his brother's eyes burned into him, he made the decision he didn't want to make.

He had to stop Marcus, even if he had to kill him.

If he still could. The wound in his thigh was draining his strength as he continued to bleed. He felt off balance as he was forced to keep his weight off the injured leg. He might not have long before he could no longer fight. *Oh, God! Please! Enough strength to finish this. For Rachel and her family. For Tertius. If I die, receive me, but first let me stop Marcus so they can live.*

Marcus began to maneuver into killing position. As Lucius tried to respond, his leg buckled. He went down, but he rolled onto his back to keep his sword facing Marcus. The sword was getting heavier, maybe too heavy to swing quickly enough to block Marcus's next strike. It was the battle with the jackal all over again, but there would be no one to rescue him this time.

◆

Celsus and his squad rounded the corner at the end of the street, but neither of the brothers looked at him. Celsus started running toward them, but it didn't really matter how fast he moved. Marcus Drusus was moving in for the kill. He was too far away to reach them in time.

◆

An odd ringing in Lucius's ears, everything starting to swirl as he stared up at Marcus...blackout was close...too close. Marcus's gloating face swam through the haze above him.

In choosing not to kill his brother, had he chosen his own death? The haze grew thicker, redder. It was almost over. He'd escaped death in the wadi. There would be no escape this time.

But what about all the innocent ones Marcus was planning to kill? His own pulse pounded in his ears, the ringing faded. Rachel. . . he couldn't let her die by Marcus's hand.

He shook his head to clear it, fought to keep his eyes open. *Oh, God! Help me. Give me strength to save them all.*

Suddenly the world stopped swirling, and renewed strength surged through him as his vision cleared.

Marcus closed in with his sword ready to strike where there was no armor...Lucius's neck just below the jaw. Fool...Marcus could have just let him bleed out, but blood lust had put him within striking range.

As Marcus began the thrust to pierce his throat, Lucius watched it in slow motion. Plenty of time to roll sideways. The sword penetrated the ground, barely missing his neck. As Marcus was pulling his sword out for another try, Lucius rose to his knees and twisted to thrust upward with his own sword. He aimed at the opening in the armor under his brother's arm, just above the seam where the breastplate and backplate met.

The blade slipped smoothly between Marcus's ribs, piercing his lung and nicking his heart. Lucius released his grip on the sword as he collapsed to the ground again. Then he rolled sideways to get out of range of Marcus's next strike and struggled to his feet. The only weapon he had left was his dagger, so he drew it. He held it ready as he stood swaying, fighting to remain standing in case Marcus attacked again.

Marcus pulled the blade out and stared at it, incredulous as he saw it coated with his own blood. He dropped the sword as he collapsed, first to his knees, then falling sideways to lie on his back, staring up at the sky.

Lucius sheathed his dagger. Pressing his hand against his own bleeding thigh, he stumbled over and knelt beside his brother.

Hatred burned in Marcus's eyes as he reached for his own dagger, but Lucius pulled it from the sheath and tossed it aside.

"Oh, Marcus. Why did you make me do this?"

Marcus was fading fast. "All for nothing. It should have been so easy here..."

A final look of hatred twisted his face as he glared at the brother who would have done anything for him. Then the fire in his eyes dimmed, and his eyelids closed.

He was dead.

Lucius rocked back on his calves. Grief and pain tore at him as he raised his eyes to the sky. His cry shattered the silence.

"Why?"

Then everything began to swirl again, and he collapsed beside his brother's corpse.

◆

Thickening darkness enveloped Lucius. Then someone knelt beside him. A jerk shot pain through him as something tightened around his thigh. A hand rested on his shoulder. Would he have one final glimpse of those cinnamon eyes of compassion and that gentle smile that had given him hope? He opened his eyes.

He only saw Celsus.

"Stay with me, Drusus. I've stopped the bleeding. I'll get you to the physician quickly."

The gruff voice was fading away, disappearing down a tunnel. Celsus's face started to dance behind little sparkles and then grow dim. Night was coming awfully early today. Maybe he should just rest awhile...

Lucius closed his eyes. Celsus shook his shoulder.

"Drusus!"

Lucius's eyes flickered open, then shut again. Somewhere in the far distance he heard Celsus's voice.

"You four, carry him to the physician. Run!"

Chapter 46

COMING HOME

Joseph had just finished making a hub ring when he heard the horse coming up behind him. When he turned from the forge to see Nathaniel, a broad smile curved his lips. It flipped to a frown when he saw the blood-soaked bandage on Nathaniel's arm.

"I'd like to come home for good, Abba, if you'll have me." Nathaniel cast his eyes to the ground. He took a deep breath before he looked up at his father and continued. "You were right all along. I was a fool to think violence was the way. I'm ready to follow Yeshua again."

Joseph strode to his side. "I've been asking the LORD for this since you left. Blessed be the LORD for bringing you home!"

Nathaniel swung his leg over his horse's neck and slid off. Joseph took the reins as he wrapped his arm around his son, being careful of the wounded arm. "How did this happen?"

"Lucas...I treated him as my enemy, and he just saved me."

Joseph stared at him. "Lucas?"

"I was right. He was that missing tribune. Another Roman just tried to kill me, and Lucas stopped him."

Rachel was coming out of the storeroom with a small bag of grain. When she saw Nathaniel, she dropped it and ran to him. "Nathaniel, you're wounded!"

"It's not bad, Rachel. Wash it, bandage it, and I'll be fine."

"What happened?"

"A Roman tried to kill me." Her eyes grew huge as her hand flew to her mouth. "But another one saved me...your Lucas."

"Lucas? You saw him? Is he hurt?" Panic filled her eyes.

"I don't think so. The Roman trying to kill me called him big brother. They were in a sword fight when I left, but Lucas was only defending so I don't think it was serious."

Rachel gasped. "It was his brother Marcus? Oh, Nathaniel! Even if his brother was trying to kill him, Lucas would try not to hurt him." She bit her lip.

He smiled down at her as he pushed a wisp of hair behind her ear. "I really don't think they were serious. He should be fine, little one."

◆

Rachel stared into her brother's eyes. He would lie to shield her, but she saw truth there. Nathaniel was a fighter, so he should know. His assurance convinced her...almost. She focused back on his arm. "Come with me and let me take care of that arm. I want to make sure you're going to be fine."

"I'm home for good, Rachel. No more battles for me. You won't have to worry about me again."

She hugged his good arm. "I'm so glad. I worried and prayed all the time while you were with the zealots. It's good to finally have you home."

As she walked her brother into the house, she gave thanks that she wouldn't have to worry so much about his safety. If only she didn't have to worry about Lucas's safety now.

◆

Dinner was a joyful affair with Nathaniel back for good. Rachel's heart sang with him sitting next to Abba again, just like he should be. Abba had offered special prayers of thanksgiving for his return and for Lucas having saved him.

But Rachel's joy was tempered by worry that Lucas might be hurt, no matter what Nathaniel had said. Hurt but not dead. She was sure she would know if he were dead. She would feel the hole in the universe if he were to die.

◆

After the last prayers, Rachel began cleaning up the remains of their dinner. While she was distracted, Simeon moved close to Joseph and spoke so only he would hear.

"Abba, can I talk with you alone? There's something I think you should know."

Joseph's brow furrowed. "What is it?"

Simeon motioned for his father to follow him away from the others, and Joseph complied. When they were out of earshot, Simeon faced him straight on.

"Lucas is in love with Rachel. He'd like to marry her, but he thought you'd never give your permission with him being Roman. He never told her because he thought it was hopeless. Rachel loves him, too. Since Lucas saved Nathaniel, would you let him marry Rachel if he asked?"

Joseph stared at his son with his eyebrows scrunched. "Are you sure of this? For both of them?"

"Yes, Abba. Lucas told me himself a week before he left, and I heard Rachel tell Daniel that she would have married Lucas if he'd asked her."

Joseph stood in silence, rubbing his bearded cheek. He had seen that Rachel liked Lucas as a friend, but if he meant more to her, she had never let it show. But then, neither had Lucas.

"It is good you told me, Simeon. I will talk with Rachel about this. If you are right, I will go to Lucas and see where his heart lies as well."

As they walked back to the canopy, Simeon was grinning.

Rachel was gathering up the cushions when she realized her father was standing with his arms crossed, staring at her with serious eyes.

"Did you want something, Abba?"

"Yes. I want the truth." He cleared his throat. "Lucas of Corinth. What do you really think of him?"

"I think he's a brave and generous man. For him to risk himself to save Nathaniel...I wish he was here for me to thank."

"That was not my question." He paused as he fixed his eyes on hers. "Do you love him as a man?"

Her eyes widened. She'd been so careful to conceal her heart from both Lucas and Abba. But Abba had asked, and she would never lie to him about anything.

"Yes, Abba. I do." A sad smile flitted across her lips before she could stop it. "I wish he'd loved me, too. I would have loved to be his wife. He had a good heart even before he decided to follow Yeshua, and afterwards...well, he has such a wonderful heart for the LORD."

"Simeon tells me he loves you."

Her eyebrows shot up. "But he never let me know. If he had, I would have asked you to let us marry. He's exactly the kind of man I want as my husband." She looked at her father with a question in her eyes. "He's the only man I do want, Abba. I know he's Roman, but do

279

you think...maybe...since he saved Nathanial..."

"Maybe I might give permission for you two to marry?" A wry smile appeared. "I have been asking the LORD to bring the right husband for you, a good man who loves Yeshua as we do. I did not expect him to bring me a Roman, but who am I to question what the LORD brings in answer to my prayers? Tomorrow, I will go speak with him to learn his heart, and then I will decide."

She threw her arms around him and hugged with the strength born of a joyous heart. "Oh, thank you, Abba!"

◆

As Joseph wrapped his arms around his precious daughter, his throat felt much too small. She had grown into a second Hannah...so gentle, so loving, so strong. How could he bear no longer having her with him every day? But then he looked at her shining eyes. She deserved a good husband and a family of her own. He had no doubt about the goodness of Lucas. If any man could deserve his treasure, perhaps it was him.

Chapter 47

The Greatest Gift

Joseph stood across the road from the garrison gate and took a deep breath. Lucas was somewhere inside, but how does a man ask to see his friend when he doesn't know his real name?

He squared his shoulders and marched toward the guard, who placed his hand on the pommel of his sword as Joseph approached.

"I wish to see the missing officer who returned a couple of weeks ago."

The guard frowned at him. "Your business with him?"

"He is a friend."

"His name?"

Joseph hesitated. "Lucas." That name wasn't Roman, but perhaps the guard knew his nickname.

"There is no officer with that name." The guard gripped his sword as if preparing to draw it.

"He spent seven weeks with us using that name. I do not know what name he uses here."

The guard began to slide his sword from the scabbard. "Go. You have no business here if you can't give me his name."

◆

Celsus was walking across the courtyard when he noticed the tension at the gate. He strode over.

"What's going on here?"

The guard's fist hit his chest in salute. "This man is asking to see Lucius Drusus, centurion. He claims to be a friend, but he didn't know his name."

Celsus scanned the brawny Jew from head to foot. He didn't look hostile, but an assassin seldom did until he struck. Drusus was his friend, and he'd told him about making wheels with the father of the Jewish family that hid him. If this man was from that family, Drusus would want to see him.

"I'll attend to this." He frowned at Joseph. "Come with me."

Joseph followed Celsus a short distance into the courtyard. The centurion turned to face him, arms crossed, feet spread apart. "Why do you want to see Lucius Drusus?"

"He is a friend, and I have something to ask him. He will want to see me if you tell him Joseph bar Jonah is here."

"Drusus is with the physician. His brother tried to kill him."

Celsus had expected some surprise on the Jew's face. His frown deepened when he didn't see any.

"And his brother?"

"Drusus killed him to save himself."

The Jew's lips tightened as he shook his head. "Then truly, I must see him."

Celsus scrutinized his face, paying special attention to his eyes. That might be true concern. The Jew might be telling the truth about being Drusus's friend. If this was the wagonmaker, it might be vital for him to visit without delay. The physician said that morning that Drusus didn't seem to care if he lived after killing the brother who betrayed him. This visitor was worth the risk if it meant his friend wouldn't give up and die.

"You can see him."

Celsus waved at one of the soldiers to summon him. "Escort this man to Lucius Drusus and remain with him while he visits." He turned intimidating eyes back on Joseph. "I want no harm to come to my friend."

◆

Joseph nodded his understanding and followed the soldier. When he was escorted into Lucius's room, his eyes narrowed. Lucius was lying on the bed, pale from blood loss, his eyes closed, and a dejected look on his face.

"Lucas."

The deep voice penetrated Lucius's darkness. His eyes snapped open. "Joseph? I didn't expect to see you. Is everything all right?"

"At my house, yes, but not with you, it seems."

The soldier had been standing with his hand resting on his sword, scowling at the Jew who claimed to be a friend to make sure he didn't attack the wounded officer.

Lucius shifted to prop himself up a little before speaking. "This man is a friend. One I trust completely. You can go."

The soldier saluted and left the room.

Joseph walked over to the bedside and smiled down at him. "Nathaniel told us you were in a fight, but I did not expect to find you like this."

Lucius's eyes widened. Joseph's smile and eyes radiated genuine warmth, as if he were looking at one of his sons.

He managed a weak smile in return, but his reply lacked energy. "I'm glad you came. It's good to see you again."

His thoughts flew to Rachel. How he wished he could see her again, too. Her laughing eyes, her joyful smile, the gentle touches on his arm...

Joseph's words pulled him back. "I came for two reasons, Lucas. First, to thank you for stopping your brother from killing Nathaniel. I know that cost you more than I can repay. To save the life of my son almost cost your own. Even more, I am thankful he has come back to follow Yeshua instead of the zealots. You helped him make that choice. The LORD used you to restore my son who was lost, and I thank the LORD that He brought you to be with us."

"You owe me nothing, Joseph. You saved my life, and then you led me to Yeshua. I owe you my life two times over. It was worth whatever it cost to help your son return to you." His smile faded as his thoughts turned to Reuben, the son he took away forever.

◆

The deep sadness in the Roman's eyes tugged at Joseph's heart. Lucas had killed his own brother to save Nathaniel. What pain that must have caused. He rested his hand on Lucas's arm. "I am sorry you had to kill your brother to save my son."

Lucius shook his head twice. "It wasn't only to save Nathaniel. Marcus was going to kill your whole family and my own younger brother and maybe my father as well. I took one life to save seven, eight if you count my own."

He pulled a deep breath before his next words. "I didn't want to kill him. I tried not to, but sometimes a man must choose what he never wanted. In the end, I had no choice. The LORD gave me the strength I needed when I had none of my own left."

Joseph gazed deep into Lucas's eyes. They were too much like his own had been when Reuben died. Lucas was tightly wrapped and suffocating in sadness, but the next thing he would tell him should help with that.

"I came for one more reason. A much happier one, I think. Simeon told me something. I came to find out if it is true."

Lucas furrowed his brow. "What did Simeon tell you?"

"He tells me that you love my Rachel. Is that true?"

Lucas took a deep breath and blew it out before answering. "Yes. She's so kind and loving and...I couldn't help falling in love with her. But I swear I never did anything about it. I never even told her."

Joseph nodded. "I believe you. You should know that Rachel loves you, too."

Lucas's eyebrows shot up. That revelation struck him speechless.

Joseph almost laughed at his young friend's astonishment. "So, since you love her and she loves you, what would you like to do about that?"

"I've wanted to marry her since the second week after I met her, but I was sure you would never let her marry a Roman."

"Any other Roman, no." He raised his hands in the pacifying gesture he often used with Benjamin. "But the LORD has provided no Jewish man who follows Yeshua who could be her husband. Maybe it was the LORD who brought you to my house for that purpose. If so, who am I to stand in the way of the will of the LORD? When you are strong again, come and ask her for her hand. When she says yes, I will as well." He grinned at Lucas as he said "when" instead of "if."

He expected this news to light up Lucas's face with happiness. For an instant, he saw the joy, but almost immediately it was replaced by sadness. That was very odd.

"What is wrong, Lucas?"

◆

Lucius swallowed hard. The moment of truth had come, the truth he had hoped he would never have to reveal.

"There's something you need to know before I ask for her hand. Something that might make you refuse to accept me as your son-in-law. Something that might make Rachel want nothing to do with me ever again."

He paused, struggling to find the words that would surely end all hope of ever having Rachel as his wife. *LORD, help me. They deserve the truth, but how am I ever going to live with the consequences?*

Joseph's smile vanished, and his eyebrows dipped as Lucius struggled with his confession. His eyes drilled into Lucius as he waited to hear what he must say.

"That day in Gath-Hepher, when Reuben was trying to get Nathaniel to come home and he was killed...I was the one who killed him. I didn't see that he had no sword until it was too late." Lucius locked his gaze on Joseph's eyes. "I still see him lying there, smiling at me, saying he forgave me. Now that I follow Yeshua, I understand why he could forgive me, but I can't forgive myself. I took Reuben from all of you."

The blood drained from Joseph's face as he stared at Lucius. The shock and pain in his eyes were beyond what Lucius had ever imagined. It was as if he'd ripped open a half-healed wound so the blood gushed out again.

Lucius closed his eyes, unable to bear looking at Joseph's pain, unwilling to see the anger that must surely follow. His lips tightened as Reuben's last smile and words of forgiveness played once more in his mind. "I would give anything to have Reuben alive instead of dead by my hand. But there are no second chances in battle, and no amount of regret can undo what I've already done."

The long silence ripped deeper into his heart than anything Joseph might have said. Then Joseph's hand rested upon his shoulder. He opened his eyes.

A trace of tears clouded Joseph's eyes as he looked at the Roman soldier who had killed one son but rescued another.

"On his cross, Yeshua forgave the Roman soldiers who crucified him. It has not been as easy for me to forgive. When Rachel brought you home, I did not want to help any Roman after one killed Reuben. She convinced me to do it for Yeshua, not you. But really, Yeshua had me help you for me, to take the bitterness from my own heart. I struggled not to hate the man who killed my son, but I did not want to forgive him. I knew I should, but I couldn't.

"But now, Lucas, I can. I can forgive you, just as Reuben did. You took Reuben, but you did not mean to, and you have given me back Nathaniel. And for that, I am very thankful. Without you, he would still be lost to me and to Yeshua."

Joseph lifted his hand. "So...if Rachel wants to marry you, I will welcome you as my son-in-law."

Joseph's words of forgiveness were rays of light piercing the shadows of guilt and regret, lifting Lucius from shade into sunshine. But one deep pocket of darkness remained.

"You'll never know how much your forgiveness means to me, Joseph." He paused, and deep sigh escaped. "But what would Rachel say if I told her? Even if she loves me now, how could she after she knows? She loved Reuben so much. I know she'll try to forgive me, but even if she can, it's too much to expect she could still love me. I wouldn't blame her if she hated me. It's what I deserve."

Joseph saw the sorrowful resignation in the young Roman's eyes, and he knew what it meant. Lucas was afraid to tell her, afraid of seeing her pain, afraid she would reject him. No matter how brave he was, he didn't have enough courage to make that revelation himself and face what it might bring.

"I think this is not something you should tell her. I will tell her for you. If she no longer loves you and does not want to marry you, I will send Simeon to tell you right away."

Lucius's whole body relaxed as relief flooded his face. His lips curved into a grateful smile.

"Thank you, Joseph." His husky voice spoke far more than the words.

A new brightness filled the young Roman's eyes, and Joseph's smiled mirrored Lucas's. It was good to spare Lucas from making that confession himself.

"But I do not think you should expect Simeon to come. I know my Rachel, and I think you will have to suffer having me as your father-in-law."

Joseph patted his shoulder, and Lucas of Corinth looked up at him with more hope than he had seen on any face in a very long time.

"I will leave you to rest now. I expect you at my house soon to propose to my daughter."

Lucius's eyes remained fixed on Joseph as he walked out the door. The cloud of guilt he'd carried for the last seven months had just been dispersed by words of forgiveness from the man with every right to hate him.

Yeshua had given both Reuben and Joseph the power to forgive the unforgivable. Though Yeshua, God had forgiven him as well.

Love was more powerful than hate, and forgiveness was the most precious gift that came from love. Surely Joseph was right, and Rachel would forgive him, too.

◆

The garrison physician's brow furrowed as he walked down the hall to check on Lucius Drusus. The young tribune's life was at risk, but the problem wasn't something a physician could fix. After having to kill his brother to save himself, he didn't seem to care whether he recovered or not. The wound in his thigh wasn't that severe, but he'd seen men die of lesser injuries when they lost the will to live.

The physician was surprised to see a brawny Jew wearing a wry smile emerge from the room as he approached. He was even more surprised when he stepped into the room and found Drusus lying there with his hands clasped behind his head and a big grin on his face.

"I was hoping you'd come soon. I need to know when you think I'll be able to ride. I have some important personal business to attend to."

Chapter 48

A True Friend

Joseph expected Rachel to be eagerly awaiting his return, and he was not disappointed. The moment he came through the gate, she dropped her shuttle and hurried across the courtyard to meet him. "Did you see him, Abba? Is he hurt?"

"I did. He did not look well when I got there, but he was much better when I left."

Rachel's hand flew to her mouth. "What did Marcus do to him?"

"He tried to kill him. He did cut his thigh, but that was not the worst. He made Lucas kill him to save our family and his own younger brother."

Her eyes widened. "Oh, no! Lucas loved Marcus. He thought they'd finally become good friends here. That must be tearing him apart."

"Perhaps when I got there, but not so much now. He was smiling when I left." He rested his hand on her cheek. "I gave him two things he needed."

She tipped her head as her brows drew together. "What did you give him, Abba?"

"My permission to ask you for your hand and my forgiveness."

He had only compounded her confusion. "What did he need your forgiveness for?"

Joseph placed his hands on her shoulders to steady her before he spoke what Lucas was afraid to. "He told me he was the one who killed Reuben." Her hands flew to her mouth. Her eyes saucered at the news, but she still stood. "But he did not mean to. He thought Reuben was

288

attacking him. He stabbed Reuben before he saw he had no sword. He has been haunted by it, even though Reuben forgave him as he was dying." Joseph reached up and pushed a strand of hair behind her ear. "I have forgiven him as well, and it was good to see the LORD lift the burden of guilt from him when I did."

Joseph's lip twitched up in a wry smile. "The LORD's ways surprise me sometimes. When I told him I forgave him, the LORD lifted a burden from my own heart as well. I refused to treat him as my friend because I only saw him as a Roman, like the man who killed my son. Lucas chose to be my friend, even though I never wanted him to. I gladly return his friendship now."

He rested his palm on her cheek and stroked it with his thumb. "He was afraid to tell you he had killed Reuben. Afraid you would hate him when you knew. I told him I would tell you for him and then see if you think you can forgive him and still love him."

"Oh, Abba! Of course I can forgive him. If Reuben forgave him, how can I do otherwise?" Teardrops glistened at the corner of her eyes. She wiped one away with her fingertip. "The week before he left, he saw me crying and wanted to know why. When I told him how Reuben died, you should have seen how it tortured him. He told me then he would do anything to bring Reuben back if he could. I knew he meant it with his whole heart. He loved us like family by then. To know he was the cause of our pain—nothing could have hurt him more. He has such a good heart..."

Joseph wiped away the teardrop at the corner of her other eye.

"So, when he comes to ask to be my son-in-law as well as my friend, what shall I tell him?"

"Yes! Tell him yes. There is nothing in this world I want more than to be his wife."

As Rachel bounced on her toes, Joseph stifled a laugh.

"I thought that would be your answer. I consider you betrothed to him now. It may be a while before he can get here with his bad leg, but he will come soon to ask you for your hand. I told him he should come ask you himself." Joseph's smile broadened as he leaned over to kiss her forehead. "I thought that was something both of you might enjoy."

He gazed down at his precious girl as she hugged him, her eyes now sparkling with joy instead of tears. She was more like Hannah every day. He had dreaded this moment, but somehow he was happy about it, too.

Joseph's brow furrowed. Lucas was the right husband for Rachel, but how to handle their marriage—that posed a problem. It would cause a stir in the village when it became known that he had betrothed his daughter to the Greek God-fearer. Lucas was liked and respected by the men in the synagogue, except for Benjamin, of course. When they found out he was really a Roman, Joseph expected that to change. Lucas of Corinth was welcome. Lucius Drusus would not be.

It had been a week since Joseph's visit, and Simeon had not appeared. Lucius was a patient man, but each new day that he couldn't go to Rachel's house to seal their future seemed an eternity. The problem was the wound in his thigh. The garrison physician told him he shouldn't even think about riding for at least four weeks after such an injury, but it was impossible to wait that long. There must be a way to get there sooner.

He hobbled across the garrison courtyard to the main gate using his crutch. It was so much easier getting around when he didn't have bruised ribs as well as a bad leg. Using the crutch didn't hurt at all. He leaned against the wall just outside the gate and watched the people passing until he saw a merchant he knew.

"Hezekiah bar Akim."

The man paused when he heard his name, then looked in the direction it came from.

"Drusus. I haven't seen you in a long time. I thought perhaps you had returned to Rome." He gazed at the bandaged leg and the crutch that Lucius held in one hand. His eyebrows rose, but he didn't care enough to ask about either.

"No, my time of service is far from over. Are you going near Jacob bar Asa's inn today?"

"I am on my way there now."

"Would you tell him that I have great need of his help and ask him to come to me here when he can?"

"Of course, Drusus."

"You have my thanks, Hezekiah."

The merchant nodded and continued on his way.

Lucius hobbled back into the courtyard and found a seat on a bench under a tree. He had been so angry and said such hateful things the last time he saw Jacob. He wouldn't blame him if he didn't come, but if his friend came, he would be waiting for him.

It was less than half an hour before Jacob entered the garrison gate and told the guard on duty that he was looking for Lucius Drusus. When he was directed toward the tree, he hurried over.

"Lucius! What happened to you?"

Lucius tightened his lips and shook his head slowly. "You were right, Jacob, and I should have listened to you. I was a fool not to see that you only spoke because you care what happens to me. Marcus tried to kill me. He did it himself this time instead of hiring someone to do it for him...and I had to kill him. He was going to kill some people I care about here and then my younger brother if I didn't stop him."

He looked down at the ground and then up at his friend. "I hope you'll forgive me for my anger when you were only telling me the truth. I should have trusted you as my friend...my true friend."

Jacob stepped close and placed his hand on Lucius's shoulder. "There is nothing to forgive. If a man cannot trust his brother above all others, who should he trust? I am just glad to see your brother failed." One corner of his mouth turned up more in a joking smile. "We need at least one good Roman here in Sepphoris."

Lucius slapped Jacob's hand in appreciation of the friendship it conveyed. "Sit with me, Jacob. I have an important favor to ask of you."

"If it is something I can do, just ask."

"I need to go to the house of Joseph bar Jonah about five miles south on the Legio road, but I won't be able to ride for at least two more weeks. I can't wait that long."

"I can borrow a cart and horse from my brother-in-law and take you there tomorrow. It would probably not be safe for you to go alone the way you are. Will your business take long?"

A crooked grin appeared. "It's not exactly business, Jacob."

"No?"

"No. I'm going to ask the woman who saved my life the first time to marry me."

Jacob's eyebrows shot up. "Does she know what you plan? Isn't she a good Jewish girl? She'll obey her father in this. Will her father say yes to a Roman marrying his daughter?"

A grin split Lucius's face. "Strange as it may seem, Joseph came here to give me his permission even before I knew she loved me. He's the one who told me she does."

The grin faded as his brow furrowed. "It's ironic, Jacob. I was so careful to hide my love from her because I thought her father would only let her marry a good Jew. I had no hope of ever being with her again after I left her father's house. She never let me know she loved me because I hid my feelings so well she never suspected them. Her younger brother told her father how I felt, and he came here to see if I loved her and wanted her as my wife." The grin reappeared. "You could say her father arranged the match. She'll only marry a man who follows Yeshua, but Joseph himself led me to believe in Him. While I was with them, her father was very cold because I'm Roman, but it doesn't matter to him now."

"And what of the men of their village? They welcomed a Roman?"

"I went to synagogue with them for almost seven weeks. Most of them welcomed me, but they think I'm a Greek that her brothers found after a robbery. They know I became a God-fearer while I was with them. Unless Joseph told them after I left, no one knows what I truly am."

Jacob tightened his lips and nodded. "I think you will wear some of my son's clothes for the trip. I will be happy to drive my God-fearing Greek friend to visit his betrothed. It would not be wise for me to drive a wounded Roman officer into any village near here. Zealots are everywhere, and you never know...The LORD has spared you from death two times. Let us not test Him by trying for three."

Chapter 49

HOW TO MARRY A ROMAN

It was midmorning when Jacob drove the cart up to the gate. Joseph was at his forge, and Nathaniel sat at the workbench. Nathaniel glanced over when he heard the creak of the cart wheels.

"Abba, he's come."

Joseph turned and spread his arms in welcome as he walked over to the cart. "Welcome back, Lucas. We have been expecting you."

Jacob hopped out and walked around the cart to help his young friend down, but Joseph was ahead of him to lift Lucas down so he wouldn't hurt his leg.

"It is good to have you with us again." He reached into the cart and took out the crutch. "We sent you off in better shape than this, but I think Rachel will be glad to help you with your crutch again, if you need her to." He placed his arm around Lucius's shoulder as he grinned at his future son-in-law. "She is in the storeroom. Go to her."

Lucius grinned back. "First, I want you to meet my good friend, Jacob bar Asa. He helped me learn Aramaic, so I owe him my life and my faith as much as I owe it to you, Joseph."

Joseph spread his arms to welcome Jacob. "Shalom, Jacob. Tie your horse and come talk a while. Any friend of Lucas is welcome as a friend in my house." He turned again to Lucius. "Now, you go. Rachel is waiting for you."

With his crutch beneath his arm, Lucius hopped over to the house as quickly as he could. Then he stood to the side of the door where she might not see him, waiting for her to emerge.

Rachel came from the storeroom with a small sack of grain. He waited until she set it down by the quern.

"Will you let a Roman with a bad leg watch you grinding today? I promise I'll rest later if you do."

She spun around. "Lucas!"

She held out her hands and stepped toward him. He let his crutch fall as he opened his arms to receive her. She flung her arms around him and snuggled into his chest. His heart pulsed against her cheek, speeding up like a stallion straining to win a race. He pulled her closer. A contented sigh escaped as he rested his own cheek on the soft pillow of her hair. After much too short a time from his perspective, she eased away from him and tipped her face to gaze into his eyes.

"Abba said you would be coming."

"Did he tell you why?"

Simeon had never come, but he wasn't sure exactly what her father had told her and how she had reacted to the news. The last time he held her like this was the day he learned he'd killed her twin.

"Yes." Her cinnamon eyes sparkled. "He told me I'm betrothed now. He finally found me a husband who follows Yeshua that he thinks is good enough."

"Are you happy about that, Rachel? Even after he told you what I did?"

Uncertainty darkened his eyes.

"Oh, yes, Lucas." She rested her palm on his cheek and stroked it with her thumb. "I love you, and there's nothing I need to forgive. You didn't mean to kill my brother. He understood and forgave you. Even Reuben would be happy to have me marry you. Someday you'll meet him, and he'll greet you gladly as his brother."

He pushed some hair behind her ear as her eyes shone with love. Her love...so much like Yeshua's that she could give it to an enemy soldier who'd murdered her brother. And with that love...forgiveness. He should have known her forgiveness would be so freely given, but hearing it spoken freed him from the last shadow of guilt.

A playful smile appeared as she traced the scar on his clean-shaven cheek with her fingertip. "You know, Lucas, if I'm to be your wife, you should tell me your real name and where you're from. Did you know you never have?"

"Lucius Claudius Drusus. The main family estates are east and northeast of Rome. I grew up mostly on the eastern estate. It was where my father lived until he arranged for Grandfather to die in the arena when I was sixteen. Then he moved into Grandfather's house in Rome. I mostly stayed at the eastern estate where my mother remained."

"So you didn't leave Corinth at seventeen."

"Actually, I did. Father took me and Marcus there for a few weeks after Marcus almost killed me when we were sparring." He dragged his thumb along the scar. "That's when I got this." His lips tightened as he shrugged. "I thought it was an accident then, but now I'm sure it wasn't. Marcus was only trying to do what Father had done." He looked away from her. "Father arranged my uncle's death to become the oldest son. Then he reported Grandfather to get him killed as a Christian so he could became head of the Drusus family."

His shoulders drooped as he spoke of what his father and brother had done.

Again she traced the scar with her forefinger. "You once told me your father taught you nothing worth learning. I see why. I'm sorry, Lucas...Lucius."

"I'd rather you keep calling me Lucas. You grew to love me with that name. I want to be the Lucas who loves you and Yeshua, not the Lucius who served Rome, no matter what she asked of me."

"I'll call you whatever you want...as long as I get to call you husband as well."

Lucius shifted his weight fleetingly onto his bad leg, then back to his good one. Her teasing smile flickered at that sign of weakness.

"It's time to get you off your leg, Lucas. Did you want to sit out here under the canopy and keep me company? I need to be grinding the flour until it's time to serve Abba and your friend something. I still have your bench here for you."

He grinned at her. "I'll do whatever you think is best for me, Rachel."

She traced the scar one more time, her eyes glowing as she gazed into his. Then she hugged his arm before she picked up his crutch and handed it to him.

"I think having you near is best for both of us."

The four men sat around the mat as Rachel served them dates and wine. Lucius's eyes kept lingering on her.

Joseph grinned. More than twenty years ago, he had looked at Hannah the same way. "So, Lucas, there are things we need to arrange if you are to wed my Rachel."

Lucius snapped his eyes back on Joseph. "I would like to marry her as soon as possible. What do I need to do?"

"I have given that some thought. Since you are only a God-fearer and not a Jew, Rabbi Eliezer may not be willing to conduct your wedding. Then again, he may. He has never been asked to celebrate a wedding with a Gentile bridegroom before. I don't know how that is to be done, either."

Lucius's brow furrowed. "I hadn't realized that would be a problem."

Jacob leaned over and rested his hand on Lucius's shoulder. "I can help you with this, Lucius. I have been to such weddings before. I have had some in my inn, and I can tell you what was done."

Lucius focused on Jacob. Here was the man who had looked past him being part of the hated Roman occupation to see a man eager to learn his language and wanting to call him friend. He cared enough to warn him about Marcus. He received only anger in return for his concern, but he still came as soon as he knew Lucius needed his help. In this land of masked hostility and fake friendliness, Jacob was as true a friend as any man could want.

"I have something more to ask of you, Jacob. As my friend, I want you with me at the wedding to make sure I do what a good Jewish bridegroom should."

Jacob's eyebrows shot up. "Are you asking me to be the shoshbin, the friend of the bridegroom?"

A sheepish grin spread across Lucius's face. "I haven't learned that word, but I think so." He turned to her father. "Am I, Joseph?"

Her father nodded. "You are."

"Will you be my shoshbin, Jacob?"

Jacob's delight at Lucius's request lit up his face. "I would be honored, Lucius. Deeply honored."

Joseph nodded his approval. "Jacob and I will make the plans, and we will get you and Rachel married very soon. There is no need for this betrothal to last a year." He flicked his hand toward Rachel. "Now go to her so the two of you can talk for a while before you have to return to Sepphoris."

Joseph stood and helped Lucius to his feet before handing him the crutch. With a broad grin, Lucius turned and headed toward the loom where Rachel was working. It was always a good idea to obey Joseph's commands promptly, and this was one command he was particularly eager to obey.

It was midafternoon and almost time to return to Sepphoris. The visit had been too short as far as Lucius and Rachel were concerned. As they began their stroll back to the cart, Nathaniel stepped in front of them.

"I need to take him from you for a moment, Rachel." He fixed serious eyes first on Lucius, then on Rachel. "There are some things I need to say to him."

Nathaniel chuckled at the uneasiness in her eyes as she wrapped her arm protectively around Lucius. "Don't worry, little one. I'm not going to hurt your Roman. You can have him back when I'm through."

She relaxed. "Just don't take too long."

Lucius's contented eyes followed her as she walked over to talk with Joseph and Jacob. Then he turned them on Nathaniel.

Nathaniel cleared his throat, then locked his eyes on the Roman's. "There's no way I can thank you enough for risking your own life to save mine, but there is something you did for me that's even more important than that." Nathaniel glanced down at the ground, then pressed on to speak the words that once would have choked him. "I want to thank you for helping me see how wrong I was to support the zealot attacks. When I learned how the tax collector's children were murdered before his eyes, I knew what I was part of could never be pleasing to the LORD. I knew I needed to return to following Yeshua. I was already on my way home when you stopped your brother."

He shook his head as he remembered. "All those dinners where I tried to force you into anger so you would reveal who you were...I was a fool. If you hadn't kept your head, I would have killed you. Instead, you showed me how a man who wants to please the LORD should respond."

He placed his hand on Lucius's shoulder. "I once told you that you would never be worthy to be with my sister. I was wrong. I'm glad you'll be Rachel's husband. She deserves the best, and she couldn't do better. I'll gladly call you brother-in-law."

Lucius placed his hand on Nathaniel's before he withdrew it. "Life is strange sometimes. What Marcus meant for evil, the LORD used for good. If he hadn't hired the assassins to throw me off the cliff, I would never have met your family. I may never have learned about the LORD and how Yeshua saved me. If I hadn't fought Marcus to save you, I would never have known Rachel loves me. I would never have known Joseph's forgiveness or had his permission to marry your sister. My own father isn't a man I can admire, but Joseph is the finest man I've ever known. I look forward to calling him father."

Lucius offered his arm to his future brother-in-law. "And I look forward to having you as my brother and friend, something my own brother never was."

A friendly smile hovered on Nathaniel's lips as he took the offered arm. Having this Roman as a brother was something even a former zealot could look forward to.

A few days later, Jacob drove the cart up to Joseph's gate again. With him, he had two versions of the marriage contract. He had crafted the first *ketubah*, the one that would be read at the wedding, to make sure no one would know who Lucius really was or how rich he would someday be. Lucas of Corinth would be marrying Rachel bat Joseph. Lucas was a skilled workman, making what a wagon maker in Sepphoris would be expected to earn.

The second *ketubah*, the true marriage contract, named Lucius Claudius Drusus, Roman tribune with a monthly income of 1500 denarii and heir to the six million denarii that was half of the Claudius Drusus fortune.

Joseph heard the cart stop and came from the forge as Jacob climbed down. "Shalom, Jacob."

"Shalom, Joseph. I have come to get your approval of the marriage contract, but there is something special we need to discuss first."

"Come to the canopy. Rachel will bring some refreshments for us."

As Jacob walked beside Joseph, he struggled to suppress a grin. He expected the expression on Joseph's face to be priceless when he read the true contract.

Rachel stood by her loom, beaming as she watched them come. In her happy eyes, Jacob saw his own daughters and their excitement over the arrival of the marriage contract. As soon as it was approved, the final preparations for a marriage could begin.

She shook the serving mat and fluffed two cushions. "It's good to see you again, Jacob. I'll be right back with some wine and dates." With another bright smile, she disappeared into the house.

They settled on the cushions, and Jacob pulled the two scrolls from the bag he carried.

"I have given this much thought, and I think we cannot risk what might happen if your village were to learn you kept a Roman officer with you and even intend to let him marry Rachel. I have found an easy solution to that problem."

Joseph's lips tightened as he slowly nodded. "I have worried about that myself. It could be very unwise. So, what do you propose?"

"I have drawn up two *ketubot*. The first is the one we will read at the wedding. The other is the real one. I can serve as one witness. Is there a man here that you can trust with a dangerous secret? If so, he can be the second witness."

"Eli is a true friend and a man I would trust with anything. He thinks well of Lucas, so I am sure he will be glad to help." Joseph's eyebrows dipped as Jacob's question drilled into his mind. "But what is this dangerous secret about the man I am allowing to marry my daughter?"

A laugh rumbled from Jacob's throat. "Not dangerous to Rachel. No, only to the peace of mind of the village. Here is the *ketubah* to read at the wedding."

Joseph scanned through it. It would seem reasonable to any of the men in the village, given what they knew of Lucas.

Jacob pressed his lips together as he handed the second scroll to Joseph, but try as he might, he couldn't quite suppress the grin. "Here is the true *ketubah*, listing Lucas's real name and what he will bring to the marriage."

Joseph began to read with a relaxed expression. As he got past Lucius's name and into the financial portions, his brow first furrowed, then his eyebrows shot up as he read further.

"Is this all true, Jacob?"

Jacob grinned. "It is. Now you see why I think two versions are such a good idea."

Joseph covered his mouth with his hand and stroked his beard. He shook his head as he read the numbers one more time before looking up at Jacob.

"So I should not have to worry about him being able to support my Rachel." He blew his breath out. "Yes, two versions are an excellent idea." He grinned at Jacob. "I think I can agree to the conditions of the real *ketubah*."

He covered his mouth and slowly shook his head as he once more read the real contract. The people of the village would die of shock if they were to know what Rachel would be receiving. He would have to warn Eli to brace himself before he saw the numbers. He didn't want his best friend to die of shock before he witnessed the contracts.

Chapter 50

FATHERS

Lucius's excitement as he stood under the wedding canopy with Jacob beside him was inexpressible. As he watched Rachel, draped in her veil, walking toward him, he could scarcely believe it was all real. She was so beautiful, and Joseph looked truly happy as he led his precious daughter to the husband God had so unexpectedly provided. Joseph released her arm and walked under the canopy.

Rachel's eyes glowed as she stepped under the canopy and walked around Lucius three times before standing at his side to face Rabbi Eliezer.

As the rabbi spoke the benedictions, Lucius could have sworn he heard her every heartbeat. Her blush when he caught her eye declared her eager awareness of him so close beside her. As they shared the first cup of wine, their eyes locked as love flowed between them.

Lucius slid the gold ring on Rachel's index finger. His gaze shifted from the ring to her glowing eyes and froze there. He cleared his throat before he spoke the declaration, "Behold, you are consecrated to me with this ring, according to the Law of Moses and Israel."

Joseph and Eli exchanged knowing smiles as Rabbi Eliezer read aloud the *ketubah* binding Lucas of Corinth to Rachel bat Joseph. Jacob managed to maintain a straight face when Lucius grinned at him as he mentally substituted the conditions of the *ketubah* of Lucius Claudius Drusus.

Lucius was beaming as he watched Rachel sip from the second glass of wine they would share that day. He flipped his head back as he drained the remainder, placed the glass cup in the small bag, and crushed it with his foot.

As the guests shouted, clapped their hands, and sang, Lucius gazed at Rachel. His brother had tried to kill him, and what had come of it? He was now married to the most wonderful woman in the world, and he followed the God who loved him enough to die to pay for his sins. He was truly a blessed man.

◆

Joseph leaned against the compound wall, a contented smile curving his lips as he watched his friends and neighbors celebrating. Rachel was as radiant as his own Hannah had been, and Lucas's beaming smiles reminded him of his own so long ago.

As he watched the wedding couple, Lucas tore himself away from Rachel's side and came to join him.

"I have something to ask of you, Joseph."

"What is that, Lucas?" He beamed at his new son-in-law.

"I have five more years to serve as tribune, but I can't keep serving in Judaea. I see nothing but growing conflict between Rome and the zealots. It's only a matter of time before full rebellion breaks out again. It could be ten years, two years, next month, but for certain it's coming soon."

The happy glow in Lucas's eyes dimmed. "It was bad enough what happened when Titus crushed the rebellion last time. Next time, it won't just be a city or two destroyed and a few ten thousand taken as slaves. Rome will crush Judaea so completely it will never rebel again. It won't matter whether a Jew is part of the rebellion or not. Everyone will be punished."

Joseph crossed his arms, and his smile drooped. As much as he hated to think about that on this day of celebration, he knew what Lucas had said was true.

Lucas's lips tightened as he shook his head. "I don't want to be part of the legions that will carry out the orders to do that. I don't want to see you and your family caught up in the destruction. I plan to write my uncle Titus to ask him to help me get a transfer from Judaea to Thracia as soon as possible. He lives in the capital and is a friend of the governor, so that should take no more than a month or two.

Lucas rested his hand on Joseph's forearm. "I want to take you and your whole family with us when Rachel and I go. I can give you the money to get started with a new shop wherever I get posted. That will probably be Perinthus, where my mother and sister are living with my uncle."

He moved his hand to Joseph's shoulder.

"Come with us, Joseph. Rachel would love to have you all near, and our children will need their grandfather to teach them to know the LORD."

Joseph first looked down at the ground, then slowly scanned the courtyard of the house that had been his home since he was a child. Memories swirled around his heart and mind. Memories of the laughing eyes and hugs of his mother, of working the forge with his father, of his years with Hannah, her smiles and laughter as she sat under the canopy with him when their children were small.

So many good memories...but they were only memories. The future was more important than the past. He would like to stay close to Rachel, and it would be good to get his sons out of a land consumed by a hatred that would never die.

"We will come with you, Lucas. You are right that the future for us lies away from this land."

The smile that lit up his son-in-law's face was almost as bright as the one on the day he told him Rachel loved him.

"I'm glad, Joseph. Now that I finally have a father worthy of the name, I'd hate to leave him behind."

Lucius Fidelis was seated in the garden of his house in Rome, reading, when a slave approached him and bowed.

"A letter for you, master."

Fidelis held out his hand. When he took the letter from the slave, he glanced at the address. Marcus had sent several letters since reaching Sepphoris. Except for the ones reporting Lucius's disappearance and return, they had mainly been complaints about conditions in Judaea.

His eyebrows rose as he discovered this one was from Lucius.

His oldest son only sent a letter every six months. It was always a very short note that satisfied Lucius's sense of filial obligation but conveyed no real information about anything. It was less than four months since his last letter, so why was he writing? Fidelis frowned as he slid his finger under the wax seal to break it. He unrolled the papyrus sheet and began to read with some concern.

Lucius Claudius Drusus to Lucius Claudius Drusus

Fidelis, my father, greetings. If you are well, then I am glad. It is with great sadness that I write to tell you what has occurred during the last three months.

Fidelis's head popped back as his spine straightened. Then he read on with foreboding.

Marcus is dead. He came to Judaea with the intention of killing me to become the oldest of your sons. Three months ago, he hired an assassin to kill me. That first attempt failed only because a Jewish family found me where I was left to die and cared for me until I recovered. Marcus then tried to kill me himself a second time. I am grieved to tell you that I was forced to kill him. As we fought, he told me that he planned to kill first me and then Tertius to become your sole heir. He then planned to hasten your death as well. While I am very sorry that I had to kill him, I have the consolation of knowing that his death by my sword has spared Tertius and you. Marcus has been cremated, and I have arranged for his remains to be returned to you in Rome.

I write to tell you happier news as well. By the time you receive this, I will have married the Jewish woman who saved me after Marcus's first attempt on my life. Also, during my time here in Judaea, I have seen that the God of Israel is real. I have become a God-fearer like Grandfather was.

The events of the last three months have made other things clear to me. I do not want to be part of the military occupation of Judaea and all the killing that I will be called to do if I continue serving in this province. I do not want to be here when the next Jewish rebellion starts, as it surely will, and so many innocent people will die by Roman and Jewish swords. I plan to finish my last five years of service in Thracia as soon as I get my transfer. That is now being arranged with Uncle Titus's help. I will let you know where I am as soon as I arrive at my new posting.

I do not know when I will next return to Rome, but

I pray that you will be well until I see you again. May
God reach your heart so you can know His blessings,
as I now do. May God guard your safety until He does.

Fidelis sat staring at the letter from his oldest son. Marcus dead.
Marcus planning to kill them all to gain the family fortune. Were he
not who he was, had he not done what he had done, he might have
asked himself how his second son could ever have decided to kill the
older brother who had only been good to him. As it was...he tried not
to ask that question. He knew he would not like the answer. He tried,
but he did not totally succeed.

He stood and stepped from the bench in the sun to sit in the deep
shade cast by the grape vines that covered the arbor. He wanted no one
to watch him as he digested what had happened. He had taken a hit
when he read the letter, but that would pass.

Fidelis heard voices approaching, but Tertius didn't notice him sitting so quietly in the dark shade under the grape arbor. He strolled past
with his best friend.

"You know, Gaius, it's just not fair. I'm sick of how fathers control
everything, no matter how old their sons might be. Sometimes Roman
law is stupid. I hear that in parts of Gaul, a father only controls you
until you marry. I wish Rome was more like that. I don't want to wait
until Father dies of old age to be my own master."

"Well, there isn't any choice, so you may as well accept it."

"No choice? That's what you think. My father chose not to wait."

Tertius and Gaius walked into the house, and Lucius Fidelis heard
no more of the conversation.

He slumped against the arbor post, but only for a moment. A surge
of regret swept through him, but he squared his shoulders as a rueful
smile twisted his lips.

His own father would have appreciated the irony.

Historical Note on Roman and Jew
IRRECONCILABLE DIFFERENCES RECONCILED THROUGH CHRIST

The challenges faced by Joseph and his family in deciding first to help, then to accept, and finally to embrace Lucius, the Roman tribune, reflect a long history of hostility between Roman and Jew.

In AD 122, the Roman province of Judaea was unique among the provinces that were not recent conquests at the imperial frontier. The initial conquests of the other provinces were brutal, with towns and cities destroyed and thousands taken as slaves to serve the new Roman masters. Still, being part of the Empire came to be appreciated by their surviving inhabitants within a few decades.

Not so the Jews. Fiercely loyal to the God of Abraham, Isaac, and Jacob who commanded His followers to worship no other gods, the Jews refused to assimilate into the polytheistic Roman world. In other provinces, where adding one more god to a person's religious rituals posed no problem, being told to offer sacrifices to the emperor and the Roman gods as a sign of loyalty was perfectly acceptable. For the Jews, it was the ultimate sin.

Romans believed their strength and security depended on proper execution of the "faithful ritual" of the civil religion of the Roman state. Even educated Romans who doubted the existence of the Roman gods were superstitious about risking their wrath by failing to perform their rituals exactly right. Belief didn't matter; perfect performance did. When the Jews and later Christians refused to take part in the national religious rites, many believed it could bring calamity by making the rituals imperfect and therefore ineffective.

Still, the Jews were allowed an exception. They were a nation following their own ancient religious tradition, and that made their refusal to worship any but the Jewish god legal lest the Jewish god be offended. Since the followers of Jesus were mostly Jewish in the first decade after the resurrection, Christianity was treated as one strain of Judaism. As the number of Gentile converts increased, the Jewish laws about circumcision and what was kosher were set aside. Roman leaders reclassified Christianity as a "new and illicit religion," and its followers lost the exception from offering sacrifices to the emperor allowed to Jews. Following Jesus became a Roman crime.

The people who heard Peter announcing in the temple that Jesus has been raised from the dead were pious Jews, many of whom had traveled hundreds of miles to worship in the holiest sanctuary of Judaism. When they returned to their homes, they would have gone to their local synagogues to share the news that the long-awaited messiah foretold by the prophets had come. The people who heard the apostles speaking in their own languages after the Holy Spirit came upon them at Pentecost had come to worship and offer sacrifices in accordance with Jewish law.

Joseph is one such Messianic Jew, and he raised his children to know Yeshua as the fulfillment of prophesy and the final perfect sacrifice for sin so the temple sacrifices would never be needed again. His love for Yeshua led him to obey Jesus's command to love his enemy even when he had every human reason to hate. But Christian love is an act of the will, not an emotion. His natural emotions after the murder of his son ran counter to that command. Pulled in two directions, he chose to do what he never wanted only because he placed Jesus above all else.

But why did other Jewish Galileans hate Rome? The first Roman armies under Pompey were invited into Judea by two Jewish brothers fighting over who should be high priest and national leader. When that civil war ended in 63 BC, Judea had been reduced to a client kingdom of Rome. Hyrcanus was only an ethnarch (not a king), and he ruled only at Rome's pleasure. Rome divided the country into five administrative districts; Sepphoris was the capital of Galilee with Herod (later the Great) as its procurator. Herod's loyalty to Rome and friendship with both Julius Caesar and Mark Anthony enabled him to become king of all Judea. When Herod died in 4 BC, rebels under Judas bar Hezekiah seized the royal armory in Sepphoris. A legion from Syria ended the rebellion, burning Sepphoris to the ground and enslaving the local population that had supported Judas.

After Herod Antipas was made tetrarch of Galilee by Caesar Augustus, he rebuilt Sepphoris in the Roman style. The new inhabitants of the restored city of nearly 30,000 were a cosmopolitan mixture of Jews and Gentiles (Greeks, Syrians, and Romans). In AD 67 during the First Jewish War, the people of Sepphoris didn't merely refuse to fight. They openly welcomed the Twelfth Legion, leading many smaller Galilean towns to stay out of the fight. Not so Jotapata, about 20 miles to the north. After a brutal siege, as many as 40,000 Galileans were killed, and 1200 women and small children taken as slaves. From all of the Roman province of Judaea, at least 100,000 were taken as slaves, and many times that were killed.

The decision of Sepphoris to stay out of the fight was regarded as wisdom by some and treason by others. While most Jewish inhabitants of Sepphoris stayed out of the battle, that did not mean affection and loyalty toward Rome. Galilee remained primed for lethal opposition to Roman occupation. Desire to cast off the Roman oppressors simmered, boiling over in guerilla-style attacks by zealot groups. Rome kept two legions in Judaea, ready for action.

Forgiven is set in Galilee near Sepphoris in AD 122 during the final years of resentful submission to the pagan overlords. Soon the Bar Kokhba Rebellion of AD 132 will lead Rome to ban all Jews from Jerusalem and merge Judaea with Syria to form Syria Palaestina to erase any memory of Judea.

For those who chose to hear, the words of the apostle Paul in Galatians 3:28 promised a better future. "There is neither Jew nor Greek, slave nor free, male nor female, for you are all one in Christ Jesus." Joseph makes the unnatural choice to treat his enemy as a friend. Acting becomes reality as shared faith in Jesus brings reconciliation between Roman and Jew.

For more about life in the Roman Empire at its peak, please go to carolashby.com.

Discussion Guide

1) When *Forgiven* begins, Lucius is a man from a warrior culture, comfortable with killing when duty to country requires it. He's also a man who wants to help Romans and Jews live together in peace. Have you or people you know had to live with that seeming contradiction?

2) Rachel's beloved twin brother was killed by a Roman soldier, even though he was a peaceful young man doing nothing wrong. Still, when faced with the choice of helping Lucius or leaving him to die, she chose to help. Why did she do that? Would you have made the same choice? Why?

3) Joseph is a man of peace, but one son was murdered by a Roman soldier while another might die fighting the occupying army. Why did he decide to help an enemy soldier? Would you have made the same choice? Why?

4) Nathaniel was raised to follow Jesus's teachings about loving his enemies, but he eagerly joined the zealots in their fight against the Romans. Why did he make that decision?

5) Lucius begins with curiosity about the Jewish religion because his grandfather had become a God-fearer and later a Christian who was killed for his faith. How did that change? Why?

6) Rachel's relationship with Lucas changed from helping an enemy out of a sense of duty to caring as a friend and more. How did that

happen and why?

7) Even though Joseph led Lucius to faith in Jesus, he struggled with having a Roman soldier in his household. Have you ever felt that way about a Christian brother or sister? How did you deal with it?

8) When Lucius learns the innocent youth he killed was Rachel's twin, how did he respond? How did Joseph and Rachel respond when they learn Lucius was the killer? How would you have reacted to such a revelation?

9) Lucius would do anything for his brother Marcus, while Marcus sees Lucius only as an obstacle to inheriting the family fortune. How could two brothers have such different values? Would you have responded as Lucius did when he learned the truth?

10) *Forgiven* is a story of hatred and love, vengeance and forgiveness, ruthless ambition and selfless sacrifice. What touched you most? What made you think about what your own choices would be?

Glossary

bet sefer	Jewish school for boys 6-10 where they learn to read and write Hebrew and memorize the Torah
bet talmud	Jewish school for boys 10-14 where they study the Jewish scriptures more deeply and learn the oral law
centurion	1st level officer over 80 men; rises through ranks based on merit
cuirass	metal body armor protecting torso
denarius	*denarii* (pl); 1 *denarius* = 4 *sesterces*; about one day's living wage
gladius	short sword used by Roman military
Kabbalat Shabbat	Friday night synagogue service
ketubah	marriage contract (plural: *ketubot*)
quernstone	a hand mill for grinding grain made of two circular stones (quernstones) where the upper rotates against the lower
Shabbat	Sabbath
Torah	The Law—the first 5 books of the Scriptures
tribune	high-ranking officer from equestrian or senatorial order
trireme	Roman warship with three banks of oars

Scripture References

Chapter 10: Lev. 19:1-4, 32-37
Chapter 18: Lev. 19:33-34, Is. 49: 5-6
Chapter 30: Lev. 25:23, 25, 28, 39, 53-55

*Formal prayers are derived from contemporary Messianic Jewish prayers found in "A Shabbat Seder: A Simplified Guide for Christians," Copyright by John J Parsons, www.hebrew4christians.com

Acknowledgements

I am so grateful to God that He's called me to write stories of love and spiritual transformation when choosing Jesus could be deadly. *Forgiven* is the first of several, and I'm so excited by this opportunity to share how Jesus can give new life and greater joy to the ones who love him above all else and follow faithfully, no matter what the cost.

I want to thank those who so willingly read earlier versions of *Forgiven* and helped me refine the story to its present form. Many thanks to my critique partner, Katie Powner, and my wonderful friends who love to read and gave me great suggestions. My deepest thanks go out to each, and here they are alphabetically: Seaborn Ashby, Susan Brockington, Andrew Budek-Schmeisser, Tiffany Coble, Gayle DeRose, Darcie Farrow, Lisa Garcia, Bonnie Marron, Antoinette Smith, and Patti Stouter. Your insights and suggestions made the characters more real and the situations more authentic. Many thanks!

My special thanks go to Wendy Chorot for her content editing and for being a sounding board for my many questions. If you're looking for an editor, Wendy is the one you should call!

I love how the cover design captures the soul of the story. Roseanna White of Roseanna White Designs is responsible, but you may have heard of her already. She's the author of several top-selling historical novels. One of her Roman-era novels kept me reading until 3:00 a.m. three nights running. Sometimes sleep deprivation is worth it!

But I especially want to thank my wonderful family. My grown kids, Paul and Lydia, are endlessly encouraging. Paul has been writing himself since 8th grade, so he's my true kindred spirit when I want to talk books. Lydia, well, there is no joy greater than having your grown daughter be one of your dearest friends.

My husband Jim keeps everything running when I submerge too deeply into my writing (which is way too often). We'd starve if he wasn't such a good cook. He says I'm incredibly lifelike when I'm working at my laptop. It's a joy being married for decades to a man who can be the model for the better parts of my stories' heroes!

About the Author

Carol Ashby has been a professional writer for most of her life, but her articles and books were about lasers and compound semiconductors (think the electronics that make cell phones, laser pointers, and LED flashlights work). Now she is having a wonderful time creating stories about human conflict and difficult friendships that grow into love as characters discover their own faith in Christ. Her fascination with the Roman Empire was born during her first middle-school Latin class. A research career in New Mexico inspires her to get every historical detail right so she can spin stories that make her readers feel like they're living under the Caesars themselves.

Read her articles about many facets of life in the Roman Empire at carolashby.com, or join her at her blog, The Beauty of Truth, at carol-ashby.com.

LIGHT *in the* EMPIRE SERIES

The Light in the Empire Series follows the interconnected lives of the members of three Roman families of the senatorial order during the reigns of Trajan and Hadrian. Join them as they travel the Empire, from Germania and Britannia to Thracia, Dacia, and Judaea and, of course, to Rome itself.

Coming in 2017
Blind Ambition

Sometimes you have to almost die to discover how you want to live.

It's AD 114 in the Roman province of Germania Superior, and being a Christian carries a death sentence. Tribune Decimus Lentulus is on the fast track for a stellar political career back in Rome. When he's robbed, blinded, and left for dead, a young German woman who follows the Way finds him. Valeria knows it's his duty to have her and her family killed, but she chooses to obey Jesus's command to love her enemy and takes him home to care for him.

It's not his miraculous recovery that shakes Decimus to his core. It's the way they love him like family and their unconcealed love for Jesus. In spite of himself, he falls in love with the Christian woman Rome wants him to kill. Can Valeria hide her faith to follow him into the circles of Roman power? Or should he abandon his ambition to help rule the Empire and choose to follow a different way?

The Legacy

What can you give your children when Rome has taken all you own?

In AD 114, Claudia loathes her oldest brother Lucius after he arranges their father's execution for his new faith in Jesus to gain the family fortune. Suicide seems her only escape from a forced marriage to a cruel Roman power broker. Then the man who secretly led her father to Jesus arranges for his son Philip to sneak her out of Rome and take her to her brother Titus a thousand miles away in Thracia.

A childhood accident scarred Philip's face. A woman's rejection scarred his heart. Claudia's gratitude grows into love, but what can a house-church leader do when the first woman who returns his love hates the God he loves even more? Can Claudia's love for the kind, brilliant man who rescued her survive her learning what he really is?

Claudia and Titus hunger for revenge on Lucius and the Christians they blame for their father's deadly conversion. When Titus buys Miriam, a secret Christian, to care for his sister, he starts them all down a path of conflicting loyalties and dangerous decisions. His father's final letter commands the forgiveness Titus refuses to give. What will it finally take to free him from the hatred that's poisoning his own heart?

Second Chances

In a world defined by class and wealth,
it takes more than love to conquer all.

In AD 122, Cornelia Scipia, proud daughter of one of the noblest Roman families, learns her adulterous husband plans to betroth their daughter to the vicious son of his best friend. Only over her dead body! Cornelia divorces him, reclaims her enormous dowry, and kidnaps her own daughter. She plans to start over with Drusilla a thousand miles away. No more husbands for her! But she hadn't counted on meeting Hector, the widowed Greek captain of the ship carrying them to their new life.

Devastated by the loss of his wife and daughter, Hector's heart begins to heal as he befriends Drusilla. Cornelia's sacrificial love for Drusilla and her courage and humor in the face of the unknown earn his admiration...as a friend. Is he ready for more?

Marriage to the kind, honest sea captain would finally give Drusilla the father she deserves...and Cornelia the faithful husband she's always longed for. She signals her desire, but he doesn't propose. There are secrets in his past and unspoken misunderstandings born of the chasms between their social classes and different faiths. Will they keep two lonely hearts from the second chance at happiness that God so unexpectedly offers?

I'd love to hear what you think!
If you enjoyed this book, I would really appreciate it if you would post a review at the retailer you purchased it from. A good review is like a jewel set in gold for an author. I'd love to hear from you.

Interested in my upcoming titles?
You can sign up for my newsletter at carol-ashby.com for advance notices of upcoming releases and other info about my latest writing adventures. I hope you will!

Carol Ashby

Made in the USA
Coppell, TX
26 May 2022

78155141R00194